W9-AVO-664

BLOODY POINT

A NOVEL

LINDA J. WHITE

RIVEROAK®

Good News in Fiction

COOK COMMUNICATIONS MINISTRIES
Colorado Springs, Colorado • Paris, Ontario
KINGSWAY COMMUNICATIONS LTD
Eastbourne, England

RiverOak® is an imprint of
Cook Communications Ministries, Colorado Springs, CO 80918
Cook Communications, Paris, Ontario
Kingsway Communications, Eastbourne, England

BLOODY POINT
© 2005 by Linda J. White

All rights reserved. No part of this book may be reproduced without
written permission, except for brief quotations in books and critical
reviews. For information, write Cook Communications Ministries,
4050 Lee Vance View, Colorado Springs, CO 80918.

Cover Design: BMB Design, Inc./Scott Johnson
Cover Photo: ©Photo Disc Collection/Getty Images

First Printing, 2005
Printed in United States of America
1 2 3 4 5 6 7 8 9 10 Printing/Year 09 08 07 06 05

Quotations from the HOLY BIBLE, NEW INTERNATIONAL VERSION®.
Copyright © 1973, 1978, 1984 International Bible Society. Used by permission of Zondervan. All rights reserved.

Library of Congress Cataloging-in-Publication Data

White, Linda J., 1949-
  Bloody Point / Linda J. White.
      p. cm.
  ISBN 1-58919-028-9 (pbk.)
  1. Women detectives--Maryland--Fiction. 2. Government investiga-
tors--Crimes against--Fiction. 3. Seaside resorts--Fiction. 4. Maryland--
Fiction. 5. Widows--Fiction. I. Title.
  PS3623.H5786B58 2005
  813'.6--dc22

                                                    2004030616

For Larry

1

*A*shadow fell over the wet, gleaming wood. Cassidy McKenna stopped her varnish brush just shy of the port side winch and looked up, squinting into the bright Maryland sky. The sailboat rocked and the sun blinded her, but she still recognized a familiar form. "Jake?"

"Hey, partner!"

She jumped to her feet. "What are you doing here? I can't believe this!" Conflicting emotions swirled in her head. How long had it been? Two months? Three? A soft breeze blowing in off the Chesapeake Bay ruffled her honey blonde hair.

"You look great, Cass."

She shaded her eyes with her hand. "How did you find me?"

"Your dad."

"He told you where I was?"

"I pressed him. Gently."

"I'm sure." FBI Special Agent Jake Tucker was not known for his subtlety, a fact she knew well. When they were partners up in Baltimore, she'd spent a lot of time smoothing the ruffled feathers he frequently stirred up. He looked out of place here at the Goose Creek Marina, dressed in his dark gray suit, white shirt, and expensive Italian leather shoes. She suppressed a smile. "Why are you here?"

But Jake's eyes had shifted beyond her, across the docks and down the creek, to a place where dark gray smoke was beginning to rise from an anchored sailboat. "Is that boat supposed to be doing that?" he asked, gesturing.

Cassie stepped out on the dock to see what he was talking about.

"Oh, my gosh!" She jumped back onto her boat, dashed below decks, and reemerged with a fire extinguisher and her cell phone. She punched in 9-1-1. "We've got a sloop on fire, anchored in Goose Creek, just off the marina. No, I don't know if anyone's on board. Yes, I will."

"Come on!" she said to Jake, grabbing two life jackets and tossing one to him.

"What?"

"I need you!" Cassie threw on a life jacket and dropped into a rubber dinghy sitting in the water, untying it as she held onto the dock. "Come on!"

Jake gingerly climbed into the wobbly boat. The outboard motor started with a roar, and Cassie steered for the craft on fire. Jake hung on, grim faced, as they bounced over the waves, trying to keep his 200-pound frame from pitching overboard. "I hate boats!" he yelled over the roar of the outboard.

"I know!" She slowed the motor as they neared the sloop. Already flames were licking out of the ports.

"Get me close! I'll climb onboard," Jake yelled.

"No! Too dangerous! It could explode." Cassie circled cautiously around the boat. "Hello? Anybody onboard? Hello!"

"Put me over there!"

"No!"

But she had swung close enough for Jake to grab the swim ladder, and he pulled himself out of the dinghy and onto the sloop.

"Jake, for crying out loud—" but he was already up on the deck. With smoke now billowing out of the starboard side, he raced down the port and disappeared down the steps of the companionway. Thirty seconds later he reappeared, a little white Maltese terrier in his hands. As he handed the dog down to Cassie, she noticed his thumb was bleeding.

"Nobody on board," Jake said, climbing back into the dinghy. "Just the dog. Let's get out of here!"

Sirens were screaming from the shore as Cassie hit the throttle.

She maneuvered the dinghy away. Waves stirred by a fresh breeze rocked the rubber craft and Jake braced himself, one hand on the dinghy, the other holding the dog. Fire engines, their lights flashing, and an ambulance edged down the tiny lane that ran next to Goose Creek. There was not much they could do. Within seconds, a tremendous explosion shattered the sailboat, sending fragments of fiberglass and wood skyward. Cassie and Jake watched in stunned silence as the boat burned to the waterline.

The Blue Goose Restaurant faced northeast, overlooking the marina, Goose Creek, and further in the distance, the Chesapeake Bay. They were sitting next to the window at a weathered table made of dark wood. "Aren't they beautiful?" Cassie said, gesturing toward the rows of sailboats and powerboats bobbing in their slips. Puffy white clouds dotted the bright blue sky, and off in the distance, a huge cargo ship churned its way toward the vast port of Baltimore.

"What's beautiful? Those boats or the one that's burned out?" Jake answered with a grin. He took a swallow of water and chomped down on some ice. His thumb bore a thick white bandage where "the little rat," as he called the Maltese, had bitten him. Cassie had made him promise to see his doctor, a promise she figured he had every intention of ignoring. The dog was up to date on his shots, the owners assured Jake when they'd finally shown up. They'd been off exploring the town of Goose Creek Landing when the boat burned and were ever so grateful to have little Max rescued.

Cassie turned her attention to her former partner. His short dark hair made him look like a Marine, and he had a perpetual tan that only deepened in the summer. He was barrel-chested, strong, and the only man she knew who could intelligently discuss U.S. foreign policy while bench-pressing 300 pounds. But why was he here? "You still haven't answered my question," she said.

He looked at her quizzically.

"Why are you here?" she repeated.

"Is it so wrong to look up an old friend?"

"Don't give me that. Something's up."

He stretched back in his chair and studied her. She felt her throat involuntarily tighten.

"How are you?" he asked.

"I'm fine," she said, too quickly.

"Really?"

"Really. Just fine." She jutted out her chin.

"Well, that's good, Skeet."

She flinched. There were only two people who ever called her that. She had earned the nickname the day she out shot both her husband and her partner at a local firing range.

Jake's dark brown eyes told her he'd noticed the flinch. Cassie cleared her throat. "And how are you, Jake? How's Tamara? And the kids?"

"The kids are fine. Growing." He took a roll from the basket, tore it in half, and took a bite. "Tamara ... well, she went through with it. We're officially divorced."

"Oh, I'm so sorry." She glanced at his left hand. The wedding band was gone, a white line testifying to its recent departure.

"Yeah. I get the kids every other weekend and once during the week. Provided I'm not working late."

A wave of sadness swept over Cassie. There were all kinds of pain out there. All kinds. So many nights when they were preparing for court or working cases together, Jake would leave so he could go home and have dinner with the kids and put them to bed. Then he'd come back and work until two or three in the morning. Whatever it took to get the job done. She'd always admired his dedication to his family. Imagining him living without them was impossible.

"I got an apartment, a two-bedroom," he continued, "about ten minutes away from the house." He crunched some more ice, pulverizing it, and stared out across the marina. "I hate it—being away from the kids."

Cassie wondered how things could change so quickly. She

had lost her husband, Mike, in an accident. Jake had lost his family ... to what? Busyness? Dedication to his job? Male inconsideration amplified over the years? Female independence and pride? Cassie unconsciously fingered the gold cross that was suspended on a chain around her neck. It had been a gift from Mike on their wedding day. She never took it off.

A middle-aged waitress took their order—crab bisque soup and Cobb salad for Cassie, soup and a complete steak dinner for Jake, who hadn't eaten since early in the morning. "I'll be right back with the soup," she said, collecting the menus.

"So, Jake—"

Cassie's question was interrupted by the approach of a man in a dark blue uniform. "Special Agent Tucker?"

"Sit down, sit down," Jake responded. "Loughlin, right?"

"Paul." The fire marshal dropped into a chair.

"This is Cassidy McKenna, a friend of mine," Jake said. "So, what'd you find out?"

"Do you want something to eat?" Cassie interrupted.

"No, I'm fine. My wife will have dinner waiting for me. Apparently the Sinclairs were cruising the Chesapeake on a three-week vacation. They'd just bought this boat through an agency in Annapolis."

"From?" Jake asked.

"We're working on that. Anyway, today was just the second day they'd been out on it. Mr. Sinclair decided to make a cup of coffee before they left on their shopping trip. He tried to light the alcohol stove, and thought he'd failed. We're thinking now that perhaps he didn't, that the flame had ignited and caught a dishtowel or something like that on fire. The flame on an alcohol stove can be nearly invisible. And unfortunately, fires like that aren't too uncommon." The fire marshal pushed his chair back. "Thank you both for jumping in and helping. The Sinclairs were very grateful that you saved their dog."

"It was Jake. Jake saved the dog." Cassie looked at her partner, who was curiously silent.

"Well," Loughlin said, rising, "I've got to go."

"Paul." Jake pulled a business card out of his pocket. "When you find out who previously owned that boat, give me a call, would you? Or if anything unusual crops up?"

"Sure," said the fire marshal, reading the card. "I'll be glad to."

Cassie just stared at Jake, with more than one question in her eyes.

As Loughlin left the restaurant, their waitress returned to the table with two bowls of steaming soup. Cassie inhaled the soft scent of crab, punctuated with just a hint of Old Bay seasoning. It was a smell she never got tired of, one that took her back to some of the happiest days of her life.

"So, you live on your boat?" Jake asked, breaking apart another roll.

"Mmm hmmm."

"How safe is that?"

"What's that supposed to mean? I'm fine. The boat's safe."

Jake doggedly worked at his soup.

"Good, isn't it?" she asked.

"Yeah."

"We've got the best seafood in the world."

Jake wiped his mouth. "Tell me about it. Your boat, I mean." He offered her the bread, and then took some more for himself.

"Well, it's an Alberg 30 ... thirty-feet long, a great boat for the Bay. It belonged to a man who brought it up from Florida. Somebody down there installed a seacock, an underwater valve, that wasn't rated for freezing weather. One cold night last winter it burst. The dockhand, Scrub—"

"Scrub?"

"Yeah, Scrub. His real name is Myron Tunney but everybody calls him Scrub. Anyway, Scrub showed up for work and found the

Alberg sunk at the dock, just the mast and the top of the main hatch sticking up out of the water."

"It sank?"

Cassie nodded. "The water's about six feet deep at the slip, so it was down and resting on its keel. Scrub called my dad—Dad befriended Scrub a couple of years ago—and the two of them spent three days raising the boat."

The waitress retrieved their soup bowls. "Your steak is almost ready, sir."

"Could I have some more water? And bread? More bread?"

"Certainly."

"Gosh, I wish I could eat like you!" Cassie said.

"So, how'd they get the boat up?" Jake asked.

"They covered the hatches and ports with plastic bags, stuck the hose of a sump pump down one hatch, and started pumping. Three days later, it was up. It was a mess, full of mud and oil, but it was up."

The waitress put another basket of bread on the table and two glasses of water.

"The owner was furious. The insurance company declared it a total loss. But Dad figured the boat was still basically sound. At his suggestion, I bought it from the salvage company, as is, for practically nothing. A lot of people thought I was crazy, but after two months of hard work, I think it's looking pretty good."

"What's with this guy, Scrub?"

"As I said, Scrub is his nickname—from his childhood. I guess he was just a little guy. His dad was over six foot, so the boy must have looked like a scrub to him." Cassie laughed softly. "One thing's for sure—Scrub's a character. Doesn't read well. Can't do math. But the man knows boats. Inside and out. Without his help, I wouldn't have the boat anywhere close to where it is today." Cassie fingered the edge of her napkin.

The waitress arrived with their order. Outside the cool April evening was drawing to a close. The sky was deep blue and the lights in the marina had come on. A flashing red marker was visible in the channel, and one lonely trawler was creeping back to its slip.

Cassie picked absently at her Cobb salad, normally one of her favorite dishes, while Jake devoured the steak. She was teetering on a tightrope of comfort and confusion, happy to see him, yet somehow resistant to his presence. She noted his eyes cataloging each person as he or she was seated at nearby tables. He never seemed relaxed. That was typical for an agent.

When he was finished eating, Jake carefully wiped his mouth and his hands. The waitress brought the check in a leather folder, which he took before Cassie could protest. He filled out the credit card slip and placed it on the edge.

"Now what?" Cassie asked, leaning forward. "Now will you tell me why you've gone to all this trouble to find me? Why you've driven all the way to Goose Creek, Maryland? Why you're buying dinner for me?"

Jake cocked his head and his eyes searched her face. His brow furrowed and Cassie could tell by the set of his jaw that he was weighing his words carefully. "When are you coming back?"

"To where?"

"To work."

"Who says I am?" Her heart was thudding.

"I thought you were on a leave of absence. That you'd be coming back sometime soon."

The familiar ringing in her ears began and she closed her eyes. How many times did she have to explain it? "I'm not coming back. I'm resigning."

The silence that followed was worse than the argument she'd had with her dad. Jake's jaw muscles flexed. She tried to read the expression in his eyes. "I ... I just don't have the heart for it anymore, Jake. No heart."

"Cass, you can't quit. You're too good—one of the best."

Frowning, she touched the cross around her neck.

"You're terrific with people. You have good instincts. You worked your informants well." He looked at her intently. "Shakes is still calling and asking for you."

Cassie snorted softly. Ol' Shakes was a busybody who'd proved very useful in the past.

"You need to come back, Skeet. We need you. I need you."

She studied his face. "No, Jake. You don't need me."

Jake got quiet. He stared at his hands before him on the table.

"Why do you need me?" She couldn't resist asking.

"It's a new case I'm working on. I got a call the other day from a woman, a friend of Tam's from college." Jake hesitated. "A guy she knew got killed a few weeks ago. Throat was slashed. It happened at a marina just north of here—Sullivan's Wharf. You know it?"

Cassie nodded. "Yes."

"This guy had a sailboat there. The woman—Tam's friend—was with him when he died. They had been sailing together for a week."

"They were in a relationship?"

"Yes, they had been, for six or eight months. Although apparently he also had a wife. Anyway, this guy left the boat for a few moments, supposedly to get some cigarettes. When he wasn't back an hour later, she went to investigate, and sure enough, the guy's dead."

"So what?" Cassie asked. "Why does the FBI care?" The FBI didn't get involved in simple murder cases.

Jake drummed his thumb on the table. "The guy, Frederick Schneider—"

"Freed-rick?"

"... yeah, that's right. The way he was killed was pretty gruesome. Schneider was a consultant, an engineer. He used to work for Tracor, a company in Delaware that has a major defense contract. They make a lot of things, but among them are control systems for missiles. Then, last week, Tam's friend was cleaning up and she found a book the guy had left at her apartment. She opens it up, and a letter drops out. But not just a letter—it was an extortion threat."

"From?"

"Unsigned."

"And the threat was ..."

Jake shifted in his chair. "It was a threat of violence if Schneider didn't provide the 'package'—whatever that was."

Cassie took a deep breath. "So somebody was threatening him, Schneider didn't produce, and he got whacked. I still say it happens all the time."

"It may happen all the time, but this time it happened at a marina and this time the victim had access to some pretty pricey technology that has national security implications and he's connected with someone who knows my wi ... my ex-wife." Jake's eyes flickered.

Cassie's heart flinched. Too many changes, too fast. She wished they could rewind the tape to about a year ago and write a different ending.

"To clinch it, the threatening letter came via the U.S. mail," Jake continued, "so we have an interest."

She took a deep breath and started to speak. Jake stopped her, holding up his hand like a traffic cop. "Just think about it, okay? Will you? I could really use your help on this case. You know all about this sailing stuff. And, Cass, I'll be honest, I'd just like to see you come back to the FBI. So just promise me you'll think about it."

Cassie couldn't speak—the words caught in her throat. She nodded wearily.

2

*T*here isn't anything to think about, Cassie told herself repeatedly as she pressed down harder on the sandpaper. The sun was hot on her back as she moved the paper over the woodwork, stripping off old varnish and weathered teak. So what if Frederick Schneider had been killed? She didn't care. So what if he had access to defense technology? It was someone else's problem now.

That's what she had told Jake, and that's what she believed—so much so that she had driven up to Baltimore that morning, turned in her gun and her credentials, signed the papers, and officially resigned.

Now Cassie had a different goal: finishing the woodwork on her boat. Countless days spent sanding, varnishing, re-sanding, and re-varnishing had transformed most of the weathered gray teak into a beautiful, mellow brown, the color of expensive racehorses, autumn leaves, and an Irish setter she'd once owned. And now she just had to complete the job.

But despite the musical clanging of halyards on masts, the companionship of the swallows that lived around the docks, and the work that was before her, Cassie's thoughts kept drifting back to Jake. Jake the strong man, Jake the tough guy, Jake the one who had stood by her through her darkest days.

They'd gone through the FBI Academy at nearly the same time. Cassie's husband, Mike, had graduated first. Jake was next, and then Cassie finished the following year. They'd known a lot of the same people. When the three met again at the Washington Field Office, they had hit it off instantly, and soon they were inseparable. Jake's wife had joined them on some social occasions, but it was mostly Mike and Cassie and Jake together, the "triple threat" as their Bureau friends called them.

Life was exciting—filled with purpose and good times. And then came November of last year. Never her favorite month, it was now destined to be on her blacklist forever.

Late on the night of November 4, Mike was driving home from an interview with an informant. As he drove through a dingy part of Annapolis, he came upon two cars stopped by the side of the road. The drivers were out of their cars. One was on the ground, the other beating him with a tire iron.

Mike radioed for help, jerked his car to a stop, and intervened. Identifying himself as an FBI agent, he ordered the attacker to stop. Instead, the man had rushed toward Mike. Thirty seconds later, the assailant was dead, his body pierced by rounds from Mike's Bureau-issued Glock pistol.

That was only the beginning of what would be the most traumatic time of Cassie's life. From the beginning, it was clear that Mike had acted appropriately—he had, in fact, saved the other motorist's life. Still, a routine Critical Incident Review had been ordered. Mike was told to take it easy for a while, but that lasted about half a day. He was annoyed at not being able to work his cases.

When a source called him with some information a few days later, Mike decided to meet with him. He told Cassie he was going out and would be back about nine. She raised her eyebrows, but there was no point trying to convince Mike he should back off a bit. From his perspective, the shooting was justified, the review was nothing more than a technicality, and he was just fine.

It was a cold, rainy night. The leaves, still bearing the bright colors of fall, had fallen on the rain-slicked streets. A frigid wind was blowing from the northwest, and streams were overflowing, leaving pools of standing water on the roads. The wind rattled the windows and buffeted the outside wall of their apartment.

Cassie was at home, wrapping packages for a Christmas prison ministry. Her favorite worship CD was in the stereo. When she noticed it was 9:30 p.m. and Mike wasn't home, she wondered where he was. By 10:30 p.m., she started to worry. When Jake appeared at her door at 11:20 p.m., her heart stopped.

Mike had missed a curve on a dark, winding road. His Bureau car had skidded, left the pavement, and rolled over and over down an embankment until it had slammed into an eighty-year-old oak. It had taken rescue workers forty minutes to cut Mike out. Now he was at the University of Maryland Shock-Trauma unit, barely hanging on to life.

The next ten days were a fog-filled living nightmare. Blurred images flashed across Cassie's memory: the ICU, the press, the Bureau bigwigs ... and Mike, lying still and helpless amidst the tubes and beeping machines. He'd suffered massive internal injuries, a broken pelvis, a fractured skull, and broken ribs. On day seven, the doctors were hopeful. On day nine, Mike was dead, the victim of sudden, uncontrollable internal bleeding. For some reason, his body couldn't recover from the trauma.

Cassie just wanted to die with him. Her whole world went black. She moved about in a daze. It was Jake who had stuck by her side then; Jake who had interfaced with the funeral home and the press and the Bureau and even the minister.

At the funeral, it was Jake who gave the eulogy, speaking eloquently about Mike, and there wasn't a dry eye in the place when he was finished. Jake had stood by her, the most faithful friend she could imagine.

But in the end, she had to get away—from Jake, from the Bureau, from the apartment—from everything that reminded her of life with Mike.

Just thinking about it now made Cassie hurt all over. Sometimes at night she would lie in bed, curled up in a ball, every muscle in her body aching.

She didn't want to start that now. She forced herself to refocus, running her hand over the wood on the boat, feeling the smooth finish, following the grain. *Forget about the accident,* she told herself. *It's over. There's nothing you can do to bring Mike back. Look—the coaming boards, the handrails, the companionway doors, the port trim all look exactly like I hoped. A warm, homey brown.* This was tangible, this was good, this was something she could hang on to.

Mike hadn't liked sailing, hadn't liked it at all. Too slow. Not enough action. So Cassie hadn't been out on the Bay for years. Returning to the place of her happiest childhood memories seemed like the natural thing to do after he died. She needed to recapture what was good in life after facing the hellish reality of her husband's death.

The boat had completely absorbed her for the last couple of months. She'd replaced all the wiring, with Scrub's help. She'd pulled up the carpet and scrubbed the underlying fiberglass. The settee cushions and V-berth mattress were new, and the teak below decks had been scrubbed off and brightened. The engine had to be hand-turned, pumped out, and cleaned, but the sturdy Yanmar diesel was running again. All the seacocks had been fixed. Little by little the boat was becoming seaworthy.

She had been content in her little corner of the world, until her former partner had showed up. Now, although she had been initially glad to see him, she felt the old stress pulling at her like an undertow. What she had done today, resigning officially from the Bureau, was like throwing out an anchor.

The air was oppressive—hot and muggy with a threat of thunderstorms—and Cassie had chosen that day to climb the mast. The anchor light needed to be replaced, so she'd conscripted Scrub to wind her up in the bosun's chair. She was up there when she saw Jake's black SUV pull into a space in the marina parking lot. Soon he was striding down the dock. He was dressed in khakis and a navy golf shirt. Cassie felt her stomach knotting up.

"Hey!" she heard him holler. "What are you doing?"

"Fixing the anchor light," she yelled from atop her perch. "Say hi to Scrub. Scrub, this is Jake. Jake, Scrub."

The wiry guy standing at the bottom of the mast grinned and nodded at Jake. He was short, maybe five feet five inches tall, and his sandy brown hair hung over his collar. He looked like a jockey with his elfin face and small frame. He had on khaki shorts and a T-shirt and his skin was brown. His arms were muscular and strong, and he had his hand on a winch handle holding the halyard, which held Cassie, suspended some forty feet in the air, next to the main mast.

"You need help with that?" Jake asked. He stepped on the boat and up on the deck next to Scrub.

"No, sir."

Jake looked up at Cassie. She was sitting in a canvas seat screwing something into the mast. The seat was swinging as the boat rocked. "What the heck is she doing?"

"Okay! Got it!" she called.

"Ready to come down?"

"Sure."

"Nice and easy."

Scrub began lowering the halyard and Jake stayed close by. Cassie could tell it was all he could do to keep from pushing Scrub aside and taking the line himself. When it was all over and she was safely on the deck, it was obvious the dockhand had it all under control.

Cassie extricated herself from the seat and smiled at Jake. "That's one of the fun parts of sailing."

"Well, Cassie, I see you're putting that bosun's chair to good use." A man in his early thirties, tall, blond, and deeply tanned strode down the dock toward them. His eyes were fixed on Jake as he spoke. He came abreast of the boat just as Cassie, Jake, and Scrub stepped onto the dock. The man leaned over and gave Cassie a quick peck on the cheek.

"Oh, hi, Rick! This is my friend, Jake. Jake, this is Richard Maxwell. He has a boat down here." She motioned toward the end of the dock.

Jake nodded, his eyes squinting. Cassie noticed him looking closely at Maxwell. He was always so suspicious!

Rick flashed a grin and shook hands with Jake. "Glad to meet you. Yes, sir, I've known this girl for a long time." He put his arm around Cassie's shoulder and squeezed her to his side. Jake shifted his weight.

Cassie smiled and pulled away. "He gave me the bosun's chair," she explained.

"On the condition she would loan it back to me anytime I needed it. That way, I have an excuse to visit her." Maxwell turned as if he'd noticed Scrub for the first time. "Scrub! How about cleaning out the bilge on my boat sometime soon?"

"Yes, sir." Scrub finished tying off the halyard and turned to Cassie. "I'll be goin' now, miss, if you don't need anything else."

"Sure, Scrub. Thanks so much for your help."

"Yes, Miss Cassie." Scrub turned and walked down the dock toward the marina office, his head down.

"It's great to have someone do my dirty work," Maxwell said, grinning. "Well, I'm off to Annapolis. Always something to buy for the boat."

"You got a job coming up?" Cassie asked. She turned to Jake. "Rick is a certified captain. He delivers boats for people, you know, when they buy them one place and want to keep them at another."

"They buy 'em, I sail 'em!" Maxwell said. "And no, Cassie, I'm staying right here for now. See you fine people later." He put his hand to his brow in an odd semi-salute, then turned and walked away.

Jake shook his head as he watched him leave. "I don't know, Skeet. He sure is different."

"Him? Why?" She cocked her head.

"Kind of prissy, wouldn't you say?"

Cassie frowned. "He's very bright. I've known him since high school."

Jake's eyes narrowed and followed Maxwell all the way to the parking lot, and even as his car was leaving. "Really? Did you date him?"

She laughed. "No, he was a player, even then. Wanted me to go out with him big time but I refused. He went to college, and spent some time in the Army. My dad said he went to the Middle East for a while. It's just a strange coincidence that he ended up working as a captain and having a boat at this marina." She turned her attention to Jake. "So what's up with you?"

"Let me see your boat," he said, avoiding a direct answer.

She realized she'd just been put off, but what could she do? "Sure," she responded. They stepped back on board, and she noticed how much smaller the sloop felt with more than one person on board. "Come on down," she said, leading the way down the companionway and below deck.

"This is called the salon," Cassie said. "Those settees—the couches—make up into beds. The head—bathroom—is in there, and I sleep up there, in the V-berth."

"It's tight," Jake grunted. At almost six feet tall, he couldn't quite stand up straight.

"Yep."

"No shower?"

"There's a shower in the land head."

"The what?"

"There's a bathroom up near the entrance to the marina. There are showers there."

"How convenient," Jake muttered.

"I take it you're not ready to sign on," Cassie said as they emerged again on deck.

He looked at her, his head tilted. "No offense ... but I don't know how you can stand it."

She laughed. How could she stand it? It was simple, that's how. No muss, no fuss, no room for anything. Alone, for the most part. No furniture to deal with, no neighbors to pretend to be friendly with, none of the detritus of life, like photos or old movie stubs. Or journals. It was simple and clean. Cassie motioned to the cockpit seats. "You want to talk?"

Jake looked around. Over sixty boats bobbed in their slips. Four slips over, on Cassie's dock, a man with a bucket was washing down his craft. Gulls sat on pilings, one after another, like peas in a pod. No other people were visible, but the hatches and ports on several of the boats nearby were open. "Let's go someplace more private. Why don't we go to dinner?"

They headed north, to a place on the Magothy River that was one of Cassie's favorites. "So what's up with you, Cass? What are your plans?" Jake asked as they drove.

"Finish working on the boat."

"And then?"

"Mike had a lot of life insurance. I can live off that until I figure out what's next." She braced herself.

His silence registered his disapproval. She felt anger rising in her, even though he hadn't said anything. Cassie shook her head hard, as if to dislodge some uncomfortable thought, and turned her eyes toward Jake.

He was focused on the road. "I got a call from Paul Loughlin, the fire marshal," he said. "That boat that burned the last time I came down? It was arson."

"Really?"

"Yeah. He told me somebody tampered with the automatic bilge switch and some hoses. The bilge filled up with water and when the switch activated, its spark set off some propane which had settled in the bottom of the boat."

Cassie frowned. "So it was intentional."

"Yes, and I just think it's odd. That guy, Schneider, is murdered in a marina. Then a boat is torched just a few miles away."

"Does Laughlin think the guy who was cruising in the boat—what was his name? Sinclair?—set fire to it?"

"I don't know."

"Who was the previous owner?" Cassie asked. "Turn right at the next exit, then take the second left," she directed.

Jake swung his SUV onto the exit ramp. Rush hour traffic was diminishing. The sun was low in the sky and humidity hung in the air in a haze. "A guy who lives in D.C. Nothing special about him."

The restaurant came in view. "Here it is, on the right."

Jake swung the car into a parking space and shut down the engine. Cassie pushed open her door, relieved to get out of the conversation.

"I'll tell you more inside," Jake said.

3

Skippy's Crab Shack was dark and loud, and later Cassie wondered if she'd chosen the place to minimize the opportunity for conversation. She made Jake try steamed crabs, ordering two dozen. The waiter spread brown paper over their table, brought hammers and picks, and dumped the freshly steamed crabs right in the middle. Then Cassie spent the next ten minutes showing Jake how to crack and eat them.

"It's a lot of work, but there is nothing else like it."

"Except maybe lobster, only you get a lot more out of it," he teased.

"I dare you to match it with something from your Midwest."

"What? Like prime beef, maybe? A Delmonico steak?"

She dismissed him with a snort. "The Bay's seafood is the greatest, and steamed crab is the best part of that. Now my dad, he loves oysters. Right out of the shell. Raw."

Jake rolled his eyes. The music began again, loud Jimmy Buffett-style beach music, and they had to eat in silence. But she noticed Jake watching everything going on in the joint, taking note of every person who walked in, even scrutinizing the waiters and busboys.

And that was the problem. When you worked for the FBI you were always on duty. In a restaurant, you automatically sat with your back to the wall. In a bank line, you scanned the other customers for suspicious behavior. When you were working a corruption case, everyone you met was a potential criminal.

You couldn't let go, couldn't relax, couldn't let your guard down because if you failed to pick up a clue on your watch, you'd never forgive yourself.

A couple of times, Jake tried to resume the conversation they'd begun in the car, but it was just too loud in the restaurant. So they confined themselves to small talk and listening to the music. They finished their meal and left. As they drove back to the marina, Jake kept the conversation light, but Cassie could sense something was brewing.

The clouds were gathering in the western sky. It was after nine o'clock and Cassie could see flashes of lightning in the distance. The predicted thunderstorms were on their way. She wanted to air out the boat before she had to batten the hatches again. It would be a long night on the boat, hot and uncomfortable. If it rained she would have to close the ports and the hatches. Inside, then, it would be stifling.

Arriving back at the marina, Jake parked and turned off the engine and Cassie reached for the door handle, hoping to make a quick escape. "Thanks for dinner, Jake—"

He touched her arm and said, "Cass, wait just a minute."

A chill ran through her.

"Cass, I want my partner back. I want you to come and help me with this case."

Cassie looked at his face, at the intensity in his eyes and the set of his jaw. She tried to picture herself going for it, strapping on the gun, pocketing the credentials, hitting the streets. And she couldn't do it, couldn't see it. "I can't do it, Jake. I can't see myself there."

"C'mon, Cass. I need you."

"No. I told you. I don't want to be an agent. I'm through with that." Her heart was drumming. Her hands involuntarily clenched.

His voice was soft. "Maybe you could pray about it, okay? Will you pray?"

She refused to look at him.

Jake shifted in his seat. The leather creaked. "Where do you go to church out here, anyway?"

Defensiveness stiffened her spine. "I don't go. Not now."

"Why not? That was always a big thing with you and Mike, wasn't it?"

Cassie unbuckled her seatbelt. Jake put his hand on her arm again and kept it there.

"I'm just not going, that's all," she said, jerking away. "And why should you care anyway? You thought all that was hooey. So what's the big deal?"

"I find it strange, that's all. Your faith was always so important to you, so much a part of who you were."

"Well I'm sorry if I'm not living up to your expectations in that area, but I'm taking a break, okay? I'm just off-duty for a while. Is that all right with you?" Cassie's eyes blazed in the dim light of the parking lot.

Jake held up his hands. "Fine, fine with me. I was just wondering."

Cassie turned away, staring out of the passenger side window, emotions she could not even name coursing through her in hot waves.

Jake sighed. He drummed his fingers on the steering wheel. "Y'know, Cass, I'm worried about you."

"Don't bother."

"I am going to bother. You're my friend! And you're making a mistake."

"I'm a grown woman! I don't need anyone telling me what to do with my life."

"Don't give me that nonsense!"

"I'm not going back to the Bureau."

"Cassie." He hesitated, reaching out to touch her hand. "I think ... well, I'm afraid for you. I think there's something else going on here. I think maybe ... you're running from something. The grief, maybe."

"What?" she exploded. "How can you say that? How dare you say that?"

He turned toward her. The lights in the parking lot lit the side of his face. His dark eyes were soft but there was an intensity in his expression that pierced her. "You are not grieving. You are cutting out everything that reminds you of your old life with Mike. Everything. The Bureau. Your apartment. Your faith. Responsibilities. Me. It's like, that whole chapter of your life is closed. Kaput. Game over." He gestured toward the docks. "This sailing stuff is nothing but an escape—an escape from pain, from life. Maybe an escape from death. I don't know. But it's an escape. It's not healthy. It's not good for you."

Cassie suddenly felt hot all over. Her anger erupted in an explosive burst of light and heat. She jumped out of the car and started heading for the boat. He followed her, as she knew he would, catching up to her at the edge of the gravel.

"Cass ..." He touched her elbow.

She pushed his hand away. "Since when have you been appointed as my shrink? Since when? What makes you think you could possibly know what's in my head?"

"Cassie, listen—"

"No! You listen to me, Jake. You might be able to work informants, but you are not working me. This is the most self-serving ... idiotic ... ridiculous way of getting me to work with you."

"Self-serving? What are you talking about?"

Cassie's adrenaline was pumping. "Your wife leaves you, right? Now you need someone to share feelings with. To keep you organized. To support your activities. And that's me. That's why you're here. Because the reality is, men don't do very well by themselves. You need me. Or somebody. I'm convenient. So you work up this cock-and-bull psychological stuff to make me feel guilty, so I ..."

Even in the dark, she could see his anger. He'd been angry before, plenty of times, but never with her. This was different, and Cassie couldn't face it. She turned and walked quickly back toward the boat.

"Cassie!" He grabbed her arm. She jerked away and walked faster.

He yelled at her. "I swear, I am thinking of you, not me. I'm worried about you! Honest!"

She was aware of him behind her. She stepped onto her boat and began fiddling with the lock to the companionway. Her hands were shaking so badly she couldn't get the combination to work. The boat dipped under his weight as he followed her. Suddenly she felt trapped—the locked companionway in front of her, him behind. Her throat closed; she didn't know if she could breathe.

"Cassie, you are in denial. And one day you're going to crash. I don't want to see that happen. And yes, I'd love to have you working with me, but Cass ... for crying out loud, would you look at me?"

She wouldn't.

"Cassie, you are going to regret leaving the Bureau. Trust me. You will. Come back now, before it's too late. Please."

A thousand arrows pierced her soul. "It's too late, Jake Tucker." She spun around. "I turned in my creds."

"You did what?" Jake hollered.

"I already quit. So it's too late."

Jake shook his head. He ran his fingers through his hair, incredulous.

"It was already too late the day Mike quit breathing," Cassie continued. "That was five months, two weeks, and one day ago. It was too late then. It's definitely too late now. Now leave me alone. Go bother someone else."

"Cass!"

"I said, leave!" Cassie shoved Jake hard. He grabbed a rail to keep from falling overboard. "Just go away!" she screamed.

He took a deep breath. His voice was shaky with anger. "All right."

"And don't come back. Ever. Do you hear me?"

"You don't mean that."

"I mean it. Find someone else. I don't want to see you again. Get out of my life!" Her head was swimming, her ears ringing. She wanted to run, to fly, anything to get away from this suffocating feeling.

He was standing silently before her, frozen in place. A rumble of thunder began in the west. She had to get him away from here. Now. "Go away, Jake. I don't care about the Bureau. I don't care about you. Now go away. I just want to be alone!"

"I can't believe this."

"Go. Before I call the police."

"Yeah, all right," he muttered, and he stepped off the boat. He turned briefly on the dock, looked at her, but then he walked away, down the dock, into the night. And her heart broke into a thousand pieces, like a fine crystal goblet dropped carelessly on a stone floor.

For the first time, the tiny cabin felt like a box, a coffin, and she couldn't stay there. She went topside, stepped onto the dock, and walked out to the farthest point from land. The wind had come up, and the thunder rumbled more frequently now. She sat down at the end of the dock, her back against a piling. The sky was black as was the water. All over the marina, boats were bobbing, tugging hard at their lines. Halyards were clanging, normally a pleasant sound, but tonight they grated on Cassie's nerves.

Cassie hugged her knees to her chest. She hated herself, hated the fight, hated the sight of Jake Tucker's back as he walked away. She hated the feelings that were swirling inside her, hated the tears that refused to flow, and hated the thought of sleeping yet one more night without Mike. Most of all, she hated the truth that kept rising like a serpent from the tumultuous seas in her mind. The effort that it took to suppress it was exhausting.

The lightning was drawing closer, bolts slashing through the blackness of the night, disappearing, then slashing again like a warrior attacking and withdrawing, then attacking again. Cassie focused on the display, as if allowing herself to be mesmerized by the raw power would take her mind off her own struggle. But in the back of her mind, she was listening to see if she could hear his car start, imagining where he would be going, wondering what he was thinking—her partner, her friend.

So when she heard footsteps approaching, her heart jumped and she leaped to her feet. When she turned, she saw Pat, the waitress from the Blue Goose.

"Are you okay, honey?" she asked.

"Yes, fine. Why?"

"A bunch of us were cleaning up, and we saw you walk out here. You shouldn't be out here with this storm coming. It's not safe."

What was the alternative? The stifling atmosphere of the boat? "I'm ... I'm fine. I was just watching. The lightning is ... magnificent."

Pat shifted position, as if she were unsure what to say. "You live on board one of these, don't you?"

Cassie nodded.

A loud crack made them both jump. "Well, honey, you need to get inside. These storms are nothing to fool with. I've got to get off this dock." Pat turned to leave. "Everybody else was afraid to come out here, but I couldn't go home without checking on you."

"Thank you. Thank you very much. I'm fine."

Pat shook her head. "Good night, then."

"Bye."

When Pat was gone, Cassie slumped to the dock again. She sat there fingering her cross and staring into the darkness as the lightning grew closer and closer, until at last the clouds burst open overhead. As Cassie sat there letting the torrential rain pour over her, she wondered at the tears she still could not shed.

The next day dawned hot and steamy, but the sky was blue and cloudless and a soft mist rose from the water. Cassie was washing her breakfast dishes and trying not to think about the night before when her cell phone rang. She glanced at her watch. It was 8:37.

"Cassie?"

It was a man. She struggled to recognize his voice.

"This is Craig Campbell, at the Bureau."

"Oh, yeah, Craig, hi." Cassie pictured him in her mind. He was an old friend of Mike's, an agent who'd shown Mike the ropes in D.C. One time he and Mike had pulled surveillance four nights in a row. Late into the night, sitting in a car in a bad area of D.C., they'd begun to open up, to talk about some pretty deep issues. That's when Mike had shared his faith with Craig. A month later, Craig became a believer. He'd transferred to Annapolis shortly after that. Now he was working in Baltimore.

"What can I do for you?" Cassie asked.

"I'm looking for Jake. Have you seen him?"

"Last night. Why?"

Campbell sighed. "We have a big powwow uptown with the Assistant U.S. Attorney and a court date tomorrow. He and I were supposed to meet for breakfast this morning. I'm getting no answer at his apartment or on his cell. I paged him at 7:45 and he still hasn't answered. So I'm just trying to backtrack, and I thought he'd said he was going out to see you last night."

"He did. We went to dinner. But he left around ten." Cassie's jaw was tight. It wasn't like Jake to miss a meeting. Or not answer a page.

"Hmmm. He wasn't having car trouble or anything, was he? Did he mention anything to you?"

"No. And anyway, he'd call, Craig. I'm sure he'd call you if something like that came up."

"Okay, well, I'm going to call his ex-wife. Maybe something happened with one of the kids. If you do hear from him, remind him we're supposed to be in town at ten."

"Yeah, sure. Give me your cell phone number. I'll call you if I hear anything."

When she hung up, she threw on khakis, a white shirt, and her boat shoes and ran to the parking lot. His car wasn't there. She scanned the ground around the space where he'd parked. There was one scuffmark, where a tire had spun gravel. He was angry. He probably had hit the accelerator hard.

Cassie felt dizzy. She knew something was wrong. Jake was

compulsively responsible when it came to his job.

What could she do? Cassie walked back to the boat. She was supposed to be changing out the galley stove today but the thought of digging into that project was impossible now. She flopped down on the settee. Her mind was racing, running in circles, and it was exhausting her.

At 8:52 a.m., Campbell called again. "Stay put; I'm on my way there," he said, and she was relieved.

Craig Campbell reminded Cassie of Jake—he had the same physicality, the same command that conveyed confidence with every step. Cassie hadn't seen him since Mike's funeral.

"Hey, Cassie," he said as he approached her on the dock.

"You haven't heard from Jake?"

Campbell shook his head. "I've asked a couple of guys to meet me here—Danny Stewart and Christopher Harding."

"Good."

"I want them to help me look. I'm not waiting. This is too unlike Jake."

"Who's the boss now?" Cassie and Jake's supervisor had retired two months ago. He had been a good friend, and Cassie often wondered if his retirement had anything to do with Mike's death. It had been traumatic for everybody.

"Schaeffer is acting, until the new guy gets here."

Over Campbell's shoulder, Cassie saw what had to be two Bureau cars enter the parking lot. Suddenly her heart was pounding. She touched his arm to keep his attention. "Craig, we had an argument."

"About?"

"Me coming back to the Bureau. And, some other stuff."

Campbell nodded, searching her face. "He left angry?"

"Probably." She had to be honest. "Definitely."

"But not depressed."

She didn't respond.

"Not suicidal."

Cassie shook her head. "No way."

"No, not Jake," he agreed. Still, they both knew the statistics for law enforcement officers. Suicide was common, and with the personal struggles Jake had experienced recently—the death of his best friend, his divorce, the resignation of his partner—anything was possible.

Danny and Christopher approached them on the dock. The sound of their heels on the wood was a rat-a-tat-tat, like the drumming of a military snare drum or a burst of gunfire on a range. The sun was bright now, at ten in the morning, and hot on Cassie's back.

Danny Stewart was an African-American man in his fifties, tall and slim. He had a reputation for being a kind and honorable man, so much so that the others called him "Deacon." A longtime agent, he'd faced his share of discrimination in some of the backwater posts he'd been sent to, and some of the big cities as well, but he'd refused to let those hard experiences sour him. Christopher Harding was a white guy, short, dark-haired, wearing a tan suit, white shirt, and loafers. Cassie didn't know him very well, but he was another runner, and Jake had spoken of him on occasion. Both were friends of Jake—they worked out together in the gym.

Craig Campbell turned around when he heard their footsteps. "Thanks for coming, guys," he said, extending his hand.

"And how are you, young lady?" Danny asked, giving Cassie a gentle hug. "We miss you!"

"Thank you," she responded. "Hello, Chris."

Campbell filled them in, and they asked Cassie a few questions. She answered them, feeling slightly dazed and disoriented.

"You say he left here around ten," said Christopher, "and he was intending to go straight home?"

"As far as I know."

Danny looked at Cassie. "Show us where he was parked."

Cassie took them back to the parking lot. They carefully studied the gravel for markings. In the grass, Campbell found a soggy napkin from the restaurant where they'd eaten that she had probably dropped when she jumped out of the car. But there was nothing to rouse their suspicions, no sign of foul play.

"He could be off the road somewhere."

"Well," said Campbell, gesturing with his hand, "I've left voicemail messages for him at home and at work. I've asked the squad secretary to keep trying his numbers. Betty's on the ball; she'll stay on top of this." He kicked at a small rock on the ground. "I don't want to be an alarmist, but I am concerned."

A white sedan, pierced by multiple antennae, had pulled into the marina parking lot. It stopped ten feet from the assembled agents and a man in a dark gray suit got out. "Craig! What in the world brings you down to our neck of the woods?" he asked as he walked toward them, extending his hand. "Good to see you!"

"You, too, Mark. This is Detective Mark Cunningham, Anne Arundel County police." Craig introduced the others.

Cassie watched the two men carefully. Craig seemed genuinely relaxed around Cunningham. She guessed they'd worked together when Craig was in Annapolis.

"So, what's going on?" Cunningham asked.

Campbell's eyes scanned his face, and it seemed to Cassie that he was carefully calculating his response. Jake could have simply forgotten their meeting. He could be drunk, although Cassie couldn't imagine that, or he could be off with some woman somewhere, although that was even less probable. Campbell wouldn't want to make public something that might embarrass Jake later. On the other hand, for Jake to miss a meeting right before a court date was extraordinary. If something was wrong, they could use all the help they could get in sorting it out.

"We may have a problem, Mark," Campbell finally said, and he explained the situation.

"Why don't you all come back with me to my office?" Cunningham suggested. "I'll check through the accident reports, and you can set up there."

"What do you say?" Craig said, looking at the other agents. After a moment, they nodded in agreement. "Thanks, Mark. We'll take you up on that."

"I want to go with you." Cassie's voice was tight.

The detective looked at her and then at Craig, who nodded his assent. "I think she should be in on it. She's his partner."

Present tense. Cassie felt relieved and saddened at the same time. She dashed to her boat, grabbed a navy blue blazer and her purse, and locked up. She needed to find Jake Tucker. Suddenly her sanity depended on it.

For the next hour and a half they pored over maps, made phone calls, and developed scenarios. Danny left to check out ditches and the areas under bridges on Jake's presumed route home. Chris called hospitals, and then went back to the marina, going from boat to boat questioning people. So far they had come up with nothing.

At noon someone called to order a pizza. Cassie couldn't even imagine eating. Campbell was on the phone again. He was keeping in close contact with Betty, the squad secretary. From the look on his face, his concern was growing.

Cassie leaned over the topographical map spread out on the table. She started to ask Detective Cunningham a question, but when she looked up, he had walked away, toward the open door. A woman and a teenage girl stood there. *Probably his wife and kid,* Cassie thought, and it annoyed her that they would interrupt them.

She looked back at the map and when she looked up again, she saw that Christopher Harding, who had just gotten back from the marina, and Craig Campbell had both joined Cunningham, surrounding the girl. Then Craig looked at her, and the expression on his face sent a shiver of fear down her back.

"Come on," he said, walking over to Cassie and grabbing his suit jacket. "I'll explain on the way."

4

*C*raig Campbell wheeled the Bureau car out of the police department parking lot, following Detective Cunningham. He picked up the radio and called Danny. "Meet me at Cedar Brook Park on Route 192."

"Right. Twenty minutes," Danny responded.

"So what's going on?" Cassie asked. Her heart felt constricted like a tight fist in her chest and her throat had closed up. She could barely breathe.

Campbell glanced at her. "The girl is fifteen."

"Cunningham's daughter?"

"Right. Last night she had permission to go to the movies with her sixteen-year-old cousin and some friends. Instead, they went to a place where the local kids go to party, an undeveloped cul-de-sac in a residential area."

Cunningham had turned on a blue light and was quickening the pace. Campbell reached under the seat and pulled out his own blue light, put it on the dash and accelerated quickly. Then he continued. "The kids parked their car on a deadend street. I guess they were drinking and listening to music, just hanging out when it started to rain."

"That would have been around ten," Cassie interrupted.

"One kid knew about a pavilion in a park, just beyond a tall hedge, where they could get some shelter. They went through the hedge, crossed a drainage ditch, came around some bushes, and then they saw a man. He was dragging a body out of an SUV."

Cassie stared straight ahead, transfixed.

"The kids saw him stab the body, over and over. The girls screamed. The man looked up. The kids beat it back to their car. They heard two shots as they ran." Campbell steered hard to the left, to head down a four-lane highway. "They were all scared to tell their folks where they'd been. But this morning, the guilt got to Cunningham's daughter. She called her mom, who brought her down to see Mark."

"Do you think this involves Jake?"

"It was a black SUV."

"Could be anybody's."

"Could be Jake's."

They rode the rest of the way in silence. Campbell sped down a side street, then finally stopped in a cul-de-sac, in front of a tall hedge. When they exited the car, Cassie looked up, and saw half a dozen vultures circling off to the west. Her stomach wrenched. She wanted to go forward, but she didn't want to face what lay beyond that hedge. She wanted to find Jake, but she didn't want to find him here.

The girl led them through a small opening in the hedge. On the other side was an open field, bisected by a drainage ditch. Beyond the ditch was a stand of tall grass and some shrubs, and beyond that, the pavilion.

The day was hot and humid. Bugs stirred up by their approach stuck to Cassie's skin and buzzed around her head. She waved them off. She wanted to race ahead of the men, to find the victim and prove it was not Jake. Not Jake. No way. But she held back and kept pace with the others.

They jogged through the field, across the ditch, and leaped over the small stream at the bottom. As they climbed the other side, Cassie uttered a soft exclamation. She saw something through the weeds.

The rest of the world disappeared. She broke away from the others and began running. Her head was pounding. She could see a piece of cloth, blue in color, just like the shirt Jake had been wearing the night before. And then, in the weeds, she saw a body lying on the ground. As she grew nearer, there was no doubt in her mind who it was. Jake.

She was vaguely aware of Campbell, who was right behind her, yelling for an ambulance as they ran. She could hear the detective and Christopher following, their feet pounding the soft earth.

Jake was lying on his stomach. His head and arm and neck looked black. As she got closer, she saw he was covered in dried blood. Flies were swarming all around him.

"Oh, no, no, no," she cried. She threw herself down on the ground beside him and gently placed her fingers on his throat. There was a pulse! It was thready and weak, but it was there. "He's alive!" she cried. How long had he been there? Desperately, she brushed the flies away with her hand. They immediately relanded. She pulled her blazer off, swatted the flies again, and draped the jacket over him.

"He's alive! Get the medics, he's alive," she repeated.

"They're on the way," Campbell responded. Jake's left hand clutched his cell phone. Campbell carefully removed it. The phone was covered with blood.

Cunningham and Christopher backed away, quickly scanning the area. They needed to establish a perimeter, search for evidence before everyone showed up and messed up the scene. The young girl stood a ways off, sobbing in her mother's arms.

Cassie focused on Jake. "Jake, it's me, Cassie. Jake, can you hear me?" She stroked his cheek, her hand shaking. The stubble of his beard was scratchy. "Jake, wake up!" *Please*, she pleaded silently, *please wake up*. "Look at me! Jake, Jake!"

His eyes flickered open for just a minute, met hers, and closed again. "You're going to make it, Jake. Hang in there. We're getting help."

"Keep talking to him," Campbell said. Already the scream of an ambulance siren could be heard. Three other carloads of agents showed up. "Mark out a landing site for the medevac helicopter," Campbell told them.

Cassie moved back when the paramedics arrived. She watched as they took Jake's vital signs, set up an IV, began administering fluids, and stabilized his head. When they gently turned him over Cassie gasped. Blood had clotted over a wound on the back of his head. Stab wounds on his right shoulder spilled fresh blood. His hands were bloody. And on the left side of his neck was an odd, inch-long cut, like an incision.

Cassie felt suffocated by fear. How much blood had Jake lost? He absolutely could not die! Life couldn't be that cruel.

The chopper would take Jake to the University of Maryland Shock-Trauma Unit in Baltimore. Campbell was going with him; he'd asked Danny to bring Cassie to the hospital and Chris to take care of his car. All the way to Baltimore, as they skimmed through the traffic on Route 2, Cassie obsessed about Jake. What if he didn't make it? What if she lost him, too?

She was consumed with guilt over the argument they'd had. Six months ago she would never have told Jake Tucker to get out of her life. Why was his presence now so overwhelming? It was like he was pulling her in a direction she didn't want to go, and she had to resist at all costs.

Only now it could cost her Jake.

Who had attacked him? Why? Why didn't Jake fight back? He was an expert in street survival. He had been on the SWAT team. How could someone have gotten the jump on him?

As Cassie rolled the questions over in her mind, country gave way to suburbs and soon the city of Baltimore appeared ahead. She could see the outline of downtown where Federal Plaza, the Inner Harbor, and Camden Yards, home of the Orioles, attracted tourists and locals alike.

The University of Maryland Hospital Shock-Trauma Center was

nestled in the heart of the city amidst tall gray buildings and traffic-clogged streets. Danny dropped Cassie off at the emergency door. "Are you okay by yourself?" he asked her. "I'll go park."

"Sure." She was clutching her blazer, the one she'd draped over Jake, like a security blanket. As she entered the hospital, nausea overwhelmed her as the familiar smell of antiseptic filled her nose.

He would be registered as "John Doe." So how could she find him? She took a guess—he would either be in the emergency room or intensive care. She'd start with the ER.

She walked past the waiting room and acted like she knew what she was doing. Someone called "Miss! Miss!" but she'd spotted Campbell down the hallway so she just kept going.

Campbell hugged her. "He's hanging in there," he reported. Then he showed her to a special waiting room they'd been assigned. It was full of agents; some she knew, others she didn't. Cassie sat down in a blue upholstered chair, off by herself, feeling strangely detached. She hugged her jacket, now stiff with Jake's blood.

Campbell squatted down next to her chair. "Are you okay?"

She nodded. "Where is he?"

"They're working on him." He put his hand on hers. "Be strong." He patted her hand, stood up, and left the room.

Be strong? How?

The thought entered her mind that she should pray, but immediately she rejected that notion. Why pray? What good would it do? Still, she tried. Silently. And she'd get about two words strung together before she just stopped. In the end, all she could say was *Oh God, Oh God, Oh God.*

The waiting went on for hours. They were trying to stabilize him, Craig said. They were giving him fluids and blood. Some of the agents had rolled up their sleeves and walked off to donate. Cassie sat huddled in her chair watching and listening. Questions ran around and around in her head, like monsters on a carousel. *Who did this? Why? How? How could I have stopped this from happening?*

A few of the agents she knew ventured over to talk to her but soon they drifted away, unsure of how to talk to this woman who spoke in monosyllables and refused to look them in the eye.

"Do you want me to call someone for you?" Campbell asked. "A female friend? Betty, or one of the other agents?"

She declined. She had no friends among the women in the office. She'd always hung out with Mike and Jake.

The daylight was fading outside the windows, the perfect blue sky deepening to azure. Like a blanket being spread over a sleeping child, night was covering the city. This is the way it was in a hospital, Cassie knew. Night and day became irrelevant; time progressed slowly if at all.

Finally, when she thought she couldn't stand waiting one more minute, Craig Campbell appeared in the doorway. Everyone in the room suddenly stopped talking and looked toward him expectantly. Cassie unfolded her legs and sat up straight. Campbell waited a long moment. Lines creased the corners of his blue eyes.

Campbell's carriage and demeanor commanded attention and respect. He looked out over the group like a general surveying his troops. "Thank you all for being here. The doctors have stabilized Jake and are preparing to move him to the Intensive Care Unit. The next twelve hours will be critical. He has sustained a severe blow to his head." Campbell pointed to the back of his own skull. "Right about here, resulting in a fractured skull. He also was stabbed six to eight times. He has defensive wounds on his hands and wrist. He's lost a lot of blood. But if he makes it through the next twelve hours, the doctors are hopeful he will live.

"Those of you who have families may want to go home and check back with us tomorrow. We appreciate everyone's continued thoughts and prayers."

Cassie pressed her fingers to her temples. *I hope he will live. He has to live, he just has to!*

"Cassie." Craig touched her shoulder. She looked up. "Let's

take a walk. Come on."

She didn't try to resist. He walked her down to the cafeteria and bought her some chicken noodle soup and a cup of tea and sat down across from her, a hamburger on the plate in front of him. She stared at his wedding ring, and she wondered for an instant if he'd called his wife to say he'd be home late, if at all. And she knew he had because he was that kind of guy, a good guy, steady and stable. Mike had said he had a good heart.

"So, how are you holding up?" he asked.

"Okay."

"So, you like what you're doing now, living down there on that boat?"

"Yeah. It's great."

"Real peaceful?"

"Uh-huh. Yes."

"Jake was kind of worried about you." Campbell kept his eyes on her as he took a sip of Coke.

"I know. You see ...." And before she knew it, she was telling him the whole story, from her husband's death to the decision to restore the boat. "It was like I needed to save it, to rescue it. It had been down three days, and when they brought it up it just seemed natural that I had to fix it, to make it right."

Campbell listened intently, his blue eyes focused on her face as he nodded in understanding.

"I named it *Time Out,* and I worked on it every day. And then Jake showed up, and I was glad to see him, but I felt like he was pressuring me, you know? Pulling me back toward a place I didn't want to be."

"Because you really don't want to resume your career with the Bureau."

"No. I just lost my heart when Mike died. I couldn't do it anymore. And Jake, he wouldn't take no for an answer."

"So you had an argument."

Cassie took a deep breath. "Yes, and I am so sorry. I ran him off.

I was so scared, and so angry. I just shoved him away, literally. I just couldn't deal with him!"

"I'm sure he felt bad about it, too."

Cassie winced at the remembrance.

"Jake thinks an awful lot of you. You're his partner. That means a lot. You're one of his best friends. Maybe the best."

She shook her head. "I didn't act like it. And now ... Craig, he just can't die."

"I know." He hesitated, as if he were unsure of her reaction. "Mike's death was hard on you."

What could she say to that? She just nodded.

Campbell began to gather up their dishes. "Come on. Let's go find out if we can get in to see Jake."

5

*T*he hospital corridors were painted a soft, pale blue and decorated with watercolors of natural scenes—vases full of flowers and ponds bordered by grassy fields. It was nearly ten at night and the visitors were gone. The only people Cassie and Craig passed were employees dressed in scrubs or brightly colored uniforms.

Craig seemed to know where he was going, a fact that gratified Cassie. He held open a double door for her. "The doctors have him heavily sedated," he said in a low voice. "They're hoping that will help the swelling in his brain go down and minimize brain damage."

"Minimize? What do they mean, 'minimize'?"

Campbell guided her to turn into a corridor. "Jake has sustained a very serious head injury. It's too soon to say what his prognosis will be, but the doctors are hopeful. He's on a respirator, because he's essentially in a coma. He won't be able to respond to you at all. You'll see tubes—down his nose, in his arm, in his side. His head is shaved and bandaged, and his arm is in a sling. I just don't want you to be surprised by his condition."

"How long will they keep him sedated?"

"We're going to get through the next twelve hours, then we'll go from there."

"Has anyone called Tamara?"

"I talked to her. She won't be coming over."

Another wave of sadness buffeted Cassie.

The pair walked into the wide bay of the Intensive Care Unit. Individual beds were placed in cubicles arranged like spokes on a wheel around the central desk. Data from each patient was displayed on monitors at the desk. At any given moment, a staff member could check Mr. Martinez' blood pressure or Mrs. Morgan's heart rate.

Craig led her through the unit to a private room. He nodded to the agent on guard as they entered.

Jake was lying motionless in the bed, strangely dwarfed by the beeping machines that categorized and calculated his vital signs. His head was shaved and swathed in white bandages, but Cassie could see bruising around his right temple and cheek, and his face was misshapen. Her stomach turned. It must have been a terrible blow to cause discoloration and swelling that far out. His right arm was stabilized in a sling and his shoulder was bandaged. A nasal-gastric tube ran into his nose and an IV pierced the back of his left hand.

She began shivering. He had the look of a corpse—he bore a resemblance to the man she'd known in life, but he was not quite right. She wondered if life was leaving him even now.

The room was dark and quiet except for the beeping and the sound of the respirator. Cassie approached the bed and touched his hand. It was cool. She cradled it in both of hers. She had to fight to keep from being overwhelmed. Six months ago it was Mike. Now it was Jake. Both men in hospital beds, heads bandaged, full of tubes ... it was all too horribly familiar. Which one was this? It was Jake, and he couldn't die. It wouldn't be fair.

Campbell came up next to her and put his arm around her shoulder. She leaned against him, finding his touch comforting. "Jake's very strong," he said.

"I know."

"He has a good chance, better than most, to make it."

Cassie touched Jake's face gently. They'd pulled off night

surveillances together, worked sources, followed a fugitive until they were both sick of the guy. She'd loved her husband deeply. Jake was knit into her soul like a brother. The three of them had been such good friends. *This isn't fair!* her heart cried.

"They've asked us to keep visits to no more than fifteen minutes every hour," Campbell said.

She looked up at him. "I want to stay. He's sleeping. I just want to stay with him for a while."

A nurse had entered the room as she was speaking. "Are you a member of his family?"

Cassie shook her head. "He doesn't really have any—just his small children and a brother in another state. I was ... I am a good friend."

The nurse looked her over from head to toe. "It's not usually allowed, but I don't see how your staying here could hurt." The nurse turned to Craig. "Maybe you could help me bring in a chair for her."

He was alive, or at least he thought he was. He was floating in a sea of blackness. To his right, and behind, was a searing, white-hot pain. He wanted to get away from it. Back and to the left was a bottomless void, and once in a while he would begin to slide toward it. That terrified him. He fought with every bit of strength he could muster to move toward the voices, away from the Pit.

He felt oddly disconnected from his body. He could feel people moving him, feel them pricking him with needles, feel hands probing him, but he could not make his own hands or feet or head move. He wanted to speak to them, to tell them he was in there, but he could not find his voice. And so he fought against the pain and the Pit, silently screaming.

At 11:00 p.m. the door opened and a man she recognized walked in. He looked at Jake, then he turned to her. "Cassidy McKenna? Do you have a minute?"

It was Special Agent Kevin DiCarlo, the case agent for the AFO—Assault on a Federal Officer. Now, he wanted to talk to Cassie. She followed DiCarlo to a private waiting room. He pulled out a notebook, a pen, and some reading glasses, which he perched on the end of his nose.

DiCarlo was about forty, with thinning brown hair. He was slightly paunchy and had an old food stain on his tie. She remembered he'd worked for years on a frustrating fraud case that had gotten hung up in the courts. It had become a standing joke in the office. Ol' One-Case DiCarlo. Other than that, she didn't know anything about him.

"I need you to tell me, Cassie, exactly what went on when Jake came to see you, before he was attacked. First of all, why was he there?"

So Cassie began to tell the story. By the time she got to their argument, her stomach was knotted and her head was pounding.

"So you argued. Did it ever get physical?" DiCarlo asked.

"No. No, wait," she instantly corrected herself. "I did push him. I was so frustrated, I shoved him away."

"Ah," he said, jotting something in his notebook. "Did he fall down?"

"No, of course not."

"Did you have something in your hand when you pushed him?"

"No."

"A tool? A purse?"

"No!" Cassie felt her irritation growing.

"What happened after you pushed him?"

"He left. I told him to leave, and he left and went back to his car."

"Did you follow him?"

"No."

"Not even part of the way?"

"Of course not! Look—"

"Did you feel intimidated by Jake?"

"No." Cassie fingered the cross on her neck.

DiCarlo looked at her as if he didn't believe her. "You didn't feel threatened by him, and yet you felt like you had to push him to get him away from you?"

"That's right." Cassie stood up and started to pace.

DiCarlo jotted down some more notes. "Your husband died how long ago?"

"The end of November."

"And how long have you been seeing Jake?"

Cassie bristled. "We aren't *seeing* each other."

"Oh, well then, how would you characterize your relationship?"

"We were partners, and friends. He was a good friend to both me and my husband."

The more questions DiCarlo asked, the less Cassie liked him. He kept coming back to her relationship with Jake, as if there had to be more to it than she was admitting. But there wasn't, and she refused to be bullied.

Finally, his questions started to take a different angle. Had Jake mentioned anyone lately that he had a conflict with? What about his ex-wife? Her boyfriend? How much did he drink? Where did he tend to hang out? Was she aware of anyone who owed him money? Or anyone Jake owed money to?

The more questions he asked, the more irritated Cassie got. Why was he only focusing on Jake's personal life?

After an hour, DiCarlo closed his notebook. He thanked her for her cooperation, and Cassie shook his hand firmly, to show him she wasn't intimidated. Then she went back to the ICU, and sat in the dim room, and watched Jake sleep.

Relentless pain consumed him, flooding his thoughts and overpowering him. It felt like a heated iron bar plunged into his head, behind and above his ear.

As the voices grew more distinct, the pain increased. And then he felt his eyes open, and he was in a tunnel, looking out. He tried to focus, to see faces and name the people around him but it was too exhausting, and in the end he closed his eyes again. If only he could let them know he was there, that he could hear them. If only he could tell them about the pain.

But he couldn't. Frustrated, soon he drifted off again, floating in a sea of blackness bordered by despair.

Craig Campbell came into the room. He looked tired.

"Hello, Cassie." He glanced toward Jake.

"Still no change," she said, anticipating his question. She leaned forward. "What's going on?"

Craig sagged down into the second chair in the room. "Not much."

"What do you have so far?"

He looked at her, measuring his response. "Let's step outside."

Cassie followed him out to the hallway. Craig led her away from the guards. He stopped near an empty gurney and ran his finger down the bed's metal rail. His hesitation was killing her. Finally, his eyes met hers. "We've canvassed the marina, and all of the houses near the park. No hits so far. We found two 40mm casings on the ground near where we found Jake. Maybe the perpetrator tried shooting him and missed. We don't know. The teens are all juveniles, but their stories are matching up. They didn't get a good look at the guy; they just know he's white and was wearing dark clothes and a hat pulled down low."

"What kind of a hat?"

"They described it as a floppy-brim hat, white or light in color."

Cassie nodded. Kind of odd for a killer. "How about his truck?"

"Jake's SUV? No sign of it. We've entered it in NCIC." The National Crime Information Center had a huge database of missing vehicles.

"His laptop was in it. I saw it."

"We were operating under that assumption. So, whoever has the car could hack into the laptop and access a whole lot of information. Maybe that was the motive."

Cassie shook her head. "This is so frustrating!"

"We'll find him, Cassie. There's not an agent out there who doesn't want to get the guy that hurt Jake. You know yourself, even the agents who hate your guts close ranks when something like this happens."

"I know, Craig. I know."

"Tell me, Cassie, did Jake mention anything to you about any of his cases?"

"Just one ... he was looking into the murder up at Sullivan's Wharf and wanted my input. Some friend of Tam's contacted him for help. I couldn't figure out why he was so concerned, but he seemed determined to pursue it."

"Okay ... thanks. We'll start checking that out."

Craig touched her arm. He looked concerned. "Cassie, there is one more thing."

"What?"

"When the evidence techs were going over the ground where Jake was attacked—"

She was holding her breath. What was he going to say?

"—they found something in the mud where Jake was lying ... a piece of paper with a partial address on it. It may have fallen out of his pocket."

"Jake was always doing that—writing addresses where he was supposed to meet people on odd scraps of paper. It drove me nuts. What was the address?"

"As I said, it was only a partial: 128, then we can't read the street, except for the letter 'S' and the letters 'A-N-N-A-P' which of course, must be Annapolis. We've got someone looking at possibilities. But, Cassie, I need to ask you something. Did Jake ever verbalize any theories about Mike's death?"

"Mike's death? Theories? What are you talking about?" Suddenly her heart was pounding.

"About how Mike died."

"It was an accident. Mike died in an accident," she asserted.

Craig looked away, and Cassie's heart tightened. She grabbed his arm. "Craig, it was an accident. The roads were slick, it was late ..." His failure to respond to her was alarming. Cassie wanted to shake him. "That's what they told me from the beginning. It was an accident. Craig, look at me! What are you saying?"

His eyes were bright and filled with compassion. "I ... well, I was never comfortable with that finding. Mike had been out plenty of times in much worse weather. He was a good driver ... I don't know. I just never bought the idea that he'd had an accident."

Cassie's heart was thumping. She wondered if Craig could hear it.

"We can read the last two digits of the zip code on that note we found. And one possibility is an address not far from where Mike killed that man."

"So what? What does that prove? How many people live in that vicinity, anyway, fifty thousand? There's no proof that Mike's accident was anything but that."

Craig swallowed hard. "I was uncomfortable, as I said, with the findings, so once I got to Baltimore, I convinced them to have the lab go over Mike's Bureau car again." He hesitated. "And they did find some green paint on the side panel."

"Green paint? How much? Why hasn't anyone told me this before now?" *Did somebody hit Mike and force him off the road?*

"No one wanted to upset you. We weren't sure what it meant. It's not much paint, just a little, from a Ford make, an Explorer most likely. It may be nothing, or —"

"Or it could be that someone killed Mike? Is that what you're saying?" Cassie's face was hot.

Campbell nodded. "I told Jake about all of this a week before he was assaulted. He was furious. And if he was looking into it himself, if he'd made contact with a source, or started asking questions ..."

"He may have stumbled onto something relevant, and that could have instigated the attack." She could barely get the words out. Her breathing was shallow, as if she dared not inhale too much air. There was a loud buzzing sound in her ears like the drone of a million bees.

"If Mike's death was not an accident," Craig said softly, "and if it was connected to Jake's assault, then we could have a very dangerous person running around out there. Someone who's willing to kill agents to cover up whatever he's doing."

Cassie slumped against the wall and Craig put his arm around her shoulder for support. A dull ache gripped her. She wanted to cling to Craig and run at the same time.

Mike murdered? Was it possible?

Craig Campbell talked Cassie into getting a room at a nearby hotel for the night, just to relax, to take a break. He drove her over there and offered to stay and talk if she needed to. But all she wanted was to be alone.

Somewhat reluctantly, Craig left. Cassie took a hot shower and curled up in bed. She lay there, wide awake, staring into the dark, mentally going over all of Mike's cases that she could remember. The drug dealers. The fugitives. A public-corruption case.

She turned on the light and found a small hotel notepad, and started writing down names, places, anything she could remember. When she'd exhausted her knowledge, she went over his hospital stay from beginning to end ... the first view of him as they were prepping him for surgery, the days and nights at his bedside, everything the doctors had said. And she started to reconsider all of that in the context of his death as a murder, not an accident.

It made her sick.

The only thing she knew for sure was that Mike was dead. Was he killed? Who killed him? And why? Is that why Jake had been bugging her so much about coming back to the Bureau? Because he suspected Mike was murdered and he knew she'd want to be in on that?

He was right. If Mike had been murdered, Cassie had to make sure the killer was found. She would not, could not allow it to become a cold case. And if the same person had attacked Jake, that was all the more reason to get the guy.

Suddenly, with a clarity she hadn't felt in months, she knew what she had to do.

6

—————

You seem in better spirits. You get some sleep last night?" Craig asked Cassie as they walked toward a hall lounge near Jake's room. The lounge was constructed in a corner of the building and had large windows overlooking the city. The afternoon sun was bright, illuminating the entire room.

Cassie stared at him intently. "I did get some sleep. But only after I made a decision."

"What's that?"

"I'm reactivating. Coming back to the Bureau. I wrote the letter last night and delivered it to the office this morning."

Craig raised his eyebrows. "Coming back? Are you sure?"

"Yes." Cassie unconsciously shifted her weight to the balls of her feet. "You told me yesterday that my husband might have been murdered. They should have done more to rule that out to begin with. They should have been more aggressive. If it hadn't been for you and Jake ..."

"You know yourself it looked like an accident."

"Doesn't matter. The finest investigative agency in the world should have pursued it."

"Yes, but Cassie, are you sure you want to suit up again? Why don't you—"

"Think about it? No, there's nothing more to think about. I've got to make this right. Mike's dead, and Jake's hurt. I'm the only one left who really cares, besides you. I have to find the person who did this. And if there's a connection, if there's any possible connection between Mike's death and Jake's assault—"

"You'd be at risk to go anywhere near the case," Craig interrupted. "The perp might already know who you are."

"You know what? I don't care. I really don't."

"They won't let you work it. They'll say it's too personal."

"I will work it. One way or the other."

An orderly passed by the doorway. Craig waited for him to get out of earshot. "You know who would be your boss?"

She tilted her head.

"Frank Foster."

Her heart sank. She didn't know much about the new squad supervisor, but what she did know wasn't good. He was nit-picky, people said. A real bean-counter who went strictly by the rules. Last she'd heard he was on a fast track upwards, so why was he busted back to squad supervisor?

"Rumor is he's being spanked for a mistake a subordinate made," Craig said, anticipating her question, "and that's why he's here. He's a by-the-book man, and even more so now that he's taken a hit for somebody else's actions."

"So he plays by the rules. I can deal with that."

"Some people say they're Nazi rules."

Cassie set her jaw. "Even if I have to work for him, I will do it. I will not let these cases get sidelined, just swept under the rug because they can't figure it out."

Craig looked off across the room, as if he'd run out of arguments and wasn't sure how to handle this worked-up woman. Cassie inspected his face, from his thick neck to the small lines around his eyes and the shape of his nose, searching for answers hidden there, as if wisdom were chiseled into his jaw and etched into his brow.

Craig turned and looked at Cassie. "It's a lot to deal with, isn't it?"

She looked away, suddenly embarrassed.

A couple came down the hall, talking intently with each other. Cassie focused on them, willing herself to calm down. She wondered what they were saying, and why there was so much tension between them. An orderly pushing a man lying on a gurney came by, and in a flash, she saw Mike, lying on that bed, fighting to live. She trembled.

"Life's pretty tough," Craig said. His eyes indicated he'd seen her stress.

Was he leading up to something? Cassie braced herself.

"Mike told me something that I've never forgotten, one time when I was going through something really hard. He said, 'You know, none of this was any surprise to God.'"

Cassie bristled. "I don't even know what that means," she snapped.

She could see the color rise in Craig's face, and then in her mind's eye she saw a picture on her aunt's wall. It said, "Trust his heart when you can't see his hands." She'd never understood what that meant. She still didn't.

Less than a week later, Cassie received a letter at her post office box. Her dad picked it up and faxed it to her at the hospital. She read it, then, seething, she called and demanded a meeting with the bureaucrat at headquarters in Washington who'd sent it to her.

The day she drove to Washington was hot and sticky. She had the top down on her Volkswagen Cabrio and sitting in the stop-and-go traffic wilted her. By the time she'd found a place to park and walked into the J. Edgar Hoover Building, she was irritable and impatient. Dealing with security only raised her blood pressure further.

Nevertheless, at 2:00 p.m. sharp she was sitting across a desk from Charles A. Caldwell, a specialist in human resources. He was looking at a file in front of him, and he was frowning. "Now, you just resigned, Ms ..."

"McKenna," Cassie said. "Cassidy McKenna."

"And you want to be reinstated?"

You bet, she thought, but she straightened her skirt and tried to relax her expression. She wanted to sound professional, in control, and positive. "That's right. I want to resume my career as a special agent."

"That's a pretty quick turnaround. You only just left." Caldwell peered at her over his glasses. He appeared to be in his forties. His face was fleshy and pockmarked, his hairline receding. There was no "SA" or "SSA" before his name on the sign on his desk. He was not an agent and that meant she couldn't play the agent-fraternity card.

"There were extenuating circumstances and, well, frankly, I realized almost immediately I'd made a mistake." She cocked her head and flashed him a smile, all the while hearing Jake's assertions playing over and over in her head. "You're making a mistake," his voice said. "You'll regret leaving the Bureau some day." She forced the thoughts to the back of her mind.

Caldwell looked down again at the papers. Behind him, on the wall, were certificates from a management-training program. *Big deal,* Cassie thought. *How impressive.*

Finally, he put the papers back on his desk. "Well, we'll see. I'll put the paperwork in. We have a normal review procedure for these requests."

Cassie felt the heat of anger rise in her blood. "How long will that take?"

The man shrugged. "The usual time frame is somewhere around six months."

"That's ridiculous. Can't you make an exception? As you said yourself, I only just resigned! It was, what, two weeks ago?"

"There are no exceptions. Sorry."

Cassie didn't want to give up. "Look, not only did my husband die, but my partner's been attacked as well, and as you can imagine, the squad is short. They need me and I really want to be back on the job, too. I can get—"

The man flipped her file shut. "We don't make exceptions. That's the bottom line. You turned in your creds and your gun. If you want them back, you'll have to wait. That's it."

She persisted. "Who can I talk to besides you?"

"I'm it."

"Who's your boss?"

"Now that would be Special Agent Carson," the man said with a half-smile, "but I'm afraid he's out of town. Sorry, Ms. McKenna."

He stood up. The interview was over. Cassie rose from her seat, started toward the door, then looked back at Caldwell. He was obviously looking her over, and a hot flash of indignation coursed through her.

"Would you like a cup of coffee, before you drive back?" he asked.

"Not particularly," Cassie retorted, and she grabbed her attaché case and walked out.

Cassie's neck was tight as she walked back to her car. *They're idiots,* she kept saying to herself. *They don't understand. They don't have a clue how the field works.*

But gradually, as she sorted her way through the increasingly dense rush-hour traffic, she reviewed her options. And on I-95, headed back to Baltimore, she swallowed her pride and placed a call. Maybe the new squad supervisor could ask the Special Agent in Charge to get headquarters to make an exception. Frank Foster might be a stickler, but maybe he'd do that for her.

He agreed to see her the next day.

The receptionist who greeted her at the Baltimore field office was new, and Cassie felt irritated at having to show her driver's license for an ID, and then having to wait to be buzzed in and be escorted by a staffer. This was her office just a short time ago. So now she was unreliable?

She had purposely worn her best navy blue suit and heels, which after months of Docksiders and sandals made her feet uncomfortable. A few people looked up as she walked down the hall, and she was painfully conscious of the large visitor's badge pinned to her lapel.

Foster had taken over her old boss's office. It had a view overlooking the Baltimore Beltway that could be quite entertaining during rush hour. As Cassie walked in she looked out the window. In the distance she could see flags whipping, announcing the kind of wind she'd love to sail in. The thought was tempting.

Frank Foster sat behind the large desk and Cassie noticed he was wearing French cuffs with gold cufflinks under his expensively tailored blue suit. He wore a Princeton tie, and on his desk was a brass sculpture of a tiger. Behind him, on the credenza, was a picture of a beautiful blonde woman—his wife, no doubt—and a second one of a shiny, red 1965 Mustang convertible.

Foster motioned for her to sit down in one of the studded leather chairs. "What did you want to see me about, Ms. McKenna?" he said, continuing to hold a sheaf of papers in his hand.

"Well, sir, I need your help," Cassie began. "After all that's happened, I've decided to ask to be reinstated as an agent. I got this," she said, handing him the letter she'd received, "from headquarters. And I went to see a guy down there. He's insisting I go through the normal review process."

Foster frowned slightly. "What does this have to do with me?"

"I thought if perhaps you recommended that I be reinstated, considering the circumstances, that might speed up the process. I could come back to work sooner." Her voice was calm but her heart was pounding in her chest and her palms were sweaty.

Foster leveled his cold gray eyes at her. He sat back in his chair. She counted the seconds in her head.

"No," he said finally. "I'm not going to do that."

"Why?" Cassie demanded.

"Don't want to."

"Why not?"

He shrugged. "There's no compelling reason for me to get involved. I'm not going to go to headquarters or the SAC for a non-issue."

Cassie bristled. "So, you don't think getting a fully trained agent back is worth a little effort?"

Again, he shrugged.

"You can't just make a phone call? Or mention it to the SAC?"

His silence told her the discussion was over. She stood up. "Well, I know I'm worth it, sir. I am worth reinstatement. And I'll get it, with or without your help."

"Fine." He tapped his pen on the desk. "Maybe you'll get it, maybe you won't."

Cassie hesitated. "Why wouldn't I?"

"Off the record?"

She nodded.

"You blinked."

"I blinked? My husband," she took a deep breath, "was killed."

"That may be."

"I think that's a good reason to reconsider my career."

"Stuff happens all the time. Husbands die. Wives leave. Kids get sick. The Bureau can't afford an agent who calls 'time out' just because of a personal loss."

Her face reddened. "That's ridiculous."

"Perhaps in your book. Not in mine. I don't like people who quit. I'm not anxious to have someone on my team who can't stick out a tough situation. Maybe you should go find another career."

Now Cassie's temples were throbbing and her face was burning. Foster's icy stare was unwavering. His phone buzzed. He picked it up and his face grew even darker as he listened. "Yes, do it. Do it now. Right now!" he said and hung up the receiver. Foster stood up quickly and moved out from behind his desk. Cassie could see he was agitated. Was it her? The phone call? "If there's nothing else, Ms. McKenna, I have work to do."

She left, and as she stood in the hallway and pressed the button for the elevator, a sickly feeling crept over her.

7

He was asleep when it started. Hands were all over him probing, adjusting, moving him. He could hear equipment being rolled away and soft, urgent voices. He forced his eyes open just as they lifted him and moved him sideways onto a stretcher that was on a gurney next to his bed. Orderlies and nurses surrounded him. A doctor gave orders. They began strapping him onto the board. He wanted to protest but he couldn't find his voice. Then he saw Craig Campbell standing by the door, his jacket pushed back to reveal his gun.

Something was up. Jake swallowed and submitted, concentrating just on breathing.

When they were finished strapping him in, the nurse stepped aside so Campbell could come near. "We've got to move you, Jake. Don't worry. We've got a helo on the roof. It'll be a quick trip through the halls and then you're out of here. We've got you covered. Don't worry."

The gurney started moving. It took a right turn outside his door, and then they began moving quickly. He could hear the creaking of the wheels, the padding of shoes on the floor, the brisk, quiet commands of Campbell. The ceiling was flying by. A hard left turn and he was on an elevator. The doors closed, the lift began.

Seconds later he was on the helo pad. The bird was cranking, the blades beating the air, wind whipping. The sun was so bright Jake squeezed his eyes shut. Hands grabbed the stretcher, pulling him off the gurney. They raced to the copter, and then he felt them strapping the stretcher down. A medic took his pulse. Off to the side, Campbell

buckled himself in the jump seat. They lifted off. Jake closed his eyes.
And the city of Baltimore dropped away beneath them.

Cassie left the FBI building angry and confused. Squinting in the bright sunlight, she retrieved her sunglasses from her purse and put them on. She had no idea what to do next. Foster had just slammed a door, one she had assumed would be open if she wanted it to be. Hadn't she been a good agent? Hadn't she won the respect of her peers and the acclaim of her superiors? Hadn't she proven her dedication and willingness to work and work hard?

So why this? Why now? Had it been a fatal mistake to ask for time to grieve? Wasn't she allowed to be human?

What was she supposed to do now? Where was she supposed to go?

A man in a dark blue suit talking on a cell phone bumped into her and walked on without apology. Other people on the steps stared at her, the only one not moving. She wanted to scream.

Cassie was preoccupied as she walked down the hallway of the hospital and didn't notice that the guards were gone outside the ICU door until she was almost at the threshold. *That's odd,* she thought and pushed in the door. Inside Jake's room, a woman in a hospital uniform was making up the bed. The monitors were gone. The extra chair was gone. Jake's IV stand, his bedside equipment, and his chart were gone. The flowers, cards, and pictures from his kids—all gone.

Cassie's chest, already tight with tension, constricted even more. "Where is he?" she demanded.

"Ma'am?"

"Where is he? The patient who was in here ... where is he?"

"I don't know. They just told me to make up the room."

Cassie spun around and stormed to the nurses' station. "Where is he? The man who was in the last room. Where did he go?"

A young nurse who looked Middle Eastern opened her mouth to respond but an older nurse interrupted. "He is no longer with us."

"Why? Did you move him? What happened?"

"All we know is that he is no longer with us."

Cassie slammed her fist down on the counter. "Just tell me! He's my friend!" *Tell me he's alive,* she thought to herself, although she could not bring herself to mouth those words.

There was dead silence, the nurses staring at her with expressionless faces. "He's not here," said the older nurse, "and you need to leave."

Where was Jake? What had happened?

She turned and left. She jogged to the elevator, pushed past an older lady, and slammed her fist into the button that would take her to the lobby. When the doors opened, she raced into the lobby and from there, went outside.

The day was still sunny, and it was hot. She moved to the edge of the sidewalk, pulled out her cell phone, and dialed Craig's cell number. There was no answer. She left a message and then called him at work. Voice mail. She called two other agents on their squad, then tried Jake's ex-wife, Tamara.

"How should I know? They didn't call me," was the chilly response.

Surely they would have notified the mother of his children if he had died! Surely they would have done that!

Cassie reentered the hospital, trying desperately to remember the name of the neurosurgeon who had been treating Jake. Dr. Ohn, that was it. Trying to look casual, she walked to a wall map of the hospital and studied the plan. Then she took the elevator to the physical therapy wing on the third floor. Walking past a small office she noticed an unattended white lab jacket and for a minute considered lifting it, slipping it on, and allowing it to be her passport through the labyrinthine maze of the hospital. But she resisted.

Instead, she decided she would just play dumb if she were caught. She walked through a therapy room filled with stroke victims, MS patients, and a brain-injury survivor or two. No Jake. She didn't see Dr. Ohn or any of the therapists she knew.

She pushed through the door on the other side and headed for the brain trauma unit on the fourth floor. Where were the doctors' offices? Did they have offices?

Carefully avoiding the nurses' station, Cassie threaded her way through the wing. Nothing. She walked past two parked gurneys and a hallway filled with monitors, took a right, and saw a small door leading to an office. The sign read, *Dr. Ohn.* The door was closed and locked.

"No!" Cassie cried. Unsure what to do next, Cassie tried to regroup. Finally, she pulled out an old business card—one that identified her as an agent—and scrawled, "Please call me" on the back, changed the phone number on the front, and shoved it under the door of the office. Impersonating an agent? Could they get her for that?

Retracing her steps, she moved back toward an elevator. Rounding a corner, she almost ran over the young nurse she'd seen at the ICU nurses' station.

"Oh!" the nurse exclaimed.

Cassie grabbed her and backed her up to the wall. "Tell me! You have to tell me! What happened to him?" Her voice was a harsh whisper.

The nurse's eyes deflected.

"Please!" Cassie begged. "Please tell me." The nurse looked up at her. "Is he alive? Please, can you just tell me that—is he alive?"

Tears came to the nurse's eyes. She nodded quickly, pushed past Cassie, and hurried down the hallway. Cassie watched her go. "Thank you," she breathed, and she wasn't sure to whom.

For the next four hours, Cassie lived in a cold sweat. She felt like she herself was hovering between life and death, afraid to move, afraid to breathe, afraid to be out of cell tower range.

When her phone finally rang, she answered it quickly. "Hello?"

"Cassie?"

"Craig! What happened, where is he?"

"Listen—we had to move him."

"To where? Why?"

"There was a credible threat against his life. Someone came into the hospital looking for him. The information clerk told him Jake wasn't registered. Later, on her break, she saw the same guy roaming the floor near ICU. She told the guard, and when he approached the man, he ran down the steps and out of the ER. Cassie, we decided he wasn't safe. We couldn't protect him there. So we moved him, by helo."

"When did this happen?" Cassie gripped her cell phone as Craig told her. It was right when she was in Foster's office. "When can I see him? Is he all right?"

"He's fine. But listen, you won't be able to see him. Not now, not for a long time."

"What?" Her head was spinning.

"We've made arrangements for him at a rehab center. He'll be there for a long, long time. It'll be months, Cassie, before you can see him again. I'm sorry."

"Why?" Cassie cried. She was standing near a brick wall in the Inner Harbor of Baltimore. She leaned back against it, as if its strength could carry her. The bricks were hot. She swore she could feel the wall swaying.

"Cassie?"

"Can't you tell me where he is? I'm his partner!"

There was a pause at the other end. "No. I wish I could. But I absolutely cannot. I'm sorry … I'll be in touch, okay?"

"Why are you doing this to me!" she yelled.

Craig hesitated. "I know you're hurting. But you know what? It's not about you, Cassie, it's about him."

Cassie left Baltimore, driving south through rush-hour traffic on Route 2. The day seemed even hotter than it was at noon, hotter and more miserable. Ahead, in the bright blue sky she could see planes making their approach to the Baltimore-Washington International Airport, just to the west. She was surrounded by commuters, all stuck in their little hot cars, waiting in line to end their day so they could begin it all again tomorrow.

What now? Where could she go? Back to the boat? No.

Her father, Jim Davison, lived in a small beach house right on the Bay, just half an hour from Goose Creek. The blue bungalow had a screened-in porch that overlooked the water, two small bedrooms, a living room, and a tiny eat-in kitchen. One of the bedrooms was a study lined with books, but its small couch turned into a bed. That's where Cassie stayed whenever she came to visit.

Her dad wasn't at home when she got there, but Mr. Henry, the yellow cat, greeted her enthusiastically in the front yard. Cassie ignored him and entered the house through the screened porch, through the door her father always kept unlocked. Once inside, she went to the kitchen, threw some ice cubes in a glass, and poured in Diet Dr Pepper. She found a lime in the refrigerator, sliced it, and put the slice and some maraschino cherries in the drink.

Her father's computer was in a corner of his bedroom. He'd used the same password since she was in high school. Cassie turned it on and logged on to the Internet. She might be out of the loop but she wasn't stupid.

When her father walked in an hour later, she was still at it.

"Cass!"

"Hi, Dad. Hope you don't mind ..."

"No, not at all." At age sixty Jim Davison was slim and fit. He had a weathered complexion and his shock of silver hair made him look distinguished and wealthy, which he decidedly was not. A retired biology professor from the University of Maryland, he had spent his life outdoors, and had passed on his love of nature to his two children. Cassie's brother was a park ranger in Utah.

Jim leaned down and kissed his daughter. He threw his hat onto the bed. He sat down and began pulling his boots off. His khaki pants were stained and Cassie knew he'd been in the field all day, working on something. He might be retired, but Jim Davison still studied.

He looked at his daughter and he dropped the first boot on the floor. "What are you up to?"

Cassie stood up and turned toward him. "Dad, something came up. They moved Jake. There was some kind of threat. I don't know what. Craig Campbell just got him out as fast as he could."

"Out of the hospital?"

Cassie nodded. "They had a helicopter and everything. Just, zoom, and off he goes. I went there after my appointment with Foster—oh, and by the way, guess what—he won't let me come back. He says I blinked." Her heart was pounding now and she began to realize how angry she was.

"Whoa, wait. The Bureau won't reinstate you?"

She waved her hand. "How's that for a crock? They say there is a mandatory six-month review process. Anyway, so after that I went to see Jake and he was gone—the room was empty. I was frantic. Nobody would tell me anything. Dad it was so scary. I didn't know if he was dead or alive."

"How'd you find out?"

"Finally Craig called, and he told me the story. Except, Dad, get this, he won't tell me where they've taken him, just that wherever it is, Jake will be able to get the rehab he needs." Cassie sat back down at the computer and her father rose from the bed. "It's probably that idiot Foster who won't let him speak. The guy's a total jerk. I can't believe it.

"So look," Cassie continued, "I'm not stupid. I'm figuring it is some place away from the population centers, away from either coast. I looked up head injury on the Net, and now I'm in the process of identifying rehab centers." She sensed her father moving close behind her. "Now, they'll register him under a false name, but the diagnosis will be the same, so all I have to do is—"

"Cass," her father said softly.

"—figure out the most likely centers. I mean, I'll check them all if I have to ..."

"Cass." Davison squeezed his daughter's shoulder gently.

"What?"

"Come here." He put his hand under her arm and guided her to her feet, then he took her in his arms and held her close to his chest. "Cass, you're going to have to let him go."

She pushed back. "What?"

"Come here, come here." He held her again. "You've got to let Jake go. They don't want you to find him. It's no use trying."

"But ..." She could feel heat rising in her face.

"Listen, sweetheart. You need to just let him go. Let the Bureau do what they need to do. Let Jake hide somewhere. Don't try to find him."

She pushed him away. "You don't understand! You don't know what I did to him—this is all my fault!"

"What are you talking about?"

"The argument we had. It was because of me—he was preoccupied I'm sure. That's why he didn't see it coming, that's why he couldn't defend himself. There's no other reason Dad. He's the best, the best at street survival. It was because of me. And the things I said ..."

"No, sweetie. No."

"Yes it was, Dad! It was my fault."

"No, Cass. You're not responsible for him being hurt. And you can't save him, either. That's up to God."

Her temples were throbbing now and she put both hands up to them as if to squeeze the anger back inside, the anger that was spilling out of her in waves. It wasn't fair. What happened to Mike, what happened to Jake—it just wasn't fair. Anybody could see that. She couldn't do anything for Mike anymore, but Jake ... that was a different story.

"He needs me, Dad. That's all I know; he needs me." Cassie

struggled to keep her voice calm.

"And don't you think that, if it was truly a matter of life and death, the Bureau would come and get you and take you to him? You don't think they care that much about one of their own?"

"Not with that idiot Foster in charge. Besides, what did they do for Mike?"

But her father wouldn't quit. He was like that—a quiet but tenacious debater. She, on the other hand, was like her mother, people said—fiery and quick-witted.

"Cass," he said, "let's just say you do your usual excellent job researching and found all the head-injury rehab hospitals. And let's just say you manage to sweet-talk the truth out of some unsuspecting registration clerk and you find out where your friend is. What then?"

"I go there. I go see Jake."

"You go see Jake. You breach security. Potentially you lead who-ever's trying to kill Jake right to him. The FBI is annoyed. More than annoyed. And then they move Jake again. Do you want his life to be disrupted that way? Is that what you want for him? Now he has to go to yet another hospital, another set of doctors, different nurses, a whole different program. That's what you want?"

Why did he have to be so sensible? Cassie suddenly felt deflated and she sagged down onto the bed. She stared at her hands, as if they held some secret, some rejoinder she could make. But her hands were empty.

"Let him go, Cass."

"How can I stand by and do nothing for him?"

Her father sat beside her on the bed. He put his arm around her and kissed the side of her head. "You can always pray for him, honey. God knows where he is."

"No, no, no," she said, and Cassie got up and walked out of the house.

8

*S*he stayed outside until after dark, walking along the sandy strip of beach along the Bay. The air, though cooler, was still thick with humidity. She walked all the way around the cove and then back again, and finally sat on a rock, staring into the distance, fingering the necklace Mike had given her. Her dad was right, she knew that, but she hated it. How could she let him go? Jake needed her, and probably she needed him. He had occupied so much of her thinking lately.

The lights from the bungalow glowed softly. She could hear Mozart being played on the stereo. A fish jumped in the water. Mr. Henry came up and rubbed against her leg.

Finally, Cassie went inside. When her dad saw her, he came to her and wrapped his arms around her.

"I'm sorry, Daddy."

"It's okay, Cass. I love you."

They had a simple dinner of grilled salmon and salad and they talked about his projects—the underwater grasses nursery program, the educational tours, the oyster garden. Her father was very actively working to save the Chesapeake Bay. It was, he said, his second greatest passion.

"Cass, why don't you spend the day with me tomorrow? A group of us are going out to Bloody Point to band pelicans. Why don't you come? It would be good for you to get out on the Bay for a day." Bloody Point was a place just off the south end of Kent Island. An old caisson lighthouse stood guard over the six-foot shallows.

Ironically, the deepest part of the Bay was nearby, a 174-foot pit everyone called Bloody Point Hole. Local tradition said that ships used to dump dead and sick slaves there, throwing them overboard before they got to the market at Annapolis. That was one of the stories, anyway.

Cassie wiped her mouth with her napkin. "No, Dad. I don't think so. There's too much to do."

He opened his mouth as if to say, "Like what?" but must have thought better of it. Instead, he kissed her good night.

After showering early the next morning, Cassie drove to Goose Creek, parked her car, and sat on a hill overlooking the marina. She watched Scrub move a sloop over next to the lift, his jon boat nudging and shoving the larger sailboat into place. She saw Pete, the mechanic, arrive in his ancient pickup truck and two fishermen she didn't know load their boat with gear and take off toward the Bay.

After an hour or so, she walked over to the dinghy rack and pulled out a sea kayak she kept there. Donning her life jacket and grabbing a paddle, she launched the craft and set off down the creek. Perhaps the wheeling gulls, or the whispers of the bulrushes, or the sound of the egrets crying from their nests on the channel markers would tell her what she needed to know.

Cassie stayed out for about two hours. The Bay was calm with light waves. She stayed close to shore, near where Goose Creek entered the larger body of water. She saw schools of little fish jump out of the water as if something bigger were underneath them, chasing them. She saw cormorants, dark duck-like birds with long necks, diving for food. And she quietly watched a blue heron stalking minnows in the shallows along the shoreline, his long, ungainly legs almost comical in their stilt-like form. She always found peace on the water. The smell of the salt, the breeze on her face, the lapping sound of the waves, the birds, the fish—they all touched a part of her soul that otherwise languished. She needed the water.

Then the wind came up strong, and the chop started to build and Cassie began paddling back up the creek. Her arms began to ache but it was a good kind of ache—from exertion, not emotional pain—and she welcomed it. Arriving at the marina she beached the kayak, scrambled out, and tugged it up on shore. She hefted it overhead, and put it back in the dinghy rack, securing it with a lock. The wind, stronger now, whipped her hair. She got in her car, and drove away. Where exactly she was going, she didn't know.

When she had driven half a mile down the road, a loud "boom" rattled her car windows and made her jump. *That's odd,* she thought, *I wonder what that was?* Still, she kept on driving. Less than five minutes later, a police car screamed past her, going the other way, lights flashing. Then there was another, and another, two more "booms" and then she saw fire trucks rolling out of a station, lights and sirens blazing.

Curious now, Cassie wheeled her car around and headed back toward the marina. Two more cop cars passed her, and then another fire truck. She accelerated in her anxiety. A block away from the marina, she saw a dark column of smoke billowing in the sky. She turned left, then right, and when the marina came into view, she gasped. Black smoke billowed from burning boats. The marina was on fire!

Cassie parked the car and jumped out. Six boats were already burning. The sloop next to the lift was fully involved. Flames were licking hulls, lines, and docks. One fire truck had arrived and was laying lines, others were arriving, their crews jumping off as the engines came to a stop. People were streaming out of the Blue Goose Restaurant.

Cassie spotted her boat. It was five boats away from the fire. Five boats. Could she save it? She had to. Adrenaline flashed through her and she began running toward *Time Out.* The boat had been resurrected once; she couldn't let it be destroyed now.

Boom! A boat exploded on the A dock, stopping Cassie in her tracks. Already she was choking on smoke. Could she get there in time? Could she save her boat?

The smoke thickened as her feet hit the dock. Her eyes began watering. She could hear the firemen yelling for her to stop. *Time Out* was halfway down the A dock. As she ran, Cassie went over in her mind what she needed to do. *Open the seacocks. Turn on the starting battery switch. Start the motor. Disconnect shore power. Free the lines.*

A brisk wind was driving the fire. Tongues of flame were leaping from boat to boat, and even the big, thick pilings were beginning to burn. *Boom!* The boat four boats down from *Time Out* exploded. Debris rained down around Cassie as she reached her slip. "No!" she yelled, kicking a flaming piece of material into the water. She jumped onto her boat. Already several sparks had singed the sailcover.

Her hands were shaking. It took her three attempts to open the companionway lock. Choking on the smoke, she jerked the boards up and raced down the stairs. Quickly opening the engine-cooling seacock, she flipped on the starting battery switch and grabbed the ignition key. Back up in the cockpit, the smoke was intensifying. She could no longer clearly see the shore. She stabbed the key in the ignition and turned it. The big Yanmar chugged a couple of times, then stalled.

No, not now, Cassie screamed inside. *This is no time for engine trouble!* She tried again. It stalled again. Then, *Boom!* The boat three slips down exploded and she felt the explosion reverberate in her whole body.

Desperate, Cassie turned the key again. For the third time, the motor chugged, then died. Her mind began racing: *Do I loose the lines and set it adrift? Get off the boat? What?*

"Miss! What are you doing? Miss!" It was Scrub. The little dock-hand, blackened with smoke with his eyes red and tearing, jumped into the cockpit.

"It's stalling!" Cassie screamed.

Scrub yelled, "Get the shore power off! I'll get the engine." He raced down below, jerked off the engine cover, and fiddled with something as she unscrewed the big cable that fed electricity to the boat. Then he leaped up into the cockpit. "Cast off!" he yelled.

Cassie jumped onto the finger pier and freed the docklines, throwing the aft line onto the boat and holding the bow line. Scrub turned the key, and the engine roared to life. He jammed the boat into forward, and Cassie jumped on as he steered it out of the slip.

The water was filled with burning debris. The sky was totally obscured by black smoke. Arches of water from the firehoses formed a tunnel and Cassie and Scrub motored through it. Tears from the smoke were streaming out of her eyes and her lungs felt seared. But Cassie was grateful as the distance grew between them and the burning slips.

Coughing and choking, the two took *Time Out* down the creek. Before the last turn, Cassie looked back.

The entire 120-slip marina was ablaze. Docks, piers, pilings.... Huge clouds of black smoke billowed in the stiff wind. Two docks filled with boats had been consumed already. She could see some of the blackened hulls still floating; others had sunk in their slips. Here and there a boat drifted, its dock lines burned through, and off in the distance a houseboat on fire spun crazily in the creek.

Two fireboats sprayed water on what was left, but their efforts were fruitless. It was clearly too little too late. Emergency vehicles, police cruisers, and ambulances were gathered on the shore, their lights sparkling like some weird celebratory parade.

Off to the right, the Blue Goose Restaurant was ablaze. Flames licked through the roof and one wall remained standing but the place was mostly gone, gutted, and all the workers could do was huddle in the distance, watching their jobs go up in smoke.

It seemed so surreal to Cassie, like a nightmare. She felt like her insides had been gutted as well. The marina, her home for these past months, was gone, just gone! Viewing the destruction she realized how fortunate she'd been. "Thank you, Scrub. Thank you!" she said. "Thank you for saving my boat!"

"Yes, miss."

They anchored the boat safely down the creek, and got in the dinghy to motor back. Skirting the edges of the fire area, they headed toward a large crowd gathered on shore. Scrub guided the dinghy to the shoreline, and secured it after they got out.

Cassie had to struggle to breathe. The smallest exertion sent her into a coughing spasm. Then she heard her name and looked up. Her father was racing toward her, his face advertising his relief.

"Cassie!" Jim Davison grabbed his daughter in a hug. "I am so thankful! Thank God you are okay! The firemen said they saw a woman running down the dock and I knew that had to be you! I was so worried!"

Cassie coughed. "I had to save the boat, Dad!"

"You scared everyone! Oh, honey!"

A huge explosion made her jump in his arms. One more boat destroyed. Flaming pieces rained down, plopping in the water and sending spectators scurrying on land. There were two more boats on that dock, just two. Suddenly, Cassie's knees felt weak.

Jim held his daughter close. Another coughing spasm overtook her. "Let's get you some oxygen," he said, and ignoring her protests, he led her over to a rescue squad truck.

Cassie sat on the ground, an oxygen mask covering her face. Her father stood nearby. Before them was the destroyed marina, smoke still rising, its piers and pilings like a charred skeleton in the water. The acrid smell of smoke filled the air, and the buzz of news helicopters overhead competed with the loud chugging of the fire truck engines. Film at eleven.

"Jim!" Richard Maxwell joined them. He was dressed in khaki pants and a bright green shirt. His face was red and his eyes snapped with anger. "This is unreal! What happened? I can't believe it! It's a tragedy, a terrible, terrible tragedy."

Cassie saw her dad look oddly at Maxwell. "No one was killed," Davison said, "at least as far as we know. So it's not the worst that could happen. Did you lose your boat?"

"Of course." Maxwell's face was hard. "How did it start? Who is responsible for this?"

"I don't think they know yet."

"You know, I told them that idiot would be trouble someday! I told them."

"Who are you talking about?"

Maxwell gestured down the hill toward Scrub, who was talking to the fire marshal. "What was he doing? What was he working on? I'll bet somehow—"

"It wasn't his fault! Scrub didn't do anything," Cassie interrupted, coughing out the words.

Maxwell turned to look at her, his anger contorting his face. Then, as if he'd suddenly removed a mask, his face softened. "I'm just glad you're okay," Maxwell said to her. "And your boat as well. Aren't you lucky?"

"It wasn't luck, it was Scrub," she asserted.

He looked at her, and she noticed how icy blue his eyes were. He turned back to look at the destroyed marina.

Off to the east, two of the fireboats had stopped spraying. The fire almost burned itself out, after devouring the docks and pilings and boats. The breeze sent another shiver through Cassie, and then another.

"What makes you think Scrub had anything to do with this?" Cassie's dad asked.

"He's simple, that's all, just simple. An idiot. The kind of person who might be careless with a torch or gasoline." Maxwell crossed his arms. "I can't prove he did it, but this one thing I know—whoever caused this blaze is going to pay. Big time." He gestured toward a police officer. "I wonder what he knows," Maxwell said and stalked off.

Cassie's dad looked back at her. She tried to stop the trembling that was now overtaking her body, but she couldn't. Maxwell's angry words hadn't helped. How could he blame Scrub?

Her dad sat down on the ground next to her and put his arm around her. "You're shaking," he said.

Cassie nodded.

"Let's go home."

She bit her lip. "I don't want to go, but I don't want to stay."

"Let's go."

Tonight would not be a night for sleeping. Long after she'd been interviewed by the fire marshal and the police, long after her father had gone to bed, long after the lights in the neighbors' houses had been turned out, Cassie was wide awake. She sat in a wicker chair on the porch, still coughing occasionally, hoping the familiar sounds she loved ... the cicadas chirping, the whippoorwills three-note call, the frog croaking in the bottom ... would drive out the images in her head. Occasionally an owl would hoot, and if she really tried, she could hear loons calling to one another.

What was she going to do now? Her marina was gone. She could move the boat somewhere else and take up residence again, but was that what she wanted? What did she really want? With Jake hurt and the possibility of a bad guy hunting agents, with the murder at one marina and now these two arsons, fixing the wood on *Time Out* just didn't have as much appeal. As midnight approached, Cassie slipped her boat shoes on, grabbed a small flashlight, and headed for the beach.

The night was still; the wind, which had whipped the fire into a frenzy, had died down to a gentle breeze. Overhead the stars sparkled like diamonds on black velvet. The moon was a giant luminescent disk, pure and white and distinct against the blackness of the night.

Small waves lapped the sand at water's edge, glistening white momentarily as they rose and crashed against the shore. Out on the bay she could see lights from a few small fishing boats, white lights on the stern, red or green lights on the bow. Larger lights, from a commercial cargo vessel heading down toward Norfolk, glided in the middle of the channel, and a red channel marker flashed on and off.

Cassie walked northward, wet sand moving under her feet, the smell of salt in her nose, the sound of a distant bell buoy playing in her ears. Sailing could be challenging but at least there were clear channels to follow and rules to observe that would get you safely home. Most of the time, at least. Red and green markers delineated the channel. "Red, right, return" was the sailor's rule: keep the red marker on your right when you're returning to port. Then you'd stay in the channel and not run aground.

But aground was where she was right now, in life if not in sailing. She'd lost her husband, resigned her job. Her partner had been seriously wounded, now her marina had burned. How many stress points was that? Enough to justify resigning from life for a while?

She was not a quitter. When her first big case with the FBI had been a tough one, confounding even the assistant U.S. attorney, she had remained on the trail, following lead after lead until she'd finally gotten an accomplice to talk. She busted the case wide open, and even long-time agents had been surprised at her tenacity.

But now she was stuck. She didn't know which way to go. Logically, she knew she couldn't do anything about her husband; Mike was dead and that was that. She still had her boat, but the marina was gone. She had no convenient place to live. And Jake? What about Jake?

It was clear what her dad thought she should do—live with him for a while, find some nice quiet little job, and just relax for a bit.

She had to respect his advice. Her mother had died when she was just two, killed in an automobile accident on the Washington Beltway. After that, her dad had moved what remained of their family to the Bay area, and he set about raising Cassie and her brother on his own, with the help of his sister, Trudy.

He'd done a good job. Both Cassie and her brother had turned out okay. And whatever trauma her dad had suffered from the loss of his wife had distilled into wisdom. Cassie valued his opinion above anyone else's.

So when he said something she didn't want to hear, she couldn't just blow it off. Jim Davison, the quiet, gentle biologist, was a force to be reckoned with, from sheer strength of character.

Cassie stopped walking and stared out over the Bay, as if to wrest the answer to her struggles from the waves, which hid the secrets of the deep ... bluefish, rockfish, flounder, menhaden, perch, silversides, anchovy, crabs, oysters, clams ... innumerable species living in silence underneath the surface. The Bay had its rhythms, just like life. What was next for her?

The following morning their breakfast was interrupted by a knock at the back door. It was Susan Whitaker, one of the bird banders, bringing some leftover supplies to her father.

"Why, Cassie! It's wonderful to see you," the woman said, standing in the open door. "I don't know if you remember, but my daughter went to school with you."

Whitaker. Whitaker. Cassie struggled to place her.

"Her name was Ellen Jessup. You may remember her. She played first base on the softball team that went to state."

"Oh, Ellen! Of course," Cassie said. "Sorry, the last name threw me off. How is she? What is she doing now?"

"She lives in Vermont. She's married and has two children. And she works part-time as a reporter for the newspaper up there."

"A reporter? Oh, wow, that's neat."

"She loves it. She gets to go around asking questions. I told her it suits her because she's always been nosy!" Mrs. Whitaker laughed. "Whatever. You just want your children to be happy, you know? Well, I'd best be off! See you tomorrow, Jim!"

Cassie and her father bid her good-bye and watched as she got into her car and drove off. And a new thought turned over in Cassie's head.

"I'm just asking you, Dad, to make a phone call. Remind Len Boyette about me, and ask him if he'll see me." Cassie stood in her father's kitchen with her hands on her hips.

"Look," Jim responded, "if you want to stay in law enforcement, do it. The University of Maryland–Eastern Shore is looking for a director of campus security. I'll put in a good word for you."

"A campus cop? Dad, I don't want to spend my time enforcing student-parking rules. Come on!"

"It would give you a break, Cass, a break from all the stress. You could live with your aunt."

"Dad, I love her, you know that. But no, I'm not going to be a campus cop, even the director of campus cops. Call Len for me, please. Please, Dad." She paced away. "Listen. Something's going on. Somebody set the marina on fire. Why? We've had two murders, an attempted murder of an agent, and two fires. What's happening? Jake obviously thought something was connecting these crimes, and I've got to find out. I can't just sit back and hope that the police and the fire marshal can put the whole puzzle together. Maybe, all of this is somehow connected to Mike's death. Please, Dad. Please. Just make the call."

Jim sighed. After a long moment, he reached for the phone. Within a few minutes, Cassie had an appointment set for the next day.

9

When Len Boyette was seventeen years old he was a state high school wrestling champion. Still a burly man, he stood about five feet eight inches tall and what hair he had left was flecked with gray. He had a no-nonsense air about him. Having spent the last two decades editing newspaper writing, he also had a tendency to edit his speech, his thinking, and his compassion. Two messy divorces had helped with that.

Khakis and a white shirt made up his uniform and comfortable shoes, usually Rockports if he could get them. His sleeves were rolled up and on his wrist he wore a gold Seiko watch that he'd bought on his second honeymoon in the Caribbean—the honeymoon, that is, for his second marriage. The marriage had lasted six months. The watch was a better deal.

"I'm not going to lie to you," Cassie said, sitting in a chair in his office. As the editor-in-chief of *The Bay Area Beacon*, the largest local paper in the region, Len was a force to be reckoned with. "I need a reason to be going around asking questions. All I'm asking is that you hire me as a reporter, that you give me press credentials that will justify my presence. That's it."

Len sat on the corner of his desk and stared at her. She felt like he could see right through her. "What you're asking me to do is perpetrate a ruse on the community. Tell everyone you're a reporter when you're not. You're also asking me to put the daughter of a good friend of mine in danger. I don't know that I can do that."

Cassie leaned forward. "Look, I can take care of myself. And, I can write. My undergraduate degree is in English. I'll be a reporter if you want me to be a reporter. It's just that I might ask a few questions that don't get written up." She stood up and paced away from Len. His office was lined with framed front pages of the paper, which had been in existence for more than 100 years. All of the great public events of her lifetime, and more, were documented there.

On the wall to the right was the newspaper's mission statement. And to the left was a framed copy of a photo—an American flag made of pictures of elementary school-aged children dressed in red, white, and blue with their hands on their hearts, presumably saying the Pledge of Allegiance.

"Look," she said, "my friend knew something that almost got him killed. What was it? My husband did get killed. If I'm going to find out why, I need your help. I need those creds. Will you give them to me?"

Len exhaled loudly, frowning. "You carry a gun?"

"Are you kidding? In Maryland?"

"Oh, yeah. Only the crooks can carry guns in this state. I forgot." Len gestured for her to sit down, then retreated to the chair behind his desk. He sat down with a thud and stroked his chin. "If my news crew finds out that you're not a journalist, they will be mad. But if they find out you used to be an FBI agent, they'll wring my neck! I'll have a revolt on my hands. They don't trust the Feds anyway. If they find you were one—"

"They don't need to find out," Cassie said quickly. "I won't mention it."

"You absolutely cannot work the crime beat. If Shonika Blackwell thinks you're horning in on her territory, she'll eat you alive. When she's finished, she'll come after me." He took a deep breath and stared off to the side toward the window, which overlooked the street. "We have a good staff here, a nice staff. Pretty much, we all get along. I don't want to mess that up."

"I understand."

There was more silence and then a heavy sigh. "All right," he said, after an eternity. "Here's what I'll offer you: I'll hire you as a reporter."

Cassie smiled with relief.

"You'll get the press pass. You can go anywhere in the Bay country and ask any questions you want. But ..." he gestured with his finger, "you'll work a specific assignment: I want you to cover some of the little festivals that go on in the Bay region for the rest of the summer. I want you to actually write about them. A story every week. And it had better be good 'cause we don't have time to rewrite lousy stuff.

"I'll pay you fifteen bucks an hour, that's it. No expenses, no car. And, in September we'll reevaluate."

He'd yielded far more easily than she'd expected. "Yes! I'll do it. Thank you!"

Len shook his head. "I hope you like crabs. How many dozen can you eat in a summer?"

Cassie grinned. "One more than you."

Len assigned Sally Randolph, a reporter twice Cassie's age, to orient her to the newsroom. Cassie instantly felt comfortable with her. "You can use this," she said, pointing to a small gray desk in a tiny cubicle. It's the one we use for summer interns. Len fired ours last week, so it's open."

Cassie raised her eyebrows.

"We all thought he was really dedicated," Sally explained, "but it turns out he was just using the computer late at night to visit porn sites."

"Terrific."

"Len gets intense sometimes but he's very loyal to his staff members. It takes a lot to get fired." Sally pushed the button and the computer came to life.

While Sally logged her in, Cassie looked around the newsroom. There were about thirty desks, all in cubicles with low walls. The place buzzed with activity. Computer keys clicked, some folks talked on phones, others were clustered in small groups, engaged in animated discussion.

The photographers' desks were in the back; she knew that from the equipment bags. Another group of computer operators was near them, but Cassie couldn't tell what they were doing.

"Okay, here you go," Sally said, stepping back. "Sit down. I'll walk you through it."

Within a short time, Cassie had learned the basics. The newspaper used a word processing system designed specifically for publishing. The stories were all kept on a central server, in "baskets." Certain key entries would format her work automatically. And she had access to the Internet. If she wrote something at home, she could e-mail it to herself at work.

All of this was good.

"You got it?"

"Yes, Sally, thank you."

Sally gave her a tour of the building and walked her through the press pass process. Then Cassie went back to her workstation. She logged on to the Internet and researched the local Chesapeake Bay activities. She was amazed at how many there were: seafood festivals, firemen's carnivals, Skipjack activities, boat-building workshops, plus many events organized and sponsored by the Chesapeake Bay Foundation. She would have plenty to choose from.

Someone entered her peripheral vision as she was reading. Cassie looked up to see Len Boyette standing over her. "You gonna be okay?" he asked.

"Yeah, fine. I can do this!"

He grunted. "Alright. Just take care of yourself. I don't want to have to explain myself to your father." He turned to leave, but Cassie called after him.

"Hey, Len, where's the police reporter?"

He motioned toward a young black woman. "Shonika is over there. And Curt, but he's out right now. Don't bug 'em."

"Thanks. I won't."

He started to leave again, then turned and pointed his finger at her. "You come in every day. If you're not going to come in, you call, okay? I don't want you disappearing and nobody knowing it."

Cassie smiled at his protectiveness. "Yes sir. Got it. No problem."

Shonika Blackwell was almost thirty and hadn't yet found a man worth settling down with. She had a reputation for being as hard-nosed as the cops she covered. Her only regret was that she was considered only *as* hardnosed, not more.

Heeding Len's warning, Cassie approached her with caution. Even from across the room she'd caught on to the young woman's acerbic nature. "Hi," said Cassie. "Shonika is it? I'm Cassie."

The young reporter looked at her as if to say, *So what?*

"I understand you're on the police beat."

"That's right. Homeboys, scumbags, and crooked cops, that's my specialty. We got your basic drunks, your basic perverts, your basic thieves, and your basic killers. All doing their best to keep me busy."

"How 'bout your basic arsonists?" Cassie asked.

"What're you talking about?"

"The Goose Creek Marina. What's the word on that?"

"Man, that Paul Loughlin, he's got lips as tight as Daisy Duke's shorts ... he's not giving me anything on that. Nothing at all. What do you know about it?"

"I had a boat there."

"Is that right? Did you lose it?"

"No, I was fortunate."

"I tell you, there's a lot of insurance money gonna get paid out." Shonika tapped her pen on her desk. "What makes you think it was arson?"

"Just a hunch. Remember the sloop that burned a month ago?"

"Arson?"

Cassie nodded imperceptibly.

"Hmmm. Interesting. Well, I just may have to look into that."

"If you do, it would probably be best not to mention my name."

"You got it, honey. Man, I gotta get me a Coke. These people are driving me crazy." With that, Shonika got up and left the newsroom. Cassie watched her go, questions popping up in her mind like targets on a shooting range.

The newsroom didn't really wake up until 10:00 a.m. or later, but folks were often still putting pages together late at night as the 11:30 p.m. deadline approached. The presses had to roll just before midnight, or the paper wouldn't be delivered to the distributors on time, and the carriers wouldn't get it to subscribers by 4:30 a.m. as promised.

Cassie was ready to leave at 5:30 in the afternoon. As she was walking toward the door, Len called her from his office.

"Where are you living?" he asked.

"With my dad, for now. I thought maybe I'd look for some place around here, though."

The stocky editor shifted his weight on his feet. "Look, I've got a friend, a rich friend, who's got an apartment above his boathouse, about ten minutes from here. I happen to know it's empty. You interested?"

"I don't know. How much does fifteen dollars an hour buy?"

"Enough. He'll rent it to you cheap."

"Well, sure, then," Cassie said, grinning. "Thanks."

The Cove was a cluster of exclusive homes located off Black Duck Boulevard not far from Annapolis. The best properties fronted onto the Bay. Len's friend, a local banker, had built a huge contemporary home of wood and glass looking out over a harbor full of bobbing boats, just down from the Eastport Yacht Club and the U.S. Naval Academy.

The boathouse was big enough for two boats plus equipment. It was made of cedar that had weathered to an elegant gray, and it stood some twenty yards from the house, far enough to afford Cassie the privacy she wanted. The second-floor apartment was airy and spacious. Light poured through huge windows on each wall, and a balcony off the great room overlooked the water. Furnished simply in contemporary casual wood furniture, the apartment was filled with decoys and wildlife prints. Cassie fell in love with the place immediately. The view of the Bay and the sky, of sailboats and seagulls was irresistible; the clanging of a channel buoy and the smell of the salt filled her with peace. Or something close to peace anyway.

"I expected my son to move back in when he finished college but he's gone off to California," the banker, Mr. Turnage, said almost apologetically. "So the place is empty."

And the rent was ridiculously cheap. "I love it," Cassie said. She scanned the cove. "Any chance I could drop a mooring and keep my sailboat out there?"

"What do you have?" Turnage asked.

"An Alberg 30."

"Why not just tie it up at the dock? We don't need both sides clear."

"That would be awesome," Cassie said and the deal was struck.

It didn't take much to move Cassie in, but her father insisted on helping. She knew it was as much for him to check out the apartment as anything and that was okay with her. A few clothes, some books, personal effects, linens, her laptop, and an inexpensive stereo were all she needed—and the approval of her father, which he gave her along with a big hug once he'd satisfied himself that his girl would be safe.

"You're ridiculous, Dad," she protested. "I'm a grown woman who can fight and shoot a gun!" But secretly, his protectiveness felt good.

When the unpacking was done, her dad left, and Cassie sat out in the big wicker chair on her balcony as twilight descended on the Bay. She finally allowed her thoughts to wander. Mike was gone. She was alone. Three years of marriage were floating into her past like an abandoned ship, loose from its mooring. And the rest of her world was turned upside down.

Mike kills a street thug, Tyson Farnsworth. Then Mike is apparently killed.... Frederick Schneider is murdered in a marina, a boat burns, and Jake is assaulted. Then the marina her boat is in goes up in flames. Was there a connection? Or were these all just random acts of violence in a crazy world? All these loose ends might not even belong to the same tapestry, but she had to find out.

Off in the distance a small boat, illuminated only by a tiny white stern light and a red bow light, skimmed silently over the black water of the Bay. It was too far away for Cassie to hear the motor. She watched the boat's progress, her vision blurred momentarily by emotion. She, too, was alone, skimming over the surface of life, with not much light to see by.

Chilled, she went inside. Grabbing a pen and a piece of paper, she began writing down questions. She wasn't ready to sleep until 2:00 a.m.

10

---

*F*or her first assignment, Cassie chose the Triton Beach Seafood Festival, an annual event drawing thousands from the Bay region as well as the nearby Washington and Baltimore metropolitan areas. As she pulled into the parking lot full of minivans and SUVs, she wondered momentarily what she was doing. Covering crab pickings was a long way away from finding out who had assaulted Jake. And who killed Mike.

Beggars can't be choosers, she told herself with a sigh. Her appeal with the FBI could take months. She wasn't willing to wait that long.

Pulling her Cabrio into a parking place, Cassie joined the stream of moms, dads, kids, and couples making their way to the brightly striped tents set up on the sand at the edge of the Bay. She was going to have to detach from her thoughts, to pretend she was just a tourist.

The day was sunny and bright. A few puffy cotton-ball clouds broke up the monotony of the dazzling blue sky. Several gulls soared overhead, looking for easy pickings at the fair.

As she entered the festival grounds the smell of Old Bay seasoning—on the crabs, in the soups, even in sauces—filled her nose as surely as sand filled her boat shoes. Oysters still in their shells lay spread out on grills sizzling in their own juices, and mounds of Chesapeake Bay blue crabs, their shells bright red and steaming, were heaped on tables covered with brown paper. Peppery coleslaw filled bowls and gallons and gallons of iced tea stood at the ready. Smiling men in white aprons and chef's hats stood under the tents preparing the food, their ample girths indicating they didn't need to eat a bite of it.

Pulling out her little reporter's notebook, with her press pass hanging around her neck, Cassie began to take notes. She jotted down her initial impressions—the colors, sights, sounds, and smells. She listed participating charities, menus, colorful images, and featured events. She sketched the layout of the tents, noted the colors of the striping, and described every barbecue rig employed.

Cassie had only two goals: to get enough information to write a story and to network. Many people from the town of Goose Creek would come to this nearby festival, and one of them might just know something. Who burned down the marina? Who hurt Jake? Who killed Mike?

It was only when he appeared at her elbow that she remembered a photographer, Brett Cooper, was supposed to meet her there. "Hi, Cassie! Sorry I'm late. The traffic—"

She dismissed his apology with a wave. "No problem. I'm just getting started."

Together they worked the crowd. A little, blonde, three-year-old girl looking curiously at the cooked crab in her hand became a photo op and a quote. The weathered crabber, in his high boots, standing behind the Ruritan booth, gave them a primer on crabs, or the lack thereof, in the Bay. And an impish African-American boy grinning from ear to ear as he ate fresh corn on the cob added a multicultural element to the story.

"Great job!" said Brett when they'd gotten all they needed. "You really know how to talk to people. Where'd you work before?"

"For the government."

"Oh, man. You will find this a lot more interesting than being a bureaucrat."

Cassie smiled. "Probably so."

Brett leaned against a wooden gate. He was tanned and athletic, nothing like the stereotypical artsy photographer. He reminded her of the fraternity boys at college. "Listen, would you like to do something now that we're finished? Go out somewhere? A movie or something?"

Was he asking her out? On a date? He was about her age, single … but no. Not yet.

"I can't do it," she said. "I want to get this done and then I've got somewhere else to go."

"Okay," he shrugged. "Maybe some other time."

"Maybe," she offered.

"Yeah," Brett said, grinning, like he knew he was being put off. He seemed like the boy-next-door type, so baseball-and-apple pie with his All-American good looks and blue eyes. "I'm guessing we're going to be seeing a lot of each other, anyway. You'll probably get sick of me. Len told me I was to cover the festivals with you all summer. He said to keep an eye on you."

Cassie smiled and shook her head. "Do I look that fragile?"

"You look just fine," he said, gathering his equipment. "But hey, see you Monday. I'll have the pictures done."

"Sounds good."

After Brett left, Cassie took one more spin around the grounds, just people-watching. She'd seen a few whom she knew, but she was looking for a hunch to play, a person who might give her a lead. Ninety-nine-point-nine percent of the people there were just Americans who were out having a good time. Most barely remembered the marina fire that took place a few weeks ago; few would have seen the obscure news story about the unidentified person found stabbed in the park some thirty miles south. Even fewer would remember the murder at Sullivan's Wharf. And Mike? He was just another accident statistic.

She walked the aisles, lingering over the craft booths, listening to the talk around her. She bought a cup of crab bisque soup and ate it leaning against the fence near a group of watermen chewing the fat. She struck up a conversation with a security guard, a heavy-set man who reminded her of a prison guard she'd known.

Putting her notebook in her purse, Cassie turned to go home. Maybe she should visit the mistress of the man who was murdered, Frederick Schneider. A "Hi, honey!" stopped her in her tracks. She turned around. Pat, the waitress from the Blue Goose Restaurant, gave her a big, broad smile.

"I thought that was you! Remember me?" she asked.

"Of course. Pat, right?" Her heart was thumping. Was it a coincidence she'd run into her?

"Right! And here you are. Feeling better, honey?"

Cassie's mind flipped back to the night of Jake's assault. After they'd argued, and Cassie had walked down the dock to watch the storm, it was Pat who had come out to make sure she was okay. "I'm fine," Cassie said. "And how are you? Your job burned down!"

"You bet it did, honey!" Pat glanced over her shoulder. Two teenage girls wearing bored expressions stood waiting for her. "I guess I'd better go before my girls have a fit. I just wanted to say hello. Glad to see you survived that storm and all."

"Listen, wait," Cassie said. "Could we get together? Have coffee or something? I, uh, I wanted to ask you about some things. About that night you saw me."

"Well, sure. When?"

They agreed on a time and place, and Pat waved good-bye. Cassie returned to her car, the framework of a story on her notepad and an appointment set for the next day.

Cassie and Pat met at the IHOP south of Annapolis on Sunday morning. "My treat," Cassie said, and the waitress ordered the Big Breakfast.

"I just love their pancakes," Pat said.

Cassie smiled. "Pat, I'm a reporter for *The Bay Area Beacon*."

"Is that so? I love that paper. I read the comics and Ann Landers every day—I mean *every* day. And the TV guide, well it's the best. It's got the soaps all summarized in there so if I have to work an afternoon I don't miss nothing and then—"

"Pat," Cassie interrupted. "What's the latest on the marina fire? Have you heard anything?"

"Honey, the word is, some dude set the thing off. Now I know Mr. Hardesty, the owner, and I'm telling you there's no way that man would torch the place. He cares too much about his people. I saw the man standing there watching them boats blow up and there was tears in his eyes, real tears. So I got money on the fact that ol' Hardesty had nothing to do with that fire."

"Any idea who might have?"

They were interrupted as their meal was served.

Pat took a bite of her pancakes. "Let me tell you who I think did it: a jealous wife."

"What?"

"I got the whole thing worked out in my mind," Pat went on. "Some man's been spending too much time on his boat. Maybe took his mistress out on it. And his wife just had enough. Set fire to the man's boat. That's my guess. Domestic violence of the marine sort."

Cassie suppressed a smile.

"Now Joe, the cook? He's of a mind that somebody had a boat they couldn't afford, and set it on fire for the insurance. That, to me, is just too boring."

"Where were you when the fire started?" Cassie asked, sipping her coffee.

"Serving up the lunch special, red snapper and rice pilaf, to a couple of businessmen. I heard the first boat blow, and honey, within fifteen minutes we knew we had to get out. Those customers took their plates with them. Stood outside watching the fire and eating red snapper!"

"Did you see anything unusual before the fire, out on the docks or in the parking lot?"

"No. It was a right windy day, and I remember thinking the

sailors would be loving it and the fishing parties would all be coming in sick. The Bay gets whipped up right good in that kind of wind, as you know!" Pat scraped the last bit of pancake off her plate and licked her fork. "That was great, honey. Thank you." She glanced at her watch. "Listen, I gotta run. My girls want to go to the mall."

Cassie raised her hand. "Just one more question, please. The night you saw me out on the dock, remember that?"

Pat reached out to touch Cassie's hand like a mother would. "Well, sure, honey, I remember that very well."

"Did you see anybody else out there that night? Anybody at all?"

The waitress withdrew her hand and her eyes grew distant, as if she were searching her memory. "No ... no ... no, wait! Yes! Yes, I did!"

"Who? Who did you see?"

"It wasn't so much who, but what. I was walking down to the dock to check on you. The thunder was loud, and it was scaring me. I saw a car pulling out of a space in the marina parking lot. And he didn't have his lights on! He started to drive away, real slow, and I was going to go rap on his window and tell him to turn his lights on. But then he sped up and zoomed away before I could get there. I never did see him cut on his lights!"

Cassie's scalp was tingling. "What kind of car was it, Pat?"

"A big, dark truck ... one of them SUVs. I don't know what kind."

"Who was driving it?" Her throat was dry.

"I never saw the person. Didn't get close enough." Pat took a big drink of water, finishing it. "Then I came down to see you. By the time it started to rain, I just ran for my car. I had had enough! People driving with no lights. Girls sitting out on the dock in the storm."

"Pat, listen. If you remember anything else, anything at all, will you call me?" She gave her a business card printed for her by the newspaper. "Call me, please."

"Will do, honey! I will surely do that."

Cassie paid the bill and the two women left. Cassie sat in her car in the parking lot for ten minutes trying to absorb what she had learned. Pat had probably seen whoever had assaulted Jake.

Monday morning Cassie sat at her desk, staring at her computer, trying to pull words from her brain to construct a coherent story. It had been a long time since she'd written anything but Bureau contact reports. She reached back into her memory to pull out what she could remember from her high school journalism class about the inverted triangle framework, creating a snappy lead, and the reporter's who, what, when, where, why, and how questions.

While she was concentrating, Shonika Blackwell appeared at her desk. "Hey, girl," she said, "you were dead right about that fire at the marina."

Cassie looked up.

"It was arson."

"How do they know?" Cassie wondered how much information they were giving out. She knew about the first boat—the tampered hoses, the propane in the bilge. Was the M.O. for the marina fire the same?

"They're not telling me. The fire marshal, Loughlin, he got a boat surveyor to go over those hulls. And an insurance investigator from New York, he was there, too. They're both saying it was definitely set."

Cassie pushed her chair back. "What was the name of the surveyor?" Anybody who hung around boats knew the local surveyors. They inspected a boat from stem to stern before it was purchased. Nobody wanted to invest thousands in a vessel just to find it was riddled with blisters or had rigging that was about to fail, so everybody tried to get a handle on who the good surveyors were.

Shonika flipped pages in her reporter's notebook. "It was a guy named Skip Shelton."

Cassie knew him. She had used him, in fact, to inspect *Time Out* for the insurance company once she'd fixed it up. With only thirty or so surveyors in the Bay region, it was a lucky hit, but not extraordinary. Skip Shelton was the best in the business, according to most of the marina community. No wonder Loughlin had called on him to help out.

Shonika went on her way. Cassie immediately called Skip's number. She caught him just finishing a boat. He was willing to meet her later that afternoon.

"Can we make it around four?" she asked.

Skip agreed. Cassie hurriedly finished the write-up on the Triton Seafood Festival, transferred it to the editing basket, and headed for the door. On the way she stopped by the desk of her editor, James Lee. "The article on the seafood festival is in editing," she informed him. "I've got to run. I have an appointment to talk to some organizers prior to this weekend's event."

"Where are you headed this weekend?" James was in his forties, with distinguishing silver temples and gray eyes. Not a bad-looking guy.

"Solomon's Skipjack Appreciation Days."

He nodded. "Okay, then."

"If you have any questions about the article, you can reach me on my cell," Cassie called over her shoulder as she headed for the exit.

"Right."

She pushed open the door to the lobby and nearly ran into Richard Maxwell. "Rick! What are you doing here?"

He smiled sheepishly. He had a piece of paper in his hand. "I came to place an ad. Some old boat stuff I've been meaning to sell. Might as well, now that the boat's been burned. Hey, your dad told me you were working here. How about that! Do you like it?"

"Yes, I do."

"What kind of writing are you doing?"

Cassie was anxious to leave but she tried to be polite. "I'm writing up festivals this summer, you know, like the Solomon's Skipjack Appreciation Days. Stuff like that." She glanced at her watch. "As a matter of fact, I have an appointment down there right now. I'd better run. See you later!"

"Sure!" Rick said, and he gave her that funny little half-salute.

Cassie pulled the Cabrio onto Route 2 and headed south for Solomon's. She glanced at her watch. It was 2:30 p.m.. Her timing should be just about right. The trip was a straight shot down Route 2 from Annapolis, through some of the most beautiful rural areas in the state of Maryland. Green rolling hills dotted with horse farms alternated with small villages full of charm.

Cassie never minded driving. To her, hitting the open road was an invitation to relax. She could think, listen to music, or just drive. This time, though, despite the beautiful scenery, peace eluded her.

The previous night, when she'd started to think about Jake and Mike, she wanted to pray, but she couldn't. What was stopping her? The truth was, ever since Mike's death the whole thing seemed like an irrelevant exercise.

Mike had been such a strong Christian. He'd been raised in the church and homeschooled until high school. He'd been in a Fellowship of Christian Athletes huddle his senior year. In college, he'd been in InterVarsity. It had been relatively easy, even for independent Cassie, to follow his lead because Mike truly lived what he believed. Cassie never doubted his integrity.

When he died, it was like the universe had played a cruel joke. Mike was one of the good guys—the best. Now, verses of Scripture Cassie had once placed her faith in sounded hollow. "Those who wait upon the Lord will renew their strength"? "Trust in the Lord with all your might"? How could she reconcile those with what had happened to Mike?

Sometimes it frightened her to think how far she'd drifted from what once had been so important to her—and to Mike. Even so, the only thing she knew to do with her internal conflict was simply ignore it. Maybe someday it would all make sense.

Cassie made it to Solomon's by 3:30. She parked her car and walked around. The village was built around an inner harbor area, a natural deep anchorage. Marinas, restaurants, shops, and some private houses filled the shoreline, along with a museum and the old Drum Point Lighthouse. The town had flourished as an oystering center in the early twentieth century. In recent years, it had shifted its focus and become a recreational boating center, resort destination, and military community, home of the Patuxent Naval Air Station.

Cassie parked her car and got out to browse through a couple of shops. At 3:45 p.m., she walked to Skip Shelton's office.

Skip was about five feet ten inches tall and wiry. His sandy-blond hair and blue eyes set off a boyish face. When Cassie first met him, he was so tan she thought he could be a California surfer, but his soft accent put his hometown somewhere in the South, not on the West Coast. He had an easy grin, and he greeted Cassie like an old friend, with a hug and a broad smile. "What brings you all the way down here?" he asked.

She told him about her job at the newspaper and the story she was going to write on the Skipjack festival. When she got him good and relaxed, she invited him to dinner. Single, he apparently had no other plans and quickly accepted.

They went to a waterside restaurant. Because it was a beautiful day, they opted for eating outside on the deck above the harbor. The clanging of halyards and the lapping of waves was all the music they needed. Boats filled with sunburned fishermen were gliding back into their slips, and an occasional sailor could be seen working on his craft. Swallows swooped after bugs and flitted between the masts and loud, brassy gulls demanded attention.

Skip wanted to hear about her boat and her father, whom he knew from the many Save the Bay activities they were both involved in. Before he'd finished his flounder, she had worked the conversation around to her primary interest, the marina fire.

"I can't tell you about that," he said.

"Why?"

"Don't you work for a newspaper?"

"Don't you think I can keep things confidential?" She flashed what she hoped was a winning smile. "C'mon, Skip. I was there! I almost lost my boat! Tell me what's going on—I won't say anything. I don't even work the crime beat."

"I can't do it."

She laughed. "Sure you can! Here, let me help ... I think it was arson."

He leaned forward, his eyes crinkling in amusement. "What makes you say that?"

Cassie didn't answer him. She just sat quietly, smiling at him.

Eventually he broke. He shook his head and grinned. "Yeah, you're right, Miss Know-It-All. It was arson."

"Really? Now how do you know that?" Cassie was toying with him.

"There were signs."

"Signs. Like traces of accelerants?"

Skip exhaled loudly.

"No, seriously," Cassie said, changing tactics. "I've always wondered about arson investigation in boat fires. I took a course at the FBI Academy and learned a little about arson in general, but, you know, with boats, it's a whole different thing." She took a sip of water. "But that's okay. I mean, I understand that you can't tell me anything. I was just interested and the rumor is that Loughlin doesn't have a clue how the thing got started and that he's stalling and keeping the insurance companies from paying off the claims—"

"That's wrong," Skip said emphatically. "We found the cause."

"You did? Oh, then I guess you do have an idea where it started ..."

"We knew the fire started with the *Lady J.*, the sloop near the lift."

Cassie raised her eyebrows. "Really? Because rumor has it that it started at the fuel dock."

"That's completely wrong! Gosh, where do people come up with these things?"

Cassie smiled. "Who knows? In any case, they're saying that Loughlin isn't capable of finding out what caused it."

"That's ridiculous." Skip dropped his voice and looked around before continuing. "The *Lady J.* burned to the waterline, but Loughlin and I climbed into what was left and started poking around. First thing I noticed, the seacocks were half open. No sailor's going to leave those valves half open like that. Next thing, we found a piece of hose that had been filed down. By this time, we're all hyper. Sure enough, we look, and the bilge pump has been tampered with."

"Wait a minute. That's the same—"

Skip tapped his forefinger on the table. "The same M.O. as the single boat that burned the month before. Somebody fixed it so that when the automatic bilge pump triggered on, it would ignite the propane we think had leaked into the bilge."

Cassie responded, "Wow."

Suddenly Skip seemed overcome with remorse. "Listen, none of this is public information and it's certainly not for print. I'm just telling you because ... well, I don't know why I just told you."

"Don't worry," she assured him, "I won't say a thing."

An hour later she was headed north, back to Black Duck Boulevard and her boathouse apartment. She rolled the information Skip had given her around in her head. So, the first fire was connected with the marina fire. Most likely it was the same arsonist. Was Jake's assault connected, too? Or Schneider's murder?

The moon was high in the sky and there was a surprising amount of traffic on Route 2. Lost in her thoughts, she drove in silence, without radio, but before long she started thinking about Mike. How she missed him!

When the monologue in her head became oppressive, and her loneliness threatened to overwhelm her, she threw in a CD and hit "play." Dave Matthews was a better companion. *Dave Matthews!*

When Mike was alive it was always Third Day or dc Talk. Always some Christian group. Now—

A bright light reflected in her rearview mirror blinded her momentarily. She glanced up. The right headlight on the car behind her was misaimed and the bright blue halogen light seared her vision. Irritated, she flipped her mirror to the side, and focused on the road ahead, waiting for her eyes to readjust.

Soon her exit approached, and she swung off the highway and into the darker side streets. Threading her way through the exclusive neighborhood toward the Turnage house, she pulled into the driveway, parked her car, and walked wearily up the stairs to her apartment. The burdens she carried were not physical, but they were heavy nonetheless.

She slipped into her flannel pajama bottoms, a tank top, and a light zip-front sweatshirt, poured a glass of water, grabbed a quilt, and went out on her balcony. It was pleasantly cool outside. Nestling into a white wicker chair, she pulled the quilt around her and watched as Orion stalked across the heavens while boats below silently slid over the black water. Off in the distance, the lights in houses on the far shore of the cove winked off, one by one, and somewhere a loon called out for its mate.

Night enveloped her, but she received no comfort from it. Dawn was a long way off. The noise in her head could not be stilled. Mike was gone. Jake was gone. The grief was like an anchor weighing on her soul.

11

He hated the probing, which began early each morning. The poking and pressing, the endless needles, the tests. They analyzed his movements, his speech, his vital signs, the read-outs on the EEG, and even his mood, which was most often described on his chart as "agitated."

He put up with it for a while, but then he would lapse into a stony silence that was only one step removed from an eruption of fierce anger.

Often, just when he thought things couldn't get any worse, it would begin. His right hand would curl, imperceptibly at first, and then he would get a metallic taste in his mouth.

After that came the blackness. Sometimes it was brief, a simple emptiness he would quickly pass through. At other times, though, it would go on and on. On those occasions the Pit would open in the back of his mind and once again he would have to fight terror and scramble to keep from sliding into despair.

When he eventually opened his eyes again, it was always to a pounding headache, confusion, and an oppressive fatigue. Retreating, he would sleep. And then, the whole process would begin again.

He was trapped. He was angry. He was afraid. He was alone. And he hated it.

The next day the newspaper office was filled with noise. Frustrated and unable to concentrate, Cassie decided to do some research elsewhere. Around 11:00 a.m. she told her editor she'd be on her cell and headed for Annapolis.

Cassie slid into a seat at Cap's Grill on Main Street in Annapolis, near the City Dock. It was a favorite haunt of hers, a place where copious amounts of good food attracted cruising sailors, midshipmen from the Naval Academy, legislators, and retired Rotarians. She'd been frequenting Cap's since she was a teenager, since before she was allowed to, as a matter of fact. The place was a touchstone for her, a nesting ground of sorts.

She had come armed with books on the historic vessels, and on Solomon's Island itself, prepping for her story on the Skipjack Appreciation Days. Hours of reading might only net a sentence or two in her article, but it was time well spent as far as she was concerned. She hadn't been happy with her first piece, although Len seemed to like it. She wanted more, and better. *Why am I being so obsessive?* she asked herself. *This job is just a cover!*

Cassie ordered a chicken pomodori sandwich. The waitress brought her a pitcher of sweet tea and a glass filled with ice. Cassie sipped the tea while she pored over her book.

Skipjacks were the traditional workboats of the Chesapeake Bay. Built between 1900 and 1956, their graceful lines, deck-sweeping booms, and huge triangular sails made them beautiful—and their design made them perfect for the Bay. They had wide decks for working and shallow drafts so they wouldn't run aground, and they were constructed of heavy oak, so they could take the pounding of the storms and handle the heavy dredges used to harvest oysters.

Skipjacks fell out of favor as the oyster population declined. As wooden boats they were hard to maintain and expensive as well. Of the one thousand or so built, only about dozen now remained, and a major restoration and conservation project had been organized to save them.

One of the few skipjacks afloat had, in fact, recently sunk during a storm. The *Rebecca T. Ruark* was considered precious enough to save and had been brought up from her watery grave by a small group of determined men and a heavy crane. Her story, published in the Baltimore papers, had caught Cassie's interest soon after she had taken on the Alberg.

Engrossed in her book, Cassie almost didn't hear her cell phone ringing. She answered it and heard Craig Campbell's voice.

"I need to talk to you," he said. "Can you meet me somewhere?"

Her heart leaped. She didn't even know Craig was back in town. "Where are you?"

"I-97 south, coming from Baltimore."

Cassie's mind raced. "Have you reached the Crownsville exit yet?"

"No."

"Take that exit, Route 178 I think it is, south and east. There's a marina down there called Carl's Cove. It should be pretty deserted today."

"Okay, right."

Cassie stood up. Her heart was racing now. Craig was back. She could find out about Jake. She quickly gathered up her books. "I should be there in about fifteen minutes."

"Got it."

A warm wind ruffled Cassie's hair as she led Craig Campbell down a long dock at Carl's. There were few people around, which is what she had expected to find on a weekday.

The dock ended in a "T" configuration and there were benches on the end that Cassie was headed for. The sailboats rocked in their slips, halyards clanking and fishing boats pulled at their dock lines. Gulls shrieked and swooped and chattered. The rough wood of the dock looked like any weathered dock anywhere.

She sat down on a bench by the water, and so did Craig. No one would hear them out here. "When did you get back? And how is Jake?" Cassie asked. Her stomach was nervous, almost like a schoolgirl on a first date. What was she stressed about? What Craig would say? What he wouldn't say?

"I got back a couple of weeks ago, actually," Craig said.

"A couple of weeks? You didn't call me! Why didn't you stay

with him?" Anger flared up in her, an anger she neither wanted nor expected.

"I couldn't. It's just too far away from my family and my job."

"So he's out there ... wherever he is ... by himself. Is that it?"

"No. A local agent is keeping an eye on him."

"But nobody he knows."

"No."

Cassie bit her lip and tried to calm down. *Craig's not the enemy,* she told herself. "Where is he?"

"I can't tell you. You know that."

"How could my knowing hurt Jake?" Cassie's voice shook.

"I don't know that it could, but Cassie, I can't fight Foster on this. Jake's location is classified. I can't divulge it."

Cassie crossed her arms and stared out across the Severn River. Framed by high, green hills, the river flowed down toward Annapolis and into the Bay. At its mouth was the Naval Academy. Up here, pricey homes and lovely riverside restaurants edged the banks. She could see a man in a fourteen-foot Catalina Capri out on the river, obviously a novice sailor, fighting to keep the small sailboat under control in the wind. Furious, she was fighting for control herself. "Well, how is he? Can you tell me that?"

"He's okay. He's in a rehab hospital where he can get the help he needs. I stayed for a couple of days to make sure he got settled." Craig grew silent, as if collecting his thoughts. "When I left he was awake and talking. His speech is hesitant, as though he has trouble coming up with the right words. And he still can't grab things with his right hand."

"Oh, great."

"There's something else, Cassie." Craig paused. "He's having seizures."

"Seizures?" A shimmer of alarm ran through her.

"He's having blackouts, and they don't know why. They think they are some kind of petit mal seizure, from the head injury, but they're just not sure."

"What are they doing for him?"

"Medication." Craig drew in a deep breath.

"What about MRIs? CT scans? EEGs? What are they doing to find out what's going on in his brain?"

"I'm sure ..."

"You're sure of what? How can you be sure? Nobody's there advocating for him, Craig! You know that's what it takes to get good medical care." Cassie kicked a shell off the dock. Her frustration was quickly building in velocity and power. Blood was pounding in her head. "I can't believe that you left him alone and that you won't tell me where he is!"

Craig sat silently on the bench, his elbows resting on his knees, staring down at the dock.

"You know, I'm beginning to wonder if the Bureau cares a rip about its agents. My husband gets killed and they do nothing about it. They call it an accident. Jake gets attacked, and he's shelved. Put out to pasture. Left alone. And they won't tell his one friend in the world where he is."

Craig looked up at Cassie. Lines of concern formed at the corners of his eyes. "Before you completely trash the FBI," he said, "may I remind you that whoever attacked Jake is still out there. And, you were the last person to see him, and you admitted the two of you were arguing."

Cassie's face grew red. Rage, like hot lead, poured through her.

"Now, I know you, and I know you aren't the person who assaulted Jake. But the supervisors are, in fact, operating out of Jake's best interest by not releasing his whereabouts. It's not their fault he has no close family members to look after him."

Cassie turned away from him. His words were like flaming arrows, but yet, deep down, she had to admit there was some truth in what he was saying. Many times as an agent, she had played her cards close to her chest with a trusted witness, sometimes even with other agents.

But if anyone was harboring even a smidge of an idea that she had hurt Jake, it was all the more reason why she had to find the true attacker.

She forced herself to calm down.

"Cassie, I called you because I wanted to see how you were doing. I felt bad that I hadn't called you. I thought you might want to get an update on Jake."

"I'm fine."

He looked at her like he didn't believe her.

"I'm fine. I'm only concerned about Jake." She worked to control her temper. Every muscle in her body was tingling with anger. She had to focus on Jake to calm down. "How is he handling the seizures?"

"He's very frustrated."

"What can I do for him?"

Craig looked off into the distance. "I don't know what we can do for him. I guess the only thing we can do is pray, at this point."

Anger, again—this time it was a furious flash that began at her heart and spread outward until her very fingertips grew hot. "To pray? You want me to pray?" Cassie paced back and forth, adrenaline coursing through her. "That's it? Pray?"

Craig just looked at her in confusion.

"I cannot believe—"

Campbell stood up and held up his hand, as if to hold off her thoughts. "What's happened to you, Cassie?" He sounded irritated, now, for the first time.

She stopped short.

"When Mike and I used to run together, we would talk about faith, about God, about all the things you were doing at your church. He loved God with his whole heart. I thought you did, too."

She flashed hot, then cold, then hot again. Her fists clenched.

"Was I wrong? What's happened to you?" he asked again.

What had happened? To her? Nothing! Nothing ... and everything. And oh, man, she was not going to deal with this. Not here, not now. "You're over the line, Campbell," she said. "That's a personal issue. I don't need to talk to you about that."

"You don't need to talk to me about anything," he retorted softly.

Why was he so ... intrusive? Cassie put her hands to her head. She was getting a headache, a bad one. She couldn't deal with this. No way!

"Look, I'm sorry if I upset you," Campbell said.

"I came here to find out about Jake, not to have my spiritual condition analyzed and judged!"

"I'm sorry." Craig sat down on the bench again.

"I'm sorry if I don't measure up to Mike's hero status, Campbell. Some of us just don't make the grade!"

"Sorry."

She turned away from him and looked toward the river. Leaning up against a piling, the wind in her face, the sun on her back, she watched as the small sailboat jibed suddenly. She saw the sailor spill into the river, grabbing the boom and pulling the boat over as he did. The Capri capsized and turned onto its side, its mast and sail on the surface of the water. The sailor swam around to the centerboard protruding from the hull and reached up to try to pull the boat upright again.

Cassie began to focus on the sailor to get her mind off Campbell, and in her heart she began coaching him. *Don't let it turtle,* she pleaded silently. *Don't let the sail get under the water. Don't let the boat turn upside down. Grab on to the centerboard ... that's it. Pull with your weight. Pull!* But the man in the water could not swing the boat upright. There was too much water in the mast, too much over the sail already, holding the boat on its side—he'd have to swim around, empty the sail and the mast, swim back to the bottom where the centerboard was, and try again, all the time hoping the boat wouldn't go totally upside down.

It was hard to recover from turtling.

Cassie bit the inside of her cheek. She turned toward Craig. He was staring straight ahead, rubbing his wrist with his right thumb. "What progress, if any, are you making on the investigation?" she asked him.

Campbell hesitated.

"Craig, you owe me that much!"

He sighed. "You didn't hear this from me."

"Okay."

He looked at her, his blue eyes clear and bright. "DiCarlo doesn't have a clue who assaulted Jake. We haven't found his SUV. We have very little physical evidence. We've been checking all the cases he was working, not just that murder. We've checked out his ex-wife, her boyfriend, Jake's friends and coworkers, his bad boys ... nothing's clicking, nothing's adding up."

"And the man Mike killed?"

"Tyson Farnsworth was a street thug. A druggie who'd spent more time in prison than out since he was thirteen."

Cassie rolled her eyes. "There's a pattern, Campbell, even though we can't see it. Jake was on to something. He was attacked because he was getting close. I know that."

"How do you know?"

Cassie hedged. "I just know."

Campbell picked up a splinter from the dock and tossed it in the water. The two stayed silent for a minute or two, sadness forming a gulf. Craig finally breached it. "What are you doing with your time, Cassie?"

She tossed her head. "I'm working."

"Where?"

"At a newspaper ... *The Bay Area Beacon.*" Immediately she regretted saying it.

"Really?"

"When the Bureau wouldn't let me come back, I had to do something."

Campbell looked at her, squinting in the bright sun. "Reporters often have an inside track on stuff going on. They can go around asking questions and use sources just like law enforcement."

Cassie refused to take the bait. "I can write, so I took the job. That's all. I did it in college."

Campbell picked up something else from the dock and threw it in the water. He looked at Cassie knowingly. "You're playing a dangerous game. If somebody connects you with Jake and Mike and you go around sticking your nose in places you shouldn't, whatever he was on to could get you in trouble."

"I can take care of myself."

"What's the status of your appeal with the Bureau?"

"That'll take forever, you know that."

Campbell shoved his hands in his pockets. He clearly didn't know what to say. "You should leave this to us."

"I want the guy who got Mike, and Jake."

"Everybody does."

"I can't just sit by."

Campbell shook his head in exasperation.

Cassie grimaced. "Foster said I blinked. He said he wouldn't take me back because I gave up because Mike died. That's my current reputation at the Bureau, Craig. I can't take pressure. I give up when things get tough." She gestured angrily. "I will not let that stand."

"What does it matter what they think? You know who you are."

"I'm not a coward, Craig. I'm not." She gazed out onto the water. Then she looked back at Craig, her eyes searching his.

"You're a strong lady, Cassie. The people who know you know that."

Her stomach quivered. She looked away. Should she give him the lead she'd brought? "I do have something for you," she finally said.

Craig raised his eyebrows. "What?"

"I talked to somebody who saw Jake's SUV leaving the parking lot that night."

"Who?"

Wordlessly, Cassie reached in her pocket and pulled out a slip of paper with Pat's name and number on it and handed it to him.

Craig took a deep breath. "Thank you."

"She didn't see the driver. Still, she's a witness."

"Good, thanks." He put the paper in his pocket, then hesitated. "I guess I'd better go."

They began the long walk up the dock toward the shore without talking. When they got to the parking lot, Craig suddenly gave her a hug. "You take care of yourself," he said softly. "We don't need you *and* Jake down for the count."

She stiffened. "I'll be fine."

Cassie watched him drive off, fingering her necklace. It was like seeing the last ship home leaving port, or the last guest at a funeral leave. He was her last, her only, connection with the Bureau and with Jake. Jake—who was having seizures now! Out there somewhere, by himself.

Her stomach was in a knot. She unlocked her car and got in. Starting the engine, she pulled her Cabrio out of the parking lot, onto the state road and right into the oncoming path of a black Mercedes. The other driver laid on his horn and jerked into the other lane. Fear flashed through Cassie. *How stupid,* she berated herself. *Why don't you just get yourself killed?* And for one brief moment, it seemed like an option.

12

*A*fter her meeting with Craig, Cassie debated momentarily. What should she do next? What could she do to help Jake? Finally, she turned north and drove toward Baltimore. She rang the doorbell to Tamara Tucker's house. Jake's ex-wife looked shocked when she opened the door.

"Tam?" Cassie said. "Can we talk?"

There was a long hesitation.

"Please? Just for a minute?"

The door swung open, and Cassie walked into Jake's old house. Everything looked the same, except that his shoes were gone from the place by the door where he always left them, and his baseball cap was gone, and the smell of his aftershave was gone.

Cassie and Tamara sat in the kitchen. The kids—Jake's kids—were playing in the basement. Cassie could hear their excited voices over the blare of the television. Tam looked pale and even thinner than Cassie had remembered her being. She nervously twisted a napkin, her reddish brown hair falling around her face.

"Why did you tell your friend, Frederick Schneider's girlfriend, to call Jake?" Cassie asked.

Tam swallowed and looked down. "Despite the problems Jake and I had, I knew that he would help her. He's all about work, and I knew he'd dive right into a case like that. I felt sorry for her, being involved with that man, then him getting killed practically in front of her."

Cassie nodded. "I'd like to talk to her. Will you give me her name?"

Tam looked away.

"Please, Tam. I just want to help find the person who hurt Jake."

Wordlessly, Tam stood and retrieved a card file, removed a card, and handed it to Cassie. Cassie copied down the information and returned the card.

"I'd like you to go before the kids see you," Tam said. "It would only upset them."

Cassie nodded. She stood up and moved toward the front door. Her heart was heavy. *Divorces break a lot of relationships,* she thought. She would have loved to see the kids, to hold them and let them know their daddy loved them. Before she left, she turned back to Tam. "Would you like to know how Jake is?"

Tam shook her head slightly.

Cassie took a breath. "He doesn't hate you, Tam. He blames himself mostly."

But Jake's ex-wife didn't respond. The gulf between them was too wide.

Driving back to Annapolis, Cassie pondered the visit. She'd accomplished her goal but sadness filled her. How did Jake and Tam's marriage fall apart? How did these lovers become enemies? Difficult questions, and maybe no real answers.

Later that night, Cassie got a call from Craig Campbell. "You've been to see Tam," he said.

"Wow! That was quick. Do you have the house bugged?" It irritated her that he knew about that.

"Tam had called me with a question before you arrived. I called her back with the answer and she mentioned you had been there."

"Do you have a problem with that?" Cassie demanded.

There was a long pause. "I just don't want to see you getting hurt."

"I'm fine, Campbell!" she snapped, and that was the end of the conversation.

For the Solomon's Island Skipjack Appreciation Days, Cassie and Brett drove down together in her car. The weather was typical for Bay country in the summer—hazy, hot, and humid—and the crowds were plentiful. They soon found themselves working like a practiced team, backing each other up and pointing out story possibilities. They got interviews with old-timers and little kids, working in a quote or two from oystermen who still plied the Bay, and got pictures of weathered faces, old boats, and crisply dressed Navy men.

Boarding a skipjack, Cassie noted again their broad decks and low, sweeping booms. Knowing how tempestuous the Bay could be, her respect was renewed for the sturdy oystermen. Working the Bay in 40-degree weather, dredging under sail, could not be easy. A sudden shift of the wind and you could find yourself in the cold water, swept overboard by the boom. Just minutes in the water at that time of the year could mean death. Cassie also knew that, strangely, many of the oystermen couldn't swim.

Working with Brett was almost fun, as close to fun as she could imagine these days. They were starting to "read" each other, Cassie noted. She wondered why he was still single and if he planned to stay at the paper for long. When he suggested they stop off at Holly Point Harbor for a quick bite to eat on the way home, she readily agreed. She wouldn't mind some more conversation. Maybe Brett knew something that would be useful.

"So, where'd you learn to write?" he asked as they settled in at an outdoor table overlooking the harbor.

She smiled. "Oh, I don't know," she responded. "I went to the University of Maryland and majored in English. That might have had something to do with it."

He laughed.

"What about you? How'd you end up as a photographer?"

"Flunked out of everything else," he said.

Cassie grinned. "No, seriously."

"Seriously. I went to college to play golf. That was it. I hated studying. Saw no point to English or history. I just wanted to play golf." He shrugged. "My dad was a photographer, though, for the *Atlanta Journal,* and I had picked up a lot from him. Back in high school, I shot pictures for the school paper and yearbook. So when a tournament was being played near my school, I volunteered to shoot some photos for our campus newspaper. I thought it was a great way to get in free, and get up close. I got a great shot of Tiger making a hole-in-one. Not only did the newspaper use it, AP picked it up and, as they say, the rest is history."

Cassie raised her eyebrows. "Not bad."

"I like working as a photographer because it still gives me plenty of time for golf."

It was his turn to ask a question. "What I can't figure out, is how come you're still single?"

"Oh, I was married. But my husband died."

"Oh, man. I'm sorry."

She waved him off. "No, no. Don't worry about it. He died ... some time ago, in a car accident." *Months, it was months ago,* she chided herself. She wondered why she'd hedged on that.

Brett fell silent, and Cassie knew he was trying to figure out what to say. She felt sorry for him. Not many people their age were confronted with her situation.

Over his shoulder, Cassie could see a crabber headed out to the Bay in his long, low-slung boat. It had a small pilothouse, just enough to shield the man from the weather a little, and low sides so he could pull up the traps, empty them, and place them again in the Bay.

Crabbers laid their traps all around the shallow water. They were marked with small buoys, often just two-liter soda bottles painted some color. The traps with their buoy lines were a major pain for sailors. They worked hard to avoid them. If a line wrapped itself around the prop, you could be in big trouble. More than once, Cass had had to dive into murky water to cut the prop loose. A few times doing that had taught her to keep a sharp eye out for them.

There were all kinds of traps in life, traps and entanglements.

They were saved from their awkward silence when the waitress delivered their food. Cassie had ordered chicken salad with melted provolone cheese on a croissant. Brett had decided to try the restaurant's seafood Alfredo. Fifteen minutes later, Cass noticed he'd mainly been pushing it around on his plate and she asked him if it tasted bad.

"No," he said, sheepishly, "I'm just … not hungry."

He looked at her and when she saw the softness in his eyes, she recognized it, and she froze inside. Love was not an option, not for her, anyway, not now.

Turning the conversation to a safer topic, Cassie got him talking about their editor, Len Boyette, and some of the reporters. The newsroom was a good place to work, according to Brett. The organization took care of its own. Len had once worked for the *Washington Post* and had downsized his career when he became tired of the hustle and bustle of the capital. The news team worked together pretty well, despite the potentially aggravating mix of older, experienced reporters and young hotheads.

While Cassie ate, she studied Brett covertly. He was a nice guy, an attractive guy, and under different circumstances she might have pursued a relationship. She could tell he was interested in her. But not now. A little conversation was all she'd wanted.

They finished their meal and left the restaurant. As they drove north toward home, both were quiet, speaking only occasionally and briefly.

On a dark stretch of road, Brett leaned forward in the passenger seat and remarked, "Man, that guy's headlights are bright."

Cassie adjusted the rearview mirror. When she did, her heart thumped. The car behind them had a misaimed blue halogen right headlight.

Cassie sat at her desk at the newspaper the next day, Sunday, writing her story while she pushed intrusive thoughts about the car with the halogen headlight out of her mind. Her dad had called and invited her to church, but she declined. Instead, she called Tam's friend, Desiree Dubois. After her story was in, she was going on a road trip.

Finishing her story, she left a note for her editor, shut down her computer, and left another note for Len. "I'll be out tomorrow. The story's done. See you Tuesday, late."

Then she went home, packed a few things in a bag, and headed north, to Harrisburg, Pennsylvania.

The trip up Route 83 north of Baltimore took Cassie through some beautiful rolling countryside. The heavy rains they'd received in the spring had left the hills green and lush. Here and there, fine-bodied horses were peacefully grazing. Mike had loved to ride. He had grown up in Oklahoma on enough land that he'd had horses all his life. He'd taught Cassie to ride Western, like he did, and they'd gone trail riding in the mountains frequently. Once when she'd visited his family in Oklahoma, she'd tried barrel riding. She remembered Mike's broad grin as he watched her successfully stay on the charging quarter horse. She remembered how proud he was of her.

Her dad always said he and her mom hadn't been married long enough before she died to have anything but good memories. That's the same way it was with her and Mike. In a way, it was a disadvantage. Who would ever measure up to him?

The sun was dropping toward the horizon as she crossed the bridge over the wide, rocky Susquehanna River. The dome of the Pennsylvania capitol building, so like the one in Washington, presided regally over the city. Cassie exited the highway, found her hotel, pulled into the parking lot, grabbed her overnight bag, and checked in.

Desiree Dubois, the late Frederick Schneider's mistress, worked as an assistant to a Pennsylvania state senator. Her office was in the capitol building, but she'd suggested Cassie meet her Monday morning at the Senate Grill some two blocks away.

"I'm not proud of this episode in my life," she began. She was tall, and blonde, and thin. Dressed in a black business suit, she played nervously with her earrings. "Despite my name, I am no floozy. My mother was a misdirected romantic, that's all."

Cassie nodded in affirmation. She wanted this girl to talk. "So, what happened?"

"I met Frederick when I went with my boss to a conference on the Bay. Frederick was one of the presenters. I was alone, of course, and one night as I sat in the bar, he slid into the seat next to me and offered to buy me a drink.

"How desperate was I, anyway?" She shook her head. "I mean, that line's not even original. Anyway, one thing led to another. We began meeting in Harrisburg, or sometimes in Maryland. I didn't have sex with him for months, I swear. He said he was really unhappy in his marriage. I felt so sorry for him. It was as if he was carrying some inner burden he couldn't lay down.

"After about six months, he told me he was going to leave his wife, and he asked me if I would marry him. I was thrilled. I was so tired of being alone! I told him yes, and the next time I saw him, he'd bought the boat. He knew it was something I'd always wanted." Desiree stirred her iced tea with the straw, then sipped it. Cassie figured she was stalling, and she was.

"So, what happened then?" Cassie prompted her.

"For the next three months, everything was great. Every time I could get away, which was most weekends, we'd meet at the boat and have the best time. We cruised up and down the upper Bay area, down to Baltimore and Annapolis, and it was everything I'd ever dreamed of.

"Then one night we were at that marina—Sullivan's Wharf. Frederick said he was going to get some cigarettes. I fell asleep and when I woke up, Frederick wasn't back. The companionway was open, so I popped my head above deck and looked around. I slipped some clothes on, and my deck shoes, and walked ashore. Then I saw something, in the weeds and I could tell right away, even from a distance, that it was Frederick."

"How'd you know?"

"I don't know ... woman's intuition, I guess." Desiree dabbed a tear away from her right eye. "His throat was slashed and there was blood everywhere. I dialed 9-1-1 on my cell phone, but it was already too late."

"That must have been a terrible shock."

"Oh, it was, it was."

"Do you have any idea who did it?"

"Frederick was a loner. I don't think he had any friends, much less any enemies. I never met his wife, but from the things he said about her, there wasn't much of a relationship. She didn't sound like the type who could do something like this. But somebody got to him. He'd been under a lot of pressure lately, I could tell. I had no idea, until I found that letter, that somebody was threatening him."

Cassie tilted her head sideways. "You didn't have a clue?"

Desiree thought for a moment. "There was one thing that concerned me. I didn't remember it at first. Two days before he died, I'd heard Frederick arguing with somebody. It was nighttime, and I was on the boat. He'd gone over to the convenience store, again to buy some cigarettes. I heard a car door slam, then voices, and as the voices got louder, I realized it was Frederick and another man. They were arguing."

Cassie leaned forward. "About what?"

"I couldn't make much of it out. I heard the word 'millions' and I got the impression they were talking about money. And Frederick refused to talk about it when he got back to the boat."

"You told the police this?"

Desiree blushed. "No, no I haven't. It seemed like such a tiny detail, and frankly, I just wanted to forget everything that happened." She sighed. "You know, I spent a year and all of my self-esteem on that man. I just couldn't deal with it anymore."

"Sometimes you just have to move on," Cassie said.

"That's right. The cops, they all looked at me like I was a

prostitute or something. But you know what? I'm just a lonely, thirty-six-year-old single girl who wanted to believe someone would choose her. I'm stupid, maybe, but I'm not a prostitute."

Later, Cassie pondered their conversation as she got in the car. She had one more stop to make. Her appointment with Frederick's wife was at 2:00 p.m. in Philadelphia.

"Frederick was a brilliant man," Mary Edgerton-Schneider said. She was sitting in a flowered patio chair at her home in Mainline, Philadelphia. Cassie sat next to her, a glass of iced tea on the table between them. "He was brilliant but stupid. He never got the hang of marriage, never understood what a woman needs." Mary paused. "At first I tried to make a go of it, but eventually I realized I had to create my own life."

"When did things really get bad, if you don't mind my asking?" said Cassie.

"He fancied himself an investor. For a smart man, though, he seemed to have little understanding of money. Some scheme of his went bad. He would never talk to me about it. That's when the affairs began. And there were many of them. Miss—whatever her name is—was only the last in a long line."

Cassie nodded. "That must have been hard on you."

"Frederick was trying to escape from life. This girl and the sailboat was just the latest attempt."

"I find it strange you didn't know about it."

She shrugged. "We kept our finances completely separate. I rarely saw him." She looked at Cassie, her eyes soft. "You're so young. I want you to know I never meant it to be this way. I don't think Frederick did either. I think we both wanted a close marriage. Unfortunately, that didn't happen for us. Maybe it was him, maybe it was me. I just don't know."

"I understand." Cassie shifted in her chair. "Where do you suppose Frederick got the money for the boat?"

"That, my dear, is an excellent question. He was always lousy with money. When I discovered he'd bought a boat, I was shocked. For a man who frequently didn't have enough money to pay his bills, it was an extravagance."

Cassie nodded. "Let me ask you a rather personal question. Could someone have threatened to reveal the affair Frederick was having to you? Could that have been a reason for extortion?"

Mary smiled and shook her head. "Too much had already happened between us for that to be a factor. He never talked about his dalliances, but I'm sure he knew I was aware of them. Frederick stopped being a husband long ago."

Cassie chewed the inside of her cheek. "When did Frederick buy the boat?"

"I'm not sure."

"Could we find out?"

Mary stood up. "Why yes, I guess so."

"Could we find out when he bought it and how he paid for it?"

"I suppose the broker would know."

"Yes, I'm sure he would. Would you mind calling him now?"

On her way back down to Maryland on Interstate 95, Cassie mused over the new information she'd gleaned. Frederick Schneider was a very average-looking, portly man; an engineer who couldn't handle money and was nearly broke; a married man who'd kept a mistress. He'd bought the boat last May, they'd discovered. And he'd paid $80,000 in cash. Where did he get that money, and why was he being extorted?

13

*T*he next day when Cassie walked in the newsroom, everyone was clustered around the television that hung high on the wall in a corner. "What's up?" she whispered to a reporter.

"The President is coming on," he responded.

Once again, a terrorist group had struck a U.S. target overseas. Would the UN do anything about it, or would the member nations just continue to point the finger at the Americans? Cassie was sick of the constant negative press directed against the United States.

She moved to her desk and tried hard to concentrate on preparing for the local beach festival coming up the next weekend, but she couldn't focus, and finally she logged off her computer and grabbed her purse. Walking briskly through the newsroom, she almost ran into Len.

"Hey! Where you off to so fast?" he asked.

She had to think fast. "Severna Park."

He squinted at her. "Be careful."

"Right."

Cassie was not quite through the door when the newsroom receptionist paged her. "Cassie McKenna, line 2 please."

Wondering who could be calling, Cassie grabbed a nearby phone receiver and punched line 2. "Hello?"

"Cassie, it's Craig. I need to talk to you."

"Now?"

"Now."

*   *   *   *   *

Cassie drove to the Annapolis Mall where she and Craig had agreed to meet. As she pulled into the parking lot, a storm was brewing with thick, dark clouds clustering off to the west. She hurried inside and made her way to the food court, which was teeming with families and teens out of school. Scanning the crowd, Cassie spotted Craig sitting at a table off by himself, drinking a cup of coffee.

Craig stood when he saw her. "What can I get you?" he asked. "Coffee? A sandwich?"

"Nothing, thanks."

"Let's go outside," he said and he picked up his cup and led her to his Bureau car, a slick black Ford Explorer. She climbed in as a bolt of lightning pierced the western sky and thunder rumbled in the distance.

Craig started the car and pulled around to the back of the mall, where they would not be noticed. The first drops of rain hit the windshield as he turned off the engine.

Cassie could read the tension in his face. "What's up?"

"We've found his laptop."

"Jake's? Where? How?"

"A kid bought it in a pawnshop in southeast D.C. He's pretty sharp. He hacked into it, saw some Bureau documents, and turned it in."

"Wow."

"He could have dumped it, sold it, used it himself, but he did the right thing. God bless him. A bunch of us are pitching in to buy him a new one."

"Have you gotten into his files? What have you found?"

The sinews in Craig's jaw flexed. "Jake was on to something, no doubt about it. The guy Schneider, who was killed at Sullivan's Wharf? He was an engineer for Tracor Enterprises. They make components for missile guidance systems. And the owner of the boat that started the Goose Creek Marina fire? That guy works for Tracor, too."

Cassie's stomach clenched. "So what's the connection?"

"They both had access to top-secret technology."

"Was the other guy being extorted? Like Schneider?"

"We don't know yet. He's not exactly being cooperative."

Cassie's mind was turning the puzzle in her head.

Craig ran his hand through his hair. Serious rain was falling now, running in sheets down the windshield. "Jake's got encrypted files that we really want to see. DiCarlo is talking about giving the computer to the lab to get some help with the password. That could take forever."

"Why not just ask Jake?"

Craig stared straight ahead. Cassie saw him frown slightly. Then he glanced over at her. "Jake ... he doesn't remember much. And when I tried talking to him, he just got frustrated."

"You don't have to bother him." Cassie pulled a small notebook out of the pocket of her khakis, along with a pen, and wrote three possible passwords: "Scooter," "Toots," and "4610." Then she tore the sheet out and handed it to Craig. "With Jake it was always about two things: his kids or football. Scooter is his pet name for his son. Toots is his daughter."

"And what's '4610'?"

"The Bears won the '86 Super Bowl. They beat the Patriots 46–10."

Craig laughed softly. "They're going to think I'm a genius." His face grew serious. "Cassie, you need to be careful. Your name, address, and phone number, even your cell phone number, were on his computer. Even your dad's number."

"That's okay. My address has changed, my phone has changed. I'm not worried."

"I am. Secondly, you need to back off whatever you're doing under the pretense of your job. This is a serious threat. And it's too dangerous for you to play with."

Anger flared up and she felt her face redden. "Craig Campbell. Six months ago I was just like you. Don't treat me like a little girl who needs protection."

"Six months ago you had the resources of the Bureau for

backup, and a gun. Today, you've got a photographer and a note-book. That's the difference."

She fumed. He had a point. "Okay, I have a question."

"Go ahead."

"If the person who assaulted Jake was part of an extortion ring, why would he pawn the laptop? This sounds more like a druggie crime."

"I agree. There are some other things that don't match up."

"Yes, like, why wasn't Jake killed?"

Craig grimaced. "We think the kids interrupted that."

"What?"

"That cut on his neck? We think he was in the process of getting his throat slashed. Like Schneider."

Cassie flinched. She looked away, suddenly sick.

Craig shook his head. "We haven't figured it all out yet. But now that we have his laptop, we're going to check out every name in there, every lead. Unfortunately, fingerprint-wise, it's clean. The only prints are from the kid and the pawnbroker."

"And how about the pawnbroker's records? Who turned it in?"

"Some guy with a stolen drivers license. But we're continuing to follow that angle."

A loud crack split the silence, and Cassie jumped. The storm was right overhead. The ornamental trees at the borders of the mall were whipping in the wind. The driving rain pelted the asphalt and drummed on the roof of the Explorer. She shivered involuntarily. "When's the last time you talked to Jake?"

"I call every couple of days."

"What is he saying?"

"Lately he hasn't wanted to talk to me."

"That doesn't sound good."

"It's not. His nurses say he's okay, the agent looking out for him insists everything is fine, but I don't know. I don't understand why he won't talk to me." Craig tightened his jaw.

For a few moments they allowed the silence between them to

grow. Both were lost in their thoughts.

Finally Cassie spoke. "Jake volunteered once to show me where Mike had the accident. I didn't take him up on it ... I didn't want to see it. Now, though ..." Her throat closed up and she couldn't say more.

"You'd like to?"

She nodded.

"You want me to take you there?"

"No, just tell me where it is. I'll go by myself."

"Cassie, I'm not sure—"

"Please. I'll be careful, I promise."

He wrote the location down on a piece of paper, and she stuck it in her pocket. At that point, she knew she should tell him about her visit to Schneider's mistress and his wife, but something held her back. What was it—stubbornness? Pride?

Cassie struggled with a vague sense of guilt. "How about if I go through Jake's computer with you? Maybe something will register with me," she offered.

"No, absolutely not. Nobody even knows we're talking," Craig responded.

Cassie grimaced. There was nothing she could do about it. She was locked out. "I guess I'd better go," she said.

Craig drove her around the mall and let her out where she had parked the Cabrio. After Craig left, Cassie sat in her car for a long time. Some threads were beginning to appear, but how were they woven together? Where did the threads intersect?

A thought popped into her head, unbidden, like an unwelcome guest at the door. Her aunt said that all of life had a pattern and a purpose. "There are no coincidences with God," she claimed. "Everything that comes into your life is filtered through his hand."

Yeah, right. Cassie twisted the ignition key and blazed out of the parking lot.

On Wednesday she returned to her office. Both Len and her editor were thrilled with the write-up on the Solomon's Skipjack Appreciation Days. Public response had also been good.

Grateful as she was for their appreciation, her mind was focused somewhere else. The event she had chosen this week was the Art on the Dock festival in Annapolis. In the afternoon, Cassie had an appointment with the director at a bagel nook at City Dock. At 3:00, she packed a notebook in her bag and headed out the door for the interview.

Jason Wheeler was young, blond, and handsome, Cassie thought as she sat across the table from him, but he acted flighty. The newest director of the Art on the Dock festival drank tea with milk in it, and insisted on jam with his croissant. Cassie ordered her coffee black and her bagel plain. She wasn't in the mood for frills.

"So, the festival will be a fund-raiser this year?" she asked.

"Yes, for AIDS research. The arts community has been devastated by this disease. For too long the government has failed to fund research. There is just no reason, in this day and age, for anyone to suffer from AIDS. It's just ridiculous. Why do artistic people have to suffer all the time?"

Cassie held her pen poised above the paper and wondered if it was too late to pick a different festival. "How many artists do you expect to participate?" she asked, struggling to manage a neutral voice.

"Sixty, including a performance artist named Speedo."

"What's he going to do?" She was almost afraid to ask.

"Well, he's going to cover himself with paint and perform a modern dance routine on a huge sheet of paper. It's going to be wonderful ... the combination of forms of expression. I just can't wait."

"Me neither," said Cassie, under her breath. Clearing her throat, she continued. "What other kinds of art will be on display?"

"Sculpture, watercolors, oils, pen and ink, jewelry, calligraphy, silhouettes, chalk ... you name it. It's a juried show, the largest in the Bay area, and we are just so pleased to be able to showcase all this talent."

"I suppose there will be a lot of boating-related work."

"Oh, I'm sure. You just can't avoid it here in Annapolis. But there will be a variety, I assure you, not just the schlock sailboat pictures. How many ways can you paint Thomas Point Light, anyway?"

"Well, thank you, Mr. Wheeler, for your time. I'm looking forward to covering your show."

"Well thank you, Ms.—"

"McKenna."

"... yes, Ms. McKenna. Let me know if I can help you out in any other way."

How about telling me who attacked Jake Tucker, she thought to herself as she walked to her car. *Or who torched the marina, or who ran my husband off the road?* She'd have to wait for those answers. For now, she had a festival to cover.

"Now grab this, Jake. No, hold on ... hold on ..."

The effort made the pain in his head feel like a bolt of lightning striking his skull. He stared at his hand, his eyes watering in agony. It was his hand, but it was a foreign object, unmoving, unresponsive. And he wanted to smash it.

"Try again, Jake. You can do it. Let' s try again."

The pain, the anger, the fear, a metallic taste, and then, the familiar blackness.

"Art on the Dock." Sixty artists of all shapes, colors, ages, and styles were set up in booths along the waterfront in Annapolis on a beautiful Saturday. With the Maryland State House standing tall in the background and the Naval Academy nearby, painters, sculptors,

pen-and-ink artists, watercolorists, and one very strange performance artist displayed their talents and plied their wares at the popular festival. A string quartet from the local high school added music,
the cheerful sounds of Bach and Mozart drifted on the breeze. Food
vendors filled the air with the smells of spicy sausages grilled with
onions and green peppers, yeasty funnel cakes, and hot dogs.

Cassie and Brett walked down the dock. She had a cup of coffee
in her hand. He was laden down with his photo gear. Her mind was
somewhere else, and Brett had to keep calling her attention to the
interesting sights they were passing.

"I really want to see Speedo," she said, "the performance artist."

"Now that is a frightening name," Brett laughed.

"When is he up?"

"In forty-five minutes, up near the dinghy dock."

"Okay, great," Cassie said. "In the meantime, let's wander." A
woman from Lookout Point who painted lighthouses and sailboats
on old windows gave them an interview, as did a man from
Edgewater who carved decoys that were so lifelike Cassie expected
to see them move at any moment. Decoys had become a popular
Bay area art form, and some fetched thousands of dollars.

But Cassie found her lead story midway down the dock at a
booth displaying a collection of pottery. Bowls, vases, pitchers, cups,
mugs, and plates in earthy reds and browns accented with blue and
green filled the tables and shelves. The natural elements of the Bay
region—sand, shells, cattails, and wildflowers—filled, surrounded,
and spilled out of the pottery. The artist had somehow been able to
capture the essence of the Bay—the browns of the earth, the blues
of the water, the color of the sky, the whitecaps on windy days—and
Cassie found the display was stunningly beautiful.

At the back of the booth sat a man wearing dark glasses. At his
feet was a yellow Labrador retriever wearing a harness—a guide dog.
Cassie looked around for the potter, but there was no one else present. "Excuse me," she said, "I'm Cassie McKenna, and I'm covering
the festival for the *Bay Beacon* along with my photographer here."

The man stood up. He had a collapsible white cane in his hand. The dog raised his head. "I'm Jess Santoro," he said, extending his hand.

"Jess, this is beautiful pottery."

"Thank you."

"Who does it?"

Jess smiled. "I do! I have a studio at my home, on the Eastern Shore."

Cassie glanced at Brett, who was already taking his camera off his shoulder. "You do it." She couldn't disguise the surprise in her voice.

The potter laughed out loud. He was young, maybe thirty years old, and had dark hair cut short, brown skin and an easy smile. "I know. You're wondering how a blind man could possibly make pots."

"Well ... yes, I am. Tell me, how do you do it?"

"Well, you begin with a lump of clay," he began and then he laughed. "I discovered pottery when I was a teenager. I've been blind since birth, and my mother introduced it to me as a way to teach me art."

"Your mother?"

"Yes, I was homeschooled. Once I discovered pottery, I found I loved everything about it—the feel of the clay, the smell, how pliable it is, what shapes it takes. I learned to use a wheel, and a kiln, and, well, here I am."

Cassie scribbled notes furiously. "Okay, and please don't be offended, but I can understand how you can build the pots, but how about the glazing? How do you get the colors so beautiful?"

"Colors? These things are colored?" Jess said, and then he laughed. "I had some coaching, and now and then I get my color pots mixed up and I think a bowl is green when it's actually blue. But I just had to learn it. I've never seen color, so my mother, and my teacher, and now my wife, have had to help me understand what I'm doing there."

"Your wife?"

"Well, yes. Blind men do get married."

All around her Cassie could hear the clicking of Brett's camera. "I'm sorry ... I ... I just can't imagine going through life without vision."

"Actually, I think I see better than most people."

"Why do you say that?"

Jess Santoro hesitated, then shrugged and said, "Maybe because God lets me see with my heart."

Stunned, Cassie remained silent. "That's amazing," she said finally. "Thank you."

As they walked away, Brett said, "Incredible guy, huh?"

"Yes," replied Cassie. She had a shopping bag full of things she'd bought ... a bowl for her aunt, and one for herself, a vase for flowers, and a mug that was a particularly beautiful shade of blue, with a white rim, like whitecaps on the crest of a wave. "He is remarkable."

After Jess, Speedo the performance artist was just a joke. Cassie dutifully took notes and Brett took photos. All the while, she could not shake Jess Santoro out of her mind. He was like a puzzle she couldn't quite figure out. *He sees with his heart.* What exactly does that mean?

Cassie didn't finish her write-up of Art on the Dock until after lunch on Monday. She was about to call it a day, when her phone rang. She picked it up. It was the front desk of the newspaper.

"Cassie? Somebody just called. Didn't want to talk to you, but he left you a message."

"What is it?"

"Come on up here. I wrote it down."

This was strange. Cassie walked through the building to the

front. Ruth, the receptionist on duty, handed her a piece of paper. On it was written:

JPT1648Franklin523Balt.

14

*J*PT1648Franklin523Balt." Cassie stared at the note. Her hands trembled. "What is this? Who called?"

"I don't know. It was a man, but he wouldn't leave his name. He just dictated that and made me repeat it back to him."

Her heart was pumping. "What did his voice sound like?"

The receptionist shrugged. "Male. Adult. American. White. I don't know ..."

Cassie took a deep breath. *Calm down,* she told herself. "Okay, thanks ... look, if he calls back, dial star-six-nine, will you? I want to know who this is."

Cassie walked quickly back to her desk. Her mind was racing. JPT had to be Jacob Preston Tucker. She picked up her purse and her attaché case and left, walking toward her Cabrio. She stood next to her car, staring at the paper in her hand, lost in her own thoughts. Brett approached her from behind and greeted her. Startled, she nearly turned around and hit him. "Brett!"

"What's up? Where are you headed?"

What could she tell him? "I'm not sure. Edgewater, maybe," she said. Maybe she'd get there sometime today.

"Mind if I come?"

Cassie forced herself to smile casually. "Normally, that would be great, but I just need to do this by myself today, okay, Brett?"

He was disappointed, she could tell. "Sure, no problem. See ya!"

* * * * *

She pulled out of the parking lot and stomped on the accelerator. The Cabrio sped down the street. When Cassie reached the 7-Eleven two blocks down, she pulled in and parked. Then she stared again at the address on the paper. She rummaged through the glove box and found a map of Baltimore. There it was: Franklin Street. Cassie threw the map on the passenger seat, pulled onto the road, and headed north.

Twenty miles up the road her cell phone rang. Craig Campbell's voice was tight. "He's gone, Cassie. He left the facility."

Cassie pressed the phone to her ear. "What?"

"Jake walked out. We know it was voluntary. He hitchhiked into town, got on a bus, and that's the last we know."

She slammed on the brakes to avoid a car cutting in front of her. "When?"

"Two days ago."

"And you're just now calling me?"

Campbell was silent.

"Are they looking for him?" she asked, as she resumed speed.

"Listen, I ... we ... it isn't widely known. That could get ugly. All I'm saying is, if you hear from him, call me, please. Okay?"

"Why would he do this?"

"Got fed up. That's my guess."

"Was he well enough to travel on his own?"

"I guess he thought so."

"What's his emotional state, Craig? Aren't you concerned about that?"

"Of course I'm concerned about that!" Craig almost snapped at her. "He's been very angry and despondent. Yes, I'm concerned."

Cassie glanced left and moved to pass a slow station wagon in the right lane. Should she tell Craig about the message she had? The coded phone message? No. Not yet. "Okay. I'll call you if I hear from him. But you do the same for me, okay?"

"Right."

"Seriously. I want to be in on this."

"All right."

As she hung up the phone she glanced in the rearview mirror, and she realized she was looking for a misaimed halogen headlight in broad daylight.

Cassie threaded her way through the streets of Baltimore, wondering what kind of fool's mission she was on. Painfully aware that she didn't have a gun, she reminded herself to stay alert.

She pulled up in front of 1648 Franklin. It was a 12-story apartment building in a gentrified section near the heart of downtown and as she cruised by it, she recognized it as the building where a fellow agent, Jeff Paulson, lived. Jeff? Could Jeff have been the caller? He was a friend of Jake's. She parked on a side street and used her cell phone to call the FBI office. When she asked for Jeff, she was told he was out of town.

Cassie considered her options. She had to go in. How she was going to get past the security door was an issue. Who or what she would face was a big question. Nevertheless, she had to go in. She stuck her wallet, a pen, and a small notepad in a belt bag and strapped it on, hoping it looked like a fanny pack for a gun. Locking her car, she headed for the front door of the building, wondering what it would take to breach security. But as she walked up the front steps a man in a business suit was coming out and he gallantly held the door open for her. Yes!

Cassie glanced down at the paper. The next bit of information was "523." That was probably an apartment number. She rode the elevator up. As it creaked and groaned, she steeled herself. Anything could happen.

*   *   *   *   *

The door was anonymous and white, a clone of every other door along the hallway. The brass numbers "523" were just above the doorknocker. A small peephole was right below.

Cassie hesitated before she knocked. She took a breath, reached for the knocker, and the sound of the brass hammering against the plate echoed the hammering of her heart.

There was no response. She tried again. Nothing. She stood on tiptoe and peeked into the peephole. She could see a light. She tried the knocker again, and then again.

There was no answer. Down the hallway an elderly woman opened her door and peeked out at her. Cassie smiled wanly, and the woman retreated. She knocked, she rapped on the door, she called out, and she did it all over again, until finally she stopped, uncertain of what to do next. And then, she heard the locks unlatching.

The knob turned. The door swung open just a few inches, and then no more. Cassie waited a moment, then cautiously pushed it open.

The apartment was empty except for one chair, a couch, a coffee table, and a TV on a cheap wooden stand. A man stood with his back to her, having opened the door and walked back into the room.

Cassie stepped in. "Jake?"

He turned around and her heart thudded. She barely recognized him. She closed the door behind her and moved toward him, feeling both relief and concern.

Jake had lost a good deal of weight, nearly thirty pounds. His hair was shaggy, over his ears, and he had a full dark beard. His eyes darted away from hers. His gray sweatpants seemed to hang on him and the white T-shirt he was wearing was thin and worn.

Jake turned and walked toward the kitchen. Cassie closed the door behind her and followed him. He turned on the tap, filled a glass with water, and stood leaning over the sink, staring into it.

"Hey, partner," she began, softly.

He raised the glass and drained it.

"Jake, how are you?"

He turned to look at her, his dark eyes flickering. He was holding the glass in his left hand. He extended his right awkwardly, and brought the glass over with his left, as if to switch hands. When he let go, the glass slid right through his grasp and shattered on the floor, flinging shards all over the kitchen.

Cassie stepped back, shocked.

"I'm great," Jake said, "just great." Then he brushed past her.

His bitterness hit her like a blow. Cassie stood rooted to the spot, her mind racing. How should she respond? What should she do?

Jake walked into the living room and stopped, hands on hips. His head was bowed as if he were thinking, then he turned to Cassie. "Why are you here? Why did you come here?" he demanded.

"I ... wanted to see you."

"The last time I saw you," he said, pointing his finger at her, "you ... you told me to get out of your life. You said ... you never wanted to see me again. You told me ..."

"The last time? No, Jake, not the last time. Not the last time."

"You said, 'Leave, Jake, go now.' You said—"

"No, no!" Cassie approached him. He moved away. "Jake, I found you when you were hurt. You opened your eyes, Jake, and you looked at me when you were lying there in that field."

He was looking at her now, only skeptically.

"At the hospital, I spent so much time in your room. Days, nights. You don't remember, because you were unconscious, but I apologized to you. I am so sorry, Jake. I was so mean to you."

He was breathing deeply now, struggling. She saw him flexing his left hand, squeezing his fist, and releasing it, over and over like he was trying to let go of the tension.

"Jake, I was with you in the hospital in Baltimore for weeks. Day and night, for weeks." Her pulse was pounding in her temples. "I was there, Jake, and so was Craig Campbell and some of the others. We were with you until they took you away by helicopter. Do you remember that? Do you remember the chopper?"

His silence was his answer.

"But Jake, look at you. You're much better than the last time I saw you. That was eight weeks ago, and now you're up and walking, you're talking, you're—"

"Who told you I was here?"

"I ... I don't know. I got a message."

Jake cursed.

"Obviously whoever it was didn't want me to know his identity, but he must care about you. He told me where you were because he cares, and so do I." Cassie swallowed. Her throat was thick, her mouth dry. "How did you get here, Jake?"

He didn't answer.

"Why did you leave the rehab center?"

Jake raised his arms in a gesture of frustration. "I can't ..." He turned toward her, eyes flashing. "... I can't do this."

"It takes time to heal, Jake. It just takes time."

"I can't ... work, I can't run, I can't ... drive ... I can't ..." He stopped, frustrated.

"What?"

"I can't think!"

"Jake," Cassie began but he would not look at her. Her eyes followed his. On the table was a handgun, a Glock pistol. A cold chill went through her. "Jake? What's the gun for?"

He remained silent.

Suicidal? Jake? No way. Still ... a hard knot had formed in the pit of her stomach. Jake was close, an arm's length away. His breath was tremulous and the sinews in his neck were standing out like cords. He stared at the gun. A drip of sweat ran down the side of his face.

"Your kids, Jake. Your kids need you."

"Tam's living with somebody."

Already? Cassie wanted to say. "They need you. They need their real dad."

"Not like this."

"They need your love, Jake, believe me, they need your love," Cassie responded. "No one else can take your place. And they'll accept whatever limitations you have, because you have not stopped being you."

He cursed again, and that was so unlike Jake she wanted to cover her ears. Cassie could feel her heart pounding, the blood racing through her body. "They need you, Jake. I need you."

"It's ..." An odd look came over Jake's face. He stared at his right hand. Then he groaned and sat down on the couch. Cassie watched, alarmed, as his face became pale, his eyes vacant. His head drooped, and he started to fall over. She caught him. His eyes were rolled back. He was passed out cold.

Frightened, she broke out in a sweat. What should she do? Call 9-1-1?

But according to Campbell, this happened all the time. Several times a day. It was normal for Jake—at least, normal right now. Cassie looked around for something to put under his head. What else should she do?

The blackout lasted seven minutes, nearly an eternity for Cassie.

"What can I get for you?" Cassie asked as Jake came out of his seizure.

"No."

She presumed he meant "nothing." He shook his head, like he knew he'd said the wrong thing.

It was painful to hear him try to speak. Jake was sitting on the couch, his elbows on his knees, his head in his hands, still dazed.

"You could tell that was coming?" she asked.

He nodded.

"How often does it happen?"

He shrugged and ran his hand over his hair. "I can't take this ... anymore."

"It takes time, Jake. You just have to be patient." But being patient was never Jake's strong suit, and Cassie knew that. Her heart ached for him.

"I'm sorry," he said and he lay down on the couch. She helped him get comfortable. Within seconds he was asleep. Campbell told her that would happen, too. The seizures left Jake disoriented and sometimes exhausted.

She had to help him, but how could she? Leaving him breathing heavily on the couch, she looked around. The apartment was spare, as one would expect. Jeff was a bachelor. Everything was strictly utilitarian: a couch, recliner, coffee table, and TV in the living room, a bed and dresser in the bedroom. Jake's few clothes were in a plastic bag on the floor—one that said "Univ. of Maryland Hospital."

In the kitchen the cupboards were bare. The refrigerator was completely empty except for a six-pack of beer. Why, she didn't know—Jake wasn't a big drinker.

A wave of fear once again swept over Cassie. It looked like Jake wasn't planning to be here long. Still, if he wanted to kill himself, why did he come all the way back to Baltimore?

Cassie couldn't take any chances. She had to do something to help him. Now.

Quietly, she returned to the living room, retrieved the gun, and emptied it, pulling out the magazine and clearing the chamber. She slipped the bullets into her purse and returned the gun to the coffee table. Then she went to the kitchen and began making phone calls.

Jake was still asleep when she returned, and something made her guess he'd be out of it for a long time. She decided to chance it. Cassie left the apartment. She slipped a napkin in the doorjamb to keep the latch from catching. She hurried down to the street.

She'd seen a small grocery store not far away.

The apartment was filled with the smell of hot bread, lasagna, and vegetables when Jake woke up. "What's going on?" he asked.

"Dinner. I'm starving. Are you hungry?"

He looked at her strangely. "I guess."

Cassie talked throughout the meal, trying to prolong it. He picked at his food and that drove her crazy—she was used to seeing him eat with gusto.

Far too quickly, he pushed back from the table. Time to talk. Now. She took a deep breath. "Jake," she began, "I'd like to help you."

"How?"

"I made some phone calls while you were … asleep. I've got an aunt—"

"No," he said, abruptly rising.

She followed him into the living room. "She helped raise me. You met her, when Mike died. Her name is Trudy. She is a terrific person, and Jake, listen to this." Cassie boldly put her hand on his arm and turned him around. "Her husband had a brain injury, an aneurysm. She took care of him for twenty years. Twenty years, Jake. She understands what you're going through and she can handle it. The blackouts, the depression …"

Jake jerked away from her.

"Come on. My aunt is by herself now, in a house on the Eastern Shore, and she said you could come there and stay with her. She'll help you, Jake. She'll cook for you, and take you to physical therapy if that's what you need. She knows the best neurologist in the country—he's in Baltimore. She's terrific, Jake, honest. You'll like her. And she wants to help."

Jake was standing over the coffee table staring down at the gun, and Cassie wondered if she'd made a mistake by leaving it there. If he found it was empty, what would he do? Fly into a rage?

"Who did this to me?" he asked abruptly.

Cassie was taken aback. "We ... the Bureau doesn't know yet, Jake. They're making progress, but they don't know."

He turned away.

"Jake, my aunt ... it would be good for her, too, to have company. She's been alone since my uncle died. No kids. And I'm too busy to visit very often."

"No."

"Why?"

"I don't want to."

Indignation rose in Cassie. "Why are you being so selfish?"

"What?" he said sharply.

"Why won't you accept some help?"

"Been there, done that. Didn't like it."

"Well, you haven't tried my aunt. You haven't exhausted all the possibilities."

Jake waved her off, dismissing her logic.

But she wouldn't let him go. She moved close to him, trying to capture his dark eyes with hers. He kept glancing down, sideways, any way but straight at her. Not one to be dismissed, she finally grabbed both his arms. "Jake, your kids need you. Please don't do this to them."

For a moment, she thought he was going to explode. His face was red, his eyes narrow, and his shoulders were hunched up.

"They need you, Jake," she whispered. "I need you. Please, please, let me help you."

He sat down on the couch and dropped his head in his hands. The room was quiet for what seemed to Cassie like a long, long time. Finally, he sat back. He looked weary and worn out, a dark shadow of the strong man she had known. "Two weeks," he said. "I'll try it for two weeks."

15

*C*assie spent the night on the couch, unwilling to leave Jake alone for a moment. She slept in her clothes and was thankful she'd worn something comfortable.

They would leave at 6:00 p.m. the next day. Rummaging through a closet she found some of Jeff's clean clothes for Jake, and she promised herself she'd remember to return them.

They got in the Cabrio, and Jake leaned his head back and closed his eyes, which was good. "We need to make one stop," she told him, and he didn't object. Nor did he notice when she pulled up to a park and stopped the car. "Just wait here," she said, patting his leg.

"What?"

"Wait here. I'll be right back."

Jake sat in the car, his eyes closed. The bright sunlight bothered him. He had a nearly perpetual headache that ranged in intensity from painful to excruciating. As it progressed in the spectrum, he would gradually pull inside himself, avoiding light and sound and fighting the nausea by detaching himself from the world. As long as he didn't sense the Pit right behind him, it was bearable.

But while sitting in the car waiting for Cassie, something made him open his eyes. He saw her striding across the park in her khakis and black shirt. She walked past the swing set, past the slide, and on toward a row of cars parked on an adjoining street.

And then he focused more carefully and he saw a familiar van, a dark green minivan, and then he saw a woman step out of it. And Jake sat up straight when he realized it was Tam.

By the time the sliding door of the van opened, Jake had begun to get out of the Cabrio. And when two little towheaded kids spilled out, Jake's heart leaped and adrenaline flashed through him like lightning.

He began to run, clumsily at first, but then more confidently. His heart pounded and his breath came hard. Halfway across the park, he fell to his knees and swept Caitlin and Justin into his arms.

"Daddy! Daddy!" Their two little voices formed a childish chorus, and he thought his heart would burst as he held them close to his chest and felt their little bodies squirming against him. Tears spilled from his eyes and streamed down his cheeks and he looked past his kids to Cassie, who was smiling broadly. And he thanked her with his look.

"Daddy, you have a beard!" said Justin.

"Yes, yes I do."

"Why are you crying, Daddy?"

Jake swallowed hard, trying to find his voice. "I'm just really happy to see you. I've missed you so much!"

For the next hour, they played.

Jake drank in the kids' giggles and fed on their laughter. For sixty minutes, he was transported beyond a fractured skull, beyond memory loss, beyond blackouts, and into a place powered by love and infused with childish innocence and hope.

When the van pulled up again across the park and Cassie saw it and said it was time for them to go, Jake's pumped-up heart ached. He kissed the kids good-bye and promised them he'd call them. And then he watched through teary eyes as they walked slowly back to their van.

"Thank you," he said to Cassie as they drove away from the park.

"You're welcome. It was worth it to see you guys together."

"I have missed them so much."

She glanced toward him. His eyes were full of tears. "In the glove box," she said.

He opened it and retrieved a napkin and blew his nose. "I'm sorry."

"That's okay."

"You know what?" he said. "Sometimes ... sometimes you just don't know how dead you've been until you come back to life."

Cassie stayed quiet, unsure how to respond.

"What ... what did it take to get Tam to agree?" he asked.

She laughed. "A whole lot of talking."

Night was beginning to fall. The sky had darkened to a deep blue and a star was visible in the west. Cassie sped down Route 2, thoughts ebbing and flowing as she weaved in and out of traffic. Jake rested his head back.

"Are you okay?" she asked him.

"Yeah, fine."

"Headache?"

"Hurts like crazy. But I don't care."

They rode in silence for a while, the car skimming through the "magic hour," that time around twilight when the world turns a soft blue. Lights twinkled on in the communities they passed while stars pricked holes in the blackness of the night sky. Cassie looked over at Jake. He was resting but awake. "What are you thinking about?"

"How big they've gotten. In just two months. And how sorry I am ... that ... that Tam and I couldn't make it work."

Cassie glanced in her rearview mirror. She'd been tracking the traffic behind her carefully, looking for a blue headlight or any sign they were being followed. It was tough at night. "It's hard, Jake. Life is just very hard."

At 8:15 p.m. they pulled into the driveway of a small, two-story farm-house set back off the road in Talbot County, Maryland. As Cassie stepped out of the car, the familiar smell of boxwoods filled her nose, and her soul clicked on something called "home." They walked up to the front porch, past planters full of petunias and impatiens and a garden edged in hostas. A metal milk can sat next to the front door. Then a black-and-white Springer spaniel appeared inside the screen door, barking excitedly.

"Jazz!" Cassie called out, and the dog, recognizing her voice, dissolved into wiggles of joy.

A woman in her sixties dressed in slacks and a white sleeveless shirt appeared. She opened the door, the dog leaped out, and the woman said, "Welcome!"

Cassie bent down to pet the dog, who responded with all the exuberance of a pup while turning occasionally to bark at Jake. Then Cassie walked up the steps. "Aunt Truly!" she said, embracing the older woman. "Aunt Truly, this is Jake. Jake, my Aunt Truly. Well, it's Trudy, actually."

Jake stood by awkwardly, the Springer bouncing all around him. "Hello."

"Welcome, Jake. I am so glad to meet you. I remember you from Mike's funeral, and I've heard about you for years."

Jake glanced at Cassie, who was busy petting the dog.

"You can just call me Trudy, if you like, Jake. Cassie just couldn't quite get that out when she was three, but you might feel a bit silly calling me Truly. And this is Jasmine," she said, pointing to the dog. "We call her Jazz. Come in, now, come on in."

Jake stepped up on the front porch. There were two wooden rockers there, and an old dresser with pulled-out drawers holding pots of red geraniums. A calico cat walked stiffly away.

Jake followed the women into the house. Just inside the front door was a small table holding a brass lamp. Next to the lamp, sitting on a piece of lace, was a small framed quote: "In all things God works for the good of those who love him, who have been called according to his purpose. Romans 8:28." He frowned.

A stairway with a dark wooden banister leading upstairs was in front of him. To the left was a small sitting room. A narrow hallway led to the rear of the house.

And that was the way Trudy and Cassie were walking, so Jake followed them. On the way, he passed two more framed verses: "I can do everything through him who gives me strength. Phil 4:10." and "Faith is being sure of what we hope for, certain of what we do not see. Hebrews 11:1." He was beginning to wonder what he'd gotten himself into.

But something smelled really good and so he kept on walking. The hallway opened into a large country kitchen with a big farm table right in the middle of it. In the center of the table was a wooden bowl holding a boxwood wreath surrounding a short, ivory-colored candle.

"Sit, sit!" Trudy said, and so Jake pulled out one of the Windsor chairs surrounding the table and sat down.

"I've made us a Big Apple Pizza," said Trudy.

"No, you didn't!" Cassie exclaimed.

"Yes, I did." Trudy opened the oven and pulled out a pizza pan. Apple slices were arranged in a pinwheel design on a piecrust, and were topped with a crumb topping loaded with cinnamon and sugar. "This was always Cassie's favorite dessert," she explained to Jake, putting the pan on a hot pad on the table. "Now, would you all like coffee? Or milk?"

While Trudy cut the dessert, Cassie filled three glasses with milk and Jake had time to look around the kitchen. One whole wall was a collection of photos, and Jake realized there were many of Cassie at all stages of her life and of her brother, father, and a woman he presumed to be her mother. There were several pictures of natural scenes on the Bay: a great blue heron stalking fish in a small cove, a sunrise over the water, two crabbers pulling in their traps, and a spectacular shot of lightning striking just behind a man fishing off a pier.

In between the photos were more verses. And on an adjoining wall was a hanging on which was embroidered the names of Jesus:

Wonderful Counselor, Prince of Peace, Balm of Gilead, Bright Morning Star, Lion of Judah, and many more. *So, Aunt Trudy has her quirks,* Jake thought and he began to brace himself.

But then Trudy put the Big Apple Pizza on the table and the smell distracted him. How long had it been since he'd felt hunger? After the first bite, Jake was hooked. The tart apples combined with cinnamon, sugar, and butter were irresistible. "This," he announced, "is really good."

Cassie laughed. "Men are really very simple creatures."

Jake consumed his first piece, then a second, while the two women talked. From listening to their conversation, he could tell one thing: Trudy was down to earth. Sensible. That was good. He'd been afraid he was getting hooked up with some eccentric old lady. Except for all the religious stuff, she seemed okay.

The two women obviously had a lot to catch up on, and Jake was only too happy to let them. Then Trudy asked him a couple of questions, and he responded with short answers. Fatigue was beginning to catch up with him. She must have noticed, because she looked at him with kind eyes and said, "Would you like to see your room?"

"Sure."

Trudy led them upstairs to the first room on the left. "This was where Cassie always slept when she came to visit," she said. It was bright and airy with many windows, including a triple bay window on one side. The walls were covered with flowered paper and the hardwood floors, partially covered by a large green-and-beige braided rug, gleamed in the soft light. Against the north wall was a dresser of dark walnut with brass drawer pulls. A double bed covered with a quilt was in the middle of the room. Off to one side was a chair and to the other was a night table. "I hope this will be okay," Trudy said.

"This is fine, wonderful," replied Jake. He looked around. There was only one verse. He could put up with that.

Next to the bed on the floor was a large cardboard box. "I had my dad bring over a bunch of Mike's clothes for you," Cassie said, lifting a stack of khakis and shirts from the box. "Is that okay? Do you mind wearing them?"

"No, no. Thanks."

"I thought they'd fit. The pants might be a bit loose. You've lost some weight." Cassie began putting the clothes in the drawers.

"The bathroom in the hallway is all yours," said Trudy. "I sleep downstairs. So you just make yourself at home."

"Okay, thank you." He rubbed his hand through his hair. "I really appreciate you letting me come here. I'll only be here for a couple of weeks, just until I figure out what I need to do." He glanced at Cassie to make sure she was listening.

"You are welcome to stay as long as you like." Trudy smiled at him. She had a pleasant face with lots of laugh lines. Her hair was gray and captured in a bun at the nape of her neck. She was suntanned, but it was the gardening-and-yardwork kind of tan, not the I've-been-on-a-cruise tan. Her eyes were gray and wise and a pair of reading glasses hung from a chain around her neck.

"Cassie, why don't we let Jake have some peace and quiet. Are you tired, Jake?"

"Actually, yes, I am." He shoved his hands in his pockets. "Cassie, did you, uh, tell your aunt ..."

"About the blackouts?" Trudy said. "She told me. Don't worry about it. Just sit down if you have to. It's no big deal, Jake. I've seen a lot worse."

He nodded.

Cassie gave him a hug and handed him a slip of paper. "Good night, partner. Here's my cell phone number. My aunt will take good care of you, but if you need me, just call."

"You make yourself at home, now, Jake. If you need something, let me know. Anytime, day or night, you just yell and I'll come, okay?" Trudy said.

"Yes, fine, thanks. Good night. And Cassie ... thanks for everything."

16

When Jake woke up the next day, it took five minutes for him to remember where he was. He got out of bed, washed his face, put some clothes on, and went downstairs. Jazz greeted him with her tail wagging and dropped a tennis ball at his feet. He'd never been around dogs much and wasn't quite sure how to deal with her.

Trudy was nowhere to be found, so Jake walked out through the kitchen door into the bright morning sunshine, Jazz dancing around his feet. The steps led into a large backyard. Off to the right were an old shed and a woodpile. To the left was a neat vegetable garden, surrounded by marigolds and zinnias. In the back was a wooded area, and one tree, a massive oak, had fallen onto the lawn. Its leaves were still green—it could not have been down long.

Once more Jazz dropped a ball at his feet, then stared at it, inviting him to play. He picked it up and pitched it with his left hand. She brought it back and dropped it at his feet once more. He threw it again. He pitched the ball to her over and over until she was panting hard. He could throw it pretty far, even with his left hand, and it felt good to him to be out there in the sun playing ball, even if it was with a dog.

"She won't quit, at least not before you do." Trudy appeared from around the side of the house. Dressed in denim capris and a pinstriped, sleeveless shirt, she was carrying a large basket in her hands. "How are you this morning? I was just taking some vegetables to my neighbor."

"I'm fine ... good."

"Did you sleep okay?"

"Yes. Thank you." Jake gestured toward Jasmine. "The dog really likes to play."

"Oh, now that she's discovered you know how to throw a tennis ball, you're her best friend." Trudy watched as Jazz dropped the ball at Jake's feet. Jake picked it up and threw it. "She's really taken to you. You must have had a dog before."

"No, not really." Jake launched the ball again, sending it in a high arch almost to the woods. "Never did have one as a kid. My dad would have beaten it to death."

"Oh, my," Trudy responded. She brushed a stray hair away from her face. "Where are you from?"

"Detroit."

"And what did your dad do for a living?"

"He was an auto worker. And he didn't have much use for pets." In fact, Jake's dad didn't have much use for anything that required affection. His main hobby was pitting Jake and his brother against each other. From early on, Jake had learned to fight. Maybe that's all he had learned.

"That's quite some tree," Jake said, gesturing toward the oak.

"Yes. It came down in a terrible storm a couple of weeks ago. I'm so thankful it didn't hit the house or the shed! I'm going to have to figure out what to do with it pretty soon." Trudy shifted the basket she was carrying. "Are you ready for breakfast?"

"Sure." Jake wiped his hands on his pants.

They walked inside, Jazz dashing between their legs. She headed straight for her water bowl and began lapping loudly.

"Would you like coffee? Bacon? Eggs?" Trudy asked, but Jake did not respond. His hand was curling and he had a metallic taste in his mouth. As he reached for the table, his vision went dark, his knees buckled, and then he fell, taking a chair down with him.

When he regained consciousness, he was aware of a cool cloth on his face. He opened his eyes and looked through a tunnel to see

Trudy bending over him. He blinked, swallowed hard, and struggled to sit up.

His vision cleared. Jazz was lying next to him, her head resting on his thigh. She raised it, watching his face.

Trudy said, "It's okay, Jake. Take your time."

"I'm sorry." He rubbed his temples. "I'm ... I'm sorry."

"Don't worry about it. I'm just glad you didn't hurt yourself."

Trudy stayed with him, talking to him gently and waiting for him to be ready for the next step, like she had nothing else to do the rest of the day. Her patience kept defusing his frustration.

There was a big, comfortable armchair in the corner of the kitchen, something he'd thought odd at first, but now he was grateful for it. When he was ready, she helped him into it, and he sat there, trying to relax, trying not to let the anger that welled within him erupt.

After an hour, he was ready to eat. Trudy made him coffee and bacon and fried eggs, over easy, just the way he liked them.

While he downed his breakfast Trudy asked him questions, and he answered them, and when she asked him if he'd be willing to try the neurologist she knew, he said yes. She told him she'd already called, and he could see Jake on Friday, and she would be glad to take him. The office was in Baltimore, at Johns Hopkins University Hospital.

"Thank you," he said. "I'm getting really tired of this."

"I'm sure it's frustrating."

"Very," he said. "The latest in a long series of frustrations."

She looked at him curiously but didn't ask more.

Cassie was late. She zipped in and out of traffic on Route 2 at well over the speed limit. When she'd gotten the call from Desiree, Cassie had thought she could leave the newspaper right away. But her editor wanted to talk to her about some story ideas, and then Brett needed her to look at some pictures. Now she had to race to meet Desiree.

She didn't want to keep Desiree waiting. The woman said she had something she wanted to give Cassie. As tenuous as the relationship was, Cassie wanted to cement the deal quickly. So she'd agreed to meet her at a restaurant off Route 83, north of Baltimore.

The good news was, Jake was settling in with Trudy. She'd checked with her aunt that morning. That was a relief.

As she approached her exit to get on the Baltimore Beltway, her cell phone rang. It was Craig Campbell. "Just an update," he said. "We've tracked Jake as far as Kansas City. Someone saw him get on a Greyhound bus ... at least, we think it was Jake. We thought we had the bus driver, but we just found out the guy we'd been talking to was a substitute. The original driver got sick and was replaced in Kansas City. We've been talking to the wrong guy for two days."

"Oh," Cassie said, glancing right so she could change lanes.

"His brother is in Chicago, so he may be headed there, but now we don't know."

"You alerted his brother?"

"The agent in Chicago is having trouble connecting with him."

"Oh, okay." A guy in a black Firebird cut Cassie off. She slammed on her brakes, moved left, and then she noticed Craig had been oddly quiet. Quiet for too long. "Okay, Craig, thanks," she said.

"Where is he?" Craig demanded.

"What?"

"You ought to be going ballistic right now, since we can't find Jake. Where is he, Cassie?"

"How would I know? Listen, Craig, I gotta go. I'm in really bad traffic. Thanks for the update." And Cassie clicked off the phone. *He's where he needs to be,* she thought, *and the Bureau doesn't need to mess with that. The ball is in my court this time.*

She ignored the arrow of guilt that stabbed at her gut.

Cassie pulled into the parking lot of the restaurant. It was 5:10 p.m. Only ten minutes late.

Desiree was sitting at a table eating an apple dumpling and

drinking coffee. Her eyes looked puffy, like she'd been crying for the last century, and Cassie suddenly felt sorry for her.

Cassie got a cup of coffee and a salad and listened to Desiree talk. The death of her lover had overwhelmed her again. Cassie was very familiar with that pattern of grief. Just when you think you're coping, bam! It hits you again, like an ocean wave you regrettably turned your back on.

When Desiree had spilled her story, she reached into her purse. Cassie thought she was going for a tissue, but instead, she pulled out a small silver Palm Pilot. "I want you to have this. It's Frederick's," Desiree said.

Cassie's throat tightened. She took the device. "Have you shown this to the police?"

Desiree shook her head. "I just found it in the couch. I want you to have it. I don't trust them."

Cassie nodded. The PDA was evidence. Who knew what information it contained? "Thanks, Desiree. I hope you start feeling better soon."

"Thanks. I hope so, too."

As Cassie drove back to Annapolis, she mulled over various scenarios. She could give the Palm Pilot to Craig. She could unlock it herself. She knew what she *should* do, but what would she decide?

Late in the evening, Jake sat on the edge of the bed, trying to clear the fog out of his brain. The day had gone badly. Was it stress? Or fatigue from yesterday? He didn't know, but he'd had two more blackouts after breakfast and then he'd developed a massive headache. Trudy had done what she could to help, but finally he'd simply decided to go back to bed, to escape into sleep.

He could hear soft music playing, something classical. Jake struggled into some clothes and went downstairs.

A few candles were lit, adding a warm glow here and there. Jazz padded out to greet him when she heard him, a ball in her mouth, tail wagging. He rubbed her ears. The kitchen was empty, and so he followed the sound of the music to another room, a room off the kitchen he had not entered before.

Trudy sat in a big wingback chair. A lamp was on next to her, and she was reading. She looked up when Jake entered the room, put the Bible down, and rose to greet him. "How are you? Better, I hope?"

"I think so," Jake responded.

The room was large with a whole wall of windows on one side and a beautiful brick fireplace at the end. A large painting of a sailboat heeling in the wind was over the mantle. Inside the door Jake had just come through was an old oak washstand with a marble top, which held a lamp and a framed picture. Jake picked it up.

Shocked at what he saw, he looked at Trudy, then down at the picture again.

Trudy walked over to him. "That," she said softly, "is my husband."

Jake's throat tightened. There was a buzzing in his ears. He wondered for a moment if he were going to have another blackout. The man in the picture was thin and pale, and he was lying in a hospital bed. His wrists were bent spasmodically and there was an odd expression of surprise on his face. "What happened to him?"

"Sit down," she said, motioning to the wide-armed couch opposite the windows, "and I'll tell you. First, though, let me get you something to eat."

Jake declined food, but was grateful for a tall glass of water. He sat on the couch, and Trudy sat in her chair. Jazz curled up on the floor between them. Slowly, the story unfolded.

"My husband, Wes, was an electrical engineer," Trudy said, brushing a wisp of hair out of her eyes. "He was very, very smart. He worked for the power company. We met in college, and got married after graduation. For a while, life was idyllic. He worked, and I taught kindergarten. When we found this house, we felt like we'd come home. It was just right for us! So, we bought it and immediately started to work on it.

"The only cloud on our horizon was the fact that no children were coming along. We had no idea what was wrong, and it was very frustrating. Still, we loved each other and had a lot of work to do on the house, so we pressed on and tried to make the best of it. Periodically, we'd talk about adopting, and as time went on we were more and more open to it. We began to think about a child from China or South America.

"For our tenth anniversary, we had decided to treat ourselves to dinner at a fancy restaurant near City Dock in Annapolis, where all the boats parade up and down. Then we were going to spend the night at a bed and breakfast on the Severn River. I had bought a new dress—a royal blue, elegant dinner dress—and Wes was going to wear his best black suit. He looked so handsome in that suit!

"I was dressed and sitting on our bed, putting on a bracelet. Wes was in the bathroom, shaving. A song was playing on the radio, an old song called "Only You." I was sitting there thinking how lucky I was to have a husband who loved me. Suddenly, Wes cried out, 'Trudy! Oh, God! Trudy!'

"I heard him fall as I raced to him. He was lying on the floor. His eyes were wide open, but he wasn't responsive.

"I called for an ambulance. It seemed to take forever for them to get here. They took him to the hospital in Annapolis. I went along, in the ambulance, dinner dress and all. I must have been quite a sight, but everyone was so concerned about Wes, nobody was looking at me.

"My brother Jim, Cassie's father, met me at the hospital. He was already a widower with two little kids, so it must have been very hard for him to drop everything and come to me, but that's the kind of guy Jim is. He was not going to let me go through this alone.

"The doctors told us Wes had suffered a ruptured cerebral aneurysm. A balloon had formed in a blood vessel in his brain, and something made it burst that night." Trudy paused, and took a sip of tea from the cup on the table next to her. She put her closed Bible in her lap and held on to it.

"At first, the doctors didn't think he would live. He was totally paralyzed, absolutely unable to move a muscle, although there was plenty of brain-wave activity. After two weeks, they took him off the respirator, fully expecting him to die. He didn't. They advised me to consider removing the feeding tube. I wouldn't.

"They moved him to a rehab center, then a nursing home. Finally, four months after the accident, Jim and Wes's dad and I sat down at the kitchen table and talked things out. I decided to bring Wes home. I just couldn't see letting him vegetate in that center.

"A group of people from my church helped Jim and Wes's dad build this room. We designed it with lots of windows, so Wes could see outside, and the big fireplace, so he could feel the warmth and smell the burning wood. We hung a TV in the corner near the ceiling and built ramps and extra-wide doors.

"I quit my job to take care of Wes. The doctors predicted I'd last six months." Trudy laughed softly. "I lasted twenty years."

"Twenty years?" Jake asked. His mouth was dry. He couldn't imagine being paralyzed and helpless for twenty minutes, much less twenty years. Nor could he imagine caring for someone who was.

"Twenty years of taking care of him. Oh, not without help. Eventually, I hired nurses to come for part of the day, so I could get out. I began teaching preschool in the mornings, just for a break. And Jim bought the house next door and he and the children helped, too. Oh, I didn't do it alone. But I did succeed in having Wes spend his life in his own home."

"And all this time, he was paralyzed?"

"Totally paralyzed and unable to speak. For years I sensed he knew what was going on around him, but his face was frozen in the expression you see there." She nodded toward the picture. "And so we had no confirmation. I would talk to him as if he understood everything. I played his favorite music. I would read the Bible to him and play tapes. I hung hummingbird feeders outside those windows, and moved his bed so he could see them. In the winter, I put a reg-ular bird feeder there and dried corncobs for the squirrels. I tried to create as stimulating an atmosphere as I could for him.

"I bought a puppy for me. With Wes paralyzed and no children around, I needed something energetic to remind me how lively things could be. I bought a Springer spaniel, Jazzie's mama, and she was my companion for thirteen years.

"And then, a few years before Wes died, technology gave us a gift. They developed a computer sensitive to eye movement. Wes was one of the first ones to try it out. He'd lie in his bed and move his eyes and spell things out. He could even play games. Oh, what an amazing thing! For the first time he was able to communicate!

"We discovered then that he had retained his full cognitive func-tion. He just was unable to move or speak."

Jake's heart literally ached. "So he was frozen in his body. That had to be awfully frustrating!"

"Oh, I know. And he couldn't do a thing about it. He couldn't even kill himself if he'd wanted to."

Jake glanced away.

"But do you know what? Wes coped. Somehow, he coped. And not only that, he still was able to love. Every morning, when he signed on the computer, the first thing he said was, 'I love you, Truly.'" Her eyes misted over. "That was our little joke, our pun. He used Cassie's pet name for me. Isn't that sweet? I felt like he cher-ished me, right up to the end."

Jake sat motionless, his elbows resting on his knees. "He must have been an incredible person. And you, too, for sticking with him."

"It's funny. I miss him terribly now." She laughed softly. "Strange as that sounds. I'm happy for him, because I know he's in heaven, totally healed, but I miss him. Every time I walk in this room, I auto-matically look for that big hospital bed. And it's not here anymore. All I have is my little Jazz."

A comfortable silence fell between them, a sacred pause.

Finally, Trudy stood up. "Jake, you must be hungry. Please let me fix you something to eat." Before he could protest, Trudy went into the kitchen and began to pull food out of the refrigerator: salad, meat loaf, potatoes. Soon the kitchen was filled with wonderful smells. Jake followed her in and stood watching her, lost in thought.

"You must have really loved him," he said.

"Loved? Oh, yes, I loved him in that young married, not-a-care-in-the-world kind of way. After his accident, though, it was often a matter of choosing to love him every day."

"Choosing to?"

"Yes. Every day." She put some biscuits in the oven. "I discovered love is an action, not a feeling. It's a commitment played out over time. It's just doing the best for somebody else day after day after day."

"But in the process, you kind of got left out. I mean, what happened to your dreams?"

"What was I supposed to do?"

"You could have divorced him. Married again."

"No." Trudy tossed the salad. "The way I saw it, I was going to honor my vows." She filled a plate with food and put it in front of Jake, who was sitting at the farm table. "For better or for worse, in sickness and in health."

"Thank you," he said, picking up a fork. "You are amazing!"

Trudy laughed.

Hours later, after Trudy had gone to bed, Jake still couldn't sleep. He wandered through the parlor and the kitchen and then was drawn to the large room where Wes had lived. Jake turned on a light and scanned the room, trying to imagine what it must have been like to spend twenty years totally paralyzed, unable to speak or move but fully aware of your surroundings. He shivered.

Trudy's Bible caught his eye. He walked over to the table by the recliner, picked it up, and opened the black leather cover. On the first page was an inscription: "To my wonderful wife, Trudy, on our first anniversary. All my love, all my life, Wes."

The poignancy of it caught Jake's heart. He sat down in the recliner and leafed through the book. Near the back, where a ribbon marked Trudy's place, he began to read.

17

The next morning, when the sun was still low in the sky and the grass was wet with dew, Jake went outside and rummaged around in the shed until he found what he wanted: some work gloves and a strap, which was actually an old dog collar. Next to the door was an axe, and the blade was still pretty sharp. He picked it up and walked to the oak tree lying across the grass.

Resolutely, Jake shoved his right hand in the glove, working to get his fingers in right. Then he fitted the axe in his hand, and wrapped the dog collar around it to hold his hand in place. He grabbed the axe handle with his left hand, and using the muscles of both arms to power the axe and his left hand to guide it, he began to chop up the fallen tree, blow by blow.

He might be hurt, but he wasn't paralyzed. He wasn't lying in a bed, totally helpless. It was time to get up and do something. Even if it was just chopping up a tree, it was time to do something.

On Thursday Cassie filled her car with two more bags of Mike's clothes for Jake. She needed to go see him. After going through Frederick Schneider's Palm Pilot, she had some questions. Maybe, if she talked to him, Jake would remember something. So she'd called in to work and told them she'd be out most, if not all, of the day. Nobody seemed to care, as long as she was getting her stories done on time.

The large majority of the names in Schneider's contact directory were normal entries: his doctor, his dentist, his wife, his brother, and so on. But four were curious. They were identified only with initials: "D," "J," "M," and "F." The first one was easy: "D" stood for "Desiree." The phone number matched the one Cassie had. The other three were a mystery. She'd called the second one: it was the cell phone of a teenage girl. Why?

She knew she was going to have to give the Palm Pilot over to the Bureau. Their access to phone information was much better than hers would ever be. Plus, it was evidence. Evidence! What was she doing holding onto it?

She crossed over the Bay Bridge, turned south on Route 50, and made her way back into the country until she drove up the lane leading to Aunt Trudy's house. When she saw the Bureau car parked in the driveway, her stomach dropped. She was in trouble. In a flash, she considered driving past the house and back to Annapolis. But she couldn't! She'd come to see Jake. She had to go in.

"Hello?" she called as she walked in the front door. Jazz came racing to greet her.

"In the kitchen, honey!" Trudy called.

Cassie hugged the bags of clothes to her chest like body armor, as though they would shield her from what was to come, and she walked back. Jake was sitting in the big chair in the corner, a pair of work gloves next to him. Aunt Truly sat in one of the Windsor chairs, and Craig Campbell, dressed in a tan business suit, white shirt, and tie, stood next to the refrigerator.

Her stomach knotted up. "Hi, Jake. Craig." She gave her aunt a smile. "Hello, Aunt Truly. Do you feel like you've been invaded?" An awkward silence followed. She put down the bags.

Craig leveled his blue eyes on her. "You should have told me, Cassie."

"I was handling it. Jake didn't want the Bureau to know where he was." Cassie opened a cabinet door, got out a mug, her favorite blue pottery mug, and poured herself a cup of coffee. The smell told her it was freshly made. She inhaled it, bracing herself.

"You put him at risk."

"I did not!" She turned to face Craig, her eyes blazing.

"You absolutely did! And not only him, but your aunt." Craig's face was tight with anger.

"I was careful. I didn't tell anyone he was here!"

"Oh, really? Like your father?"

She snorted. "Who's he going to tell? The ospreys? A few oysters maybe? Now there's a threat."

Craig pointed his finger at her. "People talk. What if someone was watching you? And followed you here?"

"Nobody followed me."

"They could have."

"I was careful!" She paced away from him. She felt the familiar anger rising. "I was incredibly careful. I was watching for that as we drove down here ... I made odd turns, I varied my speed, I looked for blue headlights—" Cassie stopped short. Why had she said that? How stupid!

"For what?" Craig and Jake asked simultaneously.

Furious with herself, Cassie didn't answer. She turned toward the cabinet and took a long drink of coffee. It was black and hot, too hot to drink that fast, but she didn't care. Why did she open her big mouth? Why?

When she turned around, Craig had his back to her and was rubbing his neck, one hand on his hip, his jacket pushed back. He was staring at the floor as if he were planning his next move.

Jake was sitting forward in the chair, focused on her, his dark eyes intent. "What, Cass? What about blue headlights?"

She could never escape that stare. Jake knew her too well. "Nothing. I was just looking for anything that ... that looked wrong. Just, you know, anything weird." She leaned back against the sink, crossed her arms in front of herself, and fumed.

"Has someone been following you?" Jake demanded.

"I've seen some headlights lately that look similar. Blue headlights. Those halogen things. That's all. It's nothing. I shouldn't have even brought it up." She shouldn't have opened her mouth, she shouldn't have come here, she shouldn't have left the Bureau, she shouldn't have to explain herself to these two men.

Craig turned around, and Cassie confronted him head-on. "Forgive me for trying to help my friend. I thought the job the almighty Bureau was doing taking care of Jake was less than effective. Inhumane is perhaps a better description. Shipping him off like that, without any kind of emotional support, as he tries to come back from that kind of injury ... it was ridiculous. Ridiculous."

She turned to Jake. "I'm sorry, Jake, if I've hurt you somehow. I was simply trying to help. And Aunt Truly, you know I would never do anything that would endanger you. I'm sorry if this has upset you." Then she pushed past Craig and walked out the back door, into the bright sunshine.

Cassie stormed out into the backyard. High in a poplar tree, a mockingbird called out. She forced herself to stand still, feeling the heat of the sun, letting it boil out her anger. What now? What was next? She heard the screen door open and shut behind her, but she didn't move.

She heard Jake's voice. "Hey, Cass," he said softly, but then he stopped, and there was an odd noise. When Cassie turned around, Jake was falling.

"Oh, no!" Cassie caught him. His weight pulled hard on her shoulders and she cried out, trying to ease him to the ground. The back door opened and Craig came running out, followed by Aunt Trudy and Jazz.

Jake laid still, his head turned to one side. Cassie loosened the collar of his blue chambray shirt, one of Mike's that she had given him, and she put her fingers on his neck, feeling his pulse, trying to calm the pounding of her own heart.

Craig bent down beside her, on the other side of Jake. He straightened Jake's legs out to make him more comfortable and felt for his pulse in his wrist. "Did he hit his head? Going down?"

"No."

Trudy grabbed a towel off the clothesline, folded it, and brought it over, and together Cassie and Craig put it under Jake's head. Jazz lay down close to Jake.

"So this is how it happens? No warning?" Craig asked.

"Yes. This is what happens. This is what he's been dealing with. Sometimes he can tell it's coming. His right hand begins to close and he says he gets a metallic taste in his mouth. But if he's distracted he may miss the signs."

Craig took a deep breath. He picked up Jake's hand again, checking his pulse at his wrist. Jazz growled softly at him. "I guess I'm the bad guy," he said.

Cassie stroked Jazz's head. Forced to focus on Jake, her perspective was returning. "No, you're not, Craig. It's been ... a difficult time." She glanced up at Trudy. "Look at how Jazz is lying on him. Isn't that odd? It's almost like she's trying to protect him."

"She doesn't usually take to men," Trudy responded, "but she's been following Jake around ever since he got here."

Craig stood up and walked to the back steps, pulled off his suit jacket, and sat down, draping the coat on the step next to him. "So now we wait?"

Cassie kept her eyes on Jake. "Now we wait." She slipped her hand into his useless right hand, and stroked the back of it. "The longest I've seen is half an hour, but often it's just a couple of minutes." She glanced at Craig.

"He's got to be frustrated with this," Craig said.

"Can you imagine, going from who Jake was, the marathon man, the one we all looked to as a role model for fitness, to not being able to walk across a yard without worrying about passing out, not being able to drive, not being able to live on your own, to ... to use his right hand ... it's got to be one of the most devastating ..." Cassie trailed off, glancing involuntarily at her aunt, thinking instantly about her Uncle Wes. Devastation came in all shapes and sizes.

Craig reached down, plucked some grass, and rolled it between his fingers. He cleared his throat. "I, uh, I think you've done a lot for him, Cassie."

She looked up, surprised.

"He wouldn't even talk to me when I called the rehab center. He was withdrawn and depressed. Now, he seems a lot healthier, mentally. Happier. He told me what you did ... getting Tam to bring the kids to the park. That was wonderful. Very kind."

Cassie nodded, grateful for his words.

"I'm sorry I was angry. I'm concerned about his safety, your safety, your aunt's safety."

"Jake would be safe in a cage, but I don't think that would be very good for him," Cassie retorted. "How'd you find him, anyway?"

"When I was talking to you on your cell phone, I could tell you weren't as concerned as you would be if you didn't know where he was. I figured somehow you knew where he was. So, I called your dad."

Cassie frowned. "Who have you told?" Did Foster know? The bigwigs at the Bureau? What would they have to say about it?

"I haven't told anyone yet."

"Why don't you just concentrate on finding out who attacked him? And let us worry about our own safety?"

Craig studied her face. It seemed like forever before he spoke. "I don't think Jake's being here is a good idea, Cassie. I'm sorry. I've got to tell the Bureau, and I'm going to find him a more secure place."

Cassie stared at him, furious.

"Mrs. Monroe," Craig said to Aunt Trudy, "you're a wonderful person. Thank you for agreeing to take Jake in. I hope you understand. As soon as I can move him, I will."

"I understand, Mr. Campbell." Trudy cocked her head and smiled softly. "But I don't agree."

Emerging from a blackout felt like slugging through a swamp in the fog. Gradually things began to come into focus, but Jake was exhausted from the exertion of it. This time when he opened his eyes, Craig was there. He kept trying to talk to Jake, but Jake couldn't make sense of what he was saying. The words were not coming through, and the sky ... the sky behind Craig was so bright! Jake closed his eyes again.

"I'll wait," Craig told Trudy. "I'd really like to ask him some questions."

"Would you like some coffee?" Trudy asked.

He readily accepted, and she left to go make it. While she was inside, Jake opened his eyes again. This time, Craig and Cassie were able to help him to a sitting position, and then to his feet, and finally into the house, where he collapsed in the armchair in the kitchen.

Cassie saw that he was okay, that he just needed to sleep it off. "I've got to go," she said abruptly, and she left, too irritated to be around Craig anymore.

She was angry—angry she'd gotten caught in her deception, angry the Bureau was now aware of where Jake was, and angry with Craig for interfering with what she was trying to do for him, angry that he was planning to take Jake somewhere else. Who was Craig to dictate what Jake should do?

Suddenly, she realized she hadn't given Craig the Palm Pilot. "Oh, well!" she muttered, and she knew immediately she should go back, turn in the evidence, let the Bureau have it, but she could not make herself turn the car around. Instead, she pressed down on the accelerator.

When Jake finally roused, he heard voices in the sunroom and smelled coffee. Glancing over to the kitchen counter, he saw the coffee pot was half-full. He stood up, fought to keep his balance, then walked slowly to the counter. Steadying himself, he found a mug and poured the steaming liquid into it. The smell of it alone helped clear his head. Even the warmth of the mug in his hand felt good. He took a big swig of it, black.

When had he lost consciousness? He searched his thoughts. The last thing he remembered was walking outside.

He followed the sound of voices to the sunroom. Craig was sitting on the couch. Trudy, who had her Bible open in her lap, was sitting in her usual chair. She closed the Bible when Jake appeared at the door, and invited him in. "How do you feel? Can I get something for you?" she asked.

"No. I'm fine. Thanks."

"How're you doing, guy?" Craig asked.

"All right."

"Come sit down!"

Craig moved to make room on the couch. "That's something, Jake, blacking out like that. It's gotta be hard."

"Yeah."

"And what's the prognosis? What do the doctors say?"

Jake gestured angrily. "They tried all kinds of drugs. Couldn't get the mix right. They say they think the seizures can be controlled, but man, they weren't making it happen." Jake took a gulp of coffee and looked around. "Where's Cassie?"

"She had something she had to do," Trudy said. "Once she saw you were okay, she decided to go." She rose to her feet. "Speaking of which, I'll leave you two alone. Call me if you need anything."

Trudy left, and Jake was alone with Craig. Seeing how healthy Campbell looked, it struck Jake that he was a long way from running down a street or kicking in doors like the old days. That was discouraging, to think about how much of his physical strength he'd lost.

He must have been scowling, because when he looked up, Craig was looking at him with concern. He felt his face flush. More than anything, he hated pity. Hated it.

Craig cleared his throat. "You feel like answering some questions?"

"Sure. Right. Go ahead."

"Tell me what you remember about the night you were attacked."

What did he remember? He'd been asking himself that question for the last month. "I ... I remember Cass and I went out to dinner. When we got back, then, I started talking to her again about coming back to the Bureau. I guess she thought I was being pushy. I remember I was angry, because she was being so ... stubborn. I followed her to the boat. We were arguing. She yelled at me to go away and leave her alone.

"I was furious. I remember the feelings more than anything we said. Finally, I did leave. I remember lightning and thunder. The air was thick. All I could think about was Cass. I was so frustrated! And I didn't want to leave her, not like that, not fighting. I stood next to my car, trying to think what else I could do, what else I could say. I watched the first drops of rain splatter on the roof ... I remember that so clearly ... those raindrops, exploding on the roof of the car. I was trying to figure how I could reach Cass, how I could ... could make it up to her. I didn't want to lose her. I was angry and sad, all at the same time. That's all I remember." Jake looked at Craig. "That's all. The next thing I knew, I was in that hospital in Montana."

"Why'd you leave the rehab place?"

"I was sick of it. Tired of all the drugs and the tests and never getting any better."

"How'd you manage to get away from there?"

"One day, I just unplugged the IV, bribed an orderly to bring me my stuff, and I walked away. I hitchhiked to town and caught a bus."

"And you didn't black out the whole time you were traveling?"

"No, I did. But I could tell when it was coming and I just leaned my head back and pretended I was asleep."

"What were you planning to do when you got back here?"

Jake's eyes flickered. He hesitated before he responded. "I don't know, really."

Campbell took a deep breath. He rested his elbows on his knees and drew closer to Jake. "Jake, I've got to ask you this. Have you been having any thoughts about hurting yourself?"

Jake's jaw shifted. "I'm okay now," he said. "I'm better."

Craig scanned his face. "Do you need to talk to somebody?"

"No."

Campbell nodded. "I'd like you to. It would be a good thing. You're dealing with a lot right now."

"I won't. I don't need that."

Craig backed off. "Well, you call me if it gets bad, okay, buddy?"

"Yeah. Okay."

"Anytime, day or night." Campbell shifted focus. "Jake, whoever attacked you—it wasn't just random."

Jake rubbed his neck. "What do you mean?"

"The attacker waited for you. He came up behind you, hit you over the head, and muscled you into your car, right? Then he took you to the park, pulled you out of the car, and stabbed you ... over and over. If he just wanted you dead, why didn't he shoot you right out?"

"I don't know."

"We found bullet casings, but he apparently didn't shoot until the kids saw him, and he was so rattled he completely missed you. He chose a very personal way of hurting you. Is there anybody who hates you that much? Anybody at all?"

"I don't know. I'm sorry. I just ... don't know." He squeezed his eyes shut and opened them again. The pain was increasing. It was right behind his eyes.

"No affairs going on, or anything like that?"

"No."

"Anybody hit on you lately, in a bar or anything? Anybody you might have rebuffed?"

Jake stared at him. What was that supposed to mean?

Craig hesitated, then continued. "What about Tam? Or that guy who's living with her? Any chance he might hold a grudge against you?"

"No." Jake squeezed his eyes shut. "And Tam may not like me, but she has nothing to gain from me being dead." He wanted to will away the pain, but he couldn't, and it was frustrating. It was growing like an ugly, malignant tumor.

Craig shifted in his seat. Over his shoulder, Jake could see one of Aunt Trudy's plaques. "I know the plans I have for you," it said, "plans to prosper you and not harm you, to give you a hope and a future." What did that mean, exactly?

"Jake," Craig said, gesturing to capture his attention. "We found a note under you in the park that made us believe maybe you were looking into Mike's death. Were you pursuing that?"

Mike's death. Yeah, Mike was dead.

"Jake," Craig tried again, "did you have contact with anybody? Question any sources?"

He frowned. "I don't know. I don't think so. But I don't know." What did he remember? Nothing. Just Mike died. That's it. No, wait. "I had a contact I was going to pursue, but I didn't get there. Over in Annapolis."

"Okay, that's good."

Jake dropped his head, rubbing the back of his neck with his left hand. His headache was getting worse.

Campbell looked at him and apparently decided Jake had had enough. He closed his notepad and put it in his pocket. "Jake, whoever attacked you is still out there. I don't think you are safe here, buddy. I think you should come with me and let me find you someplace more secure."

Jake raised his head. "What? Why?"

"It's not safe here. There's no way to protect you."

The hammering began, then at the back of his head, a relentless pounding. He could feel his neck tightening up. He stood up. "No, man. No."

"Look, I know you're comfortable here, but—"

Jake faced him. "I said, no! No. I'm staying here."

"Have you considered that you might be putting Trudy at risk?"

He stared at Craig, unwilling to accept his words. "Trudy? Trudy!"

She appeared at the doorway. "Yes, Jake?" she asked, stepping into the room.

Jake looked her in the eyes. "Does it ... worry you ... to have me here? Does it?"

"Why, no."

Jake turned back to Craig.

"Even though the person who assaulted him may try to find him?"

Trudy straightened her back. "Craig, I put my armor on every morning. You know what that means. If I'm doing God's will, whatever happens, happens. I'm right where he wants me. And I believe I am doing his will."

Jake had no idea what she was talking about, but he saw in Craig's eyes that she'd gotten through somehow. "I'm staying, Craig," Jake said.

"I don't know ..."

"Well, I do, and I'm staying! That's it!" Jake felt his face grow hot.

Craig shook his head and took a deep breath. "Okay. I'll have to figure out some way to tell the boss."

"You do that."

Cassie got out of her car. She'd driven to Sullivan's Wharf, the place Frederick Schneider was killed. She should have gone back to the office to research this weekend's story, but she'd been wanting to go to Sullivan's Wharf, and right now, as angry as she was with Craig, she just couldn't think about crab feasts.

The sun was still high in the sky. Tall cumulus clouds were building in the west and Cass wondered if they'd get storms that day.

The marina was a nice one with a landscaped entryway and a pool surrounded by a trim white fence. It was popular with sailors as well as powerboaters, and Cassie could see a forest of masts rising above the shrubs around the parking lot.

Cassie adjusted her shirt, a navy-blue polo, and smoothed out her khakis. Pulling a hair elastic from her purse, she gathered her hair in a ponytail and secured it, and then walked toward the docks.

Someone called her name, and she turned around and saw Scrub coming out of the shop area.

"Hey there! Miss Cassie! Hey!" The little dockhand broke into a half-jog, waving as he ran, a broad grin on his face.

"Scrub! What are you doing here?"

"I came to get some things for Mr. Maxwell," he said breathlessly. "Mr. Maxwell, he's buying a new boat!"

"Is that right?" Cassie was glad to see Scrub. It had been weeks.

"Yes, miss! And Mr. Hardesty, he's rebuilding the marina."

"Wow. That's good news!"

"You bet! It means I'm keeping my job!" Scrub grinned. "I miss seeing you and your boat. Mr. Maxwell, he said the same thing. It just ain't the same without all those boats and people around, you know? But boy, that fire, that was something, wasn't it? Seeing them boats explode, it was just like in the movies, wasn't it? Boom! Boom! One after the other, 'til nothin' was left but hulls, like bodies floatin' dead in the water."

Cassie agreed. "It was amazing."

"And they found one up here, did you know?"

"Found what?"

"A body! Man got killed and they found his body right over there," Scrub said, motioning toward some marsh grass. He dropped his voice. "Ain't nobody gonna ask me, but let me tell you, ever a man deserved to die it was that man."

Cass wrinkled her brow. "Why?"

He shook his head. "I ain't saying. I cain't say. But it's so, believe you me." He grinned. "Got to go! Bye!'

"Wait! Scrub!"

"Sorry, Miss Cassie, it's real good to see you but I've got to go now," Scrub said, turning around so that he was walking backwards as he moved away from her. "Mr. Maxwell, he needs these things right away."

18

*C*assie couldn't shake off Scrub's words. Why did he think Frederick Schneider deserved to die? Cassie looked over the marina, which consisted of four floating docks made of aluminum and arranged in a back-to-back E pattern. One of them was covered, and huge, expensive powerboats filled the slips there, shaded from the sun and sheltered from the rain. Of the other slips, around half held sailboats and half held powerboats. At an end slip was a large catamaran, a 40-footer in Cassie's estimation.

Cassie stepped onto the A Dock and walked up and down, looking at all the boats. When she returned to shore, she wandered into the convenience store.

"Can I help you?" The young clerk was probably a college student on summer break. She was a blonde, in her twenties. Her hair was pulled back in a French braid, and she was chewing gum while she leafed through a copy of *Sail* magazine.

"No thanks, just looking around." Cassie fingered a collection of floating key chains at the counter. "Say, I understand this place is famous."

"How's that?"

"I heard a guy was murdered here?"

The girl rolled her eyes. "Yeah. Some old guy. A professor at the college."

"A professor?" That didn't match with what Cassie knew.

"Visiting lecturer anyway, at Washington College. At least, that's what I heard."

The liberal arts college was less than an hour and a half away, in Chestertown, Maryland. Was Schneider teaching there? That would be news to Cassie. Why would an engineer be speaking there? Maybe that's where he spoke at the conference Desiree had mentioned. "What happened?"

"He had his boat here ... right down there, on D-dock. It's still there, in fact—the one with the 'For Sale' sign on it. Anyway, they found him in the grass over there. His girlfriend called the cops."

"So where was he found?"

The clerk stood up and moved toward the front window. "Right over there, where that orange buoy is lying."

"Oh, okay, I can see it. Was he shot?"

"Uh-uh. His throat was slashed. Oh my gosh, you should have seen it. I mean, his head was nearly cut off ... blood was everywhere."

"You saw it?"

"Yep. You bet. It was sick."

"But they still have no idea who did it?"

The girl shook her head. "Creeps me out, every time it rains."

"What do you mean?"

"The night it happened, it was raining. One of those spring thunderstorms we get. It was just pouring. That's why we think no one heard anything."

Cassie pondered that a moment, then smiled. "Well, thanks. Here, let me buy one of these." She handed a red foam crab key chain to the girl. On it was printed "Sullivan's Wharf Marina" and the address and phone number. "Thanks," Cassie said as she took the change. "See you around."

Cassie walked down the D-dock. The boat in slip D12 was a Catalina 320. It looked fairly new. The bright blue canvas was unfaded, the deck clean. Cassie copied down the broker's name and number off the "For Sale" sign. Then she walked back up the

D-dock and over to the grassy area where Schneider's body was found. It was eerily reminiscent of the place where they'd found Jake—knee-high grass, lots of bugs.

After she finished looking around she visited the marina office, the gas station, and the grocery store in town, striking up conversations in each place. Frederick Schneider, she learned, was a newcomer. The boat had been at the marina for only a month. He had purchased it just up the bay at Havre de Grace. Now that he was dead, he was something of a celebrity: Sullivan's Wharf had never had a murder before, and everybody seemed to want to talk about him.

He was a nice guy. Or kind of standoffish—depending on who Cassie talked to. He was pudgy and bald. Had a real looker for a girl-friend. Was cheap. Pinched every penny. He was picky. Had to have things just right but hated to pay for them.

It was 7:00 p.m. before Cassie was ready to go home. She was unlocking her car when a pickup truck pulled up next to her. Skip Shelton, the surveyor, rolled down his window and said, "Well, hi!"

"Skip! What are you doing here?" Cassie exclaimed.

He was in the area to check out a boat he was surveying tomor-row, he said, and after he and Cassie exchanged small talk, they mutually decided dinner would be a good idea. And he knew just the place. "You feel like Italian?" he asked.

"Fine," she responded and she followed him in her car to Luigi's.

Luigi's was quiet and dark, and smelled of garlic and fresh bread. Family owned, Pappa was the head chef and Momma and all the kids helped out. The decor was simple: Plastic grapevines hung over decorative wooden latticework and multicolor candles stuck in Chianti bottles sat on the tables.

Skip ordered chicken cacciatore and Cassie selected manicotti. They munched on bread while they waited for the food. He asked her about her boat and she cataloged her progress and then sought his advice on hatches and water pumps and standing rigging.

By the time their food came, they were both relaxed. They

talked about movies and the Orioles and shared crazy boat-owner stories. He told her about the club boat that he'd surveyed for a prospective buyer that had been dismasted three times by novice sailors. She told him about the boat she and her dad had chartered in the Caribbean. The bilge had filled up with water and the pump failed. With the water shimmering just below the salon floor, they'd tried to run the pump manually but it wouldn't work. The emergency manual bilge pump was also broken, as was the two-way radio they tried to call the charter company with. "I'm amazed we survived!" Cassie laughed. "It was a great trip but my gosh, what an adventure!"

"It's a good thing you all are sailors," Skip said. "Imagine being a novice and having to deal with all that."

She nodded. "Speaking of novice sailors ..." She leaned forward and lowered her voice. "How's the arson investigation going? Anything new? Just for my personal information."

Skip cocked his head and smiled. "Just a source, huh? That's all I am?"

"You know that's not true!" Cassie smiled. "You're also a good surveyor and pretty decent company over dinner."

"Well, that'll do. For now." Skip leaned forward, glancing around before he spoke. "I told you before, we discovered the two arsons started the same way, and Loughlin started looking into where the Sinclairs' boat had been just prior to the time it blew up. Turns out, it had spent the day prior at the shop at Goose Creek Marina."

Cassie raised her eyebrows. "The shop?"

"Yes. The Sinclairs had taken it there because they were having trouble with the engine's water pump. Turns out, the impeller was just bad, so it was replaced and then the Sinclairs sailed down the creek to the anchorage, where it burned just a few hours later."

"So who had access to it at the shop?" Cassie asked.

"A bunch of people." He looked away, as if he was deciding how much more to say. "Including Myron Tunney."

"Scrub? The dockhand?"

"That's the man."

"He's a suspect?"

Skip stayed silent, but it was clear he was confirming that.

"I know him, pretty well. He's the one who helped my dad bring my boat up, remember?" Cassie said.

"I'd forgotten that."

"And he helped me save *Time Out* when the marina burned." Cassie frowned. "I can't believe he's involved in this."

"Why not? A lot of guys get their jollies from setting fires."

"But he seems so good-hearted, so ... so innocent," she protested.

"Scrub's not as innocent as you might imagine."

"What do you mean by that?"

"He has a criminal record."

"For what?"

"He's been a bad boy: drug possession, theft ..."

"How long ago?" Cassie demanded.

"Ten or twelve years."

"He was a kid then!"

"Eighteen. Old enough to know better. And there's something else, too, in his juvenile files. Loughlin's trying to get those opened."

Scrub? A suspect? Suddenly Cassie's food didn't taste so good. "But this is all just conjecture. I mean, you have no physical evidence against him, right? And no evidence he was carrying a grudge against the boat owners?"

"No, we don't have anything like that, but the circumstantial evidence is pretty strong." He leaned forward. "The word we have, from interviewing people in his hometown, was the juvenile crime was arson."

Cassie's heart dropped. She'd been around Scrub a lot. Her dad had certainly worked with him closely and had known him for several years. He'd even picked Scrub up on Sunday mornings and taken him to church. The dockhand was a little slow, maybe had some learning disabilities, but he seemed so good-hearted. And he loved boats. Not only that.... "Skip, Scrub was dependent on the marina for his job. Why would he burn it down?"

Skip shrugged. "Who knows why people do things? For the excitement? Passive-aggressive behavior? Who can say?"

Cassie couldn't argue with that. "He's from the Eastern Shore, isn't he?"

"Yep. Oxford." Then Skip changed the subject. It didn't matter. He had already given Cassie plenty to think about.

It was nearly 9:00 p.m. before Craig was ready to leave Trudy's. Storms were beginning to roll in from the west, the sound of thunder announcing their imminent arrival. As he and Jake stepped outside the humidity hit them like a wet towel. Cicadas were chattering in the bushes and the calico cat scampered away as she heard their footsteps.

"You be careful, man, okay?" Craig said, walking down the front steps. "I'm doing this your way, but I don't like it." He turned to say good-bye to Aunt Trudy.

Lightning flashed and there was a roll of thunder. The heaviness of the air created an uneasy feeling in Jake. He glanced around, wondering who or what he was looking for. Was it stress? Craig's warning?

Jake propped his arms on the roof of the Bureau car, waiting for Craig. Drops of rain began to fall, huge splattering drops. They plopped onto the roof and exploded, making little circles in the dirt. They caught his attention. He stared at them transfixed. His neck tightened.

He felt like he was being transported over time, back to another rainy night. A black cloud began to cover his heart. He stared at the rain, allowing the feelings to envelop him. What was there? He wanted to remember, he needed to remember.

"Jake?" Craig stepped forward and touched Jake's shoulder.

He jumped.

"Jake? Are you all right?"

"Oh, yeah, sure, sorry," Jake responded. He said good-bye and moved aside so Craig could get in.

Craig started the car, waved good-bye, and Jake stood in the oyster-shell driveway watching as he drove away.

The rains came then, full sheets of rain pouring out of the sky. Jake remained frozen in the driveway, feeling the water beating on his shoulders, watching the lightning flash, listening to the thunder roaring in his ears. Something was back there, in his memory, something about the night he was attacked. He just couldn't quite see it. He didn't want to move and break the spell; he wanted to coax it out front where he could deal with it.

His throat was tight and his chest heavy. His hair clung to his head and rain dripped off his beard. He caught his breath. In his mind he could hear the sounds of a struggle. As he focused, the sounds became clearer—the grunts and groans of exertion, the sounds of a storm, rain on a car. Jake tried to remember a face, but he couldn't. Lightning flashed and thunder rumbled again. For a moment, he thought he saw blood pooling on the ground. Then, the memory faded.

Jake shivered and walked quickly into the house.

"Trudy," Jake said, standing in his bedroom drying his hair with a towel, "do you believe in evil?"

"What do you mean? Do I believe in evil that is the opposite of good? Of course. I think everybody knows there is good and evil." She lifted up the mattress on his bed and fitted a clean bottom sheet on it.

"Okay. I agree. But do you believe in evil personified?"

"As in Satan? Yes, I do. Do you?"

He paused and looked at her. "No, not really. But if I did, I know what it would be like to be near him. I know what hell is."

"What's hell, Jake?" she asked, stopping what she was doing.

"Hell is a black pit that you fall into. And you have no control over yourself anymore. There's no security, nothing underneath you, no way to save yourself. The Pit wants to swallow you, and you can't stop it. The pain is immense. You are totally alone in the blackness. No one can hear your screams. And it is absolutely the most terrifying thing anyone can ever experience." He looked at her. "If there is a hell, that's what it is. I've seen it."

"There is a hell, Jake. And also a heaven."

He shook his head. "I don't know about that. I just don't know," and he left the room before she could say more.

Cassie walked into the newsroom the next day, her mind flitting from subject to subject, thinking about what Skip told her, wondering about Schneider, worrying about Scrub. She knew she had to give the Palm Pilot to Craig and let the agents start unscrambling it. In the meantime, she had a job to do.

KidFest, in Baltimore's Inner Harbor, the largest of the summer festivals she would cover, would take place this Saturday. Len had okayed it as a break from the small-town gigs. She put her stuff down on her desk and flipped on the computer. Behind her a group of photographers carrying their gear were laughing and joking on their way back to their workstations. Shonika was standing at her desk, talking on the phone, gesturing with her hand. Across the room Len walked up to the city desk, looked at Cassie and nodded as if he were checking her in, affirming her presence.

Cassie sat down and forced herself to focus. KidFest was an extravagant display of child-friendly products, games, fun rides, food, hands-on art, and educational pavilions. The entire plaza would be taken over by the organizers, who expected thousands of children and adults to attend. Included in the event would be major displays on the Chesapeake Bay and the environment, model sailboat races, and a touch tank of marine life native to the Bay.

Digging around the Internet for background on Baltimore, she learned that the city had been a seaport since the 1600s. In fact, it was the westernmost port on the Atlantic coast. The town thrived during America's early years, its mills providing a ready product for shipping. The city played a crucial role in the War of 1812. The British, having already burned Washington, D.C., turned their sights on Baltimore. But the able gunners of Fort McHenry defended the town, and the victory against the British was immortalized in a poem now familiar to all Americans—"The Star-Spangled Banner."

Baltimore, Cassie learned, was currently the fourth-largest port for container shipping on the East Coast. Which would explain the huge ships she'd had to dodge when sailing up the Patapsco River and the many commercial ports she'd passed on her way to the small-boat marinas.

The Inner Harbor was part of a downtown revitalization program begun in the 1970s. A finger of the Patapsco, the Inner Harbor, was a protected basin right in the heart of downtown. Surrounded by hotels, restaurants, and attractions like the Maryland Science Museum and the National Aquarium, the Inner Harbor had become a mecca for tourists and families seeking to experience Baltimore at its best.

Cassie would join the crowd on Saturday. And, if all went according to her plan, Jake and Trudy and Jake's kids would come, too. She was looking forward to that! The kids would love the festival and Jake would love seeing them. And yes, it would mean him being out in public but hey, it was all the way up in Baltimore, there'd be huge crowds, and she was confident there was nothing to worry about.

After work, Cassie drove to her father's house. She had called earlier to see if he'd be home because she wanted to pick up some things from the garage. When she pulled up, she saw another car in the driveway, one that she didn't recognize. As she opened her car-door and got out, she saw her dad standing on the back walk, talking to Rick Maxwell.

"Hi, Dad!" she said. "Rick, what brings you here?"

"He was just asking about you," her dad responded.

Rick flashed a boyish grin. It was her dad who had put Cassie and Rick back in touch, all these years after high school. Sometimes she wondered why: Her dad didn't seem too fond of him. But they shared a lot in common. Her dad knew an awful lot about boats and was frequently in the marinas either working on one or going out with someone. And he loved to sail. She supposed her dad was trying to reach out to Rick.

"Your dad was just telling me about your place. It sounds neat. How's the sailing up there? I assume you have your boat there, too?" Rick asked.

"Yes, yes I do. But I haven't been out much. It's a little more than I want to single-hand right now. How about you? I heard you're getting a new boat!"

"Yes, a catamaran this time. I'll take delivery in the next day or so. And Cassie, that reminds me. Would you be interested in helping me try it out?"

"Maybe."

"I'm picking it up in Annapolis and eventually I want to sail it to Baltimore, to the Inner Harbor. I'm going to introduce my girlfriend to it there."

Girlfriend? Cassie hadn't been aware of any girlfriend. The news struck her as odd. Still, Maxwell was good-looking and had plenty of money. Why shouldn't he have a girlfriend? "I didn't know you were dating. Anybody I know?"

"No. Just a girl I met at a bar." Rick shrugged his shoulders. "She's not much of a sailor, and I thought, if I could get her to come to the Inner Harbor, and see it there. Just sit on it and watch all the people, the lights ... have a nice, romantic dinner at a harborside restaurant. I just think she might buy into it. But that's for later. Right now, I just want to test it, and I thought you might be interested."

"It sounds like fun. I've wanted to try a catamaran."

"Well, and this is a nice one. Really luxurious." Maxwell bowed awkwardly. "My dear, you will be treated like a queen."

She looked at him skeptically. "Yeah, well, I'd just be crew."

"Cassie is going up to the Inner Harbor this weekend, aren't you, dear?" her father added.

"Well, tentatively." For some reason, she was irritated that her dad had mentioned her plans. Why? She wasn't sure. Maybe she was getting paranoid. She turned to Rick. "Let me know when you want to go out. Dad, I'm going to get that stuff I wanted. See you later!" She quickly walked away.

"You're awfully quiet," Trudy said, glancing over at Jake. He was sitting in the passenger seat of her red Saturn sedan. They were returning from the visit to the neurologist in Baltimore, and he was pensive. "Are you thinking about what the doctor said?"

Jake adjusted himself in the seat. "Kind of. But mostly, I'm thinking about my kids."

"Have you talked to your ex-wife? Will she let us take them to KidFest?"

"I'm going to call her when we get back to your house." He stared out the window, trying to keep the bitterness at bay.

"You really love your kids, don't you?"

Jake took a deep breath.

"I can tell by the way you interact with Jazz."

"What do you mean?" Jake asked.

"The way you play with her, the way you talk to her, the way you pet her. You've never had a dog but you obviously care about her. Usually if men are good with dogs they're good with kids, too." Trudy exited onto Route 2, speeding up to avoid a large truck moving slowly in the right lane. "So my guess is, you love your kids and you're a good dad."

Jake drummed his thumb on his thigh and nodded. "It's too bad I couldn't get Tam to see it that way. But yes, I do love my kids." His marriage to Tamara had gone well at first. But then the kids had come along. After Caitlin was born Tam had gotten depressed. After a few months, she'd insisted on returning to teaching. He still didn't understand why. In his mind, the stress of two careers and two kids had been a death knell for their relationship. Tam insisted it was dead long before that. Jake sighed deeply at the memory.

"Did what Dr. Harrington say bother you?"

Jake glanced toward Trudy. "About all the tests he wants to do? No."

"So what's on your mind?"

"I don't know. Just ... stuff."

Trudy moved left, passed a white delivery van, and moved right again. "The other night, when Craig was here, you stood out in the rain for a long time."

Her voice was so gentle. Ordinarily he might have stiffened, thinking someone had been probing him, but with Trudy, somehow, he didn't take offense.

"What were you thinking about then?" she asked.

"Would you believe me if I said, 'I don't know'? I mean, it's like ... like I can almost remember something, but then, it's gone."

"Honey, that happens to me all the time!" She laughed.

Jake ran his fingers through his hair. "I just can't quite see it."

"Give it time, Jake. It'll come back. Everything you need to know will come back."

19

*L*ater that night, Jake stood in the kitchen, brushing a stray blade of grass off his pants, his head pounding. He turned toward Cassie, who was sitting at the table. Aunt Trudy stood nearby. "I'm telling you, it's not going to happen! So forget about it!"

"What did she say? What exactly did she say?" Cassie demanded.

Jake clenched and relaxed his fist over and over. "Apparently Campbell told Foster everything. So Tam had some 'visitors' as she called them, a couple of agents, and they asked her a bunch of questions. In the course of it, the idea was conveyed that there's some boogeyman after me, and Tam got scared. She even found out about the blue headlight thing! She doesn't want the kids to be out in public with me. So she said no."

"How can she do that?" Cassie spit out the words. "Don't you have visitation?"

"Sure. Sure I have visitation! But you know what? If I fight her on this, and she goes back to court and tells them the kids are at risk when they're with me ... then *pow*! That goes away."

"It's so unfair!"

"Of course it's unfair! That's why I hate this ... this whole mess! You're never really divorced if you have kids with somebody. You're tied to that person for life. You can't just ... sever that." He turned and slammed his fist into the cabinet.

"I'll call her ... let me talk to her—"

"No!" he thundered, turning toward her. "Stay out of it, Cassie!" He dropped his head and his face softened. "I'm sorry," he said, looking at her. "It's just ... please, let it be. Let me choose my battles. I'm not totally incompetent." And with that, he left the kitchen, walking out the back door, Jazz padding behind him.

Cassie looked at her aunt as the back door slammed behind him. "I didn't mean to upset him."

"It's just one more frustration," Trudy said. "That's all."

"What can we do?"

"Maybe Tam would let the kids come here. I could go pick them up or maybe she'd like to come down."

"Good idea! I'll call her—"

Her aunt held up her hand. "No, Cassie. I'll suggest it to Jake. Let's let him take the lead on this."

The thud of the axe hitting the wood was something tangible he could focus on. Something physical. Something he could control. Jake raised it over his head and felt a trickle of sweat run down his back. He brought the axe down hard, and the oak cracked under the blow. He wiped his brow with his left forearm. Even this late at night, the air was humid and thick. The sky was grayish black, a thin layer of clouds obscuring the stars, and from somewhere off in the woods came the sound of a whippoorwill.

He worked under the glare of the back spotlight, his movements making stark shadows on the lawn. The trunk of the fallen tree was about twenty inches in diameter, and he was making eighteen-inch pieces that he would then split. He would have used a chain saw to make the cuts. That would be a lot quicker. But Trudy didn't own one and so he worked at it the hard way. The feel of the wood in his hand, the heft of its weight, the way it yielded to his blows was satisfying to him, a relief from the otherwise unrelenting frustration.

It irritated him that he had to ask permission to see his own kids. Irritated him big time. And that Tam could say no so easily. And he didn't know what to do about it. So he split wood, blow after blow after blow, until sweat poured down his face and down his neck, and his chest was heaving with exertion.

Jazz was lying about fifteen feet away near an old lilac bush. Jake fingered the axe again and started to raise it, then Jazz suddenly jumped up and ran to him. She pressed her head against his knee and whined. He looked at her curiously, then felt his hand tighten on the axe and tasted something metallic. "Oh, no," he said, and his eyes rolled back and he collapsed to the ground.

Early Saturday morning Cassie met Brett and together they drove to Baltimore, her enthusiasm for the KidFest assignment dampened. Her plan had failed and that was depressing. She couldn't get Jake off her mind. Jake and the kids. They should have been able to come. And those stupid seizures. It had taken him twenty minutes to come around after the one he'd had last night in the backyard, and he had gone straight to bed, exhausted, the lines in his face deep with sorrow.

They parked the car, and as they walked Cassie willed herself to focus on her task. The Inner Harbor was the poster child for successful urban revitalization. When the Rouse Company had taken on the task of refurbishing Baltimore's central waterfront, no one realized just how popular it would become. When Cassie was a little kid, Baltimore was a smoggy, blue-collar, down-at-the-heels town. Now, it sparkled with activity and color and drew tourists from all over the world. You could rent pedal boats, take a harbor tour, watch sharks at the aquarium, or catch an Orioles game at Camden Yards. Rain or shine, summer or winter, there was always something interesting going on at the Inner Harbor.

The sun was warm and huge, puffy clouds dotted the sky. By 10:00 a.m. the Harbor was full of tourists and families and groups of children. The organizers of KidFest had done their job well. Brightly colored plastic slides and sandboxes; a huge, inflated moon bounce; an inflated sea monster called "Chessie;" exhibits and information booths filled the plaza. *Jake's kids would have loved it*, Cassie thought.

One KidFest booth had a touch tank, populated by sturdy critters that could be handled. A dad was daring his eight-year-old boy to pick up a horseshoe crab. He finally did, and Brett grabbed a picture as the large, ugly crab wiggled its legs and the kid's sister screamed. Cassie interviewed the family briefly for her story.

A few sailboats were in the harbor next to the plaza and half a dozen pedal boats moved around among them. The sun glistened on the water. Cassie shaded her eyes as she looked across the plaza, Brett clicking away behind her. The staccato rhythms of a steel band punctuated the air. Families strolled, scrambled, ran, and wandered through the exhibits. Kids seemed to be everywhere.

Watching them, Cassie felt like an outsider looking in, a person with her nose pressed to the glass of a beautiful scene, seeing it but not being part of it. Nor would she ever be. And she was aware of an empty feeling inside, one that she rarely acknowledged even to herself.

"Let's head back," she said suddenly to Brett, and the two worked their way across the plaza, doing interviews, taking pictures, and writing notes. They got some great shots in the large sandbox of families building sandcastles, and some colorful photos at the kite exhibit. Beach kites, Cassie knew, had become a captivating hobby. She'd seen people flying "theme" kites at Ocean City: barnyard animals, colorful butterflies or bugs, or dragons of all sorts. Here, the proprietor of a nearby kite shop had set up a display, and indeed, a red, green, and yellow box kite flew fifty feet above his booth, its string trailing a collection of birds: an osprey, a heron, a brown pelican, a goose, and, down at the bottom, just for fun, a pink flamingo.

Brett was having a field day, shooting little toddlers with ice-cream smeared faces and ponytailed girls getting Chessie the Sea Monster painted on their cheeks. A model yacht club was staging races in the water with their remote-controlled miniature sailboats while nearby, Maryland's Department of Natural Resources put on a safety demonstration.

"This is great, Cassie," Brett said, grinning. "It's a lot of fun."

"Yes, yes it is," she responded, but all she could think about was Jake, and Justin, and Caitlin.

By early afternoon, she and Brett had all they needed for a good-sized article. Best of all, Cassie had seven names and phone numbers of people she met who might, just might, have some information she could use on the marina fires or maybe even Jake's assault. Either they lived in the area or had boats in the marina. She had identified them as she did interviews for KidFest, although they had no clue she was interested in anything other than the event. She would call them later.

Cassie drove back to Annapolis and Brett sat in the passenger seat, reviewing the pictures he'd taken on the digital camera. While he was busy, she used her cell phone to call Aunt Trudy.

"It's all right," Trudy said. "He's had two seizures today and he's pretty down."

"Should I come over?" Cassie asked.

"Only if you want to. He'll be okay, honey." Trudy hesitated.

"What's brought this on?"

"I think it's the stress. The conflict with Tam, and Craig Campbell was over here this morning."

"What did he want?" Cassie bristled.

"He was asking Jake a bunch of questions, and Jake was getting frustrated, and then I heard them arguing over what happened with Tam, how the agents scared her."

"Oh, great."

"I just think it stressed him out. He had his first seizure right after Craig left."

That was irritating. "If you need some help, I can come over," Cassie said.

"No, honey. You've had a long day. You do what you need to do."

Cassie said good-bye and clicked off the phone. She really wanted to get going on this article so she could follow up on her leads.

"Trouble?" Brett asked.

"No, no," she said quickly. "How are the shots?"

Brett turned back to his camera. "Did you ever notice that at some of these events you see the same people, over and over, all day long?"

"What do you mean?" she asked. They were traveling south on the Baltimore-Washington Parkway, and the joints in the pavement made rhythmic thumps, like her heart when she was anxious. Which she was now.

"I kept seeing this guy everywhere we went today. He had on a yellow shirt and a floppy white hat. And sure enough, he's in a lot of these pictures. I don't know if he was trying to be, or if it was just coincidental."

She worked to keep her voice calm. "What's he look like? His face?"

"That's the ironic thing. I never can quite see his face. He's always in the crowd somewhere, half-covered."

"Then how do you know it was the same guy?"

"His shirt. And that weird hat. It's definitely the same person."

Cassie digested Brett's words all the rest of the way to Annapolis. She didn't want to clue the photographer in that something might be amiss, that it could actually have been someone following them. And probably that wasn't the case, probably it was just a couple of guys with similar shirts. Why would someone be following them? But when she dropped Brett off at the paper, she asked him for a CD of the photos he'd taken.

"All of them?" he asked.

"Yes, please. The kids were so cute! I'd just like to see what you got."

"Will do," he said. "I'll put it on your desk."

Cassie returned to her boathouse apartment, poured herself a glass of water, put some ice and a slice of lemon in it, and took it plus her laptop out on the balcony. The late afternoon was beautiful, clear and bright, and boats were beginning to parade back in from the Bay. She watched them for a little while, letting the scene calm her thoughts. Then she opened her notes on the table beside her and began to write her story.

"Back off, Barney, kids in Baltimore have a new hero: Chessie. And if painted faces are any indication, he's in for a long run as Maryland's most popular monster ..."

Gradually, sentences formed paragraphs and paragraphs formed an article. Sometimes writing was like pulling out thorns; sometimes words just flowed. Tonight, the process was a mixed bag: The words came easily, but in the back of her mind, Cassie kept thinking about Brett, and the photos, and the man in the yellow shirt. Distracted, she was having trouble coming up with a sharp ending.

"Nuts to this," she said finally, and she closed up her laptop, and took it inside. She'd finish the story later. Cassie stared at the phone, then picked it up. She'd better check on Jake.

Trudy answered. "Two more," she said in a low voice, in answer to Cassie's question. "He's had two more seizures, and the last time he fell and he may have hit his head, although he won't admit it. I really think we should call the doctor, but he doesn't want to."

"Do you want me to come over?" Cassie asked.

"No, no. He says he doesn't want to see anyone. He's pretty much sticking up in his room, by himself."

Cassie could hear the sound of clinking through the phone. "What are you doing?" she asked her aunt.

"I'm just making him some dinner. Crab Imperial, which he loves, Silver Queen corn, and peach pie."

Cassie smiled. "Oh, Aunt Truly, you are the best."

"Oh, not really ..."

"Yes, yes you are. Whenever I was having a bad time at school, I knew you'd be home, making something good. Remember those oatmeal cookies you used to make? Or those banana-peanut butter sandwiches? And how we'd have tea together?"

"Why, yes, yes I do."

"People make fun of that nowadays, but Aunt Truly, those things meant so much to me. Thank you for taking care of Jake."

"I only wish I could help him more."

Cassie said good-bye, and hung up the phone. She thought back to Brett and the photos, and she wondered if he had made the CD for her. She grabbed her purse and headed for the office. She had to see those photos. She just had to.

As she drove, Cassie wrestled with the questions that were bouncing around in her head. Why was Scrub considered a suspect? Why did he think Schneider deserved to be killed? Who was the man in the yellow shirt? Was he following her? Why? What about the blue headlights? Who was that? What did that have to do with Jake's assault? What were the connecting threads? Or were there any?

Cassie parked in the newspaper parking lot and, glancing over her shoulder, walked quickly through the dark to the door, where she used her key card and entered. Only a night editor was present. Cassie said hello and walked back to her desk. Sure enough, there was a photo CD waiting. Glancing around, assuring herself she was essentially alone, she booted up her computer and slid in the disk.

Brett had taken almost 300 pictures. Cassie quickly scanned through them, and began placing in a separate folder the ones in which she could see a yellow shirt, or a white floppy hat. At first she had thirteen, then twenty-two, then, as she went through the whole collection one more time, she found fifteen more. Thirty-seven. In thirty-seven photographs she could see a guy in a yellow shirt or a glimpse of a white hat. That was more than coincidental. That was scary.

Then Cassie noticed something else. In five of the photographs the man's face was obscured by some type of object. When she blew them up, she knew what it was: a camera. A small digital camera. Yellow Shirt was taking pictures of her. Now that was really scary.

Scary enough to put her nerves right on edge. So when the night editor walked up to her, just to share pleasantries on the way to the coffee pot, she nearly jumped out of her skin.

She quickly clicked on "desktop" to get the photos off the screen.

The editor seemed to want to talk, but Cassie gave him short answers and no eye contact. Finally he got the hint. Once he left, she returned to the photos, tried enlarging parts of them to enhance the images, but she couldn't get anything that allowed her to recognize the man. When she'd exhausted her ideas, she pulled out the CD and shut down the computer.

The FBI had access to superior photo-enhancement technology, Cassie thought as she hurried through the parking lot to her car. She'd used the lab resources before. It would be so helpful to have that backup now!

All the way home, she kept watching in her rearview mirror for lights, blue halogen headlights, one of them misaimed. She felt so vulnerable without her gun! Sure she'd had street-survival classes, sure she could fight, but her biggest defensive asset was her extraordinary ability with a gun. Skeet. That's why Jake and Mike called her Skeet. Maybe she should chance carrying one, despite Maryland laws.

Relief filled her when she was finally at the apartment. She got out of her car, locked the doors, sprinted up the steps, entered her apartment, and secured the door behind her. Heart drumming, she jumped when the phone rang.

It was Craig Campbell. "How are you doing?"

"Okay." She laid the CD on the table, but she couldn't take her eyes off of it.

He made small talk, which she recognized was a conciliatory gesture, and her animosity toward him began to dissipate. He said he'd called Jake and apologized for scaring Tam, for causing Jake more problems than he had already. And that he'd decided to back off probing Jake about the assault, or anything else. It was just too stressful for him.

Finally, he got to his point. "Cassie, I need your help."

"What are you talking about?" Her stomach ached with tension. She crossed her arm in front of her.

"I need you to open up to me. Tell me who you've been talking to about this case and what you know. Let's work together on this, Cassie."

She hesitated.

"Mike first. Then Jake. You could be next, and I don't want to see that."

"I'm not worried," she said softly. "I'm ... uh, I'm all right."

"You're not all right, you're in danger. And you're stressed."

He was right.

"So will you meet with me? Share information?"

"When?"

"How about Monday? Somewhere near your newspaper."

"Well, okay." She could hardly believe she was agreeing. But those photos ... that was eerie. Too weird. "There's a coffee shop nearby, on Taylor Street, called 'On the Bean.' Let's meet there, at nine. Will that work for you?"

"That'll be great, Cassie. Thank you. See you then."

Despite her best efforts, Trudy's plan to lure Jake down to eat failed. He declined dinner and had even come close to being rude when he told Trudy he really wanted to be left alone. Jake had sat in the chair in his room all evening, staring into space.

That wasn't like him. Sitting alone in the dark, stroking his beard, he thought, *I don't even know who I am anymore.* When he looked in the mirror the face that stared back at him was a bearded, shaggy-haired stranger. Why shave? He wasn't going anywhere. Why get a haircut? Who cared what he looked like? But where was the in-charge guy, the take-command-of-the-situation Jake? Where was the runner and the fighter, the no-nonsense door-kicker?

While he wrestled with his thoughts, Jazz stayed with him. And he had several more seizures, there alone in his room, bringing his 24-hour total to seven, his all-time record. And he was angry about that.

Night fell and he heard Trudy cleaning up the kitchen. He felt bad about not eating the food she'd fixed for him. Still, he felt rooted in his room. He listened as she got ready for bed, and finally the house grew quiet. When he was fairly sure she was asleep, he got up, and went downstairs. Turning on the back spotlight, he walked into the yard. He fitted the work glove on his hand, and strapped his hand to the axe. Then he lifted it and began splitting wood, bringing the axe down hard, over and over, scooping up the split wood with his left hand, stacking it and starting again.

He let his anger drive the axe. He hated these seizures. He hated what they'd made of him. And Tam infuriated him. She said she was trying to protect the kids, but her demands were ridiculous. Just ridiculous. The wood felt the force of his fury.

Two hours later he was exhausted. The pile of split wood had grown, but the tree wasn't finished yet. Neither was he. He wiped the sweat off his brow and looked up into the night sky. The stars were pinpricks of light in a velvet night. Orion, the Big Dipper ... he couldn't go much further than that in naming the constellations. Still, the beauty of the sky captured him. He wished he could see beyond them, to another time, another place, another way of life. This one sure wasn't all that it was cracked up to be.

He sat on the back steps for a while, reluctant to go to bed, to lie in the dark by himself, staring at the ceiling. He had no answers for his problems. None whatsoever. And, therefore, no hope.

The next day was Sunday. Jake lay in bed, awake, listening for Trudy to go off to church. But she fooled him. She didn't go. He knew she was staying home for him, and he felt guilty about that. He just couldn't stay upstairs any longer.

"Jake, what can I do for you?" Trudy asked as she put a plate of eggs in front of him.

He was sitting at the table, twirling a fork, lost in his thoughts. "I honestly don't know."

"You're frustrated."

"Yeah, I am."

"About the seizures?"

"And Tam."

"Should we call the doctor?"

"No! No ... I'm sorry. But what's he going to say? He doesn't know anything yet."

Jazz rose from her position under the table, approached Jake, and dropped a tennis ball next to his chair. Jake rubbed her ears. "You think that ball solves everything, don't you, Jazz?"

"I think ... I think she's sensing your seizures."

Jake looked up. "What?"

"Jazz. I think she's sensing when you're going to have a seizure. She gets close to you just moments before you black out. Sometimes she whines."

Jake patted Jazz's head. "Can dogs do that?"

"I guess so. I read about it, in a newspaper article a friend clipped for me." Trudy sat down across from him, a cup of coffee before her. "Jake, do you realize what that might mean for you?"

He looked at her dumbly.

"If she is sensing them, and you can pick up on her warnings, it will give you more control. You'll be able to avoid falling, and what a blessing that would be!"

That was true. Not falling would be a big deal.

"You can keep yourself out of potentially harmful situations, just by paying attention to her. You could do more things if you didn't have to worry about a seizure sneaking up on you." Trudy sipped her coffee. "Would you like to try tracking her behavior? To see if I'm right?"

"Sure, why not." He smiled wryly. "And if you are, do you think Jazz can take care of Tam? Work it out so I can see my kids?"

Trudy laughed, her gray eyes crinkling. *She has a nice smile,* Jake thought, "She's a D-O-G, Jake, not G-O-D."

He grinned.

"Let's just pay attention, and see if we can figure out her signals."

"Yeah, okay." Jake looked across the table at Aunt Trudy's hands. She was folding a napkin accordion-style, back and forth, back and forth. "I'm sorry, Trudy, about the way I behaved yesterday. I was rude. I am so appreciative of what you've done ... but I wasn't acting that way. I'm sorry."

"It's all right. I understand you being frustrated, but is there any-thing you can do that would cheer you up? I know it's got to be hard just hanging around the house. Is there any place I could take you that would be safe? Just to get out of the house?"

"I don't know." Jake grimaced. "I'll be honest. I'm not real wor-ried about being followed or attacked. Nobody would even recognize me now."

"We could go out to a mall or a park. Where there are a lot of people around. Wouldn't that be safe?"

"Yeah. But what if I have ..." His voice trailed off.

"A seizure? In public? I'll deal with it. I'm not afraid, Jake."

Trudy's toughness pleased him. "You know what ... what I'd like to do?"

"What?" Trudy said.

"Do you know where that park is where they found me?"

"Yes. It's Cedar Brook State Park. Cassie told me about it."

"I'd like to go there. It irritates me that I can't help Campbell with this investigation more. Maybe if I went there, I could remem-ber something, or figure something out. Find some bit of evidence they haven't seen."

Trudy nodded. "We could do that." She looked at her watch. "It's just nine o'clock. We could easily go there and get back by twelve or one. Let's go, and let's take the dog."

20

*C*assie decided to hang out at her apartment on Sunday and work on her boat. She needed a break. Later, she would call the contacts she'd gathered at KidFest. For right now, she needed to relax.

It was a beautiful day, sunny and warm, with a light breeze. By midday it would be hot. Cassie got a bucket and some boatwash, a brush and some rags, and began scrubbing the boat down. The decks were dirty and the woodwork, which she had so carefully varnished, had collected a layer of grime. She scoured and polished, happy to be outside, happy to have the cool water splashing around. But despite her efforts to relax, thoughts of those photos and all the other struggles in her life just wouldn't go away. She knew she couldn't escape them forever. "Today, I just need a break," she said out loud.

"Hey, Cassie!"

Startled, Cassie looked up. There, forty feet offshore, was Rick Maxwell in his new catamaran.

"How in the world did you find me?" she asked when he pulled up to the dock.

"Dumb luck," he responded, grinning.

Cassie helped him tie off. The new catamaran was a beauty. Its twin white hulls gleamed in the bright sunshine. The aqua sail cover was new and fresh.

"Come on aboard," boomed Maxwell.

Cassie stepped over the lifeline and onto the glistening deck. "This is really nice, Rick."

"It's brand-new and made to my specs," he answered. "Let me show you around."

The cockpit included a raised helm with an instrument panel and a shiny chrome wheel. Davits held a dinghy in the back. Stepping into the salon, Cassie was impressed by the arching window. What a view! And the table would easily seat six. Back to the right was a small galley, which looked clean and efficient.

"Step down!" Rick said. He led her to the right pod, where the master stateroom took up the aft quarter. It had a beautiful teak standing locker for clothes and sliding-door bookshelf-type cabinets above the queen-sized bed. The bed was made up with brightly colored sheets and a nautical comforter, which Cassie guessed came with the boat. Rick wasn't that décor-conscious, she didn't think.

"Come look at this," said Rick. The main head, shiny and clean, was in the forward part of the pod. It included a toilet and a separate, enclosed shower, an expensive luxury for a sailboat, and Cassie was very impressed. "This is really built for comfort," she remarked.

"That was the point. I'm going to live aboard. But," he said, smiling, "I'm not as intrepid as you are. I need my little luxuries." He led her to the other pod, which had two more cabins and a small head, plus plenty of storage closets.

"It's really nice, Rick," Cassie said as she returned to the cockpit. "Really very nice."

"I just took delivery on her." He bowed gallantly. "How about a little spin?"

She hesitated. Could she afford the time? "How long are you going to be out?"

"An hour or two."

"Okay, I'm ready. Just let me take care of the hose."

Cassie retreated to shore and turned off the spigot. Then she put the hose back where it belonged, and climbed aboard Rick's cat. "What do we need to do before we cast off?"

"Just that," he said. "Just release the lines. Why don't you get the bow, and I'll take care of the stern, here." He restarted the engines. Cassie walked forward and slipped the bowline off the cleat at the pier. She gave the piling a push and Rick turned the boat toward the channel leading to the Bay.

As soon as they cleared the channel and were in open water, Cassie felt the familiar calm she always experienced on the water. She was at home there, at peace, and she could almost forget the world. Overhead, some gulls screeched. They passed a fish trap, a V-shaped line of poles sticking up out of the Bay, with netting strung in between, and sitting on the poles were multitudes of fish-eating birds: herons, gulls, and especially pelicans, waiting to snare their dinner from someone else's efforts.

"Just watch for crab pots," Rick yelled, and Cassie acknowledged his request with a nod.

As they gained speed, Cassie noted the different feel of the boat. It was much more choppy than a traditional monohull sailboat. The waves caught each pontoon separately and a rock-and-roll movement was the effect. She wasn't sure she liked it.

Rick cut the engine to idle. "Let's raise the main," he said. Together they removed the sail cover, and then he put several turns of the main halyard around the winch and hauled the sail up to the top of the tall mast. He was sweating profusely by the time he was done. He smiled at Cassie when he was finished. "Maybe I should have ordered electric winches," he said.

Cassie settled back in the seat and watched him. He had been a football player and track star in high school. All the girls at one point or another had a crush on him, but he never settled on any of them for long. "Use 'em and lose 'em" was his motto, according to another classmate. It was weird spending time with someone she had known since they were that young. She wondered what he was really like. Despite all their conversations, she felt like she barely knew him now.

She tried to look at him objectively. Cassie guessed that some women would find him attractive. His money would make him even more so. He'd been in three separate, serious relationships since college, he'd told her ... but no marriage.

The wind was barely filling the sail, but Maxwell cut the engine to see if they could move without it. Since it was Sunday, the Bay was dotted with pleasure boaters—fishermen and sailors, yachtsmen, and trawler owners. Cassie sat on the back of the cockpit seat. She'd kicked her boat shoes off and was now barefoot.

"Nice boat," Cassie remarked.

"Yes, I like her."

"It feels funny, though, not to heel over."

"After a while you get used to that. And the cat design gives you so much more room! You know, I'm almost thankful for that fire. I like this boat so much better." Rick stepped into the salon. "Can I get you a drink? A soda? Tea? Water? Beer?"

"Water would be great."

Maxwell emerged seconds later and handed her a chilled bottle of water. Ahead, the crew of a huge, dark-hulled boat with a gigantic shamrock on its sail was pulling in the main. "Say, Rick," Cassie said, "what have you heard about the marina fire?"

His eyes narrowed, only slightly, but Cassie caught the change. He took a deep breath. "I am convinced that it was carelessness or an accident of some kind. With that half-wit dockhand and a bunch of idiot powerboaters running around, anything could have happened. Anything."

Cassie nodded. "So you're not buying the arson scenario."

"Never. Show me the accelerant. Show me the motive. Show me the opportunity. The fire began in broad daylight. No one saw anyone unusual around. It was not arson. I'm convinced of that. It started on the *Lady J.* and Scrub had just moved it over by the lift so they could work on it. Do you know why they were going to work on it?"

Cassie shook her head.

"The idiot that owns it was trying to install a 120-volt power inverter by himself. He didn't have all the wires terminated. My guess is, they sparked and started the fire."

"So you think the *Lady J's* owner was responsible, not Scrub?"

Rick shrugged. "I don't know. Anything's possible. Scrub's so stupid, he could have started it as well."

Cassie let the topic drop. Obviously, he didn't know what she knew, that the fires were started when propane in the bilge ignited. That Scrub was a suspect. "Hey, Rick," she said, "tell me about your stint in the Army. My dad said you were stationed in the Middle East. Is that right?"

He smiled strangely. "I could tell you, but then I'd have to kill you."

It was an old joke. Cassie just didn't find it very funny.

Rick perched on the helmsman's chair. He had the boat on autopilot and since they were moving at only three knots, he could chat and not have to focus on steering. "I spent several years there in Saudi Arabia."

Saudi Arabia? Her dad had said it was Qatar. Either she misunderstood him or he'd gotten it wrong.

"It was an interesting culture, one you'd hate," said Maxwell. "Women are treated like property, Christians are persecuted ... not a friendly place for a person like you."

"And for you?"

Richard shrugged. "I'm a man. It was no big deal. There was plenty of liquor; you just had to hide it in the orange juice. The bazaars were interesting, the food plentiful. And I don't think I'll ever get that call of the muezzin for prayer out of my mind. It was eerie and beautiful all at the same time."

They were barely moving now, the wind having died to practically nothing. So they dropped the mainsail and just motored, enjoying the sun and the conversation. Two hours later, it was time to head back. And Cassie felt relaxed for the first time in weeks.

Jake and Trudy stepped out of the car and walked toward the pavilion at Cedar Brook State Park. "I don't know exactly where they found you," Trudy said, "but it was somewhere near that drainage ditch."

Jazz bounded out of the car. The park was surprisingly empty, except for a few people playing Frisbee, so Trudy just let her run off leash.

The day was hot and still. The sun was nearly overhead and Jake shaded his eyes as he stared toward the ditch. Trudy followed right behind him while Jazz ran around, her head to the ground, sniffing.

"I remember Cassie talking about crossing the ditch and running through tall grass. I think she said you were just beyond it."

Jake squinted in the bright sunlight, straining to remember anything, anything at all. Nothing about the place looked familiar. On either side of the drainage ditch there was a ten-foot wide stand of tall grass. Jake walked to the edge of that stand on the near side. Across the ditch he could see a tall hedge. Cassie had mentioned something about that.

"You know, it's a miracle you survived," Trudy said, standing at his elbow.

"How so?"

"You should have bled to death. That one wound was so deep."

Jake stared down at his right hand. The scars from the defensive wounds on his hands were ugly, those from the stab wounds on his shoulder were worse.

"Somehow you managed to roll onto your shoulder and compress the wound yourself. It's just a miracle, Jake. A miracle."

He grimaced. "I was lucky."

Jazz was running through the tall grass sniffing and exploring. Jake fell silent, searching his memory. He walked up and down, looking for tire treads, for anything.

Nothing jogged his memory. Jazz emerged from the weeds with a tennis ball in her mouth, and she dropped it at his feet. "Where did you find that, girl?" he asked her. Then he picked it up and threw it.

Jazz chased the ball as Jake threw it over and over. Soon she was panting in the heat, her tongue dripping. "One more time," Jake said as he picked up the ball again. As he did, he touched the ground, and as his hand came near his face, he smelled earth and weeds. "Wait a minute."

Jake dropped and laid his cheek on the ground. Inhaling deeply, he closed his eyes. The smell of the earth and the marshy ditch nearby filled his nose. Jazz came up and nudged him. "Just a minute," he said, as if she could understand. He closed his eyes and let the smell carry him back. There was something ... if only he could remember.

But he couldn't.

"Ready to go?" Trudy asked softly as Jake stood up and dusted off his hands.

"Yeah." Jake took one more look around and together they walked back to the car.

A traffic jam on Route 50 east made the trip back home long and tedious. Jake leaned his head back as he sat in the passenger seat of the car. Jazz lay panting on the back seat. "Thanks for taking me there," he said, glancing over at Trudy.

"You're welcome," she responded. "What exactly are you trying to remember?"

"Anything. Anything at all." Jake shifted in his seat. He was disappointed he hadn't had a breakthrough. The headache, which had been threatening him all day, had arrived, pummeling him. He felt tired and agitated, all at the same time, and he found himself staring at the occupants of every car and truck on the road. What was he looking for? "Trudy, I've got a question for you," he said.

"What's that?" She glanced in her outside rearview mirror, put on her blinker, and moved left.

"You believe in God and yet your husband spent twenty years lying in a bed, paralyzed. Mike believed in God, but he dies at age thirty-two. I don't get that. How can you believe in God when stuff like that happens?"

She glanced at him. "What do you expect? That simply believing in God is some kind of magic shield? That nothing bad will ever happen to Christians?"

Jake sighed. That would be too simplistic. Even he could see that. "I don't know. I think sometimes about babies who die and the ones who are abused. I don't understand why God would let that stuff happen. Natural disasters, crippling diseases, even 9/11 ... why all the suffering?"

"You're asking some difficult questions, Jake."

"You know Mike was a smart guy. He always used to say to me, 'Jake, everything happens for a reason. There are no coincidences.' Mike understood this somehow." Jake drummed his thumb on his leg. "But I never asked him to explain it. There's got to be an answer; I just don't know what it is." Jake turned toward her. "You know, I was looking around your house for something to read. I couldn't even find a *Newsweek*, much less *Sports Illustrated*."

Trudy laughed. "Sorry!"

"So I start reading what's there ..."

"Like the Bible?"

"Well, yeah, some." Six months ago he would have read the phone book twice over before he'd pick up a Bible. But something about the physical frustration he was dealing with, the sorrow he felt over his kids, losing Mike ... these things had made him start to look for something else ... something that would help make sense of things.

"So what did you think?" Trudy prompted.

"A lot of what I read was not what I expected. I always thought Jesus was this wimpy, 'I love everybody' kind of guy. Way too passive and weak. But from what I read, when he was talking to some people, he could be tough. Angry even. And I have to admit, I liked that."

Trudy smiled.

"But I don't know, you tell me—if God is love, how could he let your husband suffer like that? And you? When you know darn well he could fix it?"

Trudy brushed her hair back from her face. Jake saw a tear glistening in her eye. "I'm ... I'm sorry," he said quickly. "I shouldn't have ..."

"No, no. It's okay. It was, as they say, a severe mercy." She took a deep breath. "When Wes first got sick I was so angry with God. I was furious." Trudy glanced toward Jake. "Does that surprise you?"

"A little."

"Instead of praying, I yelled at him. I asked him just that question over and over, 'How could you let this happen?' I cried, I prayed, I begged, I bargained. That went on for two years."

Jake tried to picture Trudy that angry. Somehow he could, if he thought of Cassie. The thought made him smile.

"For two years I fought with God over my husband. I lost my appetite, my hair began to turn gray. And then one day, in desperation, I pulled out my Bible, and I just started reading. I read and read and five days later, I surrendered. God was God, I decided. All through the Bible, it was clear. God was sovereign, in charge. He had allowed this illness to take place. Yet he was clearly good. I had to trust him. I decided I would find a way to make the best of the situation and worship him despite it."

Jake's jaw muscles were tight. He stared straight ahead, not daring to voice what he was thinking.

"Then I decided to look for him *in* that terrible circumstance. And that has made all the difference. The world you're looking for, Jake, the one where goodness is rewarded and disease and trauma don't affect the innocent—that's not this world. That world comes later. Sometimes God does warn us—with his still, small voice, and more often than we realize, he protects us when we don't even know we are in danger. But this world is full of sin and disease, unfairness and loss. Jesus said himself, 'In this world you will have trouble. But take heart! I have overcome the world.' Even in the midst of horrible circumstances, we can still find joy—and hope. The only real question is, will you surrender to him or fight him?"

Jake rubbed his hand on his pants leg. He was sweating.

"He loves you, Jake, and he's reaching out to you. Look at the people he's surrounded you with!"

That was true. Mike, Cassie, Craig, now Trudy ... the people he respected most shared a deep faith. "Yeah," he said, "they're Christians, but I try not to hold that against them."

Trudy laughed. She pulled up to the toll plaza at the entrance to the Bay Bridge and paid the toll, then she looked at Jake. "You know, there's only one way to get across this bridge, and there's only one way to get to heaven, to that world you want so much to see. Your toll has been paid, but you have to accept the ride, Jake. That's up to you."

As they climbed the arch of the bridge, Jake looked down on the Bay, dotted with boats. "That just strikes me as too ... exclusive. Almost arrogant. No offense." He looked at her quickly.

"I'm just repeating what Jesus said: 'I am the way, the truth, and the life. No one comes to the Father except through me.'"

Jake fell silent. In some ways, he wanted to believe. Fact was, he just didn't.

21

Monday morning, bright and early, Cassie pulled up in front of On the Bean, parked, and entered the shop. With its bright yellow walls and deep red chair cushions the place itself looked caffeinated. It had quickly become a favorite stop for her in the morning or after work. Mike had always teased her about her coffee "addiction," and for a while she had cut it out. But now she was back "on the bean" as Mike had jokingly called it. The name of the shop was a painful irony.

Craig was already there sipping a Grande Kenya black at a table near the back. Cassie walked up to the counter, ordered an almond croissant and a tall Sumatra. She joined him at the table. "You're not eating anything?" she asked.

"No," he said, "I had a bite at home." Then, after a few more pleasantries, he began asking questions.

She was hesitant at first, but the thought of Yellow Shirt and the blue headlights made her open up. She began telling Craig everything: about her conversation with Skip and her contacts with Desiree and Schneider's wife.

"How did you get to them?" he asked.

"Through Tam."

Then she took a deep breath and told Craig about the car with the headlights, the photos of Yellow Shirt, and how she was undoubtedly being followed at KidFest, too.

"And Tam knew where you were going on Saturday."

Cassie mulled that one over. Could Tam be involved? She picked up her cup and took a drink. The coffee was strong, just the way she liked it. What should she say? Could Tam really be involved?

Noting her hesitation, Craig said, "Don't worry about that right now. Tell me what you found out from Schneider's wife and mistress."

"I had to do quite a bit of talking, but finally both women agreed to see me. I think the cops scared them. I don't think either woman had anything to do with any of this. The mistress said she overheard the guy having an argument with another man, someone she didn't know, and the issue was money." Cassie played with a sugar packet that was on the table. "Craig, Frederick Schneider was terrible with money. He was deep in debt, overdrawn on his accounts ... the thing I can't figure out is where he came up with $80,000 to buy a new boat. His wife said he didn't have money for new socks. So where'd the boat come from? He paid cash for it a year ago."

"Cash? Then the broker should have reported that." Craig made a note. "We can press him if he didn't."

She took a long drink. "And there's another thing."

"What's that?"

"I went to Sullivan's Wharf and saw the place where Schneider's body was found. As I stood there looking around, I was over-whelmed with the similarity ..." She hesitated.

"To what?"

"The place where we found Jake."

Campbell's eyes grew intense. "What do you mean?"

"Tall grass, bugs, it was near the water ... when I was there, I just felt like I was in Cedar Brook Park where we found Jake. It was eerie."

Craig wrote that down.

"I also saw a boat surveyor I know there. We went to dinner. He's been helping the fire marshal investigate those boat arsons. They have a suspect."

"Who's that?"

Cassie took a deep breath. "Myron Tunney. Scrub. A dockhand."

She put her head in her hands. "I still can't believe it. He helped my dad raise my boat!"

"What do they have on him?"

She told him about Scrub's juvenile record, then shook her head. "I cannot believe it, Craig. I just can't believe it."

Craig got another round of coffee for both of them, and then asked more questions.

"I brought you some things," she said, and reaching into her attaché case, Cassie pulled out a copy of the CD with Yellow Shirt's photos on them and the Palm Pilot, and she explained to him what they were.

Craig raised his eyebrows. "How'd you get this?" he asked, indicating the PDA.

"From Desiree. Here's the passcode," Cassie said, writing it down on a scrap of paper and handing it to him.

"Okay, thanks," he said, taking a deep breath. He leveled his eyes at Cassie. "Are you ready to back out of this now? Leave it to the Bureau? I mean, you've got somebody following you, at least one person. How about letting us take this?"

Cassie hesitated. What could she say? She couldn't make that promise.

"I figured," he said, reading her thoughts and shaking his head. Then he leaned close. "Look, Cassie, I called headquarters the other day, and I tried to pull some strings to get your reinstatement through quicker."

Cassie brightened. "Thank you!" Wow, that was unexpected. Craig, going to bat for her?

"I know you're going after this guy, whoever he is, and frankly I'd rather have you doing it with a badge and a gun. I don't have any idea if it did any good, but I gave it a shot."

"I appreciate that!"

He closed his notebook and put it in his pocket. "In the meantime, please watch your back. Be careful. Please."

"I will." Cassie then asked him some questions about the FBI's

investigation of both Mike's death and Jake's assault. He gave her
guarded but clear answers.

"Fact is," he said, summarizing, "I'm not the case agent.
DiCarlo is. Foster's so mad at me he's ordered me to stay off the
case."

Cassie looked at him in amazement.

"So, I'm bootlegging just like you are."

"Really?"

"Yep. Working this on the side."

That impressed her. "I'm glad you are, Craig."

"I had to," he said, standing up. "It was the right thing to do."

Cassie had selected a festival in Scrub's hometown for her next
assignment, ostensibly just to expand her horizons a bit, but in reality she wanted to pick up anything she could on his history. She still
couldn't believe he was involved in arson, much less murder.

Rick had invited her out to dinner, and she'd said yes. Was it
because she was lonely? For two days, she'd thought about canceling.
But, one thing led to another and she'd never gotten around to it.

He said he was going to be in Annapolis, at Fawcett's near City
Dock, picking up some boat supplies. Cassie arranged to meet him at
a spot he suggested, Ceili, an Irish pub in Eastport. All the way there
she kept thinking about Jake. Her aunt said they noticed the dog was
sensing his seizures. Since Sunday, they'd been focusing on that, and
sure enough, Jazz would try to get Jake's attention moments before
an episode. If he caught her signals, he could make himself safe
before the attack came. And that was giving him a little more control,
and that was raising his spirits.

Cassie was skeptical. How could a dog predict seizures? But,
hey, if it made Jake happy, so be it.

Ceili was jammed when she walked in, full of men in Dockers
and boat shoes. Their eyes followed her as she moved past them and
she felt uncomfortable. A band was in the corner, playing traditional

Celtic music. A dark-haired young woman was fiddling for all she was worth, accompanied by guitarists and a drummer. The toe-tapping sounds filled the room.

Rick was sitting in a booth in a dark corner and rose as Cassie approached. "Good evening, my dear. Would you like a drink?" He had a beer sitting in front of him.

Cassie suddenly felt strange—what was she doing here with this guy? "Just water, please, with lemon."

But soon she forgot her discomfort. For the next two hours, the two reminisced about high school as they consumed salads and soda bread, Irish stew and shepherd's pie. Cassie discovered Rick knew a lot more about the current status of their old classmates than she did, and he was all too happy to tell her stories about them. She found out about the average guy who had surprisingly become an airline pilot, and the sweethearts who'd married and had three kids already, and the girl who'd become a lawyer.

Once she relaxed and started listening, she found she was actually intrigued by their stories, and by the end of the evening, she realized she'd temporarily forgotten her problems. At quarter 'til ten they left the restaurant. Rick walked her to her car, and she wondered momentarily if he was going to try to kiss her and what she would do about that.

He didn't. He just closed the door after she got in, waved goodbye, and walked back inside Ceili. He'd seen someone he knew on the way out, and he wanted to go talk to him.

Rain was predicted, so she wasn't surprised when, by the time she hit Route 2, the heavens opened. She flipped her wipers on high and leaned forward. In the dark it was really hard to see. Her windshield was smearing. She was always forgetting to clean it.

Focused as she was on the road ahead, Cassie was oblivious to what was behind her. When she sat back in her seat, however, a headlight blinded her. It was blue and it was misaligned.

Cassie's heart began to pound. Panicked, she fumbled for her cell phone, but it slid out of her grasp and onto the floor on the passenger side. Glancing quickly around, she realized they were the only two cars on the road. What should she do? Pulling over was not an option.

She decided to just keep driving. Gradually she increased her speed. The car behind her kept pace. She estimated it was about fifty yards behind her. The headlights were squarish ... she memorized the pattern.

Keeping one hand on the wheel she leaned over and tried again to reach her cell phone on the floor. She couldn't do it. Frustrated, she sat up and inadvertently jerked the wheel. The Cabrio swung back and forth momentarily, and adrenaline shot through her. She got it under control and glanced in the rearview mirror. The car was only twenty-five yards back.

The rains were coming harder now, hitting the windshield like pellets, drumming on the roof in a staccato barrage. Cassie's hands were sweating and her throat was closed up. "Please go away, please go away," she said, over and over. She tried to remember the road ahead. State Route 2 would wind all the way down to Solomon's. In no event was she going to exit anywhere near her home. Was there a state police barracks or a truck stop ahead? Yes, she remembered one. How many miles was that? She increased her speed. Maybe a cop would pull her over.

The car behind pulled a little closer. She strained but could not see what kind it was in the dark. When she refocused on the road ahead, she saw a small, leafy branch in the road. "No!" she yelled, and she held on tight as the little Cabrio rolled over it. The branch thumped and thudded under the car.

"Okay, okay, okay, stay calm," she told herself, but her hands were shaking and her knees were weak. And then she looked up. Straight ahead a deer was standing in the middle of the road, illuminated for a moment by lightning. "No!" she screamed. She instinctively pulled right. The Cabrio went on to the shoulder. Cassie hit the brakes, then she hit the accelerator again. The car skidded, fishtailing on the wet pavement. She fought for control. It pulled to the right and the right wheels dropped part of the way into a ditch. The car shuddered and shook and Cassie gripped the wheel. Bushes and weeds flapped against the windshield, while sticks and rocks rattled against the underbelly of the car.

As the Cabrio finally rolled to a stop, the car behind her whizzed by. Cassie looked up just in time to see a flash of lightning illuminate the passenger compartment. The driver was wearing a floppy light-colored hat.

Cassie's heart was in her throat.

Shaking, Cassie unbuckled, retrieved her cell phone and called the State Police. Her car was down in the ditch. She was in too deep and couldn't get out. Then, her mind churning, she called information, got the number for Ceili, called it, and asked for Rick. Maybe he could help her.

"Sorry, he's already left," the bartender said, shouting over the music. "You just missed him."

Cassie hung up her cell phone, locked her doors, and sat back to wait for the police.

"I ... I think it's okay. I just need a tow," she said to the trooper when he arrived. They were standing in the rain, looking at the little Cabrio.

"It was a deer, you say?" he asked her, shining his flashlight in her face.

"It was right in the road." She shivered involuntarily.

"Have you had anything to drink tonight, miss?"

"Yes. A tall mocha latte. And water with lemon."

He laughed. Fortunately. And then he returned to his cruiser and called a tow truck.

It took an hour to get the car out and by that time, the rains had slowed to a gentle sprinkle. Once it was back on the pavement, Cassie was happy to find the Cabrio was drivable. It was scratched up, but no major damage was done.

"You drive carefully now, miss," the trooper said, and Cassie waved good-bye with relief.

Later, when she got into bed, she pulled the covers up to her chin and stared into the blackness. When she closed her eyes, all she could see was a misaimed blue halogen headlight. Had the car tried to run her off the road? No, it was the deer, she kept reminding herself. She'd had to brake for a deer. But alone in the dark, fear began to play tricks with her mind. Was she run off the road? Or was it just an accident?

Wednesday morning Jake sat in the kitchen, lost in thought. The doctor's office had called. The tests had found a spot on Jake's brain, damage from the blow he'd taken, that might be causing his seizures. The doctor would like to talk to him right away about brain surgery.

Brain surgery? That was not something Jake wanted to talk about at all. No thank you ... the risks were too high. But what were the alternatives? Living like this for the rest of his life? Trying yet another medication?

Sighing, Jake pushed himself out of the chair. Trudy would be down in a minute. He had a short time to consider his options ... what should he do?

Stepping outside he threw the ball for Jazz over and over. Finally, she grew tired, and he sat down on the back step.

Panting hard, Jazz sat down in front of him. He scratched her ear with his left hand. "What do you think I should do?" he said. "Go for it?" Jake looked into her dark brown eyes as if there was an answer hidden there. Suddenly, he stopped petting her. He stood up. He broke into a sweat.

"Are you ready?" Trudy asked, stepping through the door.

"Trudy!" Jake responded, turning and grabbing her arms.

"What? Are you all right?"

"He was wearing boat shoes. Those brown boat shoes."

"Who, Jake?"

"The guy who hit me!" Jake paced away. He rubbed the back of his head. His heart was pounding. "He was wearing brown boat shoes, and on one of them the front eyelet was pulled out!" He looked at Trudy.

"That's wonderful, Jake! You remembered something! You need to tell Craig."

"You bet!" Impulsively he kissed her on the cheek. "I'll call him on the way to the doctor's."

"Mr. Tucker, what I am suggesting is this: we open the skull, excise this bit of tissue, and close."

"And I would be awake during the surgery?" Jake sat in Dr. Harrington's examining room, staring at films illuminated from behind by a bright white light. The films were of his head, and he could clearly see a dark area on his brain, at the impact point of his injury.

"Yes, you'd have to be awake, but you would feel no pain. It would take a couple of hours, and then we'd keep you for a few days while you recuperated."

"And ... what are the risks?"

"Any brain surgery is a high-risk procedure. If we go too far, you could lose some motor function. There's obviously the risk of infection. That's normal with any surgery."

Jake exhaled loudly. "I don't know, Doc."

Dr. Harrington sat down on the small, wheeled stool. "How often are you having seizures?"

"At least once a day."

"And, at worst?"

"Seven. I've had seven in one day."

"And is that the way you want to live?"

Jake rubbed the back of his neck. "It's not living. It's not living at all."

Oxford, Maryland—Scrub's hometown—was first designated a port of entry in 1683 and for many years rivaled Annapolis as a shipping center. Located on Town Creek off the Tred Avon River on the east side of the Bay, Oxford's commercial trade had begun with cordage and hemp and had graduated to tobacco, then oysters. As the oystering fell off, the town began to decline. These days tourism provided the biggest influx of cash, and the town was a quiet, picturesque escape from 21st-century life.

Cassie wanted to see the area by boat. It was quicker to cut across the Bay than to travel by car north to the Bay Bridge and then south to Oxford. And although she would not admit it, going by boat made it less likely she'd be followed.

Early in the morning she'd driven to her dad's house, pulled Mike's SUV out of the garage where it had been stored for the last six months, and put the Cabrio in its place. She didn't want to deal with the body damage right now.

The night before she had called in a favor from a friend and arranged to borrow his powerboat, a solid Grady-White fishing boat. This morning she had driven to a marina in Herring Bay, south of Annapolis, parked the SUV, picked up the boat, and headed out over the Chesapeake.

The day was already hot and still. Humidity hung heavy in the air, forming a gray haze. Dodging crab pots as she went, Cassie negotiated the channel and headed for the open water. Traveling at twenty knots in the powerboat was a lot different from moving at the four or five knots she could usually expect on her sailboat. The world seemed to fly by.

Up ahead, a pair of pelicans was diving for food. Pelicans had all but disappeared from the Bay after World War II. Scientists thought it was because the DDT they had ingested made their eggshells too thin, killing the babies. Now that DDT was outlawed, they were thriving in the region once again. Cassie looked ahead and watched the pterodactyl-like birds wheel and spin overhead. When they saw a fish, they'd drop headfirst into the water like they'd been shot. Cassie never got tired of watching them.

A line of bluefish just under the surface formed an arrow-like ridge in the still waters of the Bay. Just off to port, a sailboat sat, becalmed. Cassie waved as she went by. In the shipping channel a large cruise ship was headed north, back to Baltimore, which had become a new port for the industry with the construction of a large cruise terminal. Behind it, a gigantic cargo ship filled with container-ized freight churned on.

Cassie's plan was simple. She had told Len she would not be in tomorrow. Instead, she would spend the night at a bed and breakfast in Oxford, preparing for this week's festival. When he'd protested the expense, she'd waved him off, saying she was paying for it and she just needed a change of scene.

He'd bought it. In reality, Cassie expected it would take very lit-tle time to explore little Oxford. The rest of the time she would spend poking around, searching for answers to the question: could Scrub be a serial arsonist?

Cassie flew south, past Thomas Point Light and then Bloody Point. Then the leaning lighthouse, Sharps Island Light, came into view, and she rounded the lower end of Tilghman Island and headed into the mouth of the great Choptank River. She waved to a few fish-ermen and several crabbers in their low-slung workboats and fol-lowed the channel markers up the Choptank. How different it was not to have to think about depth or wind direction in the shallow-draft powerboat. It almost made things too easy. Traversing the Bay in the Grady-White had taken an hour. In her sailboat it would have been a half-day trip.

There were three major tributaries of the Choptank on the north side, before the Tred Avon River. She decided to explore the first one, Harris Creek, before proceeding to Oxford. It was not yet noon, she wasn't starving, and the weather was good. She turned north, up the broad, sparsely populated waterway. The wind on her face was refreshing, and the smell of salt comforting. *This is my element*, Cass thought.

A few houses were beginning to be built in the Harris Creek area. The whole Bay area was becoming popular, especially as a retirement location. Off to starboard a contemporary home with huge windows facing the water sat on a cliff. Down below, at water's edge, was a dock with a sailboat tied up and a small boathouse with a ski boat on a lift.

A "creek" in Bay country was no little waterway. As wide as many rivers and deep enough to accommodate good-sized boats, Harris Creek ran along the east side of Tilghman Island, a traditional waterman's community. It offered shelter from the Bay when the Chesapeake became stirred up by storms. Near the north end of the creek it broke into two branches. As she neared the fork, Cass slowed the engine down even more. When she hit a dead end, she reversed course.

She made her way back down the creek, diverting into Cummings Creek, and Briary Cove, Waterhole Cove, and Dun Cove, a favorite anchorage for sailors. Then she turned east again, toward Oxford, the laughing gulls overhead offering commentary on her journey.

Cassie pulled into the marina at Oxford. Stopping first at the fuel dock, she filled the tanks, grimacing as she did so. The sailboat took, at most, $10 worth of diesel. She could run all day on that. Powerboats in contrast were gas hogs, or "stink-pots" in Chesapeake Bay vernacular. Shelling out $150 for fuel was not Cassie's idea of a good time.

Cassie secured the boat, grabbed her backpack, and headed for the bed and breakfast, the Sally Johnston Inn, which was within walking distance. The inn was operated by two sisters. Catherine and Emily, both now well into their sixties, had been in business for ten years since Emily's husband died. It was a place she'd always wanted to visit with Mike, and she'd called and made reservations there for herself.

The Inn was a turreted Victorian house, painted blue with white gingerbread trim. The walk up to the spacious front porch was lined with perky petunias. Two planters stood near the front steps, filled with red geraniums and trailing ivy. Cassie walked up the steps, opened the front door, and walked in.

When the screened door closed behind her, Cassie felt like she'd entered a different world. A glossy dark staircase led upstairs. To the left was a room with a medallion sofa, marble-topped walnut tables, and an oriental rug on the floor. Soft music played in the background and a rose-scented candle filled the air with a heavy, sweet fragrance.

Catherine greeted her at the door. "Welcome, dear. We're so glad to have you!"

"Thank you," Cassie said. "I'm glad I finally made it."

Catherine showed her to her room, a large, airy bedroom with a queen-sized pineapple bed and a large wardrobe. Challis curtains covered the windows, two of which looked out on the water, and a comfortable rocker sat in the corner.

"This is nice," said Cassie, "very nice."

"You make yourself at home. The bath is in there." Catherine pointed to a door within the room. "We serve breakfast at seven-thirty. But anytime you're hungry, you just come down to the kitchen and we'll find you something, honey."

"Thanks, thanks very much."

As soon as Catherine left, Cassie undressed and showered, then lay down on the bed for just a moment. She fell asleep, which shouldn't have surprised her, but she was annoyed when she woke up and discovered it was nearly dinnertime and she'd wasted several hours. Irritated with herself, she slipped on a summery dress and sandals, fixed her hair and makeup and sprayed on a bit of perfume. Then she left the B&B and walked to Hilda's, a restaurant at water's edge, for dinner.

It was hard eating alone. She ordered crab cakes and Cobb salad, which were very good, but she had a difficult time enjoying them. Mike should be here. Mike should be sitting across from her eating steak, smiling and laughing.

Cassie tried to refocus her thoughts, concentrating on the conversations around her. Somebody's granddaughter was headed off for college. There hadn't been a summer like this in years for tomatoes. The Baptists never did know how to put on a strawberry festival.

Life goes on, thought Cassie, *even when marinas are being burned and people are being killed.*

"Excuse me, miss." The waiter was a young man in his twenties. "That gentleman over there—" he nodded toward a slim dark-haired man in his forties wearing a dark blue suit, "—was wondering if you would like some company."

Cassie froze. "No, tell him, thank you, but no."

She watched the waiter go back to the man, who nodded and lifted his drink toward her. Cassie looked away. She paid her bill and walked back to the B&B, tired and discouraged. How was she going to find out about Scrub? The shops were all closed, no one was around. How much time could she spend in the morning? "All day, if I have to," she muttered out loud.

The evening was still steamy and there was heat lightning in the distance. The two sisters were sitting on the front porch as she walked up, and they invited her to sit with them.

She accepted, and Emily insisted on getting her a glass of cold lemonade. The crickets were chirping in the grass as twilight yielded to night. The old ash rockers on the porch were comfortable. Citronella candles in clay pots kept the mosquitoes away. Soon Cassie found herself engaging in small talk with the two older women. What did people do in Oxford for fun? Did they grow up here? What was the job situation like?

They, in turn, managed to extract from Cassie the fact that her husband had died and that she'd grown up near Easton. She told them she was worried about a friend who'd been hurt, and about her job with the newspaper, which they thought was very glamorous.

"So, you'll be back down for the Heritage Festival?" Catherine asked.

"Yes, but just for the day. I'm coming with a photographer to cover it."

"Well that's just wonderful, honey. You be sure to stop by and say hello."

Cassie smiled. "I will." She smoothed her dress. "Say, a guy I know is from around here somewhere. His name is Myron Tunney, but everyone calls him Scrub. He helped me fix my sailboat. Either of you ever hear of him?"

Catherine and Emily looked at each other. "Oh, yes, we know the Tunneys," said Emily, leaning forward, "but the one that knows them best is our brother, Billy Thompson."

"Any chance I could talk to Billy?"

"He should be 'round for breakfast in the morning. Seven-thirty, he'll be here," Emily promised. "You can't find a better man than our brother. The only thing is ... if you want him to talk, you have to get him out on the water. Only thing that loosens his tongue is boats."

"He's a waterman?"

Catherine nodded. "Crabber. Fisherman, too."

"Would he take me on one of his runs?" She could get some good story ideas from a trip like that.

Emily giggled. "Most likely."

"I'll look forward to meeting him," Cassie said, and she excused herself, went upstairs, and climbed into bed, tired and not just a little lonely.

And, as had become her habit, Cassie took the extra pillow, and held it close to her chest until she fell asleep. It was a poor substitute for Mike. But it was all she had.

Billy Thompson was a waterman, born and bred. Perpetually sunburned, his large hands bore testimony to years of hard work, pulling crab pots and nets full of fish up from the waters of the Bay.

His face was broad and open and his forehead was covered by a shock of white hair. His eyes were bright blue, like the sky and the sea on a perfect summer day.

He sat across from Cassie, devouring a tall stack of pancakes drowning in syrup. "I know'd there was something afoot when I heard about them fires." Billy took a large gulp of coffee, which he drank black.

"So what do you think happened?" Cass asked. On her plate was an elegant breakfast of crepes and fruit. Billy had laughed when she chose that. "But then, you is a girl," he had said, his eyes crinkling in amusement.

"My guess is," Billy said, "a boy mad at the company done it. Either that or—" he leaned close to Cass, "—somebody was looking for insurance money."

She nodded and cut a slice of Eastern Shore melon with her fork. It was tender and sweet. "I'm coming over to do a story on the Heritage Festival. It would add a lot if I could include some first-person information on crabbing. Your sisters said maybe you'd let me go out with you."

Billy laughed uproariously, a big belly laugh that made everyone in the B&B turn around to look. "Lord, my wife would kill me! She'd cut me up and use me for chum, yes she would!" He shook his head, still laughing. Then he noticed she was staring at him intently. "You's serious 'bout this, ain't ya?" Billy sat back, hooked a thumb in his belt, and studied her.

"Yes, sir. And I'll speak to your wife if you'd like. I just think it would make a great story."

"Aw, she don't care if I take ye," he said, laughing. "Tell you what. You get Miss Catherine to make us up some of them ham 'n' onion sandwiches I like, and I'll take ya along. I'll show ya them crabs."

"Deal," said Cassie.

"Meet me at the marina in half an hour. Slip 42." Billy winked at her. "An' don't forget them sandwiches."

22

*E*verybody at the marina knew Billy Thompson, that was clear. Cassie could hear Billy's boisterous laugh as she walked down to the slip. As she drew closer, she could hear the friendly calls and shouts of others. "Yessiree, you all are my witnesses," he said. He raised his hand like a preacher blessing a crowd. "This here young lady wants to go out with me and I could not resist, so help me God. So, here I go. And if my wife asks, tell her I've gone to church, okay?"

The other folks at the marina laughed. She waved as she approached and dropped her backpack and the small cooler Catherine and Emily had given her into the boat. Billy started the engine, cast off the lines, and then they were off, edging out of Town Creek and into the Tred Avon River, the wind in their faces, leaving a trail of white wake behind them.

By the time the sun was high and hot, Cassie and Billy had pulled fifty-two crab pots, dumping their contents into the hold of the low, beamy boat, and then replacing them in the water. Billy had showed her the place he once bagged six canvasback ducks, the location of a wrecked airplane, the place he liked to bring kids crabbing, and the marsh where once he found a dead turtle whose shell was five feet in diameter.

He was a wealth of knowledge. "D'ya know why they call it Bloody Point?" he asked her, wiping his brow.

"Because of the slaves?"

"Nah. That's just a story. Back in the day when skipjacks was the way to get oysters it was hard findin' crew. Ya had to go out in October and November. It gets mighty cold out on the water then. Them skipjack cap'ns, they'd sail up to Bal'mer, and go in the bars and get some of them fellas drunk. Then they'd Shanghai 'em, and put 'em on their boats. Weren't nothin' for them boys to do then but work 'til the oysters were in.

"The rule was the catch got divided up between the cap'n and crew. Now, it don't take much figurin' to realize the fewer the divide, the better, so when the hold was full and they's on their way back to Annapolis or Bal'mer, often as not them boats would take a bad gust o' wind 'round Bloody Point. They'd jibe, and that big sail and the low boom would come across the deck, and sure 'nough, some o' them fellas would get swept right into the Bay."

Cassie's eyes were wide. "You have got to be kidding. They'd just knock them into the water?"

"You bet they would. Them skipjacks got them 'deck-sweeping booms.'" Cap'n Billy grinned at her. "But don't you worry, little lady. You's too pretty to toss overboard."

She laughed. "Thanks. Thanks a lot."

After the last crab pot had been emptied and reset, Cassie finally asked him about Scrub. Billy wiped his brow and squinted off into the distance, and for a minute, she wasn't sure he was going to answer. But then he set the boat's engine on idle and pulled out a ham and onion sandwich, sat down on an upturned bucket, and began to talk.

"Scrub's daddy," he began, "was a friend of mine. We played football in high school and joined the Navy at the same time. We fished together, crabbed together, chased women together, and got drunk together.

"Then we settled down, got married. And it took with me ... for all my jokin' my wife is the best thing about my life. But Scrub's daddy, Frank, he, I don't know, he just never could make the switch.

"He started cheatin' on his wife before the weddin' cake was set up. One woman after another. It near to drove his wife, Betty, crazy.

Then the baby come along. They called him Myron, but everyone called him Scrub. He was a little guy from the beginnin'—only half the size of his daddy."

Billy took another bite of his sandwich. "Frank laid off the women for a time, but then, when the boy was thirteen or fourteen, he started in again. The boy, he'd see him with these other women around town, in the boathouse, goin' into bars. And he'd see his momma cryin' and cryin'. Then one night, when Scrub was sixteen and he'd just gotten his driver's license, his momma got sick, and Scrub had to take her to the hospital in Salisbury 'cause nobody knew where his daddy was. Scrub came home, then, and he found his daddy drunk with some floozy right in the house, right in the very bed his parents slept in, with his momma's nightgown on the bedpost. And Scrub jus' lost it. He started swingin' a baseball bat, breakin' everythin' in sight. He was headed right for the bed, right for his daddy. Ol' Frank, he managed to get up and run, and the woman did, too, but Scrub, he took a swing at his daddy and missed ... hittin' an oil lamp they had lit on the night table. That started a fire and the next thing you know, the whole house burned down."

Cassie listened, transfixed. "What happened then?"

Billy shook his head. "The woman, she took off. By the time the sheriff and the fire trucks got there, it was just Frank yellin' that his crazy, stupid son had done set the house afire on purpose. Next thing you know, poor Scrub, he was locked up in juvenile detention. Charged him with arson."

Arson! And that was why Scrub had said Schneider deserved to die: because he was having an affair, like Scrub's own, no-good father. That was it!

"There Scrub sat, in juvie, with his momma in the hospital dyin' of a burst appendix. They let him out for the funeral. Took him in shackles to the church." Billy wiped the corner of his eye and Cass realized it was a tear he was wiping away.

"And what happened to Frank?" she asked.

"He took off, to Bal'mer's what I heard. Got a job delivering stuff to grocery stores. I don't know. We just kind of gave up on him. Scrub, he left, too. But every once in a while, he calls me, and we talk, and I think the boy's doin' okay. From what I can tell, anyway."

The two sat in silence for a while.

Cassie cleared her throat. "I know Scrub."

Billy raised his eyebrows. "You do?"

She nodded and told him her relationship with him.

"Well, I'll be," Billy said, delighted. "You know, he was like the son I never had. He helped me crab from the time he was eight, ten years old. He got so good, I thought I had me a partner."

"He knows everything about boats, everything," Cassie said.

Billy beamed. "You tell that boy to get hisself back over here to see me. You tell him we love him, you hear?"

Cassie nodded, grinning. Billy stood up and started the engine, and in silence the two made their way back to Oxford.

"Don't forget my message," Billy said as Cassie stepped off the boat. She noted the suspicious moisture in his eyes and assured him she wouldn't.

All the way back across the Bay in the lightning fast Grady-White, Cassie kept thinking about Scrub and his childhood. And she just knew, somehow, he wasn't to blame for the marina fire. He'd put the Bay between his past and his present, and he wasn't going back there.

She was convinced. Scrub didn't do it. But who did?

By the time she got back to her apartment it was dark. A sliver of moon hung in the sky and stars glittered in the blackness. As she walked up the stairs to her apartment she thought again about how much she loved the water, and how peaceful it was living near it. She inserted her key in the lock and stepped inside her dark apartment.

Immediately she sensed something different—a heavy odor hung in the air. She sniffed again; she recognized the smell—it was Polo cologne.

Cassie froze and listened intently. She flipped on a light. The place looked empty. Without closing the door, she walked through quickly, peering into closets and under the bed. There was no one there. Puzzled, she shut the door. Why would her apartment smell like Polo?

23

*S*weat ran off Jake's brow and down his cheek and into his mouth. It tasted salty and good, like hard work or a great run. He swung the axe high and brought it down on the oak, watching with satisfaction as the log split in two pieces. He propped one of the pieces on end, split it again, and then repeated the process.

Jazz lay nearby, chewing on a stick. He had to admit, he felt better since he'd started picking up on her warnings about his seizures. Just getting thirty seconds advance notice was a huge help. It gave him a little more control.

But being dependent on a dog wasn't exactly the lifestyle he was looking for. He was hoping to have a slightly more significant job than cutting up wood. And driving! He so missed the independence of being able to drive!

At least he had remembered about the boat shoes. He'd passed that information on to Craig. A lot of people wore boat shoes, but Craig was going to start calling shoemakers around Annapolis to see if anyone had brought a pair in to have the eyelet fixed recently. It was something.

The tree lay nearly cut up at the back of Trudy's yard. He was about to begin taking the limbs off the top. She had told him where to make a stack of the small wood that would be useful for kindling. The rest would go in a pile to be burned.

Shirtless, he could feel the sun burning his back. He hoped the heat and the physical activity would take his mind off the future. He had two weeks before the surgery. His goal was to finish the tree.

"Jake, are you sure you'll be okay?" Trudy asked, emerging from the house a short time later. She had promised to help a friend. She'd only be gone two or three hours at the church, but she hated leaving Jake alone. He'd been having many seizures, and even though he was getting good at reading Jazz's warnings, he still was at risk.

"Go," Jake said. "I'll be fine."

"I'd feel better if you put that axe away."

"I'm just about to quit."

She looked at him apprehensively, but then handed him a slip of paper. "Here's the church number, and my cell phone number, and my friend's cell phone number."

Her excessive concern cracked Jake's shell. He stared at the paper and then grinned at her. "Yes, ma'am. Aren't you going to give me the number for 9-1-1?"

She laughed.

"You take your time," Jake said, and he gave her a quick hug and a peck on the cheek. "I'll be fine."

Trudy backed her car out of the driveway and took off. Jake turned back to the tree. He had been thinking about quitting for the day, but what would he do in the house? Sit around and think? That wasn't a good idea. He'd limb the tree, he decided, and create the burn pile, and then that would be it.

"I'm telling you, you will love Oxford," Cassie said. She was sitting in the passenger seat of a company car on Saturday morning. Brett was driving. It looked like it was going to be a beautiful day. They were headed for Oxford Heritage Days.

"Small towns, small minds, I say," Brett said, switching lanes to get around a slow pickup truck. "Give me Baltimore any day."

"You don't know what you're missing," Cassie said, and she settled back in her seat, and began going over her plan for the day.

The *Rebecca T. Ruark* was the centerpiece of the festival. Maryland's oldest skipjack, it had been used for dredging oysters under sail. Just a few years before, the boat had been caught in an unexpected, freak November storm at the mouth of the Choptank. Winds climbing to sixty knots had torn her sails, sheared off her boom, and then she began to take on water. With waves cresting over her bow, the skipjack finally went under and didn't come back up.

As the boat was floundering, the captain had called his wife on his cell phone. She, in turn, alerted other watermen, who managed to rescue the captain and the three crewmen. But the old boat lay submerged in twenty feet of water.

She was not finished, however. A group of people got together to try to save the historic vessel. Three days after she went down, the state of Maryland committed funds to bring her up. A couple of days after that, the *Rebecca T. Ruark* was once again afloat and was towed into port for repairs.

As Cassie stepped onto the broad deck of the old skipjack she felt a sense of kinship and nostalgia. Hard work had restored the *Rebecca T. Ruark.* She was now, again, a functional, beautiful boat, fitted for oystering and educational trips, cruises, and crabbing. The broad white deck seemed to stretch forever and the huge wooden rings that stretched the sail out along the boom were glossy. The small yawl boat on the davit at the rear of the skipjack had a fresh coat of paint.

"She's just like my boat," Cassie muttered under her breath.

"What?" Brett asked.

"Nothing. I was just thinking, you can't keep a good woman down."

The gleam in his eye revealed a sharp comeback, but before he could say it, the captain of the *Rebecca T. Ruark* yelled, "All hands cast off!" They left the dock for her thirty-minute cruise and the captain started talking about the Bay, and oysters, and the way things used to be. Both Cassie and Brett turned their attention to him.

Jake had created a good-sized pile of kindling and a mound of twigs ready to burn. Most importantly, he'd almost managed to avoid thinking for a while. And he hadn't had a seizure—in fact, he felt pretty good.

Satisfied with his work, he put the axe back in the shed and went inside. He poured himself a glass of lemonade from the refrigerator. As he stood in the kitchen drinking it, his eyes fell on a box of large kitchen matches on the back of the stove. It was supposed to rain later this afternoon. Why not just burn the branches now?

But what would Jazz do around the fire? Would she be safe? He didn't know enough about dogs to know. "You'd better stay here," he said to her, and he left her in the kitchen while he went back outside.

Jake found a gas can in the shed, sprinkled some gas on the pile, and threw a match on it. It ignited with a "whoosh" and he stood watching as the flames attacked the wood voraciously. Smoke curled upward and the smell of burning wood made Jake think of Boy Scout camp.

He'd been allowed to go one summer, just one, and then only because his mother begged his father to let him. He'd earned the money himself, cutting grass and washing cars. He was twelve years old and desperate to see someplace beyond the blue-collar neighborhood in Detroit where he lived.

He had been equally desperate to get out of his house. By then, his father had become a full-blown alcoholic, a drunk who picked fights with the neighbors and dominated Jake's mother. He had already decked Jake twice when he'd tried to intervene. The one thing Jake couldn't stand was seeing the fear in his mother's face when his father was bellowing at her, and he honestly wondered if he'd kill his dad before he was old enough to leave home.

A sappy piece of wood popped loudly, snapping Jake out of his reminiscing. He walked to the shed and retrieved a rake so he could keep the fire well-contained. As he raked the fire together, he began to think again. Jake guessed he'd gone into law enforcement because he wanted justice: he wanted his dad locked up and his mother happy. In reality, it hadn't quite worked out that way. His dad had died of a heart attack and his mom had a few years of peace before she died of breast cancer. And while Jake had worked quite a few successful cases in his career as an FBI agent, he had quickly learned that injustice was impossible to eradicate.

Losing his good friend was an example. Mike's death had hit Jake hard. Why did he have to die? And to think he was murdered made it even tougher to swallow. Who killed him, and why?

And then there was his divorce. Jake knew he could make it okay without a wife, but the kids, oh, how he missed the kids. How he wanted to be there for them every day, to be the kind of dad that he'd never had. And now ...

Stop, he told himself. *That trail is too painful to go down. Think about something else.*

And he tried concentrating on the Orioles and the upcoming NFL season, and then a movie he'd seen once, and then Cassie and what she was doing with her life. He was working so hard to keep from thinking about his kids that he didn't notice the metallic taste in his mouth, or the fact that his hand was curling around the rake, nor did he hear the sound of Jazz, barking furiously inside the kitchen door.

But then the darkness came, descending on him like a closing curtain, and once he realized it was coming, he fought it, but he couldn't prevail. His knees buckled. He dropped the rake and fell to the ground with a thud. And as he did, his left arm came to rest against a burning piece of wood.

It was the incessant barking that roused him. It was so loud! And the pain! There was unspeakable pain, but in the blackness, he couldn't see which way to move to get away from it. It was like being in a dark theater with all of the exit lights burned out. Which way should he go?

What hurt so much? When he could finally move, he pulled himself forward and rolled to the right. Then his vision began to clear and he was able to pull himself to his knees and then he realized it was his left arm that hurt so much. It felt like it was on fire! He looked. A long, deep, raw burn had branded his forearm. He curled his body over it, cursing, tears streaming down his face, his heart pounding. He had to get away from the pain. He lurched to his feet. He stumbled inside. What should he do? He couldn't remember first aid for a burn but he wanted relief and wanted it now, and he flipped on the cold water at the kitchen sink and stood there, his arm under the flow, Jazz dancing around his feet.

When Trudy came home she saw thin wisps of smoke rising from a pile of ashes in the backyard, and she was surprised Jake had decided to burn the pile. She thought he'd intended to wait. She parked the car and as she went up the back steps she saw the screen was pushed out, like Jazz had broken out. That was so unlike her! Trudy went inside. Jake was leaning over the kitchen sink, Jazz at his feet, and when he turned and she saw his face, she ran to him.

At the end of the day, sunburned and somewhat tired, Brett and Cassie left Oxford. Cassie had pages and pages of notes, and she leafed through them talking enthusiastically about the day while Brett drove. He suggested they stop for dinner and so they did, at a waterside seafood restaurant on Kent Island. Over a dinner of grilled tuna and Caesar salad, hot rolls and white wine, Cassie and Brett talked comfortably while the evening slipped away.

"We really need to get home," Cassie said, and Brett agreed. Leaving Kent Island, they drove over the Bay Bridge. The water beneath them was black, dotted here and there with the tiny running lights of an occasional boat. Cassie settled into her seat and leaned her head back. Soon her eyes were drifting shut as sleep overcame her. She never heard her cell phone ringing, and Brett didn't bother waking her up.

Jake refused to allow Trudy to take him to the hospital, but she got stubborn as well, insisting he at least go see her doctor. He finally consented, and the doctor told him he ought to go to the hospital because he probably needed a skin graft. But Jake's heels were dug in, so the doctor had settled for giving him a painkiller and an antibiotic to ward off infection. Jake was so angry he could barely speak to the man, and he had to stifle the impulse to run, run, run away from this pain and this life, and oh, man, it hurt so much....

It was almost eight by the time they got home. Trudy stayed up well into the night, saying she wanted to read for a while, but Jake knew it was to keep an eye on him.

Anger possessed him, a fierce anger and helplessness and the sort of despair that is both lightning hot and intensely black at the same time. He got up and walked quickly toward the backyard with Jazz at his heels, and as he did, he bumped his arm against the open door. A searing pain shot through his body and.he cursed over and over, his fury barely contained.

Standing on the back step, cradling his arm against his body, and trying to settle his breathing back down to normal, he heard a noise and Trudy was right behind him.

"Jake?" she said softly. "Are you all right?"

How was he supposed to respond to that? No, he was not all right. He was angry and frustrated and lonely and scared to death that he was going to lose the use of the only hand he had left. Not only that, he was furious, absolutely furious, that ... that he couldn't do the simplest thing—not even burn a pile of wood. His life had been taken away from him!

But he could not lay all those burdens on Trudy. He just couldn't. "I'm fine," he said, clearing his throat. "Just looking at the stars."

It was clear she didn't believe him. He felt so guilty for bringing all this into her life.

"I should never have left you," she said.

"You have a life!" he retorted. Jake looked up at her, and in the moonlight he saw tears were running down her face. She dabbed at them with a tissue. She looked so sad. And he made a decision then and there. He needed to leave. He just wasn't being fair to her.

It took another hour to convince Trudy to go to bed. Jake told her he was fine, his arm didn't hurt that much, it just looked bad, and he was getting tired. He smiled, swallowing the pain, and told her she could stay up all night if she wanted to but he was going to go to sleep. Then he went up to his room, where he sat on the bed, clenching and reclenching his fist, until he heard Trudy go into her bedroom. Finally he heard the click as she snapped out her light.

He waited another half hour, then crept down the stairs, avoiding steps five and three, the creaky ones. He stopped in the kitchen, got some ice from the refrigerator, and put it in a zippered plastic bag. The doctor had told him not to ice the burn but it hurt so much, he had to do something. He poured a glass of water, then went out into the sunroom, unsure of how he was going to get through the night between the pain in his arm and the pain in his heart.

He didn't want to leave Trudy's. There was something about her home and something about her that was like an oasis. When he thought about leaving, loneliness swept over him like a wave. The idea of going to live in a hotel room or an apartment made him feel sick.

Still he had to do it. He wasn't being fair to Trudy. Dropping his problems on her was stifling her very life and hurting her. Her sadness told him that.

He had to call Craig. He had to do it now.

There was a cordless phone in the kitchen. He retrieved it, and left a message on Craig's voice mail at work, forgetting that the next day was Sunday. Craig always checked it first thing in the morning. "Find me a place, Craig," he said. "I need to leave."

Now if he could just get through the night.

The windows in the sunroom were open. The air had become oppressive. The humidity had been building all day, and the promised thunderstorms, sure to bring some relief, had not materialized. He stood at the window, staring into the dark, inhaling the thick air. Off in the distance he could hear thunder. The gathering storm mimicked the one inside him.

Counting his losses, he stared at his right hand. Recently he'd begun to have more feeling in it, and that was good, but it was still useless. With no grip, it was almost worse than not having a hand at all. A hook would be an improvement.

And now his left arm. The burn was deep. The pain was still nearly unbearable. It would heal, but he would have a scar. Not a big deal. But burns were prone to infection and if he got one ...

The blackouts, now they were the biggest problem. Brain surgery was risky, but if he didn't have it, he could look forward to spending the rest of his life as a useless drain on people, unable to work, unable to drive, unable to walk around in public, unable to burn a pile of wood, for crying out loud.

And that, he couldn't take.

Jake sucked in a deep breath. He felt like there was a mountain inside his chest, something that was as heavy and oppressive as the air. Restless, he moved to the other side of the room. Unfortunately, the mountain moved with him, as it always did. He couldn't shake it. It was there as usual, weighing down his chest and stifling him.

He wished he knew who had assaulted him. He wished he had a name and a face to match up with the pain and the injury of it. The frustration of not knowing who had hit him, coupled with his inability to search for the perpetrator himself was like a threshing machine in his soul, constantly churning. And Mike ... had Mike been murdered? By the same guy?

Jazz looked at him expectantly. She dropped a ball at his feet. Jake patted her on the head. "It's the middle of the night," he whispered. "Not time to play ball."

The house was so quiet. Outside the sunroom, the night insects were chirping and from somewhere a lone dog barked. The sweet smell of the rose bushes right outside the window triggered bittersweet memories: his mother's funeral, his own wedding, a bouquet he'd bought for Tam in better days.

Jake turned away. His head was pounding and his jaw ached. He wanted something, but he didn't know what it was, some relief, some hope, some reason to keep living. If he couldn't work, and couldn't see his kids ...

Sensing the Pit opening behind him, he looked around for a distraction. His problems, his pain, his past, and the unknown future were overwhelming.

Jake sat down on the couch, and a groan escaped him. There was a book on the corner table, a book Trudy had left open. She must have been reading it before she went to bed. Of course it was a Bible. Desperate for distraction, Jake picked it up.

He began to read:

When they came to the other disciples, they saw a large crowd around them and the teachers of the law arguing with them. As soon as all the people saw Jesus, they were overwhelmed with wonder and ran to greet him.

"What are you arguing with them about?" he asked.

A man in the crowd answered, "Teacher, I brought you my son, who is possessed by a spirit that has robbed him of speech. Whenever it seizes him, it throws him to the ground. He foams at the mouth, gnashes his teeth, and becomes rigid. I asked your disciples to drive out the spirit, but they could not."

"O unbelieving generation," Jesus replied, "how long shall I stay with you? How long shall I put up with you? Bring the boy to me."

Jake stopped. His eyes were burning. The heaviness in his chest seemed to increase and he opened his mouth and took a deep breath. What was this? Whenever it "seized him"? Seizures? Back then?

Outside, lightning flashed, momentarily brightening the room. He continued reading.

So they brought him. When the spirit saw Jesus, it immediately threw the boy into a convulsion. He fell to the ground, and rolled around, foaming at the mouth.

Jesus asked the boy's father, "How long has he been like this?"

"From childhood," he answered. "It has often thrown him into fire or water to kill him. But if you can do anything, take pity on us and help us."

Jake slammed the Bible shut and stood up. He walked over to the windows. He realized he was sweating. He wiped his brow with his right arm and touched his chest. His heart felt like it was being squeezed. Lightning flashed again, briefly penetrating the darkness. Everything was illuminated for a moment: the trees, the yard, flowers, bushes ... then the darkness fell again.

The story was like a magnet, drawing him back across the room, but he resisted. He tried looking around for something else to do, started to leave the room ...

But he couldn't. He paced back over to where the book was and picked it up. A ribbon marker took him back to the right spot. His heart was racing. Why? He wanted to see, but he didn't want to see. He wanted to know, but something within him still resisted.

Jesus asked the boy's father, "How long has he been like this?"

"From childhood," he answered. "It has often thrown him into fire or water to kill him. But if you can do anything, take pity on us and help us."

"If you can?"' said Jesus. "Everything is possible for him who believes."

Immediately the boy's father exclaimed, "I do believe; help me overcome my unbelief."

A bead of sweat dripped off Jake's brow and onto the thin pages. *Help my unbelief. That's where I am,* he thought. *I want something. I need something bigger than this life and its problems. Something that makes sense. But I just don't believe.* He read on.

When Jesus saw that a crowd was running to the scene, he rebuked the evil spirit. "You deaf and mute spirit," he said, "I command you, come out of him and never enter him again."

The spirit shrieked, convulsed him violently, and came out. The boy looked so much like a corpse that many said, "He's dead." But Jesus took him by the hand and lifted him to his feet, and he stood up.

An involuntary cry escaped Jake's lips. He jumped to his feet. "Oh, Jesus! I wish I knew if this were true! Is this really true?" He took a deep breath. So many people believed. Mike. Trudy. Craig. Cassie, at least at one time. "If you're real," he whispered, "please help me. Please show me! Please. Oh, God!"

And then something collapsed within him and he fell face forward on the floor. Tears began to flow, and all of the frustration, all of the anger, all of the despair, all of the grief boiled up and spilled over.

"Jesus!" he cried out. The cover of the Bible was wet with his tears. "Jesus, if you could heal this kid then, you can heal me now! Oh, God, I can't live like this! I can't do it! Please, for my sake and the sake of my children, please Jesus, oh, please, please take these seizures away."

Jake lay on the floor, his tears flowing freely. He felt weak and incompetent, like a little child, at the end of his rope, broken. And then something happened. It began as a heat that started in his feet, and progressed up his legs, and then saturated his torso, and ran out through his arms, and then filled his head. And it was heat and light all at the same time, a warmth that he had never known before. His tears stopped, and he lay perfectly still.

And he knew in his heart, he was in the presence of God. No one had ever described to him what it felt like, but he knew God was there. He couldn't speak. He didn't want to. He felt incredibly calm, at peace. And there was something else ... pleasure, or joy ... he wasn't sure what to call it.

Jake just lay there, welcoming the heat, and he felt like he was being washed all the way through, inside out, from beginning to end. And after a while the sensation faded, yet he still lay there, wishing he could stay there forever, longing for more.

Finally, he raised his head. Jazz was lying on the floor six feet away, watching him intently, her head on her paws, her stub of a tail wagging madly, two tennis balls four inches from her nose.

And Jake Tucker laughed out loud.

24

When Trudy walked into the sunroom at half past seven, a bowl of cereal in her hand, she was surprised to see Jake stretched out on the couch, sound asleep, Jazz lying next to him on the floor.

She started to back out quietly, to avoid waking him up, but Jake opened his eyes. When he saw her, he smiled. "You are not going to believe this," he said, sitting up.

But she did.

Rick invited Cassie to go sailing again on Sunday, and she accepted, volunteering to bring lunch. They sailed north, toward Sandy Point, and then up toward the Sassafras River. Cassie toyed with the idea of talking to Rick about Schneider's murder, but she held back. Why ruin a beautiful day?

Maybe that was the same reason she ignored her cell phone message and her answering machine messages at her apartment. Maybe she just didn't want to ruin a beautiful day with whatever hassles those messages were bringing. Selfish? Maybe.

The cat slid cleanly through the water, picking up the sullen breeze more readily than a monohull would have. With as many dog days as the Chesapeake had in the summer, Cassie could understand why people might like the swifter, lighter catamarans.

It felt so good to be out in the sun and the air, so much better than being stuck in an office. Even when she was an agent, she'd gotten out as much as she could. There were many other boats out on the bay, white sails, red sails, gold Mylar sails reaching for the wind. An old joke asked, "What do you call two sailboats going the same direction?" The answer—"A race." And that was certainly true today. Cassie had to laugh. As the wind picked up, Rick's catamaran outran every sailboat that took them on, and she could tell he liked that.

Around lunchtime, they anchored in a cove and she pulled out the sandwiches and fruit she'd brought. They ate and talked and when they were done, they went for a swim. The water was so refreshing. When they had cooled off, they climbed aboard the cat again, and Rick raised the anchor and started the engine, eased out into the Bay and then raised the sail again. Soon they were skimming over the water with the wind in their faces.

At the end of the day, Rick suggested dinner at a local seafood place only the natives knew about, and Cassie agreed. They pulled up to the dock and tied off. Crabby's crabcakes were the best, the perfect ending to a day on the Bay.

On Monday, Cassie worked on her Oxford story, anxious to get it down while her impressions were still fresh. When the story was done she'd be free to call Craig and tell him what she'd learned about Scrub. So she worked hard and by the time she got around to listening to her messages and calling Trudy back, it was Monday evening. Cassie's heart dropped when she heard about Jake's burn. It struck her as curious that Trudy wasn't more concerned. Surely Jake was furious. Surely he needed some encouragement. Cassie told Aunt Trudy she'd be over the next afternoon, and Trudy said that was fine, Craig Campbell would be coming then, too.

When Cassie pulled up in Aunt Trudy's driveway, Craig's Bureau car was already there. It was half past four. It had taken her longer to fine-tune her Oxford story than she'd thought it would, and traffic was slow coming over the bridge.

Cassie walked in and yelled, "Hello!" and followed the sound of voices back to the kitchen.

The moment Cassie saw Jake she sensed something was different. She was expecting depression, pain, and more discouragement. But he was energized, like somebody had turned a switch on.

"Hey, girl!" he cried out, and he grabbed her in a bear hug. Over his shoulder, Cassie saw Aunt Trudy smiling and even Craig had a satisfied look on his face.

Cassie frowned slightly. "What's gotten into you?"

Jake just grinned. "Nothing."

"C'mon, what's going on?" Cassie looked from Jake to Trudy to Craig. Everyone was smiling. "Let me see that burn—for crying out loud, Jake," she said holding out his arm, "that's horrible."

"No, no, it's all right." Jake withdrew his arm and glanced at Trudy.

Cassie's heart was thumping. Something was up.

Then, standing in the kitchen, Jake told his story ... the anger, the doubt, the guilt, the Bible story, the despair, the crying out to God, and the response, everything that had happened to him. "It was unbelievable," he said. "Absolutely unreal."

There was silence in the room when he finished. Cassie's heart was beating loudly, like a war drum. Her head felt tight. She felt hot, then cold. "So you think that was God?" she asked abruptly.

"Something happened ... I don't know what. But yes, I think it was God. In fact, I know it was God. And here's the best part. I haven't had a seizure since. And I'm wondering if maybe I've been healed."

Cassie's heart twisted. "It's only been since—"

"Saturday night. Three days."

"So why would you think you'd been healed?" she demanded.

Jake shrugged. "I'm not sure, it's just ... no seizures. And I feel totally different."

"What about your hand?" She grabbed his arm. "Let me see your hand, Jake."

He pulled away. "Not the hand," he said softly. "The seizures, Cass. That's what I asked for."

Cassie opened her mouth to challenge him again but choked on her own rage. She started to turn away, then she turned back and, her anger exploding, she shoved Jake, hard, and cried out, "Why you?"

Shocked, he took a step back.

"Why you?" she screamed, and she burst into tears. "Do you have any idea how much we prayed for Mike?" Her voice grew louder, filling the kitchen and bouncing off the walls. There was no containing her rage. "Do you know how many hours people spent on their knees begging God to save Mike? Laying hands on him? Anointing him with oil? We trusted God! We believed God! But Mike died! He died! And you think you're healed? Why you? Oh, God, why you? What's so special about you?" And Cassie began sobbing.

"I'm sorry ..." Jake tried to touch her to comfort her but she shoved him away. Trudy and Craig looked at each other.

"I can't believe this!" she yelled. "Oh, God, it's so unfair! And stupid! It's unfair and stupid!"

Trudy moved to her niece and wrapped her arms around Cassie. "Cassie, honey, come with me. Stop it now. Come with me."

Cass pulled away and challenged Jake. "What makes you think you're healed? What?"

He looked at her, pained and puzzled.

"Oh, God!" Cassie yelled.

"Cass, come on," and Aunt Trudy put her arm around Cassie's waist and led her into the sunroom.

Jake, stunned, watched them go. He felt Craig's hand on his shoulder. "I never expected that," Jake said.

Cassie had to get away. Despite Trudy's protests, and Jake and Craig's attempts to talk to her, Cassie left. She could not bear to be there any longer. She drove home, tears streaming down her face, and she lay awake most of the night, just staring at the ceiling.

Jake sat on Trudy's back steps, scratching Jazz's head, thinking about Cassie. He heard the door open, and Trudy came out and sat beside him. Craig had left, and the house seemed very quiet.

The night air was chilly. "I didn't expect that reaction," Jake said, glancing at Trudy.

"She still has a lot to work through, Jake."

"When she said, 'Why you?' I realized that's something I have no answer for. Why me? Why not Mike?"

Trudy rubbed her hands, carefully formulating her answer. "Jake, God is God. He does things for reasons we can't fathom. He doesn't always do things the way we want him to. Jesus healed a blind man named Bartimaeus, but when Paul asked God to remove some 'thorn in the flesh,' God said, 'No, my grace is sufficient for you.' He has different purposes at different times for different people. Who can understand it? No one. So we accept what he gives us, and learn to trust him ... just trust him. We can't make God do things. He's God."

"How do I know if what happened to me was for real?"

"You mean, if it wasn't just your imagination?"

He nodded.

"How are you different now than you were before Saturday night?"

Jake hesitated. That was a tough question. Everything seemed different, but how could he characterize it? "I know God is there," he began, "and Jesus is real to me now. And I really want to know more about him. It's like a whole new world has opened up to me. Everything seems different. And when I was lying there, on the floor of the sunroom, feeling what I sensed was God's presence ... suddenly, my problems didn't seem so important."

Trudy smiled and put her arm around his shoulders and gave him a quick hug. "Jesus changes people's lives, Jake. That's one way you know. And we can talk about the rest later. Cassie's got to deal with God on her own. God touched you in a very unusual way, Jake. You just be grateful for that and enjoy it. He loves you very much."

Rockfish were probably the Chesapeake Bay's most important sport fish. Delicious to eat and challenging to catch, the rockfish was Maryland's state fish.

Oh my gosh, who cares? Cassie looked away from her computer screen as tears welled in her eyes. Mike. He'd never come back. She'd never feel his arms around her again, never lay her head on his chest.

Cassie got up from her desk and rushed out of the newsroom as tears began running down her cheeks. She was aware of the stares of others: James Lee, Brett, Shonika.... She hurried into the ladies' room.

Shonika followed her. "What's wrong, honey?"

"It's nothing," Cassie protested, mopping her face with a rough paper towel.

"It's got to be something, honey." Shonika hugged her.

Cassie wouldn't answer.

"Tell me. Is it about some man?" There was no answer. Shonika lowered her voice. "Is it about your husband?"

Cassie looked at her, surprised.

"Len told me. He said your husband died. That's so sad."

The tears flowed again.

"Did he know the Lord?" Shonika asked.

Cassie nodded.

"Then he's in heaven. You know that, right?"

"I know."

"Now do you think he'd want to look down here and see you crying like this?"

Cassie didn't answer.

"Of course he would, honey! A little anyway! That's what happens when we love people ... we're sad when they die. You just go ahead and cry, baby. You deserve a few tears."

"No, no," Cassie said, and she blotted her face and walked away.

Cassie lasted until noon, and then she told her editor she was taking the rest of the day off. She got in her car and turned left out of the parking lot, toward Glen Lane.

Glen Lane. The place Mike was run off the road. Jake had offered to bring her here six months ago, but Cassie was afraid to leave Mike alone in the hospital, and after he died, she lost all interest. Why would she want to visit a death scene?

And now she couldn't stay away. Mike was dead. God let him die. She had to see for herself where the murder took place.

Murder. How strange that that word would be associated with her husband! Murder was something they dealt with professionally, of course. Murder was a frequent topic of classes on death-scene investigations and forensics and evidence collection.

But now, murder was personal.

Cassie wove her way through the streets of suburban Annapolis to the winding road leading south, toward the old beaches. A tear fell onto her map. She found Glen Lane, turned onto it, and followed its twists and turns, past small Cape Cod houses and larger colonials, past parks and business clusters, ball fields and schools. Her stomach grew tighter.

It had happened in the 3200 block. She'd read the police report; Craig had gotten it for her. Seeing Mike's death reduced to a form report seemed ludicrous, like describing the effects of an atom bomb using only mathematics. As Cassie approached the scene, her mouth went dry.

She pulled off at the spot where there was a break in the trees and the edge of the road dropped off sharply. There was no guardrail there. Cassie got out and began walking along the shoulder, searching for scuff marks, gravel displacement, anything that might be a remnant of Mike's accident. She felt like she was walking in a shrine.

Leaving the road, she inched her way down the steep slope, sliding in spots, grabbing roots and rocks to steady herself. The car had flipped over and over, the report said, down this very hill. At the bottom, the woods angled over, and an old oak stood at the edge.

That was the tree. Cassie approached it cautiously, like it was a holy place, and she touched its scarred trunk. It had been six months but the marks were still there. They always would be. As her fingers traced the rough bark, she inhaled the scent of the wood. She looked at the lines and crevices as if there was a clue to the mystery in their pattern. She studied it, and then slipped down to the ground and sat beneath its branches. Leaning her cheek against it, she closed her eyes. From the branches above a bird called to its mate.

The oak would live on despite the accident. That thought kept impressing itself on Cassie's mind. She opened her eyes and touched the gold cross around her neck. She picked up a handful of soil and let it fall between her fingers. Reaching out again, her hand touched something. From under the leaves she pulled out a fragment of red plastic, perhaps a piece of brake light from Mike's car. Cassie carefully put it in her pocket, like a sacred relic.

The tree would survive despite the accident. The oak was strong, sturdy, deeply rooted. Looking up she could see an abundance of leaves and on one branch, about thirty feet up, the nest of a squirrel. She looked again at the scar on the trunk, touched once again the cross on her neck, and let her tears flow. She put her forehead against the tree and her tears bumped over the rough bark and ran like a salve across the scar. After a while Cassie knew it was time to go.

She retraced her steps to the top of the hill, grabbing branches and roots to pull herself up the steep incline. It was hard. Her muscles ached with the effort. Several times she wanted to just let go, to fall back into the ravine, to just give up. But she kept on.

Cassie made it to the top and stood next to her car and brushed the dirt off her clothes. Then she heard someone call her name. She looked up. Rick was there.

Jake called and left a message for Dr. Harrington, and when the neurologist called him back, Jake told him about the burn. Dr. Harrington said they'd have to postpone the surgery and Jake said, no, he wanted to cancel it, and he told him why. There was a long silence, then the doctor responded, "Call me in a week and tell me if you still feel the same way."

"Four days," Jake responded. "I hadn't gone a single day without a seizure since I got hurt. I'm up to four days now. When I hit ten, I'll call you so we can set up an MRI. I'll need that so I can go back to work and start driving again."

The doctor laughed. In the end, he agreed to do it Jake's way.

Rock Hall, Maryland, was located on the Eastern Shore well north of the Bay Bridge on a peninsula formed by the Chester and Sassafras Rivers. In colonial days, Rock Hall was the terminus of the Annapolis Ferry. George Washington, Thomas Jefferson, and others used the ferry to commute from Virginia when the weather was right, riding horseback the rest of the way to Philadelphia.

As Cassie drove into town she rehearsed those facts. In her heart, she knew she was simply trying to drive away her memories.

She'd been surprised to see Rick at Glen Lane, but when he told her he'd been driving back from an appointment with a new client and had seen her car and stopped, it made sense. He said he'd been there for about ten minutes, watching her, and he thought maybe she needed someone to talk to.

That was kind of him, unexpectedly so. He'd taken her to dinner, to a quiet Italian place. And that was good, because she didn't want to be alone, and she didn't want to be with anyone else she knew: not Jake, not Craig, not her dad, or even Aunt Trudy. She couldn't face any of them.

So she and Rick had had a quiet evening, and he was charming and attentive. He told her stories of some of the sailing trips he'd been on. Before long, she found she was lost in his intensely blue eyes, able to shove her sadness, anger, fear, guilt, and despair to the recesses of her mind.

By the time she got home and lay staring into the dark, her extra pillow hugged to her chest, she was exhausted. Sleep eventually came.

Now, three days later, she was driving down the main street of Rock Hall. And Rick had called her every day since then, just to be sure she was okay. She was surprised at his sensitivity, his attention. Maybe he really had grown up since his high school days.

Trudy, Craig, and her dad had called her, too, but she hadn't returned their calls. She couldn't talk to them. Not now.

Rock Hall was a neat little town. Small shops lined the main street and several beautiful marinas dotted the waterfront. A waterman's town, it was both functional and attractive, like a fine workboat.

The Rockfish Round-up was a weekend fishing event, enhanced by a Saturday festival in town for landlubbers. The contest itself would be held on the open waters of the Bay, but the town's main street would be lined with artists and craftspeople, food vendors, face-painters, and musicians.

The serious fishermen would not finish until Sunday. Their challenge was to top the Maryland record for rockfish of sixty-seven pounds eight ounces set in 1995. Rockfish, Cassie had learned, lived in the ocean, but they laid their eggs in the fresh water of the rivers and streams that fed the Bay. The baby rockfish spent three to five years in the Bay, before migrating to the Atlantic where they might live as long as thirty years. But as long as they lived in the Chesapeake, rockfish made a tasty and challenging sport fish and the Round-up celebrated that fact.

Cassie was to meet Sam Brierly, her photographer, at the Cozy Harbor Inn. Brett had said he was unavailable. She wondered why.

Brierly was a fifty-ish veteran, gray-haired, chronically late, and crusty as stale bread. While she waited for him, she sat in the inn's dining room and had a cup of tea and a blueberry muffin. The water outside the inn was smooth and slick. There was very little wind to ruffle it. It would be a hot, sticky day.

Sam finally did show up, and together they explored the festival. Walking down the main street, pausing at vendors' stalls, talking to visitors, Cassie realized how ineffective the event was in relieving the pain in her heart. The Round-up was no match for the deep sorrow she was feeling. Painted crab shells and clown faces could not ease her suffering.

She did her job and tolerated Sam in the process, but sadness stalked her every step, and she was glad when the day was finally over. Crossing the Bay Bridge as the sun set over the mainland, Cassie could not seem to stop the grief that poured out of her. Tears streamed down her face.

Seeking distraction, she reached for the CD player. As she did, she realized she hadn't touched it since she'd started driving Mike's SUV. Whatever was in there was the last music he'd listened to the last time he drove the vehicle.

As the music started and the lyrics to "All to Jesus I Surrender" began filling the car, deep sobs erupted from Cassie. Tears dripped off her cheeks and onto her shirt and she could barely see to drive. Grabbing a napkin from the glove box, she mopped her face, and blew her nose, but the tears kept coming, relentless, like the tide. *Not this,* she thought. *I don't want to surrender this to Jesus. Not this ... not Mike.*

Half an hour later, Cassie arrived home. The sky was black. She walked slowly up the steps. Outside her door was a vase filled with a dozen exquisite pink champagne roses. She picked up the card. It simply said, "Rick." And the tears flowed again.

25

On Sunday, Cassie sat on her balcony trying to write her article. Her hands and her brain seemed frozen despite the ninety degree temperature and the humidity. She began to type, deleted that paragraph, tried again ... and forty-five minutes later she threw her hands up in disgust, exited the program, and turned off the computer. It was no use.

Cassie made herself an iced tea and stood looking out over the Bay while she drank it. Her mind was elsewhere. It was on Mike, and his blond hair and blue eyes. Every sunny day reminded her of him. And it was on Jake. Dark, brooding Jake.

Why would he even think God would heal him? Mike was the one who loved Jesus. Mike was the man with the passion for God. That was one of the main things that attracted her to him. But Mike wasn't healed, despite his faith. So why would God heal Jake?

It made her mad just to think of it. Cassie tossed the rest of her tea off the balcony and went inside.

First thing Monday morning, Craig called Jake. "We've had a break," he said, and he arranged to come to Trudy's to talk.

There was a spring in Craig's step as he bounded up the front walk. Jazz gave him two quick barks and Trudy let him in. He had a map in his hand, which he began spreading out on the kitchen table.

"What's up?" Jake asked, emerging from the sunroom.

Craig turned. Speechless, he stared at his fellow agent.

"What?" Jake asked.

"You probably had to pay that barber an extra ten bucks to cut all that hair off," Craig said, grinning.

Jake rubbed his hand over his newly shaven chin. His hair had been cut, too, down to its usual short length. The barber in town, who was at least sixty-five, had been happy to "straighten Jake up" as he put it. "I tipped him twenty," Jake said, looking sheepish. "Trudy said I owed him at least that."

Campbell laughed.

"I had to do it. I didn't want to scare all her friends at her church." Jake sat down. He looked down at the map on the table. "So, what's up?"

"The fragment of an address we found in the mud where you were assaulted. DiCarlo's been checking, supposedly, and not coming up with much. We got a call three weeks ago but nobody put it together with your case. Fortunately the woman called back and the clerk told me about it."

"What woman?"

"Tyson Farnsworth's sister."

"Farnsworth?"

"The guy that Mike killed. Seems Tyson had a bankroll, a wad of about $50,000 in his bedroom when he died. The family figured, hey, we're in the money and never said anything about it. Which is probably why they never filed a wrongful death suit against the Bureau. Anyway, Tyson's little brother, Dante, decides to cash out, and about three weeks ago, he takes the money and runs. The sister, Denise, gets mad and calls us. Only DiCarlo didn't put two and two together. He didn't see the connection with Mike and you." Craig smoothed out the map. "Denise lives here, at 128 South Boulevard, in Annapolis."

"The address in my pocket," Jake said softly.

Craig looked at him. "Do you remember anything about that?"

Jake frowned and rubbed his hand over his head. He wished he did. He wished he remembered. But it was a blank.

"Don't worry about it, man," Craig said. "If anything comes to you, let me know."

"Yeah, yeah, I will."

"There's something else." Craig pressed his palms together and put them to his lips. "You want to sit down?" He motioned toward the chairs.

"Just shoot."

"Okay." Craig cleared his throat. "I pushed DiCarlo to begin Rapid Start." The computer database program allowed agents to track multiple threads of evidence, reports of contact with witnesses and informants, and other information on a case. "I had a feeling these cases were linked somehow but I wasn't seeing the connection. After we entered everything we knew about Schneider's murder, the boat arsons, Mike's death, and your assault into the database, we got a hit."

Jake took a deep breath.

"Human hair taken from your clothes matches some found on Schneider's."

His heart pounding, Jake sat down.

"It's not Schneider's hair. We also obtained a sample from his mistress, and it wasn't hers."

"Wow," Jake said.

"We're going to ask Tam—"

"She had nothing to do with it," Jake interrupted.

"I suspect you're right, but we're going to ask her, and her boyfriend anyway. We've got to cover all the bases."

Jake shook his head. "Oh, man. This is weird." He didn't know what to think. The guy who killed Schneider assaulted him also? The reality of how close he'd come to death hit him hard. He shivered involuntarily. Collecting himself, Jake looked up at Craig. "Have you interviewed Farnsworth's sister?"

Craig looked at his watch. "I've got an appointment with her in ninety minutes, at eleven o'clock."

"Let me come with you." Jake's chair scraped the kitchen floor. Craig eyed him warily.

"Craig, it's been eight days since I've had a seizure. Eight! I hadn't gone one day without one since I got hurt. I'm telling you, I'm healed. Let me go with you. I need to be in on this."

"The MRI is scheduled for—?"

"I'm calling soon to set that up."

Craig looked at him, hard. "I'm sorry, Jake. I just can't do it. If you should get hurt again, they'd have my head. Not only that, don't forget there's still someone out there who tried to kill you."

Jake sighed deeply, shaking his head. "Two weeks, Craig. I'll be back on board in two weeks. The day after the MRI. I'm not staying out any longer than I have to."

On Tuesday morning Cassie sat at her desk with the newspaper spread out before her. The article on the Rock Hall Rockfish Round-up did not meet her standards. The pictures were mundane, the writing dull. She breathed deeply, sighing in disgust.

She had forced herself to write the article yesterday, although each step of the way, her mind was distracted. Cassie felt like she had to pull each sentence out with pliers. She just could not think.

She missed Mike. She felt guilty about Jake. She was irritated with Brett. Feelings she didn't even want kept running around in her mind like spoiled food in someone's gut. Sick at heart, she could hardly function.

And then there was Rick.

Cassie closed the paper and tossed it aside. This week would have to be different. She couldn't afford a second bad job.

Len appeared at her desk. "You doin' okay?" he asked gruffly.

"Just fine." Cassie smiled. "I'm just lovin' these fairs."

The editor grunted. "I'm sure. Well, you're doin' a good job. No complaints."

"That's good," Cassie said, and turned back to her work as Len walked back to his office.

Her phone rang. It was her father. "Cassie, what in the world happened to your car?"

She stiffened. She'd hoped he wouldn't discover it. Carefully, she told him about the deer. Just as carefully, she didn't tell him about the misaimed headlight.

"You love that car! Why aren't you just getting it fixed?"

Because someone has identified it, she thought, *and is following me.* "I will, Dad! I've just been too busy." As she hung up the phone, guilt pressed heavily on her heart.

Two days later, Jake stood at the kitchen sink, washing pots and pans one-handed while Trudy filled the dishwasher. She was chatting to him as they worked. Every time she paused, the room was silent. He was brooding about something.

"So what's up?" she finally asked him. "What are you thinking about?"

Jake stopped scrubbing. He looked at Trudy. "I want to get on this case."

Trudy nodded. "Craig had big news."

"Yes. He called back after he'd talked to Farnsworth's sister and told me that nobody in the family knows where Tyson got so much money." Jake picked up a towel and awkwardly dried his hand. "You know, I want to jump back into this thing. I want to solve the puzzle. I really want to see what's going on at the office."

"It sounds like Craig is doing everything he can."

Jake grimaced. "Yes, except that there's only so much he can do. The case agent calls a lot of the shots and he's not being real effective."

"Why? They've got to find out who's behind this! You're at risk, Cassie's at risk ..."

"And sometimes that still doesn't make a difference."

"That's ridiculous!"

"I agree."

"You ought to go shake things up!"

"I think I should!"

Trudy stopped, then burst out laughing. "I think you just talked me into taking you to Baltimore."

"I think I did!" Jake grinned at her. "Thank you!"

As they rode the elevator up in the Federal Building, Jake could feel his adrenaline pumping. He was ready for work. Ready to get back to it. Happy to be here. Even though his arm still hurt like crazy. How could he care about that? That was nothing compared to no seizures. Nothing at all. The doors opened into the lobby of the FBI office. Joyce, a woman he knew well, was working reception. She gave Trudy a badge and buzzed them both in, then came around and gave Jake a big hug after he came through the security door.

From there Jake led Trudy back through a maze of cubicles and small offices. From everywhere, people came to greet him and welcome him back, and he had to explain he wasn't quite back but would be soon. By the time he ran into Kevin DiCarlo coming out of the men's room, his spirits were higher than they had been in months.

"Kevin!" Jake slapped him on the shoulder. "Kevin, you're just the man I wanted to see. I want you to meet somebody. This is Aunt Trudy!" Jake put his arm around her.

DiCarlo looked shocked. "What are you doing here? I thought ..."

"You thought I was dead, didn't you?" Jake laughed. "You'd written me off."

"Campbell said ..."

"Never listen to Campbell! Hey, man, can we talk?" Jake asked.

"Sure. Come on."

"Trudy, would you mind waiting here?" Jake pointed to a chair next to an empty desk.

"Not at all."

For the next thirty minutes, Jake sat at DiCarlo's desk listening to the progress, or lack of progress, in the investigation of Jake's assault. Jake drummed his thumb against his knee restlessly. DiCarlo was okay, but he was slow and methodical. That was fine for a white-collar crime investigation, but he didn't seem to have the intuitive sense for violent crime. After listening to him, Jake wondered why he'd been assigned the case.

"He had on boat shoes, did Campbell tell you that?" he said finally.

"Yes, he told me. I've checked the background of all the slip holders at the marina, and others that I could identify that were associated with it." He shrugged. "But lots of people wear boat shoes."

"And how about the people who hang out at Sullivan's Wharf?"

"Where Schneider was killed," DiCarlo responded.

"Right."

"All clear. We've come up empty-handed." He sat back in his chair. "I'm not sure we should put a lot of stock in that information, anyway, Jake. You were not exactly fully aware of your surroundings."

"I know what I saw," Jake bristled.

DiCarlo shook his head. "But it took you a long time to remember. I'm not sure that's a good lead."

Jake took a deep breath. His heart was drumming. He'd had enough of this guy. Still, he pressed him, about Farnsworth's sister and the marina fires and everything else he could think of. Finally, when he knew he wasn't going to get any further, "Okay, well, thanks. Let me know if I can help you," he said, standing up. They walked out to where Trudy was waiting.

"Good to see you, Jake," DiCarlo said. "Enjoy your time off."

Jake fixed his gaze on him, anger hot in his chest. "Sure, Kevin." He started to leave, then turned back. "You do the same."

DiCarlo's jaw dropped as he watched Jake and Trudy walk away.

"Well," said Jake, "that was pretty disappointing."

"He didn't know much?" Trudy whispered.

Jake raised his eyebrows. "Didn't know anything!" He grinned. "Now it's time to enter the dragon's lair." He walked up to Betty, the squad secretary, who gave Jake a big hug. "Is he in?" he asked, nodding toward a door with a sign that read "SSA Frank Foster."

"He's all yours," Betty said. "Let me warn him you're coming."

Frank Foster came to the door of his office. His eyes narrowed when he saw Jake, then he frowned as he looked over Jake's shoulder at Trudy. "Who's she?" he asked.

"Aunt Trudy," Jake replied.

It was clear Foster wasn't happy with her being in the office, but Jake invited her to sit at the spare chair at Betty's desk while he went into Foster's office. They fenced for ten minutes over his desk. "We're doing what we can," Foster said when Jake pressed him about the status of the investigation.

"I don't think so," Jake responded.

Foster shrugged. "Look, we have a lot going on."

"Let Campbell have it. That's all I'm asking."

"I decide where assets will be utilized. Not you. I need Campbell elsewhere. Now, if you'll excuse me ..."

Jake left, furious. "So now we're assets," he fumed as he and Trudy waited for the elevator. "Not people."

By the time they got to the garage he had calmed down somewhat. "Well, what do you think?" Jake asked her after they were in the car.

"A very interesting place. I can see why you and Cassie like working there."

Jake told her about his conversation with Foster.

"He sounds like a dragon, as you say." Trudy turned on the ignition and carefully backed out of the space in the parking garage. "He is the one who Cassie didn't like?"

"That's him."

Trudy pursed her lips. "Some people act big and confident but have a very shriveled character. And he seems to be mean-spirited."

Jake laughed. "You're absolutely right."

"He really didn't like me even being in the building."

"Nope."

"But you won that one."

"Yes, I did!" Jake laughed.

Trudy glanced at Jake. "Where to now?"

"It's two o'clock," Jake said, glancing at his watch. "Detective Cunningham couldn't see me until tomorrow, so we don't need to go down there. I'd like to try to see Cassie ... but maybe that would make more sense to do tomorrow?"

"Since we're in Baltimore, why don't you call your ex-wife? Let's go see your kids!"

A shadow passed over Jake's heart. "No, she'd never allow that. No drop-ins. That's the rule."

"Even if you call?"

"Even if I call."

Without speaking, Trudy just turned the car toward home.

Detective Mark Cunningham sat across a walnut table from Jake. A file was spread in front of him, and Jake was asking questions.

"Tell me again," he said, tapping his finger on the table, "exactly what your daughter saw." He was here to stir things up, and he was doing a good job.

Patiently, Cunningham went over the information again.

"So she thinks the attacker was a white guy, dressed in dark clothes. He was wearing a hat, and he was stabbing the person on the ground ... me."

"That's right," Cunningham said. "None of the kids got a decent look at his face."

Jake stroked his chin. "How much had the kids been drinking?"

Cunningham grimaced. He didn't like the question, that was obvious. "Not much. My daughter says she didn't have any." He looked Jake in the eye. "I'm not sure I buy that."

"Okay, switching topics," Jake continued, "to the Goose Creek Marina fire. I understand a man named Myron Tunney, nickname 'Scrub,' was accused of setting it."

"That's right."

"Who accused him?"

Cunningham squirmed in his seat. "I'm not sure we have that information."

Jake's eyes narrowed. "You don't have it?"

Cunningham clutched. Jake knew it was right there in front of him. "That information is significant," Jake said.

"And we are pursuing it." Cunningham flipped the file shut.

"Well, thank you for your time." Jake rose to his feet.

Back outside, Jake briefed Trudy on their meeting.

"You would think he would know right away who accused Scrub," Trudy said.

"He did know. He just didn't want to be responsible for telling me."

Settling into the Saturn, Jake said, "Loughlin is at the other end of the county. He can't see us until one. Let's go try to catch Cassie."

The newspaper office was only a few minutes away. It was a small two-story brick building with its own parking lot. Trudy went inside, and the receptionist called Cassie to tell her she had a visitor. When she told her it was her aunt, Cassie rose from her desk to meet her. The two women embraced, and Trudy asked her if she had a few minutes to talk. Cassie agreed, reluctantly, and Trudy suggested they take a walk outside.

Jake was leaning against the car. Cassie hesitated when she saw him. "Bait and switch," she said to her aunt.

"What?" Trudy asked.

"Never mind."

He was the old Jake, short hair, clean-shaven. Wearing cargo pants, probably Mike's, and a white golf shirt, he looked like her partner again. She stiffened her back, resisting the urge to run.

The air was stifling hot. The humidity made her feel like she was breathing in a steam room. "Hello, Jake," she said.

He hugged her, and kissed the top of her head. "How are you?"

"Okay. I'm, uh, sorry, Jake, for what I said." Cassie looked away. "I feel like I'm always having to apologize to you lately. I'm sorry. I just ..."

"Don't worry about it," he said. "I was concerned about you."

Cassie smiled wanly. "I'm fine. I'm ... just fine." She brushed her hair back from her face and looked him over. "You look good. Normal."

Jake grinned.

"No seizures?"

"Nope."

How long had it been? Almost two weeks? Cassie played with her necklace. "Well, what brings you two here?"

"Jake's got me on an adventure!" Trudy said.

Jake laughed. "I wanted to talk to Cunningham and Loughlin. I'm telling everyone she's my aunt."

"They're trained investigators. They'll never figure out she's not," Cassie said sarcastically. "I'm surprised Cunningham hasn't been in contact with you."

He shrugged. "Didn't have much to say, I guess."

Cassie looked at him, leaning against Trudy's Saturn, and suddenly she felt tears welling up again. She blinked them away quickly. "Look, I need to get back to work. Thanks for stopping by."

"Wait, Cass ..."

Against her better judgment she stopped.

Jake's voice was low. "Listen, I ... just want to say that, if it were up to me, Mike would've been the one healed. Not me."

Cassie struggled for control. She put her hand to her lips and nodded. "I need to go."

His face dropped. "Okay," he said, "we just wanted to check on you."

"Everything's A-okay here, partner. Just fine."

"Why do you want to know?" Fire Marshal Paul Loughlin asked. He was sitting in his office facing Jake across his desk.

"Because it's relevant." Jake adjusted his position in his chair. "If all these incidents are connected, then whoever set these fires could be the same person who killed Schneider and tried to kill me, and whoever fingered Scrub as the potential arsonist could have either been on to something or involved himself."

"Or he could be a totally innocent bystander just trying to help."

"Right. And that's actually the most likely scenario."

Loughlin sighed. He stroked his big mustache. Behind him on the wall were photos of men in uniform in front of engines and ladder trucks. There was also a plaque memorializing Sept. 11, 2001—a picture of a remnant of the World Trade Center with a trio of firefighters.

Jake read his mind. "Paul, I'm an FBI agent. I can handle confidentiality."

Loughlin nodded. He took a deep breath. "It was a slipholder named Maxwell. Richard Maxwell."

Jake's eyes stayed steady.

Loughlin picked up a paper clip off his desk and began to straighten it. "He's been around the marina for several years. Had a boat there. He's a professional captain and everybody knows him."

"What evidence did he provide?"

"He said he saw Scrub in the area of the first explosion the day of the fire. He claimed he'd heard Scrub complaining about something the marina owner had done."

"That's pretty thin, don't you think?"

"It's all we had at the time."

"Why do you suppose Maxwell would give you a tip?"

Loughlin shrugged. "He just seems like one of those people who likes to interject himself in every situation. You know what I mean? We were checking everybody out anyway and the information he gave us just turned us to this guy Tunney one day sooner."

Jake nodded. "Okay. Thanks for your help."

26

*T*he air remained stagnant all week. But the forecasters were promising a cold front would come through on Friday night, bringing more tolerable weather for Saturday. And that was great as far as Cassie was concerned. She was not looking forward to spending another day outside in ninety-five-plus degree weather.

This week she'd be covering the North Beach Bay Fest, a fun local festival in Calvert County. There'd be sailing dinghy races, sand-castle contests, live music, and great food. Best of all, Brett would be doing the photography.

It was 6:00 p.m. when she pulled into her driveway at the boathouse. The sun was still high on this hot August day, and the air was still. She set her attaché case and blazer down on the lowest step leading to her apartment, and walked out on the pier to where *Time Out* was tied up. Cassie bent down and adjusted the boat's fenders, then stepped on board.

The Alberg was small but neat. Every time Cassie boarded the boat she was glad she'd bought her. It was the one part of her life that didn't feel half-empty, the only place she could be without thinking of Mike. He'd never been into sailing—now, that was a blessing.

Cassie walked forward, to the bow, then back to the cockpit on the starboard side. She wondered if she could single-hand the boat. She thought she could. Maybe she should just take her out, even if she had to go by herself.

Opening up the companionway, Cassie went below decks. There, still in its box, was the new stove she'd bought. Scrub could probably install it for her, and he could certainly use the money. As a part-time laborer at Wells Inlet, he could hardly be making enough to live on.

Cassie made a mental note to talk to him about it. She went back on deck, closed and locked the companionway, and went up to her apartment. Ignoring the light flashing on the answering machine, she poured herself some iced tea and stared into the refrigerator for a while, before she finally decided she didn't really care about eating after all.

The phone rang. She didn't mean to answer it. But she was preoccupied and before she knew it, the receiver was in her hand, and then what could she do? Her dad tried to talk to her, but she gave one-word answers to his questions and alternated between reassuring him that she was all right and speaking in clipped tones in hopes of discouraging further discussion.

And then her dad mentioned a conversation he'd had with Rick, in which the young man had told him he believed Scrub had set the marina fire. He had, in fact, heard the dockhand complaining about the harbormaster just prior to the fire's outbreak.

"No, Dad," Cassie interrupted. "Rick told me he was sure it wasn't arson."

"What do you mean?"

"I'm saying, he told me, he absolutely positively knew it had to have been an accident."

"Well that sure isn't what he said to me."

"Maybe he thinks Scrub started it accidentally."

"He specifically mentioned arson," her father responded.

"How do you know?"

"Because he told me himself! He said he'd seen Scrub with gas cans, he'd overheard him bad-mouthing Mr. Hardesty and threatening to get even. He had access to the boat ... all of which pretty much convinced Rick that Scrub did it."

"Gas cans! Gas cans had nothing to do with the fire!"

"And I don't think Scrub did either," Jim said. "And I wish people would stop going around accusing him."

Cassie hung up the phone, feeling confused and agitated. Why would Rick say one thing to her and another to her dad?

Jake was sitting at the kitchen table in Trudy's kitchen. She was making dinner and telling him about a conversation she'd had with her brother about the marina fire.

"What's Rick Maxwell like, do you know?" Jake asked. "He seems kind of strange."

"I don't know him," Trudy said. "My brother or Cassie would be the ones to tell you about him." She placed a plate heaped with steaming spaghetti in front of Jake.

"Thank you," he said, the pungent smell of the spaghetti sauce filling his nose. "You are a great cook." Trudy made her spaghetti sauce with lots of garlic and Italian sausage, peppers and onions, and Jake could hardly wait to dig in.

"I love having somebody to cook for," she responded. Trudy placed a basket of hot bread and a bowl of salad on the table, then sat down in front of her own plate and said grace.

Jake began to eat. He was famished. "I don't think I'll be getting any information about Rick Maxwell from Cassie."

"Why not?" Trudy asked.

"I don't think she wants to talk to me. I can't tell what's going on with her."

Trudy took a piece of bread from the basket. "Cassie's going through a hard time. Losing Mike was one thing, losing her faith is another."

"Is that permanent?"

"I don't think so." Trudy looked at him. "Cassie's had a lot of losses—her mother, now Mike. You, almost. She just needs to decide whether she wants to add God to that list."

Jake winced and shook his head. "I sure hope not."

"I don't think God will let her. Once he's got you, nothing can take you out of his hand," Trudy said.

"How about if you jump?"

"No. He's faster that that."

Jake nodded. His eyes grew thoughtful. "You know, it's one thing to have something terrible happen to you when you don't believe in God. That's hard enough. But when you do believe in him, and you think he's good, and you trust him, and then your husband dies, man, that has got to be rough."

Trudy stopped what she was doing and turned toward Jake. "Good insight."

Jake mopped up the last of the spaghetti sauce with his bread. "Hey, how'd you like to go pay Schneider's mistress a visit?"

Trudy's gray eyes brightened. "Jake, I never know what you're going to say next."

"The way I look at it, if there's a connection between Schneider's murder and the attack on me, I need to know everything I can about Schneider."

"Do you think it's safe?"

"To talk to Desiree? Yeah, she had nothing to do with it."

Trudy smiled. "Then, count me in."

"Lucky me," Jake said. "It would be a long walk to Harrisburg, otherwise."

Desiree DuBois was more than happy to talk to Jake, whom she hadn't seen since his wedding to Tam. He barely remembered her.

They sat in her apartment in soft, overstuffed chairs and a chintz sofa. A jar candle flickered on the coffee table and the fragrant scent of gardenia filled the room. Jake politely engaged in small talk with the young woman as he gradually worked his way around to the subject at hand. "What was he like?" Jake asked. "What kind of person was Frederick?"

Desiree blushed. "Oh, a lot of women would call him nerdy. He was very smart, a real intellectual. And he was kind and gentle, almost too passive. We had the most interesting discussions, on the opera and musicals and theater. His career was a bit of a mystery to me—I never understood what he did and in fact, he never wanted to talk about it. But he was wonderful to me."

"Anything strange happen when you were with him? Did you ever see him act out of character?"

"Well, yes, that one time I heard him arguing with a man at the marina. And you know, I've been thinking, there was one other time."

"When was that?" Jake leaned forward.

"One night, about seven months ago, he told me he had to go meet someone. And I wanted to go with him, but he said I couldn't. He came back, six hours later, and he was very angry. The person never showed up."

"Do you have any idea who he was meeting?"

"No."

"Or where, exactly?"

"Oh, he told me that. It was the Maryland House rest area down Interstate 95." Desiree brushed her hair back from her face. "It was so odd. He was being so secretive, and the thought crossed my mind, is he seeing another woman?" She blushed. "I guess that sounds stupid, doesn't it?"

Jake sat back and glanced at Trudy. "Can you possibly tell me the date, and the time of day?"

"It was late, about ten or so, that he was to meet the person, and … let me see, where's my calendar?" She went into the kitchen, pulled an old calendar out of a drawer, and walked back into the living room, flipping the pages to November. "I think it may have been November fourth. Yes, that's right … I remember—it was a Thursday and I had a dental appointment the next day, so I was already nervous."

Jake felt his face grow hot. "November fourth."

"That's right. When he got back," Desiree continued, "he was so upset. He paced the floor for hours. The next day he left again and didn't get back until that night. He said he had business in Delaware." Desiree shook her head. "That was the only time I ever saw Frederick that upset."

Trudy voiced what they'd both been thinking once they were back in the car. "Mike killed that man on November 4th."

"Seems like an odd coincidence," Jake said, wiping his brow. His stomach was tight. Could there be a connection between the man Mike killed and Frederick Schneider? Right now, he couldn't see it. They weren't in the same social group, Schneider didn't do drugs ... what was the connection?

"Jake, what does this mean?"

"I don't know, Trudy. I really don't know."

They drove the rest of way back saying little, both lost in their thoughts. Jake called Craig as soon as they arrived. He expected to just leave voice mail but Craig was working.

"What are you doing, man?"

"Foster gave me two other hot cases so I wouldn't work yours." Craig sounded fatigued. "So I'm just doing it at night. I'm talking to every one of Tyson Farnsworth's associates that I can identify. He was well-known on the streets of Annapolis. Somebody's got to know who he was connected with. Where'd that money come from? That's what I'd like to know. And I'm also checking all the contacts in Schneider's PDA. Some of them, it appears, are encrypted."

"Thanks, Craig. I really appreciate—"

"It's nothing that you wouldn't do for me," he interrupted. "You feeling okay?"

"Yes, and listen, let me tell you what I found out today." Jake relayed the information he'd gotten from Desiree. Craig couldn't see the connection between Tyson's death and Schneider either, and maybe there wasn't any, but the common date was interesting.

"I've been trying to talk to the guy who owns the *Lady J*," Craig said.

"The boat that started the marina fire?"

"Right. He won't talk to me and I don't know why. He seems like a straight-up guy ... no criminal record, stable job, wife, two kids—

normal in other words. But he's real hinky. I left yet another message today. At some point he's going to realize I'm not going to go away."

They talked about some other possible leads and later, after he'd hung up the phone, Jake told Trudy, "Craig's getting worn out. He said he hasn't seen his kids awake in three weeks. I sure hope we break this case soon."

"For everyone's sake," Trudy responded.

Late that night, Jake stood in the sunroom, staring into the darkness outside the window, unable to sleep. Could there have been a connection between Schneider and Farnsworth? Desiree said her lover wasn't into drugs, didn't do anything illegal as far as she knew. Farnsworth was not a friend.

Jake drummed his fingers against his leg, as he did when he was hyper. He held up his right hand and looked at it. The feeling was starting to come back. A millimeter a week, that's what the neurologists had said. That's how fast nerves can heal.

Something else was bothering him. It was another memory, just a fragment of one, actually. Strangely, it was an odor, a sort of sweet and spicy smell that he couldn't identify. But it kept intruding on his thoughts and he wondered why. Was it connected to his assault? He just didn't know.

Jake lay down on the couch and he finally fell into a disturbed sleep about 4:00 a.m. He woke up around 6 a.m., restless and anxious. He'd had a dream about Cassie. He had to see her.

On Friday, Cassie worked at the office, ignoring her phone messages and refusing to take calls. Jake called repeatedly, and so did her dad, but she was not in the mood to talk to them. And although she felt guilty about it, she even ignored a message from her aunt.

At the afternoon staff meeting, Shonika came and sat next to her.

Fortunately there was only time for brief chatter before the meeting started. Cassie assumed what she hoped was an interested expression and focused on Len, who was speaking to his staff about a big fall push, but all the while other thoughts kept running through her head. *How could Rick even think Scrub had anything to do with the marina fire? Come on! Scrub had nothing to gain from it.*

The summer heat buffeted her when she left the air-conditioned building around 4:00 p.m. In his last message, it sounded like Jake might try to come to the office and she wanted to do an end run around that possibility. Why? She didn't know. She just didn't want to see him.

When Cassie got outside, she looked toward the west to see if clouds were building yet but the sky was still clear. The weather forecasters were calling for a front to come through, and in Bay country that usually meant squalls, sudden sharp storms with high winds and heavy rains.

She kind of hoped they would come. Two days ago, Rick had called. The wind instrument at the top of his mast was broken. He needed to replace it, and he wondered if Cassie could come with the bosun's chair and help out Friday evening. Scrub would be there, and Maxwell said he was going to ask her dad, too.

Cassie had agreed. That was, after all, the deal she'd made when he'd given her the bosun's chair. But the last conversation she'd had with her dad had started a different tape playing in her head, a discordant one that left her feeling uneasy about Rick Maxwell. If he really thought Scrub set that fire, why did he want him near his boat, even if just to fix a wind instrument?

She turned the SUV toward her boathouse apartment. She would change, pick up the chair, and drive to Wells Inlet. She'd eat later, she decided, after it had cooled off. Something in her wanted to get this job over with as soon as possible.

Craig called Jake late Friday afternoon. "I've been trying to get in touch with Cassie. Have you guys seen her?"

"No." Jake took a deep breath. "She's not talking to us."

"That's not good."

"I agree. Trudy says she'll come around eventually, but I don't know."

"Jake, it's just something Cassie's got to work out." Craig paused.

Jake knew he was probably right, but it didn't make him feel any better. "We're just about to leave to go by the newspaper office."

"Don't bother," Craig said. "I called there. She's left the building."

By the time Jake hung up the phone, a sick feeling had filled his stomach. Trudy had gone out to run an errand. When she got back, they'd have to talk.

Cassie entered the parking lot at the Wells Inlet Marina and pulled into a space off to the side next to a hedge. Maybe she was just tired. Maybe sadness was sapping her energy. But for some reason, she didn't want to be there.

She looked around. Scrub was nowhere in sight. Her dad's car was not in the lot, either. Why wasn't he there? Retrieving her cell phone, she called him at home. No answer. She left a message. She tried his cell number. No answer there, either. Cassie grimaced, wondering what to do.

Maybe he was in a dead zone in the cell coverage, on his way here, she decided. Taking only her keys and the bosun's chair with her, Cassie locked the SUV and walked to the marina office. "Is Scrub here?" she asked the young woman behind the desk.

"No, I haven't seen him," she said.

"How about Richard Maxwell. You know him?"

The woman smiled. "Everybody knows him. D Dock, slip 18. All the way down." She gestured toward Cassie's right.

As Cassie walked toward the D Dock she noted that the clouds were beginning to gather in the west. The heat was oppressive. *Come on, rain,* she thought. *Cool things off.* Dressed in khaki cargo shorts, a tank top, and her boat shoes, Cassie was just barely comfortable. Shading her eyes with her hand, she scanned the docks. There was no sign of Scrub or her dad. Or Rick.

"Well, hey, beautiful!" a voice said softly.

Cassie jumped and spun around. Rick Maxwell was right behind her.

27

*S*orry to scare you!" Maxwell said, laughing.

"Hello, Rick," she said.

He put his arm around her and gave her a squeeze. "You've been ignoring me."

It was true. He'd called her three times. But then, so had Jake. "Sorry, I've been busy," she said. "What did you want?"

"I just wanted to make sure you were coming today."

"Oh, sorry." Cass looked all around. "Where's Scrub?"

"He's waiting for us." Maxwell gestured toward his catamaran. "Let's go."

"And Dad?"

"Busy. But I think the three of us can handle it. I promise, it won't take long."

Cassie preceded Rick to the D Dock. For a Friday night, the marina was surprisingly empty, but the predicted weather would have most boaters waiting for tomorrow to go out. It wasn't smart to be on the Bay with a front coming through. Winds could jump to sixty knots or more, and the relatively shallow Bay could become a heaving sea in a short period of time.

As Cassie walked toward Rick's boat she looked down at the new dock, still a preweathered brown, and she wondered how the rebuilding of Goose Creek was going. She made a mental note to herself to check on it next time she was down that way.

They got to Rick's boat and walked out onto the narrow finger pier. A laughing gull shrieked at them as they walked. Cassie got to the boat and hesitated, surprised to see the lifeline on the catamaran still connected.

"Let me get that," Rick said. Three seagulls took off, squawking, from nearby pilings. Rick leaned in front of Cassie to let down the lifeline. He was wearing Polo cologne. A small alarm went off in her head.

She looked in the ports. Where was Scrub? She couldn't see any evidence of him. Why was the lifeline still up if Scrub was on board?

Her heart began to pound. "Oh, wait!" she said, turning. "I ... need to get something from my car."

"Oh no you don't," Rick responded quickly, and with that, he whipped a metal flashlight out of his pocket and hit Cassie over the head.

But Cassie was already moving and the flashlight did not connect as solidly as he'd intended. Her vision started to go dark and her knees buckled. She grabbed his shirt and tried to throw him off the dock. Her muscles seemed frozen. She had no strength. She felt like she was in a slow-motion nightmare. Still, she fought. "No!" she cried, but her voice sounded far away, even to her.

Rick cursed. He threw one arm around Cassie's neck, the flashlight still in his other hand. Cassie drove her elbow into his gut. She couldn't breathe! She needed air! Cassie stomped on his instep and tried to elbow him in the groin.

Then Rick brought the flashlight up and hit her twice more. The world went black and she collapsed.

Rick caught Cassie in his arms. He glanced around. No one was in sight. He lifted her onto the boat and carried her below decks to the berth he had prepared. When he had secured Cassie there, locking her in handcuffs, blindfolding and gagging her with duct tape, he stepped back and admired his work.

How lucky he was! The woman he'd known since high school was Special Agent Mike McKenna's wife.

Stupid Mike McKenna. The Boy Scout. The perfect little

Christian. *Well, Mike certainly paid the price for interfering with my plans.* Maxwell smiled to himself. When McKenna had stumbled on Tyson beating up that motorist, when he'd stopped and drawn his gun and shot Tyson dead, McKenna had destroyed more than the life of a street punk: he'd thwarted a plan Rick had been working on for two years. Two years! It had taken that long to get Frederick Schneider on board, to get him to agree to supply the guidance system Rick had promised to sell to the slimy little Third World dictator.

The delivery was to take place that evening but then McKenna shot Farnsworth, and the whole thing fell apart. Schneider freaked out and refused to cooperate again. And it had taken Rick another six months—and an arranged accident and a couple of arson jobs— to set the deal up again.

By sheer luck, he had discovered Cassie living at the marina. McKenna's wife! He still couldn't believe his good fortune when he was able to entice the grieving widow into a relationship.

And now all the cards were about to fall into place. Soon there would be the big payoff. He'd be able to live in the Caribbean forever. And, thanks to his good fortune and careful planning, he would get a little bonus: rape Mike McKenna's wife and then kill her when he was finished.

Ah, revenge was sweet. He was looking forward to it. He actually trembled with excitement.

Jake was pacing back and forth on the front porch when Trudy arrived home. His calls to Cassie had gone unanswered. Her dad wasn't home. He couldn't remember the name of her photographer and the newspaper switchboard was shut down for the night.

By the time Trudy walked up the front porch steps, he was in a sweat.

"Why are you so hyper?" she asked.

"I don't know. I just need to talk to Cassie."

The phone rang before their conversation could go further. It was Craig. "I just got a call from the wife of the owner of the *Lady J.* Something's up. I'm headed down towards Deale to see her."

"Alone?" Jake asked.

"Gotta be."

"Wait, no, Craig ..." But Jake couldn't think of a better plan. "At least tell me what's going on," he said.

"The husband left in a tizzy fifteen minutes ago. She's in a panic. I'm on my way there now." Craig paused. "This could be the break I've been waiting for." He explained the rest of his conversation with the woman.

"Call me," Jake said, "as soon as you are clear of there. If you can't get me here, call Trudy's cell phone."

"What's up?" Trudy asked.

Jake turned to her. His neck was tight and his mouth was dry. "The boat that started the marina fire? Craig's been trying to get the owner to talk for weeks. Finally, tonight, the guy's wife calls. He left fifteen minutes ago, saying he had to meet somebody, totally stressed out. She's scared. She'd heard the messages Craig left and used Caller ID to get his number. She's afraid her husband's gotten mixed up in some big kind of trouble."

"Oh, my," Trudy said.

"Craig's headed down to Deale. Look, Trudy." Jake put his hand on her shoulder. "We need to ... I need to do something. Will you take me to Cassie's apartment? Will you help me chase her down?"

"Of course! But Jake, I don't understand ..."

"I don't either, but I just feel like I've got to find Cass."

Trudy had an idea as they drove toward Cassie's apartment. At her suggestion, Jake called Mr. Turnage, Cassie's landlord, and he checked the apartment for them. Cassie wasn't there. Nor was her car. So Jake and Trudy went straight to Jim Davison's. He had just gotten back from the store. "I don't know where she is," he said, and his voice was mottled with concern.

The three stood in the kitchen and discussed possibilities. "She could be working. There's the photographer," Jake said, "but I don't know his name ..."

"And Skip, the boat surveyor," Cassie's dad added. "She went out to dinner with him."

"You've got his cell number, Jim," Trudy said. "He did Cassie's boat."

"That's right, I do. And I also have Len's number. He might tell us how to reach the photographer. Or, maybe he even knows what Cassie's plans were." Jim Davison reached for the phone. Seconds later, a puzzled expression crossed his face.

"What?" Jake asked him.

Jim punched numbers into the phone. "I've got voice mail," he said. "Usually the answering machine kicks in unless I'm on the Internet." Jake and Trudy stood by as he retrieved the message. Frowning, he handed the phone to Jake. "Listen to this."

Jake pressed the phone to his ear. The message was from Cassie. "Dad," she said, "I understand you're going to help us fix the wind instrument on Rick's cat. I guess you've left. I'll see you there." Jake put the phone down. His eyes were fixed on Jim's face.

"I never said I was going to help Maxwell," Jim said.

"What's going on?" Trudy asked.

Jake told her.

Jim picked up the phone again. "I don't have Rick's number. But let me try Scrub."

But Scrub didn't answer his cell phone and by the time Jim put his phone down Jake was ready to go.

"Where's this guy live?" he asked.

"I don't know, but Scrub works at Wells Inlet Marina and Rick's boat is there."

"Let's go!" Jake said to Trudy. "You stay here," he said to Jim, "in case Cassie calls."

They arrived at the Wells Inlet Marina around 8:00 p.m. When he stepped out of the car, Jake noticed the wind had come up. The sky to the west was bluish-gray. The front the weather guys had predicted was coming through.

He hitched his gun pouch to a more comfortable position. He still wasn't used to wearing it on his left. He'd practiced drawing until he felt confident he could quickly have the gun ready to shoot. Whether he could hit a target or not was an entirely different matter.

"Where do we go?" Trudy asked.

"I don't know. I'm playing this by ear." Jake led Trudy to the office, but it was locked. Then he walked down to the docks. There were four parallel piers, and Jake shaded his eyes and scanned them all. "Look! There! Isn't that Scrub?" he asked, pointing to a small figure on the B dock.

"Yes, I believe it is," Trudy said.

They walked that direction. Scrub saw them coming, and trotted up to meet them.

"Hey, Scrub. How are you doing?" Jake asked, extending his hand.

"Good, sir." Scrub nodded his head in a slight bow.

"Jake Tucker."

"Yes, sir. You're Miss Cassie's friend."

"That's right."

"And Miss Trudy. How are you ma'am?" Scrub asked.

"I'm fine, Scrub," Trudy said.

"Scrub, we're looking for Cassie. You haven't, by any chance, seen her today, have you?"

"No, sir."

"How about Richard Maxwell?"

"No ... he's not here. See over there, his slip's empty."

Jake followed his gesture as he pointed to a deserted dock. Disappointed, he turned back to Scrub. "When did he leave?"

"Don't know, sir. He was gone when I got back today."

Jake frowned, struggling to come up with Plan B. How much did

Scrub know? And how reliable was he? Lost in thought, Jake rubbed the back of his neck. Looking down, he kicked at a small stone. And then he noticed the dockhand was wearing boat shoes. And on his left shoe, the front eyelet was pulled out.

Jake's head snapped up and his eyes bored into Scrub's. Adrenaline poured through him. Instantly, he sized him up. Scrub was short and rather scrawny. He might have had the strength to reach up and hit Jake hard enough to knock him out, but there's no way he could have manhandled him in and out of the car on his own.

Jake glanced at Trudy. Her look told him she'd followed his eyes, and seen the same thing. He turned back to Scrub and forced his jaw to relax. "Nice shoes, Scrub."

The handyman smiled sheepishly. "Yes, they're new."

"New? It's looks like you've had them for a while."

"Oh no, sir, they're new. I got 'em for my birthday."

"Really?" Jake said. "When's your birthday?"

"It was three weeks ago. Three weeks ago tomorrow. And Mr. Maxwell, he gave them to me. For my birthday."

Jake's heart began pounding. "Maxwell? Richard Maxwell gave those shoes to you?"

"Yes, sir," Scrub said proudly. "He did that."

"Three weeks ago?"

"Yes, sir. After I took his car to be inspected."

"His car? What kind of car does he have?"

Scrub's eyes were bright. "A real nice Volvo, sir. Nothing wrong with it. Just a headlight out of aim. That's all."

"What kind of headlights does he have?"

"Those real ugly blue ones, sir ..."

A fire erupted in Jake's bones. He turned to Trudy. "We need to find Cass, Trudy. We have to find her." Jake's thoughts were racing. Cassie probably didn't know Maxwell was a bad guy. He had to tell her. Now.

Trudy pulled out her cell phone. She dialed Cassie's number.

"Well," Scrub said, scratching his head. "She should be here.

She's got to be here somewhere."

"Why? Why do you say that?" Jake demanded.

"Her car. Her SUV. It's right up there."

Jake followed his gesture. In the parking lot, behind some bushes, was an SUV. Was it Mike's 4-Runner? Jake charged up the hill. Trudy followed. The car was locked. Jake peered in the windows.

"That's her purse," Trudy said, in a half-cry. "There, on the seat."

Jake turned to Scrub, his blood pumping. "Scrub, did you see Cassie tonight? Did you see her get on the boat, with Maxwell?"

"No, sir. Like I said, Mr. Maxwell was gone when I got back."

Think, come on ... think, Jake ordered himself. His head felt like it was in a vise. "Do you have any idea where Maxwell might be going? What his plans were?"

Scrub smiled. "He's planning on a long trip, that's all I can say. He had me load up boxes and boxes of food in that thing. Yes, he did."

"Trudy," Jake commanded, "you keep calling ... call her dad, call her office ... see if anybody knew what Cassie was doing tonight. Scrub, let's go look at where Maxwell's boat was docked."

Scrub jogged to D Dock with Jake following him. Together they walked to the end. "How many other boats are usually here?" Jake asked, gesturing toward the empty slips.

"They all empty right now, sir. Marina's not full yet. Mr. Maxwell, he wanted to be over by himself."

How convenient.

"Here it is, sir," Scrub said, motioning toward the empty slip. "You see? The dock lines are gone. Mr. Maxwell, he's planning to be gone a long, long time. A long time."

Jake stared at the empty slip, his pulse pounding in his ears, his jaw as tight as piano wire. He would call Campbell. He would call Foster. He'd call the bureau director if he had to.

The sun burst through a small break in the cloudbank forming in the west. It's light glinted off something on the dock, something between two boards, and it caught Jake's eye. He moved onto the finger pier. He bent down. What was it? A chain of some kind?

Taking his pen out of his pocket, he carefully extracted it. And as Cassie's gold cross slid up from between the boards a jolt of fear ran through him.

"Sir?" Scrub said, snapping Jake back to reality. "I just remembered something. When I was loading them boxes, I saw a chart on the nav center. It was of Bloody Point Bar Light, sir, off the south end of Kent Island and there was a mark on it, like it was a place Mr. Maxwell was planning to go."

"How long does it take to get there, Scrub, by boat?"

"By sailboat, a couple of hours. They only go five knots or so."

"How about by powerboat?"

"You can do twenty in them, sir. Maybe twenty-five. So in half an hour, you'd be there. Maybe longer, though, with this front comin' through." Scrub shuffled his foot. "It's the deepest part of the Bay, sir. Bloody Hole."

The Pit.

The wind was starting to come up. It ruffled Jake's hair. He squinted into the distance. A few boats were out, most seemed headed back to port.

"Scrub, I need a boat."

"A boat, sir?"

"A fast boat. I think Cassie's in a lot of trouble. Can you get me a good boat?"

Scrub looked around. The A, B, and C docks were three-quarters full. Half were sailboats, but of the other half ... "Yes, Mr. Jake. I can get you a boat. But I'll have to hotwire one."

"Do it." Jake patted him on the shoulder. "Do it now. Be quick. Gas it up. I need it right away." The two men began running back toward Trudy. "Oh, and I'll need a map or directions or something, and whatever else ... a life jacket."

"I'll set you up, Mr. Jake! Meet me in ten minutes, there," he said, pointing, "at the fuel dock."

Craig Campbell pulled up into the driveway of a small, split foyer home in Deale. The front yard, fenced with chain link, was filled with kids' toys. A nondescript brown dog barked at him as he strode up the walk. He rang the bell, and Deborah Hawkins answered.

She was about thirty-five, short, heavy-set, and frightened, from the look on her face. She nervously brushed her hair back from her face, and, after he showed her his creds, invited Craig into the home. He followed her upstairs to a kitchen, which still smelled like the pizza she'd cooked for dinner.

"Tell me, Mrs. Hawkins, what's going on with your husband?"

She began to tell him what she knew and Craig took notes. Seth was an engineer for a defense contractor. He dealt with highly secure technology. After their boat had burned, he'd become brooding and suspicious, angry and depressed. "He'd forgotten to renew the insurance," she said, "and so that put us in a real hole financially.

"And then tonight," she continued, "he got a call and turned white as a ghost. He told me he had to go somewhere, and that he'd be back very late and not to wait up. He refused to tell me where he was going, Agent Campbell, but I can tell something's up. For some reason, my husband is very frightened."

"Did the number show up on your Caller ID?"

"No ... he's been getting these strange calls on his cell phone."

"What's that number?" Craig jotted down the number she gave him. "Where was he when he got this last call?" he asked.

"Why, in the kitchen ... right there, in fact. By the counter."

Craig walked over to it. Just as he'd hoped, a notepad was on the counter. Without picking it up, he bent down to look at it at an angle. There was an imprint on it, left over from the top sheet of paper. He could just barely see—it was a series of numbers. No, it was a latitude and longitude.

"Mrs. Hawkins, does your husband have access to a boat?"

"I ... I really don't know. He might. He has a lot of friends who have boats."

Craig nodded. "Tell you what. Would you start calling as many of his friends as you can? Ask them if your husband asked to borrow a boat. Will you do that?"

She would. While she used the house phone, Craig stepped outside. He had no cell phone coverage inside. Outside, it was marginal. He called the office and got the number of the Coast Guard in Baltimore. When the duty officer answered, Craig identified himself and read the coordinates he'd written down.

"That's Bloody Point Bar Light, sir," the officer responded a moment later, "on the east side of the Bay, off the south end of Kent Island."

A rumble of thunder sounded in the west. The cold front moving in was preceded by a huge cloudbank—a dark, ugly mass of lightning-filled clouds that was now within twenty miles or so. Craig could see it, standing on Mrs. Hawkins's deck, his phone pressed to his ear. "Do you have the ability to put a boat out there?"

"With this weather coming, sir?"

"If it were important?"

"Yes, sir, we can go out regardless, sir."

"Where would the boat have to come from?"

"Baltimore, sir."

"Okay, thanks."

"Yes, sir. Good evening, sir."

"Trudy, listen to me," Jake exclaimed as he rejoined her. He could see the alarm on her face.

"Is she with him?"

"That's a strong possibility. Listen. Call Campbell on his cell phone. Don't quit until you get him. Call his office, his cell, his pager, his home ... I don't care, just get him. You got some paper?"

Trudy dug in her purse and found a small notebook. She wrote down numbers as Jake recited every one he could remember, then he gave her the names of two other agents she could call.

"Last resort," he said, "if none of these work, call 9-1-1. Get

Detective Cunningham. Tell him what happened. I'm taking a boat. I'm headed south. Send somebody to Bloody Point after me. Tell them Maxwell should be considered armed and dangerous. I think Cassie is being held against her will."

"Oh, Jake!"

He grabbed her arms. "Stay strong. Make those calls. Once you get somebody here, and they know what's going on, go to your brother's and wait."

"Be careful! Please, be careful!"

Jake kissed her on the cheek. "Pray, Trudy! Pray."

She was alive, or at least she thought she was. She was floating in a sea of blackness. To her right, and behind, was a searing, white-hot pain. She wanted to get away from it.

She could feel movement, a lurching, nauseating, side-to-side motion but she could not make her hands or feet or head move. She wanted to speak to someone, to tell them where she was, but she could not find her voice. And so she concentrated on fighting the pain and fighting the nausea.

"This is the throttle," Scrub explained to Jake. "Push up to go fast, and back to reverse. In the middle is neutral. That's all there is to it. Watch out for crab pots. Try to go into the waves. Slow down if you start slapping the water. Look here, at this GPS, sir. I've entered some waypoints. Follow the arrow. It'll take you out into the Bay, then south to Bloody Point. You understand, sir?"

"Follow the arrow. Got it!"

Scrub looked up at the sky. "There's a storm coming, Mr. Jake. You sure you want to go out?"

"I have to," Jake responded. "Okay, now what am I looking for? Describe Maxwell's boat."

Scrub did just that. "Mr. Jake, you want me to go with you?"

Jake hesitated, then rejected the idea. He'd be endangering

Scrub, and he wasn't willing to do that, not if Scrub was just a pawn in this whole thing. And if he wasn't just a pawn, that was all the more reason not to have him along. "No, man, but thanks. You stay here."

"It's a Boston Whaler, sir. Very sturdy, but fast. She'll take the waves that come up." Scrub stepped off the boat. "You wear that lifejacket, sir! You don't want to be out on this Bay with no life-jacket."

"I will!" Jake threw him the dock lines. Carefully, he eased the throttle forward and began to make his way out of the marina between the rock jetties of the entrance. It was awkward, reaching over with his left hand, so he tried using his right wrist. Gaining confidence, he increased speed. The engine roared, and the boat tore through the waves. The wind blew in his face. He experimented with the wheel, turning the boat right and left to see how much it moved. Then he headed for the open Chesapeake, his jaw set, his mind focused.

Richard Maxwell would not get away.

28

Anyone who knew the Bay knew it could get very rough very fast when a front was coming through. Jake didn't know anything about the Chesapeake, but he was about to get a crash course. The boat pitched and rolled as the waves built to heights of three and four feet. Jake gripped the wheel, too focused to be nauseous. He stared into the distance grimly.

The sky was black now. A west wind whipped the waves, forming whitecaps that stretched into the distance. Waves broke against the port hull and water crashed onto the deck and sluiced back to the cockpit, drenching Jake. He licked his lips, tasting the saltiness, and shivered in the cold.

Maxwell had to be up ahead. Jake strained his eyes, looking for twin hulls, an aqua Bimini and sail cover, a boat about forty-feet long—and the only other idiot desperate enough to be out in this weather.

A loud rumble of thunder pierced the darkness. Jake clenched his jaw. The deck, rising and dropping beneath his feet, was unnerving. Dark clouds, dark sky, and the dark waters of the Bay merged into a seamless panorama accented only by the whitecaps and periodic flashes of lightning. To his left were the lights of shore, barely visible. He kept parallel to them and hoped he'd gone far enough into the Bay to miss protruding headlands.

Jake glanced at his watch. It was 8:30 p.m. He could see a lighthouse up ahead and to his left. According to Scrub, that would be Thomas Point Light, just outside of Annapolis. Stay away from it,

Scrub had warned. There were rocks around it.

Cheating the boat a bit to the right, Jake swung in a long arch, setting a southerly course. Looking ahead into the growing darkness, something didn't look quite right. When the boat lifted on a crest of a wave, Jake could make out something ... something ...

With a jolt, he realized it was a huge tanker, coming out of the darkness and headed straight for him. The ship's horn sounded, and adrenaline coursed through his body as he pulled hard right on the wheel. He hoped he'd done it soon enough.

"We can't get the helo up, Craig. The wind is too high," Danny Stewart said.

Craig pressed the phone to his ear. If he moved his head the wrong way, his cell phone dropped out. "Okay, then, listen. I need the Coast Guard to come down the Bay and pick me up in Annapolis."

"In this weather?"

"It's important." Campbell's pager went off as he spoke. He pulled it off his belt and glanced down at it. The number cited was unknown to him, but it had a suffix: 9-1-1—the signal for an emergency.

An arrow of adrenaline streaked up his back. "Gotta go, Danny. Call you back in a minute." After terminating that call, Craig dialed the number on his pager. And as he listened to Aunt Trudy's story, chills raced up and down his spine. He called Danny back. "You gotta get the Coast Guard for me. Ask them to help us. Beg them. Tell them we've got two agents in trouble out there. Ask them if they'd pick me up at City Dock in Annapolis."

"Got it, Craig. I'm on it."

The pain was unbearable. She moved her head far to the left to ease the pressure on her skull. Where was she? Why did her head hurt so much? She could not see, nor could she open her mouth. Silently, she fought to understand, to force herself back to reality.

She was lying on her back, her arms stretched over her head. Cassie reached with her hands, and realized she was locked in handcuffs secured around a metal post. Panic raced through her. Why?

Why couldn't she see? Duct tape. Duct tape on her eyes and her mouth. She could feel it when she turned her head and rubbed against the cover of the bed she was on. And then she remembered standing on the pier, and Rick Maxwell, and the panicky feeling of him choking her.

An intense fear swelled in Cassie and she became nauseous. She knew if she threw up, she would choke to death, so she forced the panic back down, forced herself to be still, forced herself to think.

Her head hurt so much. Oh, God ...

Footsteps. There were footsteps coming. Cassie lay perfectly still. She smelled Polo and grew nauseous again. And then she felt a hand on her leg, stroking it, running up and down her calf.

"Don't die yet, sweetheart," Rick said. "I wouldn't want you to miss out on the fun."

And Cassie McKenna passed out.

The engine screamed in Jake's ears as the Boston Whaler fought the waves, plunging forward, getting knocked sideways, rising and dropping with the tempest. He steered right, just missing the tanker, and headed south again.

Feeling the fatigue now of the constant battle, Jake forced himself to go on. What if they hadn't gone south? What if they'd put in at a marina? What if he'd missed them in the storm? What if?

There were too many options. Jake only knew one thing: he had to try to find Richard Maxwell, and his best guess was that he was headed south in the Bay, toward Bloody Point Bar Light. Beyond that, all he could do was pray.

The bow of the boat rose and dropped again and a wave

slammed into the hull. The boat shuddered, and tension rolled through Jake. "I hate boats!" he yelled into the wind. Straining to look ahead, it seemed that the darkness was increasing.

And then, in a flash of lightning, Jake saw something forward and to the right. It was a sail, dipping and bowing on the waves, nodding and cresting with the storm. He nudged his engine higher. If it was the catamaran, he would catch up quickly.

The rain began coming down in sheets. Within seconds, he was soaked. Shivering, he wiped the rain from his eyes. He had to find Maxwell. He had to find Cassie. He could not quit.

Danny Stewart's voice was steady. "Craig, the Coast Guard is sending a vessel for you. They'll be at City Dock within the hour, if you really want to go out. They're sending another one straight down to the waypoint you gave them."

"Great!" Campbell said. His blue light was flashing on his dashboard. "I'll be there in twenty minutes."

Again she reached consciousness, her pain and fear dragging her back to a reality she dared not ignore. Listening carefully, she guessed she was alone.

She knew now she was on Rick's catamaran, and from the feel of it, the Bay was in a tumult. She could hear thunder and the sound of the waves slapping the boat. She felt the tugging and pulling, the rocking and lurching, of the vessel as it struggled. Rick would have his hands full for a while.

She assessed her circumstances. Her feet were free, that was good. Cassie groped to feel what she could with her hands. In her mind, she could see the sliding cabinet above the bed she'd noted when she first saw the boat. The metal rod her cuffs were around? What was it? A support post?

Cassie traced the rod with her fingers. It seemed to be wedged into the wood. How far into the teak did it go? Could she pull it loose by sawing around it with the chain of her cuffs? Was it ornamental rather than structural?

Listening carefully, and hearing no one in the cabin with her, she began. She forced the chain low, against the wood near the bottom of the metal post, and she started to saw back and forth, pulling on it as hard as she could, jerking at it, then sawing again. Left, right, left, right. Eat through the wood. Loosen the post. C'mon. The pain of moving was a fire in her brain, but the rasping noise was the sound of hope.

It was a boat. Jake could clearly see that it was a boat with a mast. A sail was flapping in the wind. The sail ought to be in, that much he knew. He'd heard Cassie talking about hauling in the main and the jib quickly when the storms hit. So the sailboat was not being handled well. Jake tossed his head to fling water out of his eyes. A flash of lightning confirmed what he'd hoped. The boat was a catamaran.

His heart pounding, Jake pushed the throttle forward. In this wind, the cat might not even hear him approach. He had to hope for that.

It was half a mile ahead now, and he was gaining fast. With every dip of the Whaler, he could see the progress. A huge wave crashed into to the port side of the bow, lifting the boat, then pressing it down. Jake's stomach dropped, but he hung onto the wheel, and focused on the cat.

As he got closer, during flashes of lightning he could see someone in the cockpit. Jake hooked his right arm in the wheel and grabbed the binoculars with his left hand. Fighting the instability, he trained them on the cat. But the rain and the lurching and the darkness made them useless. Then, in a flash of lightning, he saw the cockpit was empty. The man must have gone below.

It was his chance. Jake gunned the engine. He raced forward and while he did, he formulated a plan. He was closing on the boat, one hundred yards, fifty, twenty-five. He throttled back to reduce the noise. Needing access to his gun more than anything, Jake ditched his life jacket. When he got near the back of the cat, he cut his throttle to idle, grabbed onto the catamaran, shoved the Whaler off with his foot, and swung on board.

She could hear him in the head and she lay perfectly still. She'd made progress on the teak; she could feel it with her fingers. She hoped she had arranged her hands to cover the damage.

Rick was humming to himself, an odd thing. She heard him pumping the head to flush it, and then she heard the door open and shut. Cassie lay still, breathing deeply as if she were unconscious. She heard his footsteps as he hesitated at her door, and then went back topside. Clenching her jaw, she began working again to free the post.

Jake crouched in the cockpit, waiting, gun drawn, like a cat waiting to pounce. Maxwell had to appear soon. His patience paid off—he heard a noise, then Maxwell emerged from the salon.

"FBI, put your hands up!" Jake yelled, standing suddenly, his pistol in his hand.

"You son of a—" Maxwell cursed.

"Put 'em up! Now!"

Maxwell complied, his mouth curled into a snarl, his eyes glittering with hate. "How dare you ..." he began.

"Shut up! Now put your hands on your head, and turn around slowly."

She worked quickly despite the pain and the fear. Then she heard a voice, not Maxwell's voice, but another. It sounded like Jake, and she wondered if she were hallucinating.

Her head hurt so much. Right, left, right, left. She sawed and sawed and then, finally, she felt it. The metal piece was, as she'd guessed, decorative. It was coming loose as she worked on the wood.

She redoubled her efforts. She heard Rick's voice, angry now, and another voice captured and carried off in the wind. She worked and worked. Her arms ached, her shoulders burned, and then she felt the post give way, and her hands, still in the handcuffs, were free of the constraints.

Slowly, Maxwell put his hands on his head. The catamaran rocked left and right, shuddering with the slap of each large wave. Jake's mind was racing. How could he cuff Maxwell and still keep a gun on him with one hand?

She was free ... free! Cassie sat up. Her head spun. She choked down the nausea.

With her handcuffed hands she felt for the edge of the duct tape on her mouth. She found it, and pulled it off slowly, tears forming in her eyes. When it was off, she leaned over and threw up, over and over, the nausea released at last.

Then she began to work on the tape on her eyes. Hot tears stung her eyes as she pulled it off, taking much of her eyebrows with it. She rubbed her eyes and looked around. She was in Rick's catamaran's master berth. But she was free.

Suddenly, a wave hit, hard, and Jake stepped sideways, losing his balance momentarily and taking his eyes off Maxwell.

Maxwell's hand flashed down and grabbed a boat hook. Turning, he lashed out at Jake, hitting his gun hand. The gun clattered to the deck. Jake lunged at Maxwell, who swung the boat hook again. It hit Jake in the face, opening a cut above his eye. He fell to the floor of the cockpit.

Maxwell bent over to pick up Jake's gun. Suddenly there was motion behind him. Cassie emerged from below decks, threw her handcuff chain around his neck, and pulled hard.

"Ughhhh," Maxwell choked. He put his hands to his throat. His eyes widened.

Jake pulled at his soaked pants legs to retrieve his backup weapon, a Chief Special, a small, .38 caliber revolver. Maxwell put both hands on Cassie's and leaned forward suddenly, pulling her over his head and throwing her to the deck. Maxwell ran below decks, and Jake fired as he did. Cassie lay stunned and still.

Jake wiped the blood off his face with his sleeve. The wind was howling in the mast, and the rain pelted him. He picked up his Glock, put the Chief in his pack, and cautiously moved into the salon, gun drawn. There were two sets of steps, one to the left pod and one to the right. Maxwell had disappeared to the right. Jake hoped the two weren't connected some other way.

Crouching low next to the galley stove, Jake advanced slowly. He heard a noise, then the racking of a shotgun. He fired toward the sound and dove for cover back into the cockpit, just as a loud roar erupted. A slug from Maxwell's shotgun shattered the glass in the salon ports.

Jake stuck his arm around the corner and fired back, pop-pop-pop, enough to keep Maxwell below decks. The wind whistled through the broken glass in the salon. Spray from the crashing waves was drenching the cushions. Then Jake heard the racking sound again and he fired, pop-pop-pop-pop! Maxwell's shotgun discharged. Shards of glass and pieces of fiberglass flew all around the salon. Once again, Jake fired, so focused that he never heard the roar of the gun, or felt it jumping in his hand.

"Are you Special Agent Campbell?" the Coast Guardsman yelled as Craig stepped on board the pitching vessel at City Dock in Annapolis.

"Yes, sir, I am," Campbell responded. "Let's get going."

29

Jake heard a noise in the starboard pontoon. He flattened himself just outside the salon, next to the door. Maxwell was taking a long time. What was he doing? Jake peeked around the corner, saw the muzzle of the shotgun, and he fired, squeezing the trigger of the Glock over and over, until the magazine was empty. He fumbled for his spare.

Maxwell raced up the stairs, rounded the corner, and emerged into the cockpit before Jake could reload. He started to shoot, then looked puzzled and in an instant Jake realized the shotgun had misfired. Maxwell pulled the trigger again and again. It clicked impotently. Jake threw himself at Maxwell, slamming him against the edge of the door.

The two men fell out into the cockpit, Jake's spare magazine falling to the deck. Jake went straight for Maxwell's throat, his thumb searching for a pressure point, but Maxwell jerked away and rolled out from under him. One-handed, Jake was unable to hold him.

Maxwell stood up and kicked Jake in the jaw, sending a searing pain through him. Jake jumped up and charged Maxwell again. He thought he heard a loud horn, like the tanker's horn, as he tackled Maxwell. Jake saw his head hit the cockpit seat, hard, but Maxwell continued to fight.

The horn again. Five short blasts. Jake punched Maxwell in his nose and blood gushed out. Maxwell put his hands on Jake's throat, and began to choke him.

Jake tried to pull away but he couldn't. He heard the horn continuing to sound. He tried hitting Maxwell again, tried shoving his nose up into his brain, but he couldn't get the angle, so he started working his thumb toward Maxwell's right eye. Lightning flashed, thunder roared, the horn blew again. Maxwell gripped him tighter.

And the edges of Jake's vision began to go dark.

The tugboat captain stared into the night, straining to see the catamaran, which had continued on its collision course despite his warning blasts. Had the skipper had a heart attack? Gone overboard?

"What's he doing, Cap'n?" the tugboat crewman asked.

"I don't know. Not giving way, that's for sure." They were hauling a train of three barges, loaded with sand, and it was hard enough to control them in the weather without having to avoid some fancy-pants catamaran skipper who ought to be sipping white wine in some bar rather than risking his boat on a night like this. If the guy was still alive, that is.

"He doesn't even have his main secured." The crewman trained his binoculars on the struggling cat. "What are you going to do?"

"Where's he gonna hit?"

"Behind the tug, sir. Between us and the first barge."

"Keep on the horn, and hold on. The cable will take his mast."

"Is that it? Is that what you're looking for?" The Coast Guard captain pointed toward a boat bobbing in the waves, barely visible during flashes of lightning.

"Could be," Craig shouted above the storm.

Then in the distance they heard a horn. The sound was being whipped away by the wind, but it was definitely a horn, sounding short blasts. The captain trained his binoculars forward to the starboard side. "Something's out there," he said, "but I can't quite see what."

"Cap'n," the mate said, "we're getting a Mayday just up ahead. Tug says a cat's headed for a collision."

"Let's go!"

Jake brought his knee up, hard, into Maxwell's midsection. He heard the horn again. The bow of the cat lifted, and he and Maxwell slid aft. Then there was a screeching, tearing, groaning, sound coming from the very frame of the catamaran itself. Maxwell stopped. He loosened his grip on Jake. He looked over his shoulder. And as he did, the tow cable of the barge brought the mast crashing down to the deck.

It missed them by inches and filled the cockpit with line and shredded sail, entangling Maxwell. Jake scrambled from beneath him, grabbed the Glock pistol, shoved the new magazine in, and, as Maxwell stood up, he pumped six bullets into his chest.

Maxwell looked shocked. He put his hand on his chest, then took it away, looked at the blood, and looked at Jake. He staggered back, his face contorted with anger, and then he fell, backwards, over the aft rail, and disappeared.

Jake raced to the rail and in a flash of lightning saw Maxwell sinking beneath the black waters of the Chesapeake Bay, his eyes wide with shock, his mouth open.

"Jake? Jake?" Cassie called.

He turned to her. His face was bloody, his mouth swollen and he was shaking with adrenaline. "Cass!" He exclaimed. Then he heard a roaring sound. He peered into the dark, saw the lights of the tug, looked the other way, and in a flash of lightning saw the attached barge bearing down on the cat, about to overrun it.

"No!" he yelled. Jake jumped toward the helm, climbing over sail and line and the downed mast. Instinctively, he pushed both throttles full forward, and turned the wheel hard left.

"Jake!" Cassie screamed as the leading edge of the barge loomed over them.

Would they get clear? A loud crunch confirmed Jake's worst fears. The boat leaned over as the barge pressed the starboard pontoon under water. "It's going down," Jake screamed. "Cass! We've got to jump!"

"What?"

"It's sinking!" Jake grabbed Cassie's arm and shoved her forward away from the barge, climbing up the slanting pontoon. He grabbed the horsecollar life ring, and pushed Cassie up and over the rail. "Jump!" he yelled. He pushed her into the cold waters of the Bay and leaped in after her.

"What was that?" Craig asked. "Thunder?"

"Look! It's a flare." The Coast Guard captain trained his binoculars northward, into the night. "Full throttle! Let's go! Go!"

Jake and Cassie both went underwater, then surfaced. Cassie sputtered and coughed. Handcuffed, she kicked her feet and struggled to keep her head up. Jake grabbed her and pushed her toward the life ring. She reached for it and clung to it desperately. "Hold on!" he screamed at her. He wrapped his arm around her and began kicking away from the barge and the damaged catamaran. He kicked and kicked until he thought his aching legs would just break off. *Keep going, keep going, just hold on,* he told himself.

Waves sloshed them around and the rain pelted down. Twenty yards from the boat, safely away from the barge, Jake had to stop. He was exhausted.

Cassie's teeth were chattering. Her eyes were wide. Jake looked around. They were clear of the barge. How far were they from shore? How far could he swim? His boots were weighing him down and he could feel the cold in his bones. The water temperature wasn't lethal, and he was a good swimmer. Still, he had to fight three-foot waves while supporting Cassie and he wasn't sure how long he'd last.

The tug, whose horn Jake had heard when he was fighting Maxwell, was sounding short blasts over and over. It fired a flare, then another. He thought he could see it turning around, making a wide arc in the Bay. But it was hard to tell ... the tug was so slow and the high waves gave him only momentary glimpses.

"Jake!" Cassie gasped. She grabbed for him, but he shoved her hands away.

"Hold on to the ring. Hold on!" How long could he last? Already he was gripped with fatigue. Blood still trickled from the wound on his brow and he could taste it in his mouth. His legs were cramping. His right hand was useless and the burn on his left arm hurt like crazy. Rain was still coming down hard, splatting on the water around them and running down their faces. The lightning was becoming less frequent, but the waves were still buffeting them.

Cassie was trembling. She was dressed only in shorts and a tank top. Was she cold? In shock? Terrified? Or all three?

He had to get her to shore. *Oh, God*, he cried silently. *I need help! Now!*

Yet another wave rose into the night and crashed over their heads, and the two resurfaced, choking and coughing. Cassie lost her grip on the ring. She started to slip under. Fear seized Jake and he grabbed her and pulled her up again.

"Oh, God!" he cried. "Help us!" He couldn't hold on much longer, and Cassie wouldn't make it on her own.

The mate on the Coast Guard boat was in radio contact with the captain of the tug. "He said there's two, maybe three in the water, sir," he yelled, "and the catamaran's taking on water."

"Tell him to stay in the area," the Coast Guard captain responded.

"He's shining a searchlight in the direction of the people, sir."

"Good! Let's get there!"

Jake saw a bright light, and then, in the distance, another one bouncing on the waves, but growing larger by the minute. "Hey!" he yelled. Then he could hear the high whine of another engine, a smaller one than the tug. Lightning flashed. He saw a boat headed for the catamaran. The cat was listing badly, rolled over with just one pontoon still on the surface, its broken mast flat on the water. A powerful light began sweeping the waves, edging closer and closer to Jake and Cassie.

"Oh, God, please, please," he gasped. Cassie's eyes were closed and her head was falling back. "Oh, God ..."

And then, the light fell on them. Jake yelled and threw his hand up in the air. The light stopped its sweep. Hope flared in Jake's heart. "Hey! Over here!"

Rising and dipping, the boat plowed through the waves. It was headed their way. Jake gripped Cassie. "Hold on, Cass! They're coming! Hold on."

As the boat drew near, someone on board threw a life ring out, and then he saw swimmers hit the waves. "Take her!" Jake shouted as they drew close. He let go of the life ring and pushed Cassie toward the men. Cassie, scrambling for survival, put a foot on Jake and shoved off of him.

As she kicked, Jake went down. When he surfaced a wave hit him, smacking him in the face. Gasping, he swallowed saltwater. He began floundering. Then both legs cramped, and the sharp pain crippled him. He thrashed around and felt himself going down again. The water closed over his head. His chest was tight. He opened his eyes wide and stared into the blackness. He was disoriented—where was the surface? He needed air, and needed it now.

This is it. I'm going to die, Jake thought. Then a hand grabbed his collar, and he felt himself being pulled up. His head cleared the surface and his mouth ripped open as he desperately gulped air. Seconds later, he was lying on the floor of the cutter, vomiting saltwater. And for the first time ever in his life, he was thrilled to be on a boat.

30

*T*he bright sunshine seemed overdone, as if nature were doing penance for last night's storm. Cassie sat on her hospital bed, a glass of ice water on the small table next to her. Her father stood next to the window, Aunt Trudy was seated in a chair. Jake was slouched in a second chair, two butterfly bandages on his brow. He was wearing khaki shorts and a blue golf shirt, and his gun was in a pouch on his side. Cassie suspected he wouldn't be far from that for a while.

The last twelve hours were a blur. After being plucked from the Bay, she and Jake had been rushed to the hospital. She'd had x-rays and a brain scan and received treatment for exposure and exhaustion. An IV to replace fluids had been her companion all night. Now she was waiting to be released. Just a concussion, the doctor had said, ordering her to rest for a few days. And she was happy to comply—more than happy.

Jake was telling a story, and Cassie turned her eyes toward him. He was sitting up and was gesturing with his hands, a grin on his face as he spoke. He was so animated, so full of gusto. Images from the preceding night came into her head and she shivered involuntarily. If it hadn't been for him ...

The hospital-room door opened. Craig Campbell walked in, dressed in his navy suit and white shirt. *It's Saturday*, she thought. *Doesn't he know it's Saturday?* But then she realized he'd probably been at the office already this morning, writing out a report, filling out forms, accounting for the business last night on the Bay. Lines of fatigue creased his eyes. "Good morning," he said. "How are you all today?"

"Happy to be alive," Jake said. "Literally." He stood up and shook Campbell's hand and gave him a slap on the back. "Thanks, man, for coming out after us last night. If it hadn't been for you ..."

"I had nothing else to do," Craig replied, grinning. "My boss hates me. My family doesn't recognize me anymore. So, I decided, there's nothing like a spin on the Chesapeake Bay for a relaxing evening." He shook hands with the others and gave Cassie a hug. "You know, you two are a sure cure for boredom." He leaned against a wall.

"Let's get you a chair," Jim said, crossing to the other side of the room where there was an empty bed.

"Don't mind if I do." Campbell took a seat in the chair Jim dragged over. "How's the head, Cassie?"

"I have a slight concussion. Slight."

"Which only proves her head is harder than mine," Jake added. "Something I've been saying for a long time." He grinned at his partner, then turned back to Craig. "So, what all went on last night?"

"We saw quite a bit of action, on a couple of fronts."

"Tell us," Jake said.

"About the time I got the call from Trudy about Cassie, I was at the home of Seth Hawkins, an engineer who was the subject of an extortion attempt by Maxwell. Maxwell burned his boat, then threatened to kill Hawkins's family if he didn't produce the guidance device that Maxwell wanted to sell. Apparently the same one Schneider failed to deliver.

"I knew Hawkins might be headed toward Bloody Point Light. When I got the call from Trudy, I raced back to Annapolis, caught a ride with the cutter, and that's how we found you."

"What happened to Hawkins?"

"He borrowed a boat from a friend and was headed out to meet Maxwell. Halfway there, the second cutter found him. He's still being interrogated."

Jake shook his head.

"Hawkins had no insurance on the *Lady J*. He'd forgotten to renew it. So Maxwell had him over a barrel. His wife, who was none too happy that he'd bought the boat to begin with, was really upset at having to make payments on a nonexistent craft."

"So he thought he'd just get the device for Maxwell, take the payment, and get out of his financial hole."

"And protect his family at the same time."

"And Tyson Farnsworth? How did he link in?"

"He was the courier. He was supposed to take the rest of Schneider's money to him and pick up the tracking device. But he lost his temper when he got into an accident, and then Mike intervened."

"And Maxwell was angry enough to go after Mike."

"Right." Craig opened his mouth as if to say more, but then he must have thought better of it.

Meanwhile Cassie was strangely quiet. She was focused on the floor. Suddenly, she sat up straight. "You know what, Jake?"

"What?"

"You shot him with your right hand."

"What are you talking about?"

"Maxwell. When you shot him that last time, you shot him with your right hand."

Jake stared at her. He looked down at his hand, and he tried to clench his fist. He still could not. "What?" he said to her again.

Cassie's face was intense. Everything seemed so clear now. She could see it in her mind like a movie. "No, really, listen. Jake, you were in the cockpit. You scrambled out from under Maxwell when the mast came down, then you grabbed your gun, jammed in the magazine, rolled, and shot him. Jake, you shot him with your right hand. I saw you." She looked at the others. "Don't look at me like I'm crazy!"

"No, we're not," they demurred.

Craig held out his hand. "Grab it," he said, but Jake couldn't. Jake frowned. Craig cocked his head. "Adrenaline, maybe?"

Before Jake had time to answer the doctor came in. The three men excused themselves and filed out of the room. Jim left to get a cup of coffee, and Craig and Jake walked down the hall.

"The Coast Guard went back after what was left of Maxwell's catamaran," Craig said. "They were going to tow it in to Baltimore. Danny was with them. Fortunately, they decided to check it out first. Good thing they checked. In the port-side pontoon, in the forward cabin behind boxes and boxes of food that Maxwell had packed, they found some explosives, ammo, all kinds of stuff."

"He wasn't coming back. He was just going to take off," Jake said, and the thought of what could have happened to Cassie made him shiver.

Campbell put his hand on his shoulder. "You okay, bud?"

Jake nodded. "Yeah." He drew in a deep breath. "I'm okay." He smiled softly. "One more bad guy."

"It's never-ending. It's like picking up garbage. There's always more the next day," Craig grinned.

The doctor said she could go home, and Cassie started to get dressed but then sat down again, tears spilling from her eyes. Her aunt quickly sat down on the bed next to her and put her arm around her. "Are you okay, honey?"

"Oh, Aunt Trudy, last night, last night when we were in the water ... I got so scared!"

"Well of course, honey."

"No, no ..." Cassie shook her head. Her aunt handed her a tissue, and Cassie blew her nose. "We were in the water and the waves kept hitting us. I couldn't catch my breath, and I couldn't swim. My head hurt so much and I couldn't tell where I was, I just kept getting jostled and shoved underwater, and if it hadn't been for Jake—"

"I know, honey."

"It was so scary, like not being all the way awake, and so you're not sure where you are or what's happening but you're terrified and you can't get control ..."

"Like in a dream."

"Right. Like a really, really bad dream." Cassie's tears were flowing freely now and a mound of tissues was beginning to grow in front of her. "And Aunt Trudy, I was so scared I was going to die, and I knew I wasn't ready ... I wasn't ready ..." She couldn't get the next words out.

"To see God?" Trudy prompted.

"Yes!" Cassie looked at her aunt, at those gray eyes, now brimming with tears, and her kind, gentle face, her well-earned wrinkles and her gray hair. "I wasn't ready to face God. To go into Eternity. Or even to see Mike again. I wasn't ... right."

"Oh, honey! Let me give you a hug. We need to pray."

Epilogue

The September sun was hot on Cassie's face as she scrubbed the cockpit in her Alberg 30. The rhythmic movement, the sound of the brush, the slight breeze was relaxing to her. She was so focused on what she was doing that she didn't look up, until a shadow fell across her work. Shading her eyes, she lifted her head and saw a familiar figure standing on the dock.

"Hey, partner!" Jake grinned at her.

He looked good, in his cargo pants and navy-blue shirt. His tan had deepened and his eyes looked darker than ever. But it was the expression on his face that encouraged her. The bitterness was gone and in its place was the cheerful confidence that she knew so well.

Cassie stood up. "Hey! What are you doing here?" She wiped her hands on a rag and stepped up onto the dock. She gave him a hug.

"I'm just enjoying my last few days of freedom, before I become a working stiff again."

"You're going back active?"

Jake nodded. "Yep. Oh, they're limiting me to office work for now, till this comes back all the way." He raised his right hand. "But you know, I can Xerox discovery files with the best of 'em."

"That's great, Jake. I'm happy for you."

His eyes were bright, sparkling even, in the sun, and Cassie thought, *It's been a long time since I've seen him happy. A long time.* "Did you get the results of your MRI?"

"All clear. The lesion's gone. And the docs can't figure it out."

He took a deep breath. "What about you, partner? You still a boat babe?"

Cassie rolled her eyes. "I've never been a boat babe, Jake. Just a boat owner."

"Oh, yeah. Sorry." He smiled boyishly, feigning innocence.

Cassie tossed her head. "They're letting me reactivate. I got my letter yesterday."

"Whoa! Congratulations!" Jake grabbed her in a bear hug. "Way to go, girl! I knew they'd want you back!"

"Yes. It was a mistake to resign. I missed it."

"Oh, so I was right?"

Cassie blushed. "Well, I don't know ..."

"No, no, I was right, wasn't I, about you coming back?" Jake pressed.

She hesitated.

"C'mon, Cass. You can do this. Admit it. I was right."

Cassie took a deep breath. She was having a hard time not laughing. He was so silly, and it had been a long, long time since either of them had felt this comfortable with each other. She trained her eyes on his. "You were," she said, "absolutely right—"

"Yes!"

"—although your timing was off. By several months."

"And a catastrophe or two," Jake added. "Still, I was right."

Cassie nodded and laughed, and he gave her another hug.

"You talk to Campbell lately?"

Cassie shook her head. "No."

"They got some more information on Maxwell. He didn't leave the military; he was kicked out. For sexual misconduct. And a woman he was involved with in Saudi Arabia disappeared. They can't pin it on him, but he's the prime suspect. He had a huge collection of porn, and some strange souvenirs in his boat—women's underwear, some earrings, and necklaces."

Cassie flinched.

"They're going back to reconstruct every bit of his life that they can. They're thinking maybe he was responsible for a bunch of homicides. Rapes, too." Jake looked at her, squinting slightly. "You okay?"

Cassie inhaled deeply. She still couldn't believe she'd ever trusted that man. How could she be so stupid! "Yes, fine," she said resolutely, tossing her head. "He was a scumbag."

"Yep," Jake replied. His eyes searched her face. "Y'know," he said, "we work well together."

"Yeah, we do," she admitted.

Jake cocked his head. "Do you think, maybe, once we're both back, maybe we should team up again?"

Cassie looked at Jake, first with her eyes and then with her heart. She swallowed. There was a lump in her throat.

"We were good, you and me. We did good work. I think we should do it again."

"Yes, Jake," she said, "I think we should." Then, because her eyes were tearing, she turned away from him and started to walk down the dock.

He touched her shoulder and turned her around. "You did good, Cass. You never gave up. Mike would be proud of you."

"Thanks." Her voice was soft. "I just feel ... stupid."

"About Maxwell? Don't even think about it. He was a master at charming people."

Cassie cocked her head. "What are you going to do now, Jake?"

"Job-wise?"

"Personally."

He shoved his hands in his pockets. "I ... feel like I need to go back to Tam and see if there's anyway she'd want to get back together, to be a family again."

Cassie nodded.

"She kicked the guy out who was living with her. Still, I don't think she's going to want to have anything to do with me. If nothing else, though, I need to apologize to her for all the stuff I did wrong." Jake kicked a pebble off the dock.

Why was her heart pounding? Cassie tried to still it, but it was beating wildly.

Jake squinted at her in the bright light. "How about you, Cass? Think you'll start dating again?"

She held up her hand. "No, Jake. There's just no room for another guy. That's one thing this little incident has taught me." Cassie tossed her head. "There will never be another Mike." Brushing her hand through her hair, she said, "I certainly don't need a man to be happy. I'm perfectly fine on my own."

Jake pursed his lips and nodded, then he walked to the end of the dock. Cassie watched as he stood, head down, staring at the water, his hands shoved into his pockets. What was he thinking? Then he turned around suddenly and started back toward her. She looked away, pretending she hadn't been watching him.

"Good-bye, Cass," he said, smiling and giving her a quick hug. "See you at the office soon!"

"Yeah, sure," she responded, her stomach churning. She stood frozen while he walked toward his car, throwing his keys in the air and catching them, as she'd seen him do so many times before. She saw the bounce in his gait, the way he carried his shoulders, the shape of his head, the thickness of his neck, his broad shoulders.

She remembered what it had been like to be in the waters of the Bay, at night, in a storm, handcuffed, and how Jake had been there for her. He had always been there for her. She'd helped him, too, when he was so full of despair he had no hope left.

Suddenly, she could not stand still any longer. "Jake, wait!" she cried out as he opened the driver's door. "Wait." She ran to him. Brushing the hair out of her eyes, she looked straight into his. Her throat was tight, her heart pounding. "If you ever want to do something together, just as friends, you know we could. That would be fine."

A broad grin filled his face. "Okay, good. Hey," he said, his eyes sparkling, "you want to take *Time Out* for a spin?" He nodded toward her boat.

"You hate boats!"

"I know. But you love 'em. So, do you want to take her out?"

"Now?"

"Now."

Cassie smiled at him, tears in her eyes. "Yes, Jake, that would be fun."

The wind was out of the south, blowing at a steady fifteen knots as they left the dock and motored into the channel. The land slipped away behind them and an osprey nesting on a channel marker eyed them warily. Reaching the open Bay, Cassie turned into the wind. Jake took the helm while she went forward to raise the mainsail. "Okay, turn to port," she called out once she had it up. As the boat turned, the sail caught the breeze. Cassie returned to the cockpit and pulled out the jib. Gently, the boat heeled over five, ten, then fifteen degrees. And Cassidy McKenna trimmed the sheets and set a new course.

Readers' Guide

For Personal Reflection

or Group Discussion

Readers' Guide

1. At the beginning of *Bloody Point*, we find that Cass has suffered a great loss—the death of her husband. What has been her reaction to that loss? Has Cass moved toward God or away from him as a result of this crisis?

2. Have you suffered a great loss? How have you handled it?

3. Cassie remembers a plaque her Aunt Trudy has. It says, "Trust God's heart when you can't see his hands." How might that apply to Cassie's situation?

4. How do these verses apply?
   a. "And we know that in all things God works for the good of those who love him, who have been called according to his purpose" (Rom. 8:28).

   b. "I have loved you with an everlasting love" (Jer. 31:3).

5. What would be a wise and loving way to treat a grieving friend who is stumbling in his or her faith? How do Cassie's aunt and dad treat her?

6. We may give up on God, but God never gives up on us. How do these verses confirm that statement?
   a. "If we are faithless, he will remain faithful, for he cannot disown himself" (2 Tim. 2:13).

   b. "For I am convinced that neither death nor life, neither angels nor demons, neither the present nor the future, nor any powers, neither height nor depth, nor anything else in all creation will be able to separate us from the love of God that is in Christ Jesus our Lord" (Rom. 8:29).

7. At the beginning of the book, Jake seems to have no perceived need of God. Was there a time in your life when that was true of you?

8. Jesus says, "No one can come to me unless the Father who sent me draws him, and I will raise him up at the last day" (John 6:44). Can you see the hand of Providence working in Jake's life, "drawing him," before he became a believer?

9. Looking back, can you see how God was drawing you to himself even before you knew him?

10. Jake admits he is surrounded by friends who are Christians. Do you remember anyone who influenced you before you came to Christ?

11. A major trauma starts Jake on the path to find God. Was there an incident that triggered your spiritual search?

12. Jake asks one of the most common questions nonbelievers ask: "I think sometimes about babies who die and the ones born with defects, the ones who are abused. I don't understand why God would let that stuff happen. Natural disasters, crippling diseases, 9/11 ... why all the suffering?" How would you answer Jake's question? How do these verses apply?

a. "In this world you will have trouble. But take heart! I have overcome the world" (John 16:33).

b. "We know that the whole creation has been groaning as in the pains of childbirth right up to the present time" (Rom. 8:22).

13. Trudy struggled with a monumental problem: the debilitating illness of her husband. She tells Jake, "...one day, in desperation, I pulled out my Bible, and I just started reading. I read and read and five days later, I surrendered. God was God, I decided. All through the Bible, it was clear. God was sovereign, in charge. He had allowed this illness to take place. Yet he was clearly good. I had to trust that he was good. I decided I would find a way to make the best of the situation and worship him despite it." What's been the circumstance of your deepest surrender to God? What situation or problem have you had to yield to him, trusting in his character?

14. Trudy continues, "Then I decided to look for him *in* this terrible circumstance. And that has made all the difference." Compare her assertion to the situation faced by a familiar Old Testament figure. Joseph was sold into slavery by his brothers, yet eventually he was able to say to them, "You intended to harm me, but God intended it for good to accomplish what is now being done, the saving of many lives" (Gen. 50:20). What positive things can come out of deep suffering?

15. After building a relationship with Jake, Trudy shares the Gospel, telling him there is one way to get to heaven: through faith in Jesus Christ. Jake says that

seems too exclusive to him. How would you respond to his objection?

16. In the depths of his despair, Jake has a very vivid, intense experience with God. We may not have had that kind of startling encounter with him but most of us have had moments when we knew God was present—in worship, while in prayer, in the middle of a difficult situation, or in a holy moment, like the birth of a child. Can you recall such a circumstance?

17. How does Cass respond to Jake's assertion that he's been healed? Can you identify with that? How would you respond to a friend who was struggling with that same issue?

18. As Jake begins to move toward God, Cass runs even further away. Jonah, too, became angry with God. What did he do? How did God respond?

19. From the belly of the whale, Jonah cried, "You hurled me into the deep, into the very heart of the seas, and the currents swirled about me; all your waves and breakers swept over me ... but you brought my life up from the pit, O Lord, my God" (Jonah 2:2, 6). How would you characterize God's response to Jonah's anger? Judgment? Condemnation? Discipline? Love? Redemption? A combination of these?

20. At the end of the book, after nearly drowning, Cass knows she is not ready to face God. How about you? Is there sin to confess or a relationship to mend before you stand before him?